The
Good
Mother

Kim Lock

sphere

SPHERE

First published in Australia in 2016 by Pan Macmillan Australia Pty Ltd
First published in Great Britain in 2016 by Sphere

1 3 5 7 9 10 8 6 4 2

A CIP catalogue record for this book
is available from the British Library.

ISBN 978-0-7515-6530-0

Typeset in Baskerville by M Rules
Printed and bound in Great Britain by
Clays Ltd, St Ives plc

Papers used by Sphere are from well-managed forests
and other responsible sources.

MIX
Paper from
responsible sources
FSC
www.fsc.org   FSC® C104740

Sphere
An imprint of
Little, Brown Book Group
Carmelite House
50 Victoria Embankment
London EC4Y 0DZ

An Hachette UK Company
www.hachette.co.uk

www.littlebrown.co.uk

For Stace

Kim Lock was born in Mount Gambier in the 1980s. After living and working in Darwin, Melbourne and Canberra, Kim returned to home soil in South Australia, where she lives in the Barossa Valley with her partner and children, a dog and a couple of cats.

Her writing has also appeared in, amongst others, *Daily Life*, *The Guardian*, *The Sydney Morning Herald online* and *Essential Baby*.

1

Now

From inside the handbag trapped between her hip and the front door, Fairlie Winter's phone begins to ring.

She curses as she knees at the door, swollen in the heat and stuck to the jamb. For the third day in a row, she has forgotten to buy cat food. Fumbling her keys around an armload of groceries, she hopes Yodel won't mind having Corn Flakes for dinner again.

Her breath labours as she props the screen door open, the phone in her handbag maintaining its clamour against her side. The fabric straps of the grocery bags cut into her fingers; the flyscreen bounces on her arse. Wincing, she kicks at the inner door but the weight of the bags tugs her off-centre and the keys slip from her fingers and jangle on the doorstep. A box of cinnamon donuts that was supposed to be her dinner escapes a bag and tumbles onto the ground, spitting out a puff of sugar. A single fat donut lolls out onto the concrete. Exhausted, the phone goes silent.

'Shit,' Fairlie whines.

Although it is after six in the evening, dull heat radiates from the front wall, the taupe bricks baked by a January sun. As she stoops to retrieve the keys, Fairlie catches a heady whiff of sweat from under her arms. There's a rip in the hem of her navy crepe work pants. The sight of it makes her sigh; her mother will surely berate her for her untidiness, *tsk-tsking* as she nimbly sews up the hole with cotton thread and affectionate rebuke.

'Twenty-six years old and still ripping clothes like a toddler,' Fairlie mimics.

Across the road, naked and scrawny sheep bleat plaintively, small hooves scuffing the dusty bare earth. A dog barks twice, sounding bored.

'Well, Yodel,' she says to the plump ginger cat oozing from the couch, roused by her untidy struggle through the doorway, 'it looks like we're both having Corn Flakes for dinner.' A limp brown curl falls across her eyes and she backhands it away. 'Why doesn't Mrs Soblieski leave a casserole on my doorstep when we actually *need* one?' Leaving the donuts she scrambles inside, ducking away from the screen door as it slams shut, the sound reverberating through the pokey front courtyard of the six-unit complex.

The phone begins to ring again.

'Where's the bloody fire?' she mutters. Brushing aside a rolled-up *Penola Pennant* to dump her grocery bags on the kitchen counter, Fairlie scrabbles through her handbag.

The number displayed on the caller ID causes her a flicker of hesitation. Accepting the call she blurts, 'Hunks of Spunk, you've reached Dominic.'

Apart from a strange grating noise, there is silence.

'Hello?' Fairlie says. 'Jen? It's me. I was kidding.' As she begins banging cupboard doors she feels a bit like Old Mother Hubbard, searching for something to feed the cat winding around her ankles. Eventually Fairlie says, 'You drop the phone or something?'

A throat clears down the line. 'It's me. Ark.'

Surprise halts her by the open pantry door. To combat the brief awkward silence she forces a casual cheer into her tone. 'Oh, hi.' Her voice sounds squeaky. 'Long time.' She can't help it.

'It's Jenna,' Ark says. 'She's –' His voice tears off.

'What?' Fairlie clutches an open box of breakfast cereal. 'What about her?'

Flakes of rolled corn scatter across the linoleum as the box falls from her hand when Ark says, 'She's dead.'

Fairlie's mouth feels like sand. It's over a year since she's been here but from the outside little has changed.

Late afternoon light fades across the front of the long,

limestone home with its maroon corrugated iron roof; shadows from two ancient red gums fall across the cluster of sheds behind the house. Orange sunlight slinks through row after row of grapevines bordering the house and driveway, dripping with lucrative clusters of purple-black fruit, limbs like gnarled and groping old fingers searching for a way out. A roller-doored shed sits alongside the house, and Fairlie can see the lawn has long ago reclaimed the wheel ruts that once marked a permanent car park by the shed wall. Now, a blue-netted trampoline stands there instead, a Tonka truck stalled by the stairs.

A stranger's car is parked at the end of the sweeping crushed gravel drive. A late model Holden Commodore, its paint white and nondescript, sits with two wheels on the dry clipped grass under a wattle tree.

Fairlie feels herself moving out of the car. She hears her footsteps echo across the timber decking of the vast, dim verandah as she catches a sickly breath of the young jasmine that winds up the verandah poles; she and Jenna had planted it in an old wine barrel an earlier spring, using a two-dollar bag of chook poo they'd hauled into Jenna's hatchback from the side of the road. The saccharine scent of it makes her head spin. It feels so long ago.

The front door is ajar, bordered by a shaft of weak light from inside. Fairlie knocks softly then pushes the door open and steps into the hall, purposefully stepping on the board that squeaks to announce her entry.

'Ark?'

Light spills from the lounge room with the low rumble of male voices. She finds Ark with his back to her, staring out the window into the darkening evening. Another man is seated on the couch, hands clasped loosely between his knees. The flow of this other man's words halt mid-sentence as Fairlie steps into the room. The stranger's head swivels to her.

'Ark,' Fairlie says.

Muscles stiffen across the slab of Ark's back. Arms like tree branches are clamped tightly behind his body, as though handcuffed, one hand clenched white around the opposite wrist. Coiled as tensely as he is, Ark's presence still balloons in the room. He doesn't turn or offer her acknowledgement.

'You must be Fairlie.' The other man stands. When he comes to her, he limps with an old wound – the favour of a limb with a calcified joint, not in pain. Generous streaks of silver brush the dark curls at his temples. Above a strong nose his eyes are widely set, kind, the surrounding skin webbed with lines. He regards her intently.

'I'm Detective Dallas Morgan,' he tells her. 'I'm from the Mount Gambier Criminal Investigation Branch.' He takes her hand in his palms; his skin is even darker than hers.

Criminal investigation? Fairlie snatches her hand away.

'I'm sorry for your loss.'

'Wait. What?' Fairlie frowns.

Finally Ark turns to her. Lips clamped thinly, a betrayal

of emotion in the swollen red rims of his eyes and the damp cling of hair at his neck. Obscenely, his T-shirt is inside-out and the exposed seams hit her with a pang of embarrassed sympathy, like a glimpsed nipple. It's wrong. Everything is wrong.

As they stand in an awkward triangle, paused somewhere between approach and escape, the detective speaks again but it sounds distant.

Jenna can't be dead, Fairlie decides as she steps towards Ark. *She can't be dead.* She resolves it isn't true as she searches his expression and finds it numb with pain.

Jenna can't be. Dead.

Her rib cage feels too small for her beating heart. Ark's shoulder hitches. A stunned silence swells between them and in that moment, in that onion skin shaving of time, Fairlie comes to the sickening realisation that she isn't dreaming.

'No,' she whispers. 'Oh *no*.'

There is quiet authority in the detective's voice and something else she can't quite place. Regret? Resignation? He speaks slowly and evenly as he explains that he has finished with his investigation of the scene, that Fairlie will need to make a statement before he can prepare a full brief for the state coroner.

A statement? Coroner? Fairlie shakes her head. 'I don't believe it.'

'Jenna killed herself,' Ark says plainly, like pointing out the time.

'But she couldn't have,' Fairlie argues. 'I sent her a message today. Before work. She actually wrote back. We talked about casserole. My neighbour, Mrs Soblieski ... ' She tosses an apologetic glance at the detective, excusing the stranger who won't understand the inside joke. 'She thinks I'm useless. Because I'm single and twenty-six and I live alone.' Her voice breaks on that last word. 'It ... it must be a mistake.' *Twenty-six. We're only twenty-six.*

'I'm sorry,' Detective Morgan says with sympathy. 'You were very close with Jenna.'

'Yes.' Glancing down at her hands she adds, 'We were. I mean, lately ... But I've known her forever.' Ark clenches his stubble-lined jaw. 'She's my best friend, that never changed.' Looking from one man to the other, Fairlie implores, 'What happened?'

Ark picks a glass from the coffee table, a slosh of brown liquid in the base. 'In the bath. She ... she cut her wrists.' He swallows the drink in one gulp.

If she were to take a dozen steps down the hallway and turn left before entering the open-plan kitchen, she would walk into the bathroom.

Fairlie moves down the hall: tentative, unconscious steps. What would she see if she went into the bathroom now? Where she'd once squatted on the floor, painting Jenna's toenails bright purple when her belly had grown too large to be able to bend and do it herself. Back when they still saw each other.

The bathroom looms closer. Does Jenna's blood still

line the white insides of the tub, like a bone sucked of its marrow?

Where is Jenna? Where is she now? An image of the cold steel of the morgue at work flashes before her.

A frigid elastic squeezing her snaps tight, jerking breath from her lungs. Her muscles slacken and her bones liquefy as the floor begins to rise and rush towards her face. But before it can hit her, everything goes strangely, silently, black.

'Ms Winter?'

The voice comes to her from far away, like a dream. On the creaking deck of a ship she lies, gulls reeling on currents above. It looks so calm up there, the graceful sea-birds stretch-winged against fluffy clouds. The voice comes to her again, a man's voice, and her body begins to rock, the warm slats beneath her sway and roll.

'Ms Winter? Can you hear me?'

Whose voice is that?

'Fairlie, come on, get up.'

Why is Ark Rudolph on the boat?

A hand closes over her elbow and, as she struggles to sit upright, reality comes sweeping back. Ark's breath is a wash of just-mouthed alcohol. *Jenna is dead.* A thin moan escapes her lips.

'Here, let me help you.'

The detective takes her other arm and together the older man and Ark haul Fairlie to her feet. Ark grunts and hisses, carrying on like a weightlifter, but the detective is polite and silent in his labour. Upright, saliva floods her mouth, then the contents of her stomach splat onto the hall runner. Ark swears, jumping backwards.

'I'm sorry,' Fairlie says weakly.

'Don't worry about it.' The detective's tone is practised reassurance. Taking her arm, he drapes it over his shoulders and steers her into the living room. 'Here, sit down,' he says, lowering her to the couch. 'Put your head between your knees and take some slow, deep breaths. I'll be right back.'

Fairlie complies. With her arse sinking deep into the leather and her body folded forwards, her heart thuds against her legs and the beat of it pulses through her whole body, rocking her head hanging pendulum-like between her knees. The detective places a towel next to her and presses a glass of water into her hands. A bucket surreptitiously nudges against her ankle.

Lifting her head, she sees Ark staring out the window again, motionless as a tree stump. His hands are clasped behind his body, the hands that she imagines had lifted Jenna's wet, bloodied and lifeless body from the water.

Jenna is dead. Jenna has killed herself.

The words don't make sense in Fairlie's head. Nausea lingers and a morphine-like numbness washes through.

Jenna has killed herself. Slit her wrists open in the bath.

The body has been removed. Carted away in an ambulance, its lights extinguished and sirens muted, unhurried – no point in rushing, no point cutting corners and stopping traffic when life's already spent, drained away down the plughole and dissolved like greasy soap foam.

'What now?' Fairlie hears herself croak. *Does it matter? It's too late.*

'Well,' the detective begins, seated on the edge of an armchair adjacent to the couch, 'as I said, I'll need you to come to the station so you can make a statement about Mrs Rudolph –'

'Jenna,' Fairlie corrects automatically.

'Jenna.' Dallas Morgan leans forwards in his chair and fixes her with a steady look of concern, elbows on his knees, blue shirtsleeves over dark skin. 'It won't take long, I just need to ask you a few questions.'

Cold fear threads down her limbs. 'What kinds of questions?'

'Very simple questions, I promise,' he answers. 'Just to get to know a little more about Jenna, and her mental state.' He adds this last sentence with great care.

Fairlie pushes her fingertips into her eyelids until painful stars explode.

She should have seen this coming.

Ark, like that ambulance, is voiceless – pathetic and resigned. Fairlie can't look at him. Her gaze moves away, taking in the peach-coloured walls Jenna wanted to repaint a butter yellow, the neatly stocked bookshelf, the

10

arrangement of dried banksias filling the unused open fireplace. To Fairlie's right, an upright piano waits against the wall, timber panels gleaming, hinged lid closed over keys like a row of pearly teeth. Once, she'd watched Jenna play 'Chopsticks' on it. After three ciders, the tune had been less than flawless.

Hastily, Fairlie looks away. Under the bay window that Ark stares through, a row of wicker baskets holds Henry's toys. Some have escaped, coloured blocks and an overturned plastic truck scattered on the carpet. Fairlie's spine snaps straight. 'Where's Henry?' Had he followed his mother to the bathroom, where she'd locked the door on him? Had he cried for her, waiting outside the door?

'He's asleep, now,' the detective answers.

'But where was he when —'

Ark turns on his heel. 'It was hours ago, Fairlie. I was working. Henry was fine when I got home, playing with some blocks or some shit while she ... ' He clenches his teeth and stares back out the window. 'I know as much about this as you do.'

Hours ago. Leaping from the couch, Fairlie stumbles across the room and along the hall. In the second bedroom, she holds her breath as she takes in the space where the cot used to be. In its place is a small single bed, low to the floor. Crossing the room in the dim light, Fairlie kneels alongside the bed. Pastel cotton sheets are crumpled around a stuffed giraffe, a colourful clump of Duplo.

He's grown so much.

Henry sleeps peacefully. Little arms flung out, cherubic cheeks rosy, strawberry curls fanning around his head. He wears lime green pyjamas with blue elephants printed across the fabric. Beneath his pyjamas she can see the padded bulk of the nappy he still wears at night. As she stands, hovering over Henry's bed, the detective asks her something: he wants to know how Jenna was with her son.

In his sleep, blissfully unaware, the two-year-old grumbles and shifts his head.

'She loves him,' Fairlie whispers. Her throat feels as though it might fold in on itself. To convince herself, she repeats it: 'She loves him.'

Detective Morgan apologises again and Fairlie wonders when she will wake up from this bizarre and nonsensical nightmare. Recently Jenna mentioned that Henry had blossomed through the language explosion young children have, confident yet clumsy blurted sentences that unroll like a verbal carpet for the rest of his life. So Jenna couldn't be dead, because Henry needed to talk to her.

Sensing their presence, Henry's fine limbs begin to move restlessly, and he blinks and cries. Subtle at first then growing more insistent. With trembling hands Fairlie reaches down and lifts him into her arms. Quietening, Henry studies her face. A kind of breathless silence falls as Henry stiffens, staring at her. Then he relaxes, even smiles a little.

Ark stands in the doorway, so Fairlie holds the child towards him. Henry yawns and says, 'Mummy?'

'Ark?'

Ark's face is impassive as he stares at his son. Henry pats Fairlie's face, as though re-familiarising himself with its fleshy contours. Fairlie exchanges a glance with the detective.

'How did we get here?' Ark says quietly, his hands limp at his sides. 'She was my everything. My life started when she arrived. How do I get that back?' He looks at the child for a long moment before finally he says, 'I can't right now. You take him.' Then he turns and strides from the room.

Henry stills in Fairlie's arms as the front door slams.

The sound jolts Dallas Morgan into action. 'Mr Rudolph,' he calls, tearing from the room, footsteps pounding across the verandah boards. 'Mr Rudolph!' His voice is drowned by the sound of Ark's LandCruiser roaring to life: the frenzied, labouring whine of a diesel engine in reverse, then the noise disappears down the drive.

The detective returns to the bedroom and looks at Fairlie, standing helplessly by the bed and holding the small child.

'Mummy?' Henry says inquisitively, then with more conviction: 'Mummy.' He gazes brightly about, waiting for her to appear.

Trying to keep the desperation out of her voice, Fairlie says, 'I'm so sorry. Mummy's not here.' Drawing back to look at Henry's face, she forces a smile. 'Want some food?'

Henry shimmies from side to side, his hands playing with the buttons on her blouse; she's still dressed for work.

'You want a banana?'

Vehement nod. 'Nana.'

In the kitchen, Fairlie slips Henry into the chair with the thick padded cushion at the table. The bananas in the fruit basket are perfectly ripened, a pile of fragrant bright yellow crescents alongside mandarins and green apples. Next to the fruit basket is a loaf of fresh bread in a wrapper, a bowl of grapes and a jar of strawberry jam. There's something repulsive in the fecundity of this image, Fairlie thinks, because who will eat all this food?

Once Henry is settled with his banana, attentively peeling away strips of skin, Fairlie asks the detective to watch him for a moment and then says to Henry, 'This is Mr Morgan. He's Mummy's friend. I'll be right back, okay? Just have to get something from my car.'

Quietly, so as not to alarm the child, Fairlie slips from the room, then she turns and thunders down the hall. Her palms smack the screen door and it snaps back against the wall as she bounces from the verandah and skids in the gravel at her car. Stuffy air envelops her as she rummages on the passenger seat, locates her mobile, and swipes the lock screen.

The sun has slunk to a violent slash of orange on the horizon. Grapes splashed dirty with shadow tremble in the breeze as Fairlie holds the phone to her ear. One ring, two rings; seven rings, then Ark's recorded voicemail.

'Fuck,' she mutters, her thumb slicking across the screen. Redial. Ark's voice again, asking her with

14

enthusiasm to leave a message, promising to return her call as soon as he can.

'Ark, it's Fairlie. Where the fuck are you? Come back. Immediately.'

Mobile clasped in her palm, she hurries back inside. Henry is pasting the remains of his fruit onto the tabletop with his fingertips. Detective Morgan leans against the island bench in the centre of the room. 'Did you get hold of him?'

Fairlie shakes her head. 'Voicemail.' She brings the phone to her ear again, but still no answer.

While Henry devours another banana and a box of juice, Fairlie tries to reach Ark. The first seven calls go unanswered. But on the eighth call, the line diverts straight to voicemail. 'Ark, please,' she hisses beneath her cupped hand, her back to the child at the table, 'when are you coming home? Let me know, so I can at least take care of Henry.'

'He's switched his phone off,' she tells the detective. 'Shit.' Lowering her phone she stares at its blank screen yet again.

Long moments of silence tick by, punctuated by the sticky sounds of Henry making his way through the fruit, and the zip of fabric between Fairlie's thighs as she paces back and forth across the tiles.

At length, the detective speaks up. 'I'm sorry, but I really have to go.' His tone is apologetic and he indicates with a tip of his head towards the toddler, who fusses and rubs at his eyes. 'Do you have anyone you can call for help?'

Fairlie feels abruptly exhausted. 'My parents are just in Mount Gambier.' But the thought of her mother and father invokes an image of Evelyn Francis, Jenna's mother. Jenna and Evelyn will never recover – forever now, they will remain estranged. It strikes Fairlie like a punch in her gut.

Keys jingle in the detective's hand. 'Can you stay the night?'

A picture of Jenna's spilled blood cooling in the drains beneath the floor. The bathroom – the bath – where Jenna had walked in and would never come out. This enormous house amongst the grapevines to where Jenna had flitted, arm-in-arm with the man who became the person Fairlie couldn't be.

'Mummy?'

Fairlie smiles at Henry through her tears. 'I'll take him to my place.'

The next morning, with Henry balanced on her hip, Fairlie pushes her hand into the back of her letterbox. She ignores the busy drone of bees in the thicket of lavender she has to stretch over. Vaguely, she wonders if the bees will sting her. Would she feel it? Would her nerves register the prick of their tiny barbed stingers, the sharp ache of their venom?

Beneath her feet the pavers are rough and already warm. As she bends awkwardly around the toddler's weight, her phone falls from the pocket of her pyjama shorts and clatters onto the pavers. With a groan, she sets Henry down and retrieves the phone, swearing at the fresh cobweb of cracks trailing across the screen.

Jamming a fist into the hem of her singlet, she scrubs at the screen. The phone appears to still work, so after sending Ark yet another undeniably concise and rather colourful text message, she jams the phone back into her pocket and looks over in time to see Henry lurch forwards and disappear amongst an undulating cloud of bees, his hands thrusting out to grab at the fragrant purple fronds. Mortified, Fairlie takes his hand and ushers him backwards. 'Sorry, buddy. Better get out of there.'

Last night, Henry had been hesitant to leave his house, and had asked frequently after his mother. Murmuring reassurances, Fairlie had brought him to her cramped flat and his bottom lip had quivered as she'd tucked him into her own sheets. But in the dark he'd threaded his small arm around her neck and he'd slept, and all night Fairlie had lain, slipping in and out of sleep, unsure of what images were real and what were not.

As she trudges back along the short drive the sun beats down overhead, spreading indolent heat across her shoulders. In the weedy strip of paddock next door, two dirty-cream alpacas stretch giraffe-like necks above the fence to glare at her. The minuscule town of Penola is sleepy and quiet. Birds chirrup in the trees, a car door thuds, a cow gives a morose low. Overhead an aircraft tows a silent foam contrail across a sheet of ocean-blue glass. The world is oblivious to yesterday's tragedy, time marches on. Birds chirp and planes fly and the earth and its ever-watchful moon circle the sun but Fairlie is stuck in a numb still-life of pain and bewilderment and, yes, denial.

This isn't happening.

Inside the flat, the curtains are drawn and it takes a moment for her to readjust to the dim light. Henry clings to her leg and takes some coaxing and promises of a treat before he toddles away to try to reach the cat staging a protest beneath the couch.

The sound of her phone's ringtone jumps through her like an electrocution. *Ark*, she thinks. But it's not Jenna's husband, it's Fairlie's mother.

'Is Henry still with you?'

'Yeah.' Fairlie tosses the mail onto the kitchen counter and opens the fridge. 'Poor baby.'

Her mother sighs heavily down the line, her breath *whooshing* against the speaker. 'I'm just putting a few more things in the car and then I'll be right up. An hour at the most.'

'Okay,' Fairlie says. The remains of a three-day-old Betty Crocker box mix Devil's Food Cake sit beneath cling wrap in the fridge. 'Thanks.'

'What is Ark doing?'

A cheap ceramic parrot on a magnet slides to the floor as she slams the fridge door. 'Fuck knows.'

'Fairlie.'

'Sorry.'

'Sit tight. I'll be there soon.'

A search through the drawers heralds no clean forks. She locates one in the sink and wipes it on a towel, then peels the plastic wrap from the plate. It comes away with a chunk of icing. The cake is slightly stale, but cold and richly chocolate. She sets the plate next to the unopened mail. After breaking off a small lump of cake to hand to Henry, she is on her third mouthful when her phone rings again.

'Ms Winter, Detective Dallas Morgan – Mount Gambier CIB.'

It takes Fairlie a moment to recognise the name but when she does she grits her teeth against a painful flash of the previous afternoon: egg-yolk light spilling from the lounge room; the vision of the empty, blood-stained bath; Henry, rousing from innocent sleep and asking for his mother.

'Have you heard from Mr Rudolph?' There is the buzz of voices and rustling in the background; a telephone warbles.

'No,' Fairlie says, chewing slowly. 'I don't know where he is.'

A muted sigh. 'Keep trying.' He hesitates, gives a small

cough. 'Have you called on your own support? Your parents?'

'I'm fine with Henry,' Fairlie says, 'until Ark shows up. I'm sure he's not far away. Probably went to the pub, slept in his car.' As her hand smooths the fine curls on the crown of Henry's head, the idea of handing Henry – Jenna's flesh and blood – back to his father fills Fairlie with sadness.

'Thank you, Ms Winter,' Detective Morgan says. 'I'll be in touch.' After a pause he adds, 'Are you sure you're okay?'

'No,' Fairlie says softly. 'But I don't have any other choice.'

She hangs up. Atop the pile of mail is a Telstra notice. The blue envelope signifies her bill is overdue. When they lived together, Jenna used to take care of all that. They often joked that Jenna was the husband of the pair, financially responsible and ordered, while Fairlie was flippant and hopeless. *You can't tie me down*, Fairlie would say. *I'm rootless, baby.*

It's a mocking kind of blue, that overdue notice. Pastel, the shade of a spring dawn sky, so the recipient can't get angry. But what kind of an arsehole sends a notice about fifty-two dollars and eighty-nine cents that's twenty-one days overdue when a woman has just killed herself? And not just any woman – a mother. A daughter, a wife. A best friend.

With the side of her hand, Fairlie sweeps the mail from

the bench and it scatters across the floor like autumn leaves. Henry watches as she kicks it all angrily beneath the couch, tears blurring her vision.

It's because of those tears that she misses the envelope – she doesn't see her address penned in green ink, in handwriting as familiar as her own.

2

Then

His skin was pale. Even in the murky light of the swarming pub, it shone cool white. Along with his plait-belted jeans and popped collar, he wore a lively, unbridled self-assuredness and he laughed fearlessly, with his head thrown back. Backlit by the bar, his hair glowed in rakish, burnt gold spikes. But later, as she drew closer to him, Jenna saw it was a deep shade of rusty auburn.

At first, she hadn't noticed the tall stranger's gaze fall on her as she'd slumped after Fairlie into the crowd.

'Just a few drinks,' Fairlie had assured her, tugging her towards the bar. 'It'll help take your mind off things.'

And then Jenna glanced to her right, and he was watching them. No, not *them*, Jenna realised – *her*. The man, standing half a head taller than the group of blokes packed around him, had his gaze fixed on Jenna alone. His look was steady and curious. As Jenna returned his stare he lifted his left shoulder and his head tilted, ever so slightly, and he smiled. Revellers in varying stages of drunkenness seethed between them like penguins gathering on ice – honking, waddling, jostling for space – but for a moment that all fell quiet.

Fairlie, observing this brief unspoken dialogue, delivered a poignant, raised-eyebrow look at Jenna and her sashay disappeared. 'That was fast,' she said.

Out of the side of her mouth Jenna reminded Fairlie, 'We don't come all the way to the Mount for *just* "a few drinks".'

'Fine then,' Fairlie said. 'Drinks for me, and you can admire the scenery.'

Strangers, drinking and laughing in their dozens, were exactly what Fairlie had insisted Jenna needed right now. Although Jenna knew there was little point in arguing with Fairlie, she had still voiced her dissent during the forty-minute car trip to Mount Gambier as she stared unseeing out the window. Instead of watching the streaky white and grey gums flash by, her mother's face had haunted Jenna's vision. While Fairlie employed a multitude of conversational tactics to pry Jenna's grief open, her mother's words had knifed inside her.

Now, the man's smile broadened and he nodded at her over the swarm of heads, a wordless greeting.

At the packed bar, Fairlie caught the attention of a hassled-looking young barman with tattooed forearms. She grinned at him, batting thick, blackened lashes and pulling her elbows together either side of her breasts to exaggerate the depth of her cleavage. But his expression was neutral as he slid over their drinks and asked bluntly for twelve dollars.

'Darn, Jen, the puppies didn't –' Fairlie began.

Then, there he was. Standing alongside Jenna, as though he'd always been there. At the moment he appeared, two women behind him yelped and hugged each other with a physical vigour that displaced everyone within a metre radius, like a blast zone, and the man was pitched bodily into Jenna's space.

'I'm so sorry,' he said.

The heat in Jenna's cheeks flushed up a notch. He stood so close that she had to tip her head back to regard him, and the damp warmth of his breath blew on the exposed hollow of her throat. Goosebumps rippled across her skin.

The man leaned towards Jenna, reaching past her shoulder. Jenna's breath caught as he carefully pulled her shirt away from the back of her neck and peered at the tag.

Muscles tensing, her hands curled into loose fists. 'Can I help you?'

He drew back with a wry smile. 'Just checking,' he said with a shrug.

'For what?' Jenna's hand floated to the back of her neck.

Moving towards her again, he said, 'To see if it says *made in heaven*.'

Fairlie chortled beside her. 'Please!' she scoffed, drained her vodka and signalled the barman again.

Jenna's immediate reaction was to turn away. To roll her eyes and laugh with Fairlie, likely utilising the sentiments *dick* and *head*. But she hesitated, as though her entrenched, lifelong reactions to any given situation had been flung off-kilter, like a needle jumped from a record's tracks.

So, in spite of herself, Jenna snorted, then smiled. 'That was terrible,' she said. 'Really, really bad.'

He laughed, and the sound was so self-deprecating that Jenna smiled again.

'I apologise,' he said, genuinely, then made to move away. 'Have a good evening.'

It happened before she knew what she was doing. Jenna put her hand on his arm.

He stilled, not quite turned away from her. Leaning closer she said, 'Try again.'

He dropped his head, his shoulder shaking as he laughed again. When he looked up at her he was biting the side of his lip, sizing her up.

'All right,' he said and extended his hand. 'Hi there. I'm Ark Rudolph. I'm a dickhead when a pretty woman smiles at me.'

Jenna shook his hand. 'I'm Jenna,' she said. 'I'm a nurse with a hair-trigger crankiness for hangovers in progress.'

Ark Rudolph held her gaze, an inquisitive half-smile

drawing up one corner of his lips. He held his beer towards her and, after a hesitation, she raised her glass and he clinked it, softly. He watched her as he took a long drink.

Letting the crowd blur and melt around her, Jenna held the man's enigmatic attention and felt the lump of shock inside her become bearable. She knew that Fairlie wanted to keep her close, balm her unspoken wounds with drink, carry her home and keep trying to lever the truth from her but it occurred to Jenna at that moment in a flash of furious inspiration: *what is true anymore? Does* anyone *know?*

Christina Aguilera's 'Dirrty' belted out over the sound system, bodies bumped and whirled and grinded around them as the room thickened with heat and alcohol-fuelled hormones. Fairlie settled herself on a bar stool and buried her face in her glass, throwing pickup lines at the tattooed barman that became increasingly tawdry as the evening wore on. Occasionally she tossed curious glances in Jenna's direction, her face arranged as if to say, *Well, this is new.* And it was precisely because it was new, and thrilling, and narcotic, that Jenna continued. She let it carry her along like rapids, just to see where it went.

Ark's head tilted towards her as he spoke in her ear. She was acutely aware of the heat of his flesh, the alcohol-sweet scent of his breath, the bass throbbing through the floor and up the soles of her feet. When she made him laugh, she felt the shudder of it through his chest. Later, when she let him slide his hand into the back pocket of her jeans, pulling her closer still, she felt the heady curl of desire spool between her thighs. When she stepped back, reopening the briefest of spaces between them, he smiled at her so hungrily she felt her throat constrict.

After a while Jenna turned from Ark to see Fairlie teetering on her stool, giggling as she stuffed handfuls of straws into her empty glass. Black tubes littered the bar and Fairlie leaned awkwardly to grab the last of the straws from the holder, bosom flattening out over the timber. From the other end of the bar, the barman suddenly noticed her and swore, his hands busy with the beer tap. Jenna raised a hand, signalling an apology. 'Come to the bathroom,' Jenna yelled at Fairlie over the din, carefully extracting straws from her hands.

'Hey matey.' Fairlie whistled at the barman, who looked at her and shook his head. 'Watch my sculpture, would ya buddy?' She gestured to the straw-filled glass. 'It's *art*. Will be worth a fortune when I'm dead. Like a van Gogh.' Rolling from her bar stool, her neckline slipped aside to reveal a wide beige bra strap digging into soft brown flesh. She gave Ark an enormous grin. 'It's spelt kind of like *cough*, but it's pronounced like *go*. What's that about? Anyway, back in a sec, homie.' She grazed her outstretched knuckles across Ark's shoulder.

Jenna wove their way through the bodies, obscenely patterned carpet sticky under foot, air fusty with cigarette smoke, beer and perfume. Inside the bathroom, light glared artificially white and the din from the bar was muffled, bass beating dully through the walls. Jenna hurried to a stall and shimmied down her jeans, not bothering to close the cubicle door.

'Is that dude's name seriously "Ark"?' Fairlie asked, leaning against the door frame.

Jenna shrugged, ripping off sheets of toilet paper. 'I suppose so, why?' She grinned. 'Does it even matter?'

Fairlie looked sceptical. 'You're going to pick him up? You?'

Jenna shrugged again, said nothing. But a brief smile played over her face.

'It's about bloody time,' Fairlie said. 'I'm working on Tatts behind the bar, but he's playing hard to catch. But you – really? You never . . . '

'You're making me sound like a nun.' Jenna stood and wriggled her jeans up, the pale blue denim tugging smoothly over her narrow hips like a second skin.

'Close enough,' Fairlie said, turning to the mirror. Her black T-shirt stretched tight over her breasts; her shirt had ridden up on one side and a thick roll of skin slunk over the top of her jeans. She smacked it with a palm then yanked her top down. 'You've had two steady boyfriends, both of whom you met at work, neither of whom rocked your socks.'

'My socks are fine, thank you.'

'And remember that guy at The Tavern last year? You kneed him in the nuts.'

'I didn't knee him in the nuts, I slipped.'

'Upwards? Against gravity?'

'He grabbed my boob.'

'It was the most sex you'd had in a year.'

'It was unwanted.'

'You've given this guy more than three seconds of your time. So do it. Better yet, go do it in the alley, *al fresco*, then bid him *adieu* and come back and help me out with Tatts.' Fairlie was inspecting her face in the cloudy mirror, avoiding a suspicious greasy substance smeared across one corner of the glass. 'Ark Rudolph,' she said, enunciating its syllables. 'Sounds made up.' She squinted at the reflection of her short brown curls sticking out at strange angles. 'My skin looks weird,' she declared. 'It's the colour of cold coffee, don't you think?'

Jenna rinsed her hands without replying.

'All those night shifts this week – I look tired,' Fairlie went on, peering into the mirror. She pushed her eyelids up with her fingertips. 'Better.' Turning back to Jenna, her fingers still prying her eyes open, Fairlie repeated, 'Ark Rudolph. What – is he in the nativity scene?'

Jenna wiped her hands on her jeans. 'Actually, he lives up the road from us. He owns a winery.'

'What's it called – Glowing Noah's?'

Jenna laughed. 'ArkAcres. Remember that place?' She extracted a lip balm from her purse and slid it across her lips. 'It used to be Stone Block Estate. They sold it a couple of years ago.'

Recognition dawned on Fairlie's features and she gave

a low whistle. 'Yeah, ArkAcres. Shit, really? Remember the rumours of how much that place sold for?' Gazing into the mirror again, Fairlie pinched at her cheeks. 'Hope that enormous limestone gateway he installed isn't compensating for a lack in the pants area.'

Jenna caught a glimpse of her own reflection in the mirror: blondish skin over jutting cheekbones, pointed nose and narrow nostrils, straight black fringe brushing into round blue eyes. Bony shoulders, more nipple than breast, shadows pooling in the dip of her collarbones. Against the red of her sleeveless shirt her complexion was stark. She looked away, quickly.

Fairlie clasped Jenna's shoulders tightly with wet hands and fixed her with a stern expression.

'I've gotta say it. You wouldn't normally be interested in him if . . . you know.'

Jenna stiffened under her grasp, but said nothing.

Carefully, Fairlie released her grip. 'You're probably feeling a bit vulnerable since this morning with your mum –'

'Don't, Fro.' Jenna silenced her with the palm of her hand, turning her face away.

'But Jen, she's your mum. She's all you've got.'

Jenna felt a flare of irritation. 'Just because my dad moved out when I was a toddler doesn't mean I need *her* for anything.' She straightened, tossed long hair behind her shoulders. 'Besides, you should know better than anyone.'

'Know what?'

'That blood doesn't matter. It can still fuck you over.'

Fairlie's jaw clenched. 'At least you know where yours comes from.'

In the dirty light they stared at each other, the bass pumping through the walls and a sweaty disinfectant stink rising from the floor.

'I'm sorry,' Jenna said eventually. She pinched the top of her nose and shook her head, hard. 'I don't know where that came from.'

'I'm sorry, too,' Fairlie said. 'You're right. You can be as mad as you want at your mum. Who am I to judge?' With a sigh, Fairlie turned to open the door but instead she clutched uselessly at the air. 'Bloody thing,' she cursed. 'Why'd they put a fake handle on the door?'

The bleat of Jenna's laugh echoed around the bathroom as she wrapped her arm around Fairlie's shoulders and took hold of the door handle. With Fairlie slumped against her, they made their way back to the bar. Jenna's heart juddered as she spotted Ark seeking her out in the crowd.

Raising her voice above the din, Jenna told him, 'We need to go.' Fairlie seemed to be falling asleep against her. She smiled and pressed her cheek to Fairlie's curls. 'I have to work with this one tomorrow.'

'Darn,' he said, slowly. 'Too soon. Hey, are you going to be right with her?'

Fairlie murmured something, and leaned more of her weight into Jenna's chest. Jenna struggled to stay upright.

'Can I help?' Ark held out his hand and after a hesitation, where Jenna's muscles quivered, Fairlie groggily lifted her elbow into it. Between them, they navigated Fairlie through the crowd and out into the street.

Outside, the air was dampening and cool. Halos of mist rimmed the streetlights and the abandoned street thrummed with the bass from the pub. A filmy midnight breeze coaxed a shiver from Jenna's skin as they shuffled around the building to the darkened car park behind the pub. Only a few cars were still parked in the spaces; scruffy callistemons growing between the rows cast long fingers of shadow across the grubby asphalt. At Fairlie's car, the night air finally seemed to rouse Fairlie and she lifted her head to drag her gaze from Ark's feet to his head.

'I'll be damned,' she said, slumping against the car. 'You coming home with us?' As Jenna slipped Fairlie's bag from her shoulders to search for her keys, Fairlie closed her eyes, her head falling again, and mumbled, 'Nun.'

Something in the throwaway comment rankled Jenna. She watched Ark carefully tuck Fairlie into the passenger seat. Lean, strong arms, long legs, shirt stretching across his back as he apologised to Fairlie and reached around her body to clip in the seatbelt. Once Fairlie was safely dozing on the seat, her head drooping, Ark shut the door and turned to Jenna. He opened his mouth to say something and that was when Jenna kissed him. Firmly.

Stretched up on her toes, she pressed him back against the car with her body, hips on hips, chest to chest. Her fingertips sought his warm throat. There was a pause as he was caught off guard, before he kissed her back with equal strength.

Lust rose in her, a swift and fierce thing. She ran her hands down his stomach and hooked a finger into the buckle of his belt. She pulled the strap free.

Ark broke away, surprised, laughing softly. 'Easy,' he said. But his hand slid beneath her shirt to cup her breast, and his tongue pressed against hers, so she lowered his zipper. Her fingers found him hard, his pubic hair brushing her knuckles. The night air carried the sounds of laughter, the staccato thuds of car doors, and Jenna thought of her and Ark cloaked in shadows nearby, furtive and breathless. She drew away from his mouth as his breath quickened. Her teeth grazed the soft pulse beneath his jaw until he finally shuddered and coated her fingers with hot wetness.

Jenna leaned sideways against the car as the strength left Ark's body. He pressed his face into her neck, laughing breathlessly. Flicking her fingers at the ground, she wiped her hand on his jeans, and he reached down to circle her wrist with his thumb and forefinger. With his other hand, he dug his phone from his pocket.

'Please. I've gotta have your number,' he said.

Jenna looked at his face. Pupils so dilated his eyes were a soulful black, lips flushed and parted. She took his phone and her thumb hovered over the screen. Then she quickly keyed in her number.

The car door flung open. Fairlie leaned out and said, 'Jen, I think I'm gonna –'

Then she vomited on Ark's shiny black RM Williams.

Jenna struggled awake, roused by the buzz of her phone on the bedside. Fumbling in the dark, she flipped the screen up and squinted at the painful stab of the bright display. An unfamiliar mobile number. She considered letting it go to voicemail, but it was possibly someone from work, so she answered reluctantly.

'Hey.' The man's voice was soft. 'Did I wake you?'

Something duck-dived beneath her ribs. 'Um . . . yes.'

'Sorry.' He didn't sound it. His voice lowered even further. 'You know only ninety minutes ago, we were at the pub?'

Jenna lay back on her pillow, the hawk and rumble of Fairlie's snoring coming through the adjoining wall. A pang of mortification came to her with flashes of writhing bodies and thumping bass, the muscular press of the man's body firm against hers, his semen cooling stickily on her fingers.

'After driving home, and hauling Fro into bed, I've been asleep for all of –' she brought the phone briefly from her ear and glanced at the screen '– about thirty minutes.'

'I couldn't wait,' he said.

'Until?'

'Another eight hours.'

Jenna paused. 'What happens in eight hours?'

'We're meeting at the Valley Lake for a picnic.'

'We are?'

'Invite your friends.'

Jenna's grin felt reckless, her pulse beat thick in her throat.

Somnolent afternoon sunlight raked fat golden fingers through the oak leaves. Children's voices rang out from the playground and a humid, grass-scented heat rose from the lawn as Jenna crossed her legs beneath her, the faded tartan blanket bunching beneath her bare ankles.

Ark was laughing. 'More water, Fairlie?'

From beneath an enormous floppy hat and oversized sunglasses, Fairlie winced as a toddler's shriek carried across from the swings.

'I'm fine,' Fairlie answered, lowering herself to her side, voluminous maxi dress billowing about her. 'Don't you worry about me, sunshine.'

'Fairlie Winter, eternal optimist,' said Abbey Manfried, a friend of Jenna's and Fairlie's since they'd all studied their diplomas together at TAFE. Gazing through black-rimmed glasses balanced upon a stubby nose, Abbey said this as she reached across the remains of the food in the centre of the rug for the last softening wedge of brie.

'Just don't expect her to remember to pay the rent on time,' Jenna said. 'Or at all.'

'Meh.' Fairlie was attempting to tug her hat lower, but her curls kept pushing it back up. 'Life's too short to remember things like rent,' she declared, giving up on the hat and tossing it aside.

'I'm not sure your landlord would agree,' Abbey said, sliding the slice of brie between the moustache-trimmed lips of her boyfriend, Damon, and following it with a liberal kiss.

Fairlie wrinkled her nose at the display. 'That's what I have Jenna for,' she said. 'She remembers stuff.'

Watching ants crawl into the leftover smears of tzatziki, Jenna felt the striking weight of Ark's gaze on her, his fingers casually stroking her knee, the brush of his body as he reached for food or leaned back to laugh. His presence numbed the mental strobe of her mother's face, dulled the sharp rap of yesterday's revelations. Closing her eyes, she remembered the surprised jolt of his body as she took his pleasure for herself. Heat welled inside her, an internal cringe.

She stood. 'I'm going for a walk. My legs are going to sleep.'

'I'll come with you.' Ark jumped to his feet.

'Well, *I'm* going to sleep.' Fairlie rolled onto her back, flopped an arm over her face.

From beneath the shade of the oaks, the lawn sloped down to the edge of the crater lake. Jenna and Ark made their way lazily across the lawn, Jenna tapping her fingers on her legs in time with her pace. Sunlight sparkled off the bottle-green surface of the water, mallards drifted amongst the reeds and three black swans coasted towards the thin grey-sand crescent of beach, triangular wakes streaming behind. A narrow timber boardwalk was set out over the water, following the lake's edge through the reeds and disappearing out of sight behind a drooping willow that dipped long, trailing limbs to comb the water.

Jenna pointed out the swans. 'Did you know black swans are only found wild in Australia?'

'You're kidding,' Ark said. 'They're everywhere. Aggressive bastards, I once had one chase me down and steal my sandwich.' He gave the birds a thorough side-eye.

'They're protected,' Jenna added. 'So I guess they're entitled to your sandwich.'

As they stepped onto the boardwalk Ark's fingers brushed hers, setting off sparks of electricity across her skin. Their footfalls were hollow on the sun-bleached timber. Reeds clacked against the boards with the push and tug of the breeze on the water.

'Check them out.' Ark pointed to a water-skier on the far side of the lake, where the shadowed limestone edge of the crater rose from the water's edge to thrust up into the sky. As Jenna looked over, the skier was tumbling over a whitewash of water; the boat's engine lifted then fell as it circled back.

'Graceful,' Ark said with a laugh.

'Ever tried water skiing? It's impossible,' Jenna said. 'All I could do was scoot along on my bum.'

Ark stopped, turning to her. Having passed around the willow tree they stood out of sight over the water, amongst the reeds. Insects clicked in the hot air and the lake gave off a pungent, muddy scent.

'Nothing's impossible,' he said, his hands resting lightly on the small of her back.

'Look, about last night,' Jenna began. 'What happened at the car. I'm . . . a little embarrassed.'

A slow grin spread across his face. 'Why?'

'It was a little bit public. I'm not usually so brazen.'

Ark's shoulder hitched and he chuckled softly. 'And I usually last longer than fifteen seconds.' Jenna's cheeks flamed and he took up her hand. 'It was nice,' he said softly. '*Very* nice. I went to sleep smiling.'

Jenna didn't know what to say. She licked her lips, looked out across the water.

'Hey.' Gently, Ark touched the strap of her dress. 'Why an elephant?'

Jenna glanced down to the top of her breast to where her tattoo peeked out from under her straps. 'I've always loved elephants,' she replied, giving a small shrug. 'They're enormous, powerful beasts, and yet they're entirely peaceful – gentle and majestic. Did you know that a herd of elephants is led by a matriarch?'

'Really?' A smile played at the corners of his mouth, his fingertips still lightly grazing her skin.

'It's true,' she told him, rambling now. 'Usually the matriarch is the oldest, wisest cow. Elephant herds are

38

amazing – they maintain these beautiful bonded relationships and relate to each other with compassion and
respect. The matriarchs teach this compassion and care
to the younger elephants – their daughters – and, in turn,
these skills of nurturance and leadership get passed on
from generation to generation. I think,' she finished, with
another lift of her shoulders, 'maybe we could stand to
learn a thing or two from them. Start a few less wars.'

He was studying her intently; maddeningly, her cheeks
continued to burn.

'Anyway,' she said, gently shoving his chest. 'You
wanted to know –'

Something smacked against her cheek: a tiny, sharp
flick. She jumped and flung her hands to her face as the
insect dove again, this time grazing her forehead. With a
shriek, she took an involuntary step back.

'Jenna!'

The boards disappeared from beneath her feet. Air
rushed around her before she slapped against the water.
Fizz rushed in her ears, reeds needled and scraped against
her skin and the murky, green-algae scent of pond water
filled her nose. Coughing, Jenna's feet found the muddy
bottom and she lunged to the surface.

There was a loud splash beside her. A percussion of
water slammed against her, shoving her back to her
knees.

'I'm okay!' she spluttered, scrambling to find the bottom
again.

But before she could, she was lifted into the air. Strong arms wrapped beneath her back and the crook of her knees and she was placed carefully on the boardwalk. Water streamed from Ark's body as he clambered back onto the boards alongside her.

'Are you okay?' Brows furrowed, he swiped at the water dripping into his eyes.

'I'm fine,' she replied breathlessly, wiping water from her face. She didn't know whether to laugh hysterically or wither from embarrassment. Her dress was sodden and tangled high up her thighs. Greenish mud smeared down her shins. Looking up at him, his face crowding out the sun, her mirth won over and she began to laugh.

After a beat of concern, Ark joined in. A dark pool spread onto the dry timber around them as water sluiced from their bodies and they doubled over, gasping for breath. As their giggles subsided, Ark took up her hand. He laced his fingers into hers, kissed her knuckles. Leaning in, he touched her face gently with his free hand, as though to stroke her, but instead he plucked a long string of pond weed from her cheek.

And then he tugged her to her knees, wrapped his arms around her and kissed her, his body pressed close and their clothes clinging to their skin, and his mouth tasted redwarm, of promise and of possibility.

'You're telling me a bird did this to you?' Jenna asked, pulling on a pair of gloves.

'Actually the cat did this,' Mr Ryland answered, 'while I tried to stop him from *eating* the bird.'

Jenna pulled a stool alongside his wheelchair and the old man winced as she gently swabbed antiseptic over a series of deep gouges on his cheek. His skin was craggy and thin, spotted with age.

'It's not even my bird, you see,' he continued. 'I'm looking after it for a mate.'

'Perhaps owning a cat isn't the best prerequisite for being a bird-sitter, Joe,' she pointed out.

'Not my cat, either.'

Jenna laughed. She instructed the 77-year-old to hold still as she applied butterfly tape to his wounds.

'Right you are, nurse.'

'So who came first, the cat or the bird –'

Stella, the registered nurse on shift, popped her head around the door frame. 'Jenna, what are you still doing here? Your shift finished fifteen minutes ago.'

Jenna smiled and nodded. 'We're almost done. I couldn't leave without catching up with Mr Ryland again, right, Joe? It's been, what, a week since we last saw you in here?' When she checked her watch, her blood quickened. Forty-five minutes until Ark would be picking her up. Hastily she finished dressing Mr Ryland's wounds, tossed her gloves into the bin and scrubbed her hands at the sink.

'Nurse?'

Jenna's head snapped up.

'I need to whiz.' Joe Ryland whistled, and swept his hand away from his crotch in a fountain-like curve.

Jenna glanced again at her watch. Forty minutes. 'Of course,' she said. 'I'll take you.'

She couldn't find her earrings. Fairlie was at work, so Jenna couldn't recruit her in the search.

Jenna tore around the flat, flinging books and DVD cases and the odd shoe looking for the pair of oversized silver hoops she'd purchased from a street vendor a year ago on a boozy weekend to Ballarat with Fairlie.

'Shit,' Jenna muttered, thumping into the kitchen. 'Bloody hell.'

She rifled behind the spice rack, slid aside two hardback cookbooks, wrinkled her nose over the precarious stack of grimy dishes in the sink. She even shoved her fingers into the damp maidenhair fern on the windowsill, grown too big for its pot and overflowing onto the benchtop.

'This place is a *mess*.'

In the lounge room, she dropped to her knees and thrust her hands beneath two clothes racks laden with stiffening laundry, her fingers skimming the carpet as she resolved that as soon as Fairlie was awake tomorrow they would tidy up.

'Yes, Fro,' Jenna said aloud to herself, hurrying to the bathroom. 'We clean all day at work. But I'm scared one of us is going to catch Ebola at home.'

There they are! Triumphantly, she pulled the hoops from inside the glass jar holding her toothbrush. Just as she threaded the bars into her earlobes, there was a knock at the door. With her stomach flip-flopping, she returned to the kitchen and pulled open the front door.

'Hey, Jenna.'

'Hi,' she replied. 'I'd invite you in but, frankly, I'm too embarrassed by the state of our house.'

He laughed then peered over her shoulder. 'I'm not here to judge your housekeeping skills.'

'Lucky,' she told him. Taking a step forwards, she made to move through the doorway but he took her hand.

'This is for you,' he said, handing her a small white box, loops of pale blue satin spilling from its top.

Jenna felt a stab of self-consciousness. 'You shouldn't have,' she said, her fingers hovering over the ribbon.

'I couldn't show up empty-handed to our second date. Chivalry isn't dead,' he told her, 'despite what they say.'

Inwardly cursing the burn in her cheeks, Jenna untied the bow and opened the box. Inside was an exquisite white silk scarf. Fringed with soft threads, the fabric billowed and floated as she moved it through her fingers.

'It's real silk,' Ark said. 'According to the lady at the shop.'

'Thank you,' she said, taken aback. 'It's beautiful.' She

wrapped the scarf around her throat, it whispered like breath on her skin.

Ark smiled and thrust his hands boyishly into the pockets of his jeans. His hair was raked into spikes and, with skin clean-shaven, he smelled alpine, fresh. He looked at the floor, shuffling the toe of one carefully shined shoe.

'It looks great on you – I knew it would.'

Jenna collected her bag and Ark held the door as she stepped outside. The air was delicate and aromatic with the smoky scent of summer-dry grass. Magpies warbled from the eucalypts. Parked at the kerb, a silver Mercedes glinted, dappled with gum tree shadows. Jenna felt her nerves twang.

As he opened the passenger-side door for her, she was careful to tread directly onto the spotless mat in the footwell. The last man she had dated was a painfully reticent dairy farmer from Kalangadoo named Ron who drove a battered old Ford Falcon ute and always smelled faintly of cow dung. Ron's parents were old friends of Jenna's mother; she had only agreed to go out with Ron a few times after her mum had impressed upon her that his dog had been trampled by a bull and had to be euthanised, and they were all worried for his mental health. The contrast with Ark was stark, but the thought triggered her mother's voice again. She swallowed it away.

'I had a great time on Sunday,' Ark told her. 'Your friends are fun.' He pressed the ignition button and the car purred into life. 'So you and Fro are pretty close, huh?'

'Since we were babies,' she said, without thinking. 'Our mothers have been friends since before we were born –' She stopped, closed her mouth.

'Small town,' he said lightly. 'Limits your social options a bit?'

She regarded him. Was he teasing her?

'You lived in Adelaide – I suppose you have thousands of friends?'

He tipped his head with a laugh, glancing to give way to oncoming traffic. 'I actually grew up in Tanunda, in the Barossa. Didn't move down to Adelaide until I was eighteen. My parents,' he stopped to clear his throat, tapping his mouth with a loose fist, then went on, 'they owned a winery up there. Pretty typical childhood – went to an expensive private school that didn't exactly keep me out of trouble.'

'Do you have any brothers or sisters?'

'Sister. Younger.' He smiled then. 'Much younger. She makes me want to move back home, just so I can sit on the front porch with a shotgun, you know? Scare off all the blokes.' He laughed. 'But don't tell my mother that – she'd be straight on the phone whining for an ETA in writing.' Sunlight and shadow strobed across his face as the car sped up. 'You?'

She wanted to change the subject. 'Just me,' she answered quickly.

'You're more than enough.'

Startled, she looked at him, thinking it was an oddly

fascinating thing to say. He didn't go on, just smiled at her, and after a moment she settled back into the seat, running her palms over the fabric of her skirt. The engine hummed softly and Ark drove one-handed by resting his wrist on top of the steering wheel, fingers relaxed, the other hand draped across his lap. Sculpted biceps stretched against the sleeve of his shirt. She was filled with an urge to trace her fingertips along the sinuous veins in his forearms. The interior of the car felt humid and she loosened her scarf.

'Why'd you move to Adelaide?' she asked.

'My dad died when I was fourteen, and after a few years I just needed to get out for a bit.'

'Oh, I'm so sorry.'

'Hey, not at all.' He offered her a smile before his attention returned to the road. 'It was a long time ago. My history is mostly uninteresting. I'd rather hear about you.'

'Growing up on a winery doesn't sound dull.'

'Far more dull than having a local TV celebrity for a mother.'

Jenna's fingers tightened on her knees. 'It's not as exciting as you might think. And I really am sorry about your father. That must have been rough.'

'It was, but, you know. Time heals wounds and all that.' This time, the smile he gave her was heart-stopping.

'Where are we going?' she asked.

'I've got it all planned out,' he told her with a grin. 'I hope you don't mind,' he added, accelerating to pass a log truck that lumbered in their lane. 'We've got pizza at

46

The Wooden Spoon, then I've got tickets for the movies in Mount Gambier.'

She let her head rest back on the seat, her eyes stealing to the side of his face to watch him as he drove. At the tender hollow of his throat she imagined she could see his pulse; she could almost taste his skin, salty on her tongue. He'd planned out a date: polite conversation, dinner and a movie, but all Jenna wanted to do was screw him against a wall.

What was happening to her?

r—O

River red gums, so tall their branches plucked the clouds, shed rags of bark onto the white gravel drive. Two low walls of limestone flanked the entrance to the driveway, ARKACRES in brushed steel lettering affixed to the stone.

The indicator ticked as Jenna slowed down and pulled from the highway onto the drive. The gums gave way to vines as the car crunched along the gravel. Jenna rolled down her window and breathed in the sweet bite of fertile earth and eucalyptus in the morning air. The land undulated softly and the rows of vines dipped neatly into hollows and climbed over ridges. Dots of sheep grazed the bright green strips between the grapes. Was this *all* Ark's?

The car rounded a curve and the gravel driveway opened out into lawn that sprawled before a long limestone home. Dark red iron roof, chunky timber architraves and a wide, shadowed deck running the length of the house. A purple-green Cootamundra wattle dropped browning balls of blossom onto the lawn. Sheds and outbuildings of multiple sizes were dotted around the property.

Unsure where to park, she rolled to a stop next to a new-looking shed alongside the house. Nervously, she applied the handbrake and stepped from the car. Sunlight broke from between the clouds and warmed her scalp.

'Hey,' Ark called out to her from the verandah.

'Is this *all* yours?'

'Eighty-two acres,' he replied. He strode to her, kissed her cheek. 'The vineyards all butt up together around here so it looks like hundreds of hectares, but yeah, pretty much everything you can see.' He leaned close to her, bringing a scent that kicked the backs of her knees. He pointed back down the drive. 'See that line of pine trees?' He indicated a dark line in the middle distance. 'That's my northern boundary. The highway is another boundary, the back you can't see from here and the southern edge is down near Hollick's.' His breath smelled of peppermint.

'And your grandmother left you this?'

He shook his head. 'Grandma left me an inheritance. I bought this with it.'

'Some inheritance.'

He laughed. 'I'm very lucky.'

'And you live here alone?'

'Well, for the last few months, yep.'

'I'm sorry,' Jenna said, warmth rising in her cheeks. 'That's so nosy.'

'Not at all.' He waved away her embarrassment and took up her hand. 'Come on, I'll give you the grand tour.'

Inside, the house was as beautiful as the outside suggested. Light and airy with open spaces; slate floors and plush carpet and fresh paint. Although Ark lived alone, she sensed the uneasy ambiance of someone recently absent. Ark's solitude was evident yet he didn't seem lonely. If she breathed deeply enough, she might be able to catch a whiff of her: shampoo or perfume perhaps, a ghostly trail left behind.

After making tea, they sat at a wooden table on the back deck. The view rolled down towards the highway: more grapes, more gum trees, more broad expanse of lawn. In the middle distance, a ute moved stutteringly through the rows of grapes and a man heaped mulch over the roots of the plants.

Curiosity eventually got the better of Jenna. 'How long ago did she move out?'

Ark looked thoughtful. 'I've tried not to think about it, to be honest. Three, maybe four months.'

Jenna waited for him to offer more.

'The whole thing was a mistake,' he told her with a smile. 'Don't worry, she's gone for good. Her family came and got her – they could never keep out of things. Always interfering. She's back in Perth now. Deleted me on Facebook.' He gave an exaggerated shudder. 'She wasn't a very nice person. Showed her true colours quickly. Don't know what I was thinking,' he said, shaking his head. 'I dodged a bullet.'

Jenna gave a short, nervous laugh and looked down into her tea, embarrassed. Was he analysing her? Sizing up whether this woman was different? A grey edge of self-doubt crept in and, with a sudden fury, she wanted the feeling gone.

Slowly, deliberately, Jenna lifted her eyes, gazing at him from beneath her lashes.

He was drinking her in. An inquiring tilt of his head, a restrained smile in the corners of his lips, as though he knew something about her that she didn't, as though he was peering into her, undressing her slowly. The sensation began in the centre of her chest and unfolded deep within her belly. Heat rose from her chest, warm fingers upon her collarbones.

Ark wrapped his hand around the arm of her chair. He tugged her closer and she shoved her way around the corner of the table, so there was nothing between them. He dragged her closer still, until her knees were pressed to his.

A part of her wondered what she was doing. It felt rash and irresponsible: rebellious. Alone with a man she barely knew, possessed by her own uncertainty and pain, and aware that he, too, was hurting. A diversion in the heat of his fingers on her thighs; distraction in his lips pressed into her neck. Belief in the hands that encircled her, the breath that consumed her.

'I'm really falling for you.' His words slipped beneath

the surface of her skin, a gift. Hands on her hips, he lifted her effortlessly towards him and, as she straddled his body, he rose to meet her, his radiant warmth filling the space between her arms, her thighs, her knees.

He was an analgesic, a penance and an offering, and she accepted it with welcome greed.

It was midnight when Fairlie returned home from her shift. Jenna lay awake in the dark, blankets kicked to her ankles. She listened to the sounds of the front door push open then fall softly closed, keys and bags being dumped, shoes kicked across the floor. The kettle clicked on and water rushed as it boiled. Bright light shot in from under her bedroom door.

Jenna sat up. Squinting, she pulled open the bedroom door and shuffled into the kitchen.

Fairlie was pouring hot water into a cup. 'Hey, what are you doing up?'

'Hard to sleep with all the noise you're making.'

'Sorry.' Fairlie sipped her drink. 'Didn't realise I was being loud.'

Jenna lifted Fairlie's jacket and bag from a chair to sit down but the bag tipped upside down and its contents strew across the floor. Purse, balled tissues, sticks of lip balm, faded and crumpled receipts.

'Bloody *hell*,' Jenna cried. She wheeled on her friend and

saw Fairlie's eyebrows rocket up, her cup paused halfway to her mouth. 'Why can't you clean your shit up?'

'Huh?'

'Seriously, Fro. I can't live in this pigsty.'

Fairlie's gaze swept the kitchen, the lounge room. 'It's not that bad,' she countered. 'What's wrong?'

'This mess! It's everywhere. There's clothes, dirty dishes. Just . . . shit. Everywhere.'

'Jen –'

Jenna couldn't look at her. 'It's not big enough for the two of us.'

Fairlie set her cup down, firmly. 'All right, what's going on?'

'Nothing's "going on". I'm just over the mess.'

'We've lived together for a year. This is exactly how it's always looked: lived in.' Fairlie crouched and swept the contents of her handbag into a pile. 'Sure it's messy but we're not wallowing in squalor.'

It was as though Jenna was looking through a lens and the focus telescoped out. Her peripheral vision blurred, and Fairlie shrunk away. Jenna blinked and saw Fairlie, grown robust, secure and affectionate with the love of two parents. Fairlie, a mess who didn't care what people thought. And next to her, Jenna saw herself: a broken sidekick, bitter and bewildered. Uncertain. Seeking and craving. The thought repulsed her.

'I love you,' Jenna said, her voice cracking. 'But we're not the same.'

'That just occur to you?' Fairlie huffed as she rose to her feet, setting her bag back on the chair. 'Haven't noticed that for twenty-odd years, I've been obese and black and you're skinny and white?'

Jenna softened. 'You're not *obese*.' She sighed, lifting Fairlie's bag from the chair and setting it on the table. 'Just a little pudgy, maybe.' She sank onto the chair and scrubbed at her face, trying to slough away the thoughts in her mind.

'Fine. I'm a well-risen soufflé.' Fairlie sat beside her, frowning. 'You've never said anything like this before.'

Jenna's gaze slid to the ceiling, to a lace of cobweb quivering across the cornice. She felt trapped by that ceiling; she wanted the roof to lift off so she could soar out into the night.

'Jen?' Fairlie prompted quietly. 'What's going on?'

'I don't know,' Jenna said, 'I don't *know*.'

Dear Jenna,

I don't know if you'll read this. Perhaps you're still too angry, or confused, or hurt. I understand — really, I do. But I want to tell you everything. There's so much more to the story than what you've heard. All I can do is write, and hope that maybe one day I'll have the courage to send you this letter.

Over the years I've tried to figure out the moment when it all changed. I've tried to pinpoint that mark in time where everything began to run in a direction entirely out of my control.

No. That's not quite right. Forgive me. Saying it like that, it sounds as though I'm trying to absolve myself of responsibility. Of course it was all within my grasp; everything happened as a direct result of my actions. I know that now, and so do you, obviously, as you haven't spoken to me for a year.

But I need to begin somewhere, so where better than the day that it all changed?

I felt particularly ebullient after work one day in late May. I'd wanted to leave work early but that day's recording had dragged — the cameraman was new, and I'd had to recite the headlines a few times before he'd managed to get it right. Eventually, with that evening's news recorded and ready to be broadcast, I dashed from the studio.

That night, I was going to tell him.

I tried to imagine the look on Stephen's face, tried to picture what his reaction would be. His firm had just taken on a lucrative new client and your father's hours had recently soared. Back then, we would always smile at each other – even if it was close to midnight, and even if we'd forgotten the last time we had done something as simple and reassuring as washing the dishes together.

You wouldn't remember any of this, of course. All that ease, all that contentedness – that was all long gone by the time your earliest memories would begin to set. But there was a time, Jenna, when your father and I . . . well, we just worked.

I swept through the entire house – six bedrooms, two living rooms and the echoing foyer, the type of place that I had never dreamed myself living in – snapping on all the lights; I wanted warmth, I wanted brightness. I wanted my soul to sing with my news so I could feel nothing but the elation it deserved. I would have touched up my lipstick, teased up that dark brown perm that was so fashionable in the 80s.

I was thrilled that for once my insistence that morning had worked and Stephen kept his promise – he was home in time for dinner.

Austerity was a notion incompatible with Stephen Walker. The charisma in his speech, the joviality in his short, muscular stature. That strip of moustache that always, somehow, accentuated the depth of the words he spoke. It was what had first piqued my interest: the effervescence of his prose seemed animated by the line of hair atop his lip.

How can I begin to describe that attraction to you? I suppose you could say I was a flower-child, blown into Mount Gambier in a rattling banana-coloured Kombi at the age of fifteen with your grandma and grandpa and our two pet budgerigars. How could I not find Stephen's worldly charm novel and irresistible? It wasn't about the money – despite what they all said. I loved that Stephen had bucked the trend of his family's haulage company and chosen instead to practise law. It wasn't about the money, Jenna, it never was. You must believe that.

As we sat down to eat, Stephen smiled and said, 'You're hiding something. What's going on?'

Involuntarily, I winced at his choice of words. Hiding something.

And then I told him: 'I'm pregnant.'

There. I've told you the moment when it all changed. For now, I will leave you with this. But there's more, Jenna, so much more.

If only I could know if you will ever hear it. And so, until next time.

Love, Mum

3

Now

The day grows relentlessly hot. One of those scorching summer Fridays when living creatures grind to a halt and exhausted eucalypts discard limbs like clothing.

With a finger, Fairlie lifts the gauze curtain aside. The windowsill digs into her chin. Yellow-brown paddocks shimmer across the road, crispy-skinned from the sun. Heat touches her face through the glass. Town is silent; no cars slip along the road, her neighbours are bunkered inside their houses. Not that Penola is usually a hubbub of noise – the length of the main street, doubling as the highway between Adelaide and Mount Gambier, can be strolled in a pinch of minutes.

By Fairlie's feet, Henry selects another crayon and waves it blithely across a piece of paper. Crayons spread in a shattered rainbow between the couch and the television cabinet. Yodel, having decided to drop the offence, squints indifferently atop a pile of unfolded laundry on the couch. Fairlie's attention wanders to a comet-shaped brown stain on the carpet, stretching from the couch almost to the centre of the room: a cup of coffee kicked over as Jenna had fled the room. The stain is only a couple of weeks old. Panicky sobs threaten to rise, and she presses a hand to her mouth to restrain them.

A car pulls into the drive. Hearing the sound of the engine, Henry pauses mid-scribble and asks hopefully, 'Is Mummy?'

Fairlie cups the crown of his head with her palm. 'No, love, not your mummy.'

The front door clicks open and the round moon of Pattie Winter's face leans into the room. 'Did you know there's a veal parmigiana and passionfruit sponge cake on the step here?' The beads of her mother's necklace clack against the door.

'Hi, Mum,' Fairlie says, picking her way over crayons, sultana boxes and balls of paper. 'Mrs Soblieski must have dropped them and ran.' Poking her head outside, Fairlie squints across the bright courtyard. 'Usually she at least knocks on the door.'

Pattie heaves a grocery bag inside, its fabric sides

bulging as she sets it down. Stooping, she collects the fragrant bounty from the step.

'There's enough food here for ten people!'

'Sounds about right,' Fairlie replies absently, bending to effuse over Henry's proffered artwork before collecting the grocery bag.

Fairlie sets the bag on the kitchen counter and her mother busies herself emptying its contents. Milk, cheese, eggs and bread sail into the fridge, rice crackers and two-minute noodles into the pantry while Fairlie mumbles her gratitude.

'Dad sends his love,' Pattie is saying. 'He's stuck at work, but he'll be up as soon as he's done. They're grading a bunch of unsealed roads out at OB Flat. *Again.*' She gives Fairlie a look of wretched apology before turning her gaze to Henry. Pattie folds her hands in front of her waist, almost respectfully, as though standing in front of a war memorial. Her thin arms, covered with fine hair and over-crowded with freckles, are pale against a floral sleeveless dress. Her waist is still trim despite age oozing inches onto her hips. Hers is the prim, neat countenance of a 1950s housewife, despite being born in 1961. A weighted silence passes between them.

'I'm sorry I couldn't get here earlier,' Pattie says. 'I came as quick as I could.'

'He seems fine enough,' Fairlie tells her as they watch the child pull washing from the couch onto the floor. 'It hasn't even been a full day yet, I guess he's still waiting for her. He hasn't been too shy with me, I thought he'd treat me as a stranger . . . ' She lowers her voice and adds, 'He keeps asking for her, though.'

'Have you heard from Ark yet?'

'No.' Fairlie sighs. 'What am I supposed to tell him?'

'Henry?' Her mother frowns. 'You don't have to tell him anything – leave that to Ark. I just can't –' she breaks off, contemplating the scope of it. 'I can't believe it. What was she *thinking*?'

A mental flash: blood ballooning into bath water. When she sliced her forearms open the pain must have been indescribable.

'Maybe she wasn't,' Fairlie says. 'Maybe she wasn't thinking at all.'

Silently, they watch as Henry moves around the lounge room: he lunges at the cat, who disappears in a ginger streak; he smears his fingers across the black television screen. Picking up the remote, Fairlie flicks to ABC2 and *Peppa Pig* appears on the screen.

'I can't help but wonder,' Pattie says, 'this – is it unexpected?'

Fairlie meets her mother's gaze, says nothing.

'I'm sorry, honey, but I have to ask,' her mother begins as she makes her way to the couch. 'Did you have any idea that she might be considering . . .'

A fresh stab of guilt thuds into her. 'No,' Fairlie answers, but it feels like a lie. With a hint of desperation she repeats, '*No*. Despite everything, despite her fading away into herself this past year or so, I never saw that it was . . . this bad. I know she had some rough days – the baby, Ark working all the time. But . . . ' She tips her face to the ceiling, hands limp at her sides. 'I failed her.'

'Fairlie –'

'I should have *done* something.'

'What could you have done if she didn't tell you anything?' Pattie says, and starts to sort washing into piles. 'Maybe she . . . ' Her mother stops, looks at her pointedly. 'Maybe it was a spur of the moment thing?'

'Pretty fucking impulsive thing to do.'

'Fairlie.'

'Sorry.'

'Look.' Pattie picks up a singlet and folds it neatly in her lap. 'She's always been a bit flighty. Done things rashly, you know.'

Fairlie frowns. 'She's not "flighty", she's . . . ' *What?* she thinks, *Lonely?*

'She flew off the handle at Evelyn and never spoke to her again,' her mother is saying, 'then she got married on a whim and even you've said over the past year she's disappeared –'

'All right, enough,' Fairlie interrupts. 'I'm not going to judge Jenna because we can't understand. Obviously, she was *hurting* and no one paid enough attention.' The cushions give out an arduous huff as Fairlie slumps onto the couch. 'If we're going to judge anyone, it needs to be the people around her – the people who *failed* her.

Starting with me. Why didn't I see how desperate she was?'

'Because she loved you.' Pattie avoids her gaze, hands busy with a towel. 'If she wanted to do this, the last person she'd tell would be you. Obviously, you'd have done something about it.'

'This is my fault.'

'Don't even think that. It's ridiculous.'

Henry whines, hurrying over to clutch at Fairlie's knee. 'Mummy,' he says, looking longingly towards the door. 'Where's Mummy?'

Fairlie pulls him into her lap. But Henry resists, his chubby body stiff and uncompliant as he gives a frustrated yelp. 'No! Mummy!'

Fairlie lets him sit rigidly on her knee, carefully murmuring kind, empty condolences that skirt purposely around the truth. 'Mama's not here right now,' she says. 'Don't worry. Daddy will be here soon.' Sliding from her knee, Henry wanders to the door and peers out the window, as though standing sentry to Fairlie's insincere assurances.

With Henry out of earshot, Fairlie says, 'I don't understand how she could leave him.'

There's a heavy pause, the room thick with unspoken obviousness. Almost before Pattie opens her mouth, Fairlie knows what her mother is about to say.

'It can be the hardest thing in the world,' her mother says, 'to leave a child. But sometimes, there are reasons.' Briskly, she snaps the wrinkles from a crumpled T-shirt.

'We might not understand a mother's motives. We might not even agree. But we should always forgive. Besides,' leaning across the pile of washing, Pattie gives her daughter's hand a pat, 'sometimes, the most wonderful things come of it.'

Fairlie doesn't know whether to smile or feel enraged. 'You can hardly compare adopting me with Jenna's suicide.'

A ghost walks across Pattie's face. If Fairlie didn't know differently, she might suggest her mother was frightened. But this is a look she has seen before, the quiet reclusiveness of internal conversation.

At length, Pattie's face relaxes and she offers Fairlie a tired smile. 'We've always tried to be honest with you,' she says, smoothing out a pair of shorts, 'but there's things we don't know.'

Familiar with this vein of ambiguous introspection, Fairlie lets it drop. She opens her arms for Henry and he climbs onto her lap again, rubbing his eyes with clenched fists and leaving biscuit crumbs on his lashes.

Pattie continues, 'Sometimes, we just have to accept that people have their reasons.'

'I know.'

'Life is complicated, people are complicated.'

'Yes, I know.'

'Sometimes acceptance –'

'Mum,' Fairlie stops her. 'Please, can we not do this now?'

'Fairlie –'

'You'll listen to me now, then?' Fairlie snaps. 'Is that it? You're feeling sorry for me so you'll actually consider my side?'

'I've always considered your side.'

'Growing up different to your own parents? Feeling like a white person even though you're black?'

'I –' Pattie's mouth opens, then closes. She shakes her head.

'But that's right, I'm supposed to be grateful. To feel *lucky*.'

'You *are* lucky.' Her mother's voice has taken on a sharp edge.

Sighing, Fairlie drops her head back against the cushions. The conversation is over; her mother marks it with a small nod. Setting aside her pile of folding, Pattie stands.

'Right. I'm going to get started on your dishes. It looks like it's been a while since you did them.' As Pattie moves past, she bends to kiss the top of Fairlie's head. 'My goodness, what happened here?' Her mother is pointing to the coffee stain on the carpet.

'I knocked over my drink.' To Fairlie's surprise, the lie comes out like a reflex action.

Pattie tuts at her. 'You should have put some bi-carb on it straightaway.'

Fairlie stares at the stain, hoping the brown smear might offer some answers, relieve her of her guilt. Because she tried, didn't she? But Jenna had fled.

'I'm sorry,' her mother says softly. Fairlie acknowledges the olive branch by returning the apology. Pattie squeezes her shoulder, then touches the top of Henry's head and moves into the kitchen.

Fairlie sinks deeper into the couch. Never again will Jenna's shriek of laughter contagiously set off her own, never again will they quote lines in unison from films or make each other exactly the right drink without asking first. As Henry slumps disconsolately onto the cushion alongside her, Fairlie feels a yawning black hole of awareness move across her.

Oh God, Jenna. What have you done?

─○

Finally, as filmy-gold light spills through the front windows onto the carpet like paint, Fairlie hears the rattle of Ark's LandCruiser out front.

Twenty-four hours have passed since Jenna died. Waiting for Ark's silence to break, Fairlie has held Henry, confused and whimpering, clinging to her skin as though his mother might be hidden inside it. But as the day has worn on, Fairlie has begun to wonder if perhaps it isn't she clinging to Jenna's child as though his weight might counterbalance her guilt.

Watching Jenna's husband cross the driveway – his sullen gait, the drop of his head and shoulders – part of her wants to reach out and hold him. But another, more surprised and cautious part of her wants to hate him, to blame him. This conflict feeds her angst like kindling.

Opening the door, Fairlie snaps a finger to her mouth before Ark can speak.

'I've just gotten him to sleep,' she hisses. 'He's been so unsettled, I had to lie with him for over an hour.'

Ark fills the tiny space. He flashes her a glance: a brief, blue-eyed instant analysis. Ark Rudolph is striking, it's undeniable. But Fairlie struggled to see what Jenna did. Tall, but not exceptionally. Strong and artfully shaped through hard physical work, but he's no body builder. There was always an effortless exaggeration in his presence, a command of attention without trying. Now he's dishevelled in a faded orange T-shirt, cheap rubber thongs on his feet, rusty hair in wild spikes. No RM Williams or Country Road today.

Fairlie allows her anger to well up, an ephemeral, junkie-like fix for the waiting grief. 'Where have you been?' she demands, fists propped on her hips.

'When my wife dies, I'm sure it's within my rights to take some time to grieve,' he says.

'Ark, you walked out on your kid.'

'I know.' Abruptly he looks wretched. 'I just couldn't . . .' He takes a few uncertain steps across the room, placing his feet with caution. His gaze flits across the crayon and cracker mess on the beige carpet, the bookshelf overflowing with creased paperbacks, to alight on the wall dividing the kitchen and living room: rows and rows of photographs, crookedly hung, frames mismatched and touching at the corners. Jenna's face peers out of so many of those pictures: jubilant, serious, laughing, contented. A selfie of them both atop a sand dune on the Coorong where the Southern Ocean thunders onto the shore, their faces wind-whipped and sand-stung, they squint, cheek to cheek, hair in each other's mouths. An eerie, voyeuristic peek back through time.

'Thanks,' Ark says, turning away from Jenna's faces. 'Thanks for taking him. Where is he?'

'He's asleep, like I said. But,' she hesitates, 'don't you think we should talk first?' Taken aback by his look of helplessness, she steps towards him, feeling the urge to snatch up his hand in hers. With a start, she recognises empathy: she knows how it feels to be abandoned by Jenna.

He stares at her. 'Why do you want to talk about it?'

'Because I want to know why.'

'There's nothing to talk about, Fairlie. My wife just died. I'm sure you can appreciate that I'm not in the mood for discussion.'

In the centre of the room he stands motionless apart from that occasional, almost imperceptible twitch of his left shoulder; a slight lift and fall, as though tugged by an invisible string. Once, she'd asked Jenna about that shoulder twitch. Was it a nervous tic? An old injury? Jenna had shrugged and playfully answered, *It doesn't keep him from dishing out the good stuff.* Fairlie had prodded for further details, but Jenna had winked and clammed up.

'I . . . I should have seen it coming,' Fairlie says finally. 'I should have helped her.' She aims her words at the carpet. There's a little finger smear of peanut butter not far from Ark's foot, and the sight of it makes her stomach curl. 'I wish she'd said something – been more honest.'

Ark looks about to open his mouth but then seems to decide against it. He snorts.

'We could have helped her,' Fairlie goes on. It feels incongruous to be speaking this way, uttering grief clichés like a Department of Health brochure in the Medicare office. Anger stabs at her. Turning away from Ark to flop onto the couch, she finishes, 'We have to tell her mum. We need to call Evelyn.'

He doesn't answer. Somewhere outside, a galah screeches over the far-off drone of an exhaust brake on the highway.

'Is this our fault?'

He is silent for so long, Fairlie begins to doubt she asked the question aloud.

'No,' he says eventually. 'No. It's not *my* fault.' He shakes his head, finally unfreezing. 'This is typical fucking Jenna, thinking of no one but herself.' Ark takes two strides and stands before her. 'Don't make me blame anyone else. I can't, Fairlie. It's too hard.'

'We knew she was hurting –'

'And no, I'm not calling her mother. Have you forgotten what she did to Jenna?'

'I don't *know* what happened –'

'No,' he growls. 'Just stop. Let me grieve – nothing else. Okay?'

'Ark, I'm sorry. I know this is hard.' Why is she apologising to him?

'Leave it,' he pleads. 'If you want to go searching for answers, fine. If you want to blame yourself, fine. And yeah, maybe you should ask yourself some serious questions but don't bring me into it. Let me grieve in peace. My wife just died.'

'Tell me one thing: did you see this coming?'

'Did *you*?' His expression could cut glass.

Heat creeps up Fairlie's neck. 'She didn't say anything, other than that you'd fought. She only stayed two nights, then she went home.'

Ark sighs and stuffs his hands into his pockets. 'She'd been troubled for so long, with the postnatal depression. I tried to help her.'

'Wait – the *what*?'

Postnatal depression? Her thoughts reel back over the past two years, dragging up scenes and snapshots. Jenna's pregnancy hadn't been easy, and after the birth she'd quaked a little into motherhood – but no more, Fairlie considers, than any other new mother. She recalls flashes of conversation over cups of coffee, text messages received at all hours of the day and night, typically amiable or mundane Facebook statuses.

'Depressed?' Fairlie echoes, her voice thin. 'She told me she'd been to the doctor, but she . . . ' Fairlie looks at him again. 'She kind of laughed. Brushed it off. Said she was tired and that her doctor was a notorious over-prescriber.' Fairlie chews the inside of her cheek. 'And I know that doctor. He *is*. So I . . . I didn't . . . ' Her sentence dies on her tongue.

Ark pinches the bridge of his nose. 'Fairlie,' he says, 'I appreciate you watching Henry today. But I know my wife.' He steps back, looking around. 'Now, I have to go. Henry and I need to be alone together to grieve. My family are supporting me at this time.'

Just like that? Fairlie thinks. Jenna dies; Ark disappears, and then returns with a dismissive *leave us alone to grieve?* She hesitates and her thoughts drift to the child sleeping in the bedroom, his body exhausted and confused. In the late afternoon, after Pattie had reluctantly left at Fairlie's disingenuous urges, Henry had cried on and off, frustrated and bewildered, longing for his mother's arms. Was he thinking of her soft voice, her familiar scent? Did he crave the comforting sound of her heartbeat?

Don't let him take Henry.

The thought slips into her mind so clearly that she jumps. Her limbs tingle, and something like terror rolls over her. Ark is going to take Henry, her only link to Jenna. She can see that now as clearly as though it were printed on his forehead.

Fairlie falters, clearing her throat. 'Are you sure? Do you need some more time?'

'No, but thank you.'

If he takes the baby, Jenna is gone and you'll be alone forever.
'I know it's hard right now,' she says. 'So much to think about. I'm happy to mind him for a while longer.'

'Fairlie, look.' He exhales. 'I appreciate you babysitting Henry today while I took a moment to arrange a few details. It's important to protect him from those sorts of things, he's only a child.'

Fairlie wonders what the hell Ark thought *she was* doing today. Playing Mary Poppins?

'But I need to go now,' he continues. The mood in the room has shifted; Ark seems taller. 'My family and I need to grieve.'

'Henry's in the spare room,' Fairlie tells him with some reluctance. 'Jenna's old room.'

A pang twists in her chest when Ark returns a few moments later. Henry, still sleeping, is draped upon Ark's shoulder, his small body limp and relaxed. Another brief moment of panic seizes Fairlie as she watches Henry's face.

Ark says, 'See you later, Fairlie.' Then he pauses and adds, 'I do appreciate your help. Really.' Tears well in his eyes.

She can't bring herself to respond. Instead she offers a weak smile and raises her other hand, as if to reach towards the child who looks exactly like his mother right now – skin like cream, closed crescent eyelids with thick dark lashes, small blunt chin tucked down. Sleeping so innocently. Her hand stays forwards, fingers outstretched as the door swings shut, and they are gone.

The voice is thickly accented and the background is filled with the burble of other voices and the purr of telephone rings.

'Can I speak to Ms Winter please?'

Fucking telemarketers. Fairlie inserts two corn chips into her mouth and says around the crunch of them, 'Speaking.'

'I'm calling from Telstra regarding the fifty-two dollars and eighty-nine cents outstanding on your account.'

'Oh, right. Shit. Sorry.' She isn't sorry. She turns up the volume on the television and pops in another corn chip.

'We need payment of the outstanding amount within the next twenty-four hours, otherwise this call is to notify you that your account will be disconnected.'

'Yeah right. Okay. Thanks.'

Fairlie hangs up. She finishes the bag of chips in eight minutes. It's a personal record.

Although she walks past it almost every day, Fairlie has never been inside the Penola police station. A renovated old stone cottage with cream walls, sharply peaked Colorbond roof and the unmistakable blue and white POLICE sign jutting out above the front door that inspires the involuntarily jerk of passing motorists' feet from the accelerator.

Her thongs slap against her heels and her dress brushes against her ankles. A narrow concrete path lined with balls of dwarf diosma leads from the footpath to the door. A kookaburra mocks her from above. Glancing over her shoulder at the road, she wonders who will drive past and see her. What would they think? *Fairlie Winter, drunk in public again?* Or, *Hey, that's the nurse who wiped my arse that time I had gastro. Guess even nurses are fallible.* Or more likely, *Poor Fairlie, I heard about that girl who killed herself.*

Inside, the station is quiet and smells of paper and air-conditioning and starched cotton. A young-looking officer with a crooked, pink-tipped nose comes to the reception counter. No smiles as he asks, 'Can I help you?'

'I'm here to see a detective,' Fairlie says. 'His name is Morgan – Dallas Morgan.'

'You are?'

'Fairlie Winter.'

'He expecting you?'

'Apparently.' She fidgets, feeling guilty of an unknown crime. 'He told me to meet him here.'

'Take a seat.' He gestures and leaves, and Fairlie perches nervously on the edge of a cracked vinyl seat. A bead of sweat trickles down her spine and she reaches back, awkwardly, to flap her dress away from her skin.

Postnatal depression. It's needled at her since Ark left last night with Henry. How many times had she reassured Jenna over the phone, over coffee, late into the evening when Ark was away, that Jenna wasn't doing anything wrong? How often had she winced, or frowned, or snapped with outrage at something Jenna quoted Ark had said in a burst of anger? Henry was healthy, it was normal to feel tired, and Jenna was doing the best she could – she recalls repeating those lines more than once.

But.

But then. It got worse – didn't it?

'Fairlie.' Detective Dallas Morgan's voice breaks into her reverie.

Jumping to her feet, Fairlie takes his outstretched hand. Today, the detective seems more ordinary, gentler.

'Come through,' he says, holding the door open for her. 'How are you?'

When the detective smiles at her, it's with a sympathetic warmth that constricts her throat. Two days ago this man had stood with Ark and watched Jenna's body leave. He'd picked Fairlie up after she'd fainted in Jenna's kitchen; he hadn't flinched at the sight of her vomit.

'Thanks for coming in so soon,' he says. 'This won't take long, I promise.'

Fairlie follows Detective Morgan through the station. The back of his shirt is creased from sitting down. His footfalls are heavy onto his left foot, he swings his right leg outwards slightly, as though his knee is stiffened. His gait is awkward, but swift and practised and it doesn't slow him down at all – a very old injury. He leads her to a small, cramped room in the back of the building.

'Take a seat,' he tells her, and they sit at opposite sides

of a crowded desk. A tall filing cabinet presses towards the detective's elbow, a towering tray of paperwork spills tongues of paper onto the desktop. On the wall, a decidedly amateur crayon rendition of a police vehicle is affixed with taped corners.

Fairlie gestures to the drawing. 'Your grandkids?'

'No,' he answers, smiling. 'From a school visit a few months ago. No grandkids for me yet.'

He takes her through a series of questions: the standard personal particulars of her full name, age, address and marital status, and it begins so benignly that the swift change of his next question catches her off guard.

'Tell me about your relationship with Jenna.'

Fairlie's head jerks up. He watches her, hands poised over his keyboard, reading glasses balanced on the end of his nose. 'I've known her all my life,' she answers at length. Dallas Morgan nods, smiles kindly, and begins to type as she condenses twenty-six years into a few sentences. 'Our mothers are friends – since before we were born. We grew up just around the corner from each other.'

The detective looks interested. 'Lucky, living so close to your mate.'

Blinking furiously, Fairlie is determined not to cry. 'We were one hundred and fourteen steps from each other. It was shorter if we cut through the backyard of the Millers – they lived right on the corner of our streets – but Mrs Miller didn't like that. Said we scared her Chihuahuas.' The detective has stopped typing, but listens with genuine interest. 'But we knew it had nothing to do with the dogs. It was because Mrs Miller once caught us laughing at her giant underwear hanging on her washing line.' She flushes then, realising how similarly ample her own underwear is now. Perhaps that is her karmic payback for stealing an armload of Mrs Miller's underpants that one day, that day she'd fought with her mother and wanted to do something bratty, something to be *noticed*, because a lady at the shops had bent down to her level and cooed, 'Aren't you cute? Little chocolate baby.' And Fairlie, eight years old, definitely not a baby and *definitely* not a confection, had blurted out a sentence that had brought a feverish red to the lady's cheeks and sent her stomping away with her hand to her throat as though garrotted.

'We went through school together,' Fairlie goes on, 'then TAFE . . . we lived together for about a year, here in Penola, before she met Ark. And then . . . ' Fairlie trails off.

When she remains quiet the detective prompts, 'So you were very close friends.'

'Yes,' Fairlie answers. 'We are.' Her eyes return to her hands knotted tightly in her lap. 'We were.'

'When did you last see Jenna?'

There. Right there. The guilt drops a claw into her insides and twists her innards like a skein of wool.

'A few weeks ago,' she tells him.

'How did she seem?'

How can she answer that? If she tells the truth, she may as well admit responsibility. As though she'd been there in the bathroom with Jenna, handing her the razor. The claw in her gut twists harder. 'I hadn't seen her as much of late,' Fairlie says, evasively.

'Why not?'

'She always had excuses – Henry, or something with Ark.'

'Why do you think she was making excuses?'

'I don't know.'

'So, if I can take you back to the last time you saw her,' Detective Morgan says, gently. 'How did she seem to you?'

Fairlie's mind races. In the early years of Ark and Jenna's relationship, she had watched the gradual metamorphosis of her friend into someone she wasn't sure she knew so explicitly. Over the years Fairlie had tried to pinpoint the moment Jenna went from Jenna to ... *not* Jenna. When had she gone from the woman who'd flipped the bird at a carload of men wolf-whistling at her, to the woman clutching Ark's hand and gazing up at him fondly?

The day she'd met Ark in the pub.

Fairlie shakes her head. Hadn't she always told herself that those feelings of discomfort towards Ark were an offshoot of her own envy, a symptom of some kind of unhealthy attachment to Jenna? Was a lot of Jenna's most recent detachment Fairlie's own fault? Had Fairlie been unable to allow her friendship with Jenna to evolve into an accommodation of Jenna as a wife, and a mother – and not just her childhood friend?

And when Jenna had walked out that last time, only a few weeks ago, what had Fairlie done to make up with her? Nothing. Can she tell the policeman that? Can she admit that despite twenty-six years of friendship, despite watching her friend change from afar, she'd stood by like a useless, gawking bystander and done nothing? And equally frightening, how can she smear Jenna's memory? If she tells the truth, it will affect Detective Morgan's notes, paint his impression of Jenna. Recorded forever for the coroner. She can imagine the look on the detective's face: a sad nod of knowing. *Poor girl*, he'll think. *Yet another statistic for mental illness.*

'She was fine.' Fairlie looks directly at the detective and delivers the untruth. 'Perfectly happy.'

The detective thanks her, and as he explains that her statement is done, Fairlie knows that his opinion to the coroner will state unequivocally that on a sunny Thursday in summer, with her bathroom door locked from the inside and twin purposeful, surgical scalpel slashes opening her forearms from wrist to elbow, Jenna Rudolph committed suicide.

As he walks her back to the reception, Dallas Morgan says, 'Fairlie, I am truly sorry for your loss.'

It catches her off guard, the way he looks at her then. Like he knows her. Like he really *is* sorry.

'Yeah,' Fairlie says, taking his outstretched hand again. 'Me, too.'

He clasps her hand tightly, then lets it go. 'Take care,' he tells her.

She waits until she is out in the sunshine before wiping her knuckles across her cheekbones, her hand coming away wet and shining with tears.

Dear Jenna,

I've never told you the story of how I came to buy those teacups. You know the ones that sit on the dresser in the hallway? As a kid, you always wanted me to get them down and use them. We did sometimes, for special occasions; we once used them for a picnic under the oak tree on your birthday.

They came from a new store tucked into an alley off Commercial Street. It was owned by a woman whose ladies-wear store had recently folded after twenty years of dressing the gentlewomen of South Australia's southeast. I'd heard that the owner of the store had divorced her husband, that he'd taken off with a much younger woman – a kindergarten teacher – also taking with him most of her money and forcing her to sell up. I stood in the cramped space of her new store and gazed around at the collection of scented candles, tiny blown-glass figurines and whimsical ladies' hats and scarves, feeling a pang of sympathy. It was all tainted with rumour and scandal. Shoppers would go in to poke their noses amongst the knick-knacks and hope to glean a scrap of gossip they could feed on, like a magpie with a rind of bacon. That's how it works in this town, that's how people live their lives – always knowing, always talking. Very little personal information is sacred – especially if you're well known or successful.

But this, you know by now.

Something caught my eye. A teacup with a sweet picture

painted on the side: an angel resting on a red rose. The painting was intricately detailed, with fine strokes in metallic gold edging the angel's wings. I remember thinking I could take it to work; I could gaze at it through the day – the cherub seated atop the bloom as though the world was nothing but a bed of roses.

The saleswoman must have been close to sixty years old. I didn't even know her name – I certainly didn't know her ex-husband – yet I still saw a vision: a flash of young, firm flesh, gazelle-like limbs wrapped around a man who would break his wife's heart.

'You like the cup?' she asked. 'We have matching plates – three different sizes.' She beamed. 'I could do a special price for you, Evelyn. Are you looking for anything in particular?'

I didn't know how to answer that question. It felt loaded with far more meaning than she had intended. What was I looking for? And more importantly, how would I know when I found it?

Stephen had reacted to the news of the pregnancy with delight. He had beamed and gushed at the prospect of becoming a father. He had even broached the topic of marriage yet again, and laughed knowingly at my usual hesitation. Any excuse for him to propose! De facto was a difficult concept for people to grasp back then – especially here, in this town – but I've never felt the need for that piece of paper, that certificate that essentially changes nothing.

Once again, I feel a pang of sadness that these frequent proposals and my frequent good-humoured rejections – these are the loving, delicate, idiosyncratic interactions between your father and I of which you were deprived. I will always be so sorry that you missed the real us.

And it was precisely because of your father's excitement over the pregnancy that I felt so anxious.

Because I had begun to feel fear, Jenna – what would we do if it all fell apart?

Indicating the cup with the angel and its matching saucer, I told the saleswoman, 'This tea-set. I'll take the lot, as well as any other matching crockery.'

Fifteen minutes later, I felt the saleswoman's eyes trained on my back all the way out the door. I knew I had just given the older lady three weeks worth of gossip: the Channel 8 news presenter Evelyn Francis came into the shop today; she bought two hundred dollars worth of teacups! Her friends would all titter and speculate, undoubtedly, over whether or not I even made my own tea, or had a maid do it for me. The small-town grapevine could work one of two ways: in my favour, it could enhance my reputation, but more often than not, it was the alternative – all that talk, all that word-of-mouth – nothing more than a gossip-fuelled thorn in my side.

But even now, I say these things and I wonder if you would believe me.

I slipped into a nearby coffee shop to escape the cold, seating myself by the window. I slid the box of crockery under the table and placed the cup from the shelf – the one with the angel painted on the side – onto the table. I asked the waitress to fill it with a cappuccino, then I watched her return behind the counter, lean over and whisper something in another waitress's ear. Both women then turned to me, glanced down at the teacup in the first waitress's hand, and smirked.

Then, I heard his voice.

What can I say here, Jenna, to help you understand what that voice did to me inside? How can I convey the feeling of being simultaneously twisted into a knot and yet pulled apart, splintered into a thousand pieces? A feeling of wanting to leap for joy, yet run and hide?

Have you ever felt that way? Perhaps not. I realise that I have no place to give you maternal advice but let me tell you this, my darling: I wish you nothing but love. Love that is free and honest and out in the open. Because to have to hide it, to have to fight it? Love hurts so much that way.

'Aren't you supposed to be working?' I asked.

'Aren't you?'

'I'm on assignment,' I said. 'The outrage of local cafés selling coffee at a five hundred per cent mark-up.'

When he sat down, I felt the eyes of the waitress burning into my back before she appeared beside the table and placed down the angel cup filled with foam-topped coffee. Alongside the saucer she slid a slice of cinnamon tea-cake, explaining that it was 'on the house' with a jerk of her head at the kitchen, where a gentleman offered me a wave.

Then I noticed a group of three adolescent boys at a table nearby glowering at my companion's back. One of them mouthed the words ' f---ing pig'.

I thought I might be sick. Imploring him that he shouldn't be here, I shoved the slice of cake across and told him to take it.

He chuckled, that broad grin showing perfect white teeth. I could see those other feelings in his face that day – invisible to others, hidden behind those captivating black irises: a sadness, a frustration.

I insisted that he go. I said, 'People are looking.'

He nodded and stood, placing a hand on my shoulder, and it was everything I could do not to lay down my cheek on his hand as his fingers brushed the nape of my neck.

Picking up the tea-cake, he took a bite of it straight from his hand as he moved away through the tables. I watched the teenage boys snigger behind their hands as he passed their table.

And then I was alone once more with the angel on my teacup, a box full of useless charity at my feet.

I look back over this letter and hope you can see that I'm trying to paint you a picture, my darling. I'm trying to show you why.

Until next time.

Love, Mum

4

Then

Between the rows of vines, Ark knelt on the ground and dug his fingers into the earth. The summer had been so long and dry that already the leaves of the grapes were lacklustre, not yet autumn-red but having lost their plump summer green. A cool breeze rattled through the leaves and lifted Jenna's hair from her neck.

'Here.' Ark scooped up a handful of red soil. Thin streams the colour of dried blood ran through his fingers. He brought his cupped hands to her face. 'Smell this.'

Jenna shot him a look of surprise then reluctantly lowered her nose. Quickly, she sniffed at the soil: one cursory, halfhearted intake of breath.

'You call that a smell?' he teased. 'Try again. Take a big lungful. There, can you taste that? In the scent?'

Jenna straightened up. 'It smells like dirt,' she said warily, rubbing her nose. 'What am I supposed to be tasting?'

Stepping closer, Ark licked his finger, then pressed his fingertip into the mound of soil on his palm. 'Open up,' he instructed.

'Are you serious?' She laughed, pushing his hand away. 'I'm not going to *eat* it.'

'Come on.' He grinned at her, holding up the red tip of his finger. Touching it gently to his own mouth, he traced a rusty smear across his lower lip. 'You know you want to,' he said softly, letting the soil stream from his other hand and scatter across the grass with a soft ticking noise. He lifted her hand to his lips and ran the end of her index finger across the trail of dirt.

'There,' he said. '*Terra rossa* – it's Italian for "red soil". Now try it.'

Jenna's breath came shallow as he gently steered her fingertip to her mouth. Relaxing her jaw, her lips parted and then she tasted the dirt on her tongue: earthy and metallic.

'It's ... ' She licked her lips, giving a self-conscious laugh. 'It tastes kinda rusty.'

'Nice.' He nodded appreciatively. 'It *is* rusty.'

Jenna wiped the back of her hand across her mouth. 'The dirt is rusty?'

'In a way, yes. This strip of red clay here,' he swept his arm out along the length of the vines, following the highway, 'is on a shallow limestone ridge, only about fifteen by two kilometres. The drainage is superb for Cab Sav grapes. After the limestone has weathered, what's left over is clay. The clay is susceptible to oxidisation – rust. It forms in the soil, giving it that rich, red colour.'

'I see.' Jenna nodded, pressing her lips together; she could still taste the gritty earth between her teeth. 'And is that what we're having for lunch?' She gestured to the cooler bag at his feet.

'Nah,' Ark said, leaning in close to gently kiss the last traces of soil from her lips. 'Thought I'd feed you something a little more palatable. Come on. It's not much further.'

Clutching her free hand, he swung her arm gently as they walked. Dry stubbled grass crunched under their feet as grape tendrils plucked at her shoulders.

'Such a beautiful property.' Jenna turned to gaze over the gentle rise they'd been slowly climbing. Vines unrolled in sweeping rows, their leaves scuffling in a breeze that carried the scent of far-off rain on parched earth.

Ark squinted, his face cast golden by the setting sun. 'Sometimes I forget to notice it, you know? Have to remind myself.'

Jenna picked her way carefully around knotty tufts of grass. She ignored the voice in her head that asked her how blind *she* had been. Instead she concentrated on the lilting bass of Ark's voice, the feel of the vines stretching to stroke her elbows, the clouds painted amber on the horizon. One foot after the other she pressed up the hill, striding away from it all. Reminding herself to think only of him. Here. Now. All this. Here, she could be hidden away from all of it.

'I'm too busy to stop,' Ark was saying. 'I don't *want* to pause, I want to rake in what I've worked for, what I deserve, you know?' He squeezed her hand and a thrill shot up her forearm. 'When I was a kid my dad called all the shots. He ruled with an iron fist, I guess you could say. God help me if I didn't eat everything on my plate, if I wanted to go to a friend's house, or if I got a B on my report card. I like having the freedom now, all this is mine.'

Jenna watched his pensive expression.

'I knew Grandma would want me to do something productive with my inheritance,' he said. 'As soon as I saw this place for sale, I knew. And besides,' he smiled crookedly, 'it was the perfect excuse to get away from memories of my dad.'

'You didn't like him?'

'No, no, I did,' he hurried to answer. 'But I wanted to start my own life. My own empire. My mum laments me being so far away. But . . . ' He went quiet. 'There reached a time when I couldn't keep . . . ' He sighed.

'Keep . . . ?'

'Picking up after her.'

'In what way?'

'Don't get me wrong, she's a great woman,' he said

hastily. 'She's smart and she works really hard at keeping the house perfect. She always made sure we had good food for school, stuff like that. She'd do anything for us. But if I'd let her, she would have kept me there forever. She could be a bit smothering. My dad was tough on her sometimes, he expected everyone to do their part around the place and could be . . . ' he struggled to find the word, '*tactless* at letting everyone know. Especially her.'

'Your parents fought?' Jenna asked. Memories of her own father were affectionate, pleasant, even though her parents had separated before she could remember.

'Hell no.' Ark laughed abruptly. 'Mum knew better than to answer back.'

Jenna started. 'He didn't hit her, did he?'

Ark shot her a quick sideways look. 'Nothing serious, he wasn't a wife beater. He was a good man. And never in front of us – she only told me about it later. Think he just pushed her a few times. But you know, I had a good childhood.'

She waited for him to go on, but he seemed to have disappeared inwards. His jaw went firm, he dropped his gaze to the ground.

Responses tumbled through Jenna's head, but nothing seemed right. So she just squeezed his hand.

He looked at her strangely. 'Don't move.' Setting the cooler bag on the ground, he dug into his pocket and withdrew his phone. 'I want to take a photo of you in this light. You're glowing – the sunlight on your hair.'

As the shutter clicked, Jenna laughed, embarrassed. She shoved him playfully, stooped to pick up the bag of food and strode ahead of him.

'The end of this row?' she called over her shoulder.

'Yep, up there. There's a great spot we can sit. Oh, wow,' he gave a low whistle, 'this angle is great, too.'

Heat flushed her cheeks and she broke into a jog as the edge of the row came into view ahead. A couple of wrens started into the air, chirping indignantly. Nearing the top of the rise, Jenna slowed. The breeze swirled low through the leaves. As she crested the hill a fresh gust swept sidelong and she grimaced as she caught an unmistakable foetid, rotten-sweet scent.

'Ugh.' She glanced around. 'We might have to pick another spot.'

Ark, still a little way down the hill, hastened to catch up. 'What's that?' he called, grinning. 'Didn't hear you.'

'We might have to find somewhere else,' she repeated, louder, waving her hand beneath her nose at a fresh putrid wave. 'A dead kangaroo or something –'

Midstride, Ark froze. His face drained of colour.

Jenna's smile faded. She took a step towards him. 'Ark?'

Dropping the cooler bag to the dirt, he stumbled backwards several steps, his eyes wide and darting around.

'What's wrong?'

'I can't.' He was struggling for breath; his face had turned white. 'I can't.'

'Hey, what's the matter?' With a frown, she went

towards him, whipping her head around to follow the direction of his gaze. 'What is it?' Her own heart picked up. Had he seen a snake?

'Shit,' he croaked, grabbing at his neckband, still walking backwards.

'Ark? Are you okay?'

Turning away from her, he tripped over a rock, dropping to one knee before clambering to his feet.

'Hey!' She dashed to catch up, warily putting her hand on his arm. His skin was clammy.

'I'm so sorry,' he breathed. His eyes were closed and he took frantic gulps of air through his mouth. 'I have to go back.'

Inside, Ark's house was dim and cool beneath evening's shroud. Despite his insistence otherwise, Jenna steered Ark to the lounge room, watching as he humoured her ministrations and lowered himself to the plump leather couch with an exaggerated sigh.

'I'll get you some water,' she said, then added as he opened his mouth, 'look, just sit there.'

He held up his hands. 'Fine,' he said. 'I won't argue with the nurse.'

Her footsteps were muffled on the long hall runner. The last of the afternoon light pressed dimly through the window, across the old-style ceramic sink and granite benchtops. Searching the overhead cabinets, she found a glass and filled it with water from the tap. She took in the view through the window. A sweeping lawn of lushly watered kikuyu split by a path of russet pavers, leading down a gentle slope towards a row of soaring red gums. The gums' vast creamy-brown striped trunks acted like oversized fence posts, separating the garden from the front forty acres of shiraz and cabernet grapes that rolled between the highway and the house. Evening shadows dropped across the lawn, long and blur-edged like strokes of watercolour. Looking around the kitchen, Jenna shivered, trying to imagine calling this home. She pictured her own photographs on the wall, filling the gaps where recently removed frames glared like extracted teeth. Sitting in the tall-backed chairs at the dining table, eating breakfast or sipping coffee. Inside these huge rooms, between these solid stone walls, she could be free.

Free of what? Guilt? The torment of the inexplicable crawling-skin feeling?

Jenna swallowed, placing the filled glass momentarily on the counter to wipe clammy palms against her jeans. She turned away from the window and hurried back down the hall.

On the couch, Ark had his head in his hands, elbows on his knees. Biceps swelled against short sleeves, a streak of red dirt up the inside seam of his jeans against his boots. Discarded in the doorway, the cooler bag wilted with its unrealised bounty of leg ham, crusty white bread, potato salad and a dry McLaren Vale semillon.

Hearing her approach he straightened, swiped a thumb beneath his nose and sniffed surreptitiously.

'Okay?' she asked.

'Yeah, thanks.' His fingertips brushed hers as she handed him the water. Beneath the bold line of his jaw, his pulse flickered in his throat. 'I'm sorry,' he said. 'Jeez,' he gave a soft laugh, 'talk about embarrassing.'

'Don't be embarrassed,' she said. 'Panic attack?'

He pulled her down alongside him and nodded once, quickly. 'Yep. Would have been worse if I'd let it.'

'What set it off? It wasn't something I did, I hope.'

He shook his head. 'No, God no. It's just a phobia,' he confessed, playing with her fingers. 'Nothing too serious.'

Jenna nodded and waited for him to go on.

'It's not a big deal. I keep it under control, mostly.' He ran his thumbnail delicately over the back of her hand and she shivered. 'I have necrophobia,' he said.

'A fear of death?'

'Sort of. Dead things. Reminders of death – cemeteries, funerals, and in this case, dead animals. I've had it since I was a teenager.'

Jenna wanted to ask him about it. She had the sudden urge to delve into this crack in his exterior and find a tender pulse to press. The release of sweet pain. But the clench of his jaw stopped her.

'You're perfect, you know that?' His voice was low, tentative, as though tasting the words.

She tugged her hand away. 'Far from it, I'm afraid.'

'You're wrong,' he said, and he leaned in to her. The couch whispered as his weight shifted, his hand curling over her hip. Reaching her mouth he waited for her, an invitation in his pause, and she found herself drawn to him, moving those last few beats to kiss him.

When he broke away he whispered, his lips millimetres from hers, 'We are going to be great for each other.'

She believed him.

When he asked her the first time, he phrased it so casually that what escaped her lips was almost the truth.

'What happened with your mum?'

His head rested on her belly; he was looking up at her in the dim light. They'd drawn the curtains against the late summer sun. Sheets clammy with sweat were tangled around her legs and his breath tickled the underside of her bare breasts.

The past two months were like a blur; Jenna felt consumed with a kind of fever, an almost out-of-body experience. Ark Rudolph had sauntered into her life and she couldn't recall the breadth and meander of her days before him – like that irrevocable change he'd shyly implied at the pub a handful of weeks ago. She felt as though she was reeling, blissfully off-kilter, ecstasy-drugged and invincible.

'She lied to me.' The words snuck out before Jenna was aware of them. The ceiling fan hummed, stirring the temperate afternoon like liquid candy and keeping the flames of the candles he'd arranged across the top of his dresser in a lazy flicker.

'What did she say?'

'It's hard to explain,' Jenna said. 'Just . . . she's the most selfish fucking person on the planet.'

He remained silent as he gazed at her, drawing circles in the hollow of her elbow with a fingertip.

She took a breath. 'Have you ever taken something for granted, known it so completely and without question, only to find out that it's all . . . ' She struggled for the right word. 'Fake?' Her gaze settled on the grey-white stripes of the bedsheet. 'I look back and it all looks like a sheet of rice paper. Transparent, brittle.'

'What did you take for granted?'

'Everything,' she said. 'Every single day.'

He didn't say anything at first, his fingers moving to stroke the length of her forearms. 'I know what it feels like to be hurt by someone you trust, if that's what you mean.'

Jenna laced her fingers into his hair. 'Something like that.'

'Must be hard though. From what you've told me, you used to be pretty close.'

'We were.'

'Have you tried talking to her?'

Jenna listened to the rhythm of the fan, the gentle draw of Ark's breath, the peaceful quiet of his house. They could be the only two people in the world.

What more could she tell him? What could she give him, this enigma of a man who heated her flesh like flames and somehow cupped her heart – what could she offer that would be enough? The whole story swelled inside her, pressed out from her bones. She wanted to tell him that, at first, she'd simply been too angry and bewildered to speak of it, desperate to make sense of it herself before she could speak to others, before she could find the strength to look her mother in the eye again. But with the pass of the weeks, and as Ark heated her from the outside, she found her mother's revelations growing cold within her. She hadn't intended for her initial silence to morph into complete severance – it had just happened. Could she tell him that she only wanted to hide, with him, and not to think?

Ark lifted to his elbows. 'Move in with me.'

There. He'd said it. Wasn't that what she wanted?

'Why?' she asked him, smiling.

'I want you,' he said, lips brushing her breast, 'because you're you.'

'And what's so good about me?'

Ark rose onto his knees, slid his hands beneath her hips and drew her underneath him, covering her body with his weight. He kissed her, and her own breath came back to her sweet and hot from the hollow of his neck. And as his skin burned the length of her, he rolled her over and pulled her astride him.

'I can't bear to be apart from you,' he said. He gave a low groan as she slipped over him.

He dug his fingers into the aching muscles of her thighs and she knotted her hands over his, as though to anchor herself as the earth dissolved. She decided then that it didn't matter, it really didn't matter what either of them said.

Dear Jenna,

I need to backtrack now. I have begun this letter maybe a dozen times only to delete it moments later. But this part is important. I'm sorry. So, here goes.

It was merely one day, in the scheme of things. The space of a few hours, really. But that was all it took to turn something that I fooled myself into thinking was harmless, beautiful and transient, into a series of events that wrenched apart so many lives, I wonder if I'll ever forgive myself.

I was with him. In the afternoon light of his house – the time of day most easily snatched for us both. The weight and smell of him – so familiar and yet somehow foreign, exciting. You probably wish me to omit such detail, but I need to convey how happy I felt, how thrilled and alive and real I felt with the press of him. Is that so hard to understand?

He asked me when Stephen was returning home, and when I answered, 'Tonight,' he sighed and rolled onto his back.

'Do you ever think of telling him?' he asked.

In the beginning, I had assured myself that I didn't intend for it to last, this thing with him. Whatever others might call it, the word 'affair' never rang true. An affair is a seedy, insidious act and its constituents lie and hide. I never thought of myself as doing those things. I look back now and see the heavy rose tint of the glasses I wore. How very naive! But I truly hadn't meant for it to last; I hadn't meant to maintain anything underhanded. It was just fun. It was just affection. It was just two people living moments of shared pleasure. In a world sorely lacking in love (and I reported as such to the community, every afternoon) I told myself that the expression of a little more could come to no harm, right?

What had begun as an innocent coffee together after a brief interview had turned into several balmy spring afternoons. Sometimes at my house, but later, more often, at his little place, a stone's throw from the main corner. These afternoons were snatched under the guise of a late lunch break, before I'd return to work smooth-cheeked and poised, while my insides swam giddy. He had come into my life seamlessly. The first afternoon I had invited him home seemed so natural; as expected and sure as the sunrise.

So as we lay there, his question about telling Stephen dissolving harmlessly into the afternoon, what could I do but simply stare back at him, take in the beautiful contours of his face, the rich darkness of his skin, the lines of his collarbones.

How long had it been now? A year? More? It couldn't be; it felt like weeks. But I knew the rough and soft of his body like my own. I knew he could never completely finish a tub of ice-cream – he always wanted to leave a little in the freezer, just in case. I knew that his mother had died young from lung cancer when he was only twelve and he had been returned to Adelaide to spend six restless years with his father. I knew that at eighteen he joined the police force and, as soon as he could, he moved back to Mount Gambier, his home, where his mother was buried.

He asked if I was bored with Stephen. Bored: he actually used the word. It irritated me and I drew away from him — he'd crossed a line. But if I'm honest with myself, I think the reason his flippant comment irked me was because it was rooted in some truth. Maybe I was bored. Never could I have the courage to face nor admit that, though, for isn't that the most shallow and callous thing?

I argued that I cared for Stephen deeply. That I loved him. But then I grinned at him, and told him that I loved him, too.

He laughed and kissed me and said, 'I'm going to make you choose, one day.'

'Liar,' I said. 'You'd be too scared I'd pick him.'

'You can't have it both ways,' he said. 'Not forever.'

Why not? I wanted to know when monogamy become the rule. What ensued was a lengthy philosophical rant about love and affection and the narrow-mindedness of religion and how the sexual revolution would, ultimately, lead to a better world.

He told me to get out of my parent's Kombi.

'This has got nothing to do with Stephen,' I told him. 'This is about you and me.'

He pulled me close as he said, 'It can't be about only you

and me — it doesn't work that way, Evvie. He'll always be in the middle.'

I told him that he was wrong.

But he was right.

Until next time.

Love, Mum

5

Now

Her underwear spools up on itself, her skin sticky from the shower. Walking spread-legged across her bedroom floor, Fairlie plucks at seams that ride up and feels a wave of misery roll down from the top.

The mirror's reflection regards her coolly, a familiar stranger. She puts her hands over her belly, cupping the soft bulge of herself, digging her fingers into the skin as she leans forwards and lets the weight of her flesh fall into her hands. The heft of it. Leaning forwards she has four breasts, two within and two spilling from the top of her bra. Calves curving like overgrown marrows. Tears glistening on plump cheeks.

One year in early primary school a new playground

had been installed on the edge of the oval. Ecstatic children had swarmed over monkey bars, a swing set with *four* swings, a tunnel slide that curved like a snail shell. And set off to one side, firmly dug into the mounds of pine chips, was a seesaw. Long and painted red, like a giant pop stick. Derek Shannehan, a boy who killed flies with his ruler and kept their tiny, papery corpses in his pencil case, asked Fairlie to play on the seesaw. Having already given up on the monkey bars, flabbergasted at how the other kids were able to propel themselves along hanging by fingers, and fearing the tunnel slide with visions of corks in bottlenecks, Fairlie had agreed eagerly. She mounted one side and Derek the other and she kicked off, again and again, but Derek couldn't reach the ground. He began to laugh, swinging his legs, then three other boys had popped from the bottom of the tunnel slide like a SWAT team – one after the other, pop, pop, pop – and grabbed at Derek's legs, dragging him back to earth. As Fairlie had shot into the air the boys had leapt away and Fairlie had crashed, her teeth clacking and the sharpness of blood on her tongue. Jenna had chased Derek with handfuls of pine chips, hurling them at the back of his head and calling him a *stupid wussy boy*.

Staring into the mirror, Fairlie swipes a hand beneath her nose and sniffs, hard. A glance at the clock reminds her that her mother will be here any minute. Pulling open the wardrobe, she yanks the simple black dress from its hanger and steps into it quickly; her mum will zip it up for her.

—o—

Fewer people are here today for Jenna than at her wedding.

Sunlight falls from a blue-white sky in columns through the trees, burnishing the lawn and the headstones. The breeze tugs at Fairlie's curls, dragging the desiccated scent of summer from across the country.

Fairlie squints behind her sunglasses; a strand of hair alights upon her lip and she bites at it. The air is hot, filled with the ghosts of the bodies turning to bones beneath her feet.

Six days have passed since Jenna died. *Let's get this over with*, Ark said. Now, Jenna's body is lowered into the earth where she too will disappear into the dirt. Fairlie is struck at the knees by the waste.

She has tried to acknowledge everyone, tried to offer smiles, but what's the point? Although she told herself it shouldn't matter, earlier in the chapel she couldn't help but take a head count. Twelve. There are only twelve to mourn Jenna. For the first time in her life Fairlie wishes that she and Jenna had siblings. Perhaps then, there would be more people here, more living bodies pulsing with blood and murmuring, 'What a loss,' and crying tears onto the grass. More people to remind Jenna what she'd left behind.

Beneath a spray of white lilies and roses, Jenna lies in a slick mahogany coffin – its glossy polish seems like an obscene contradiction. Across the other side of Jenna's coffin, a green-faced, dressed-in-black Ark sways on his feet. His gaze seems singularly focused on his shoelaces and he gives off an air of both wretchedness and stupefied terror. Between the celebrant and Ark is Ark's mother. The woman seems small and faded, but she appears to have a shield around herself, hard lines around her mouth, elbows locked at her sides. Fairlie has only encountered Ark's mother twice before, and now she tries to recall her name. Margarita? Margarita Rudolph? Hidden slightly behind Ark's mother is his younger sister, a diminutive girl who looks to be in her teens. A wisp of a thing with bright orange hair raked back, a black slip dress and bowed legs. Next to her towering older brother, it's hard to imagine they're related. But they share the same eyes – clear, wide-set and so softly blue beneath prominent brows and that pale, pale skin. The girl clutches her mother's arm with both hands.

The rest of the meagre crowd have their faces lowered, hands clasped decorously. Self-effacing sniffs. A colleague – a nurse from the hospital – dabs at her eyes with a crumpled tissue. A little way from the nurse, Abbey Manfried alternates between sobbing and silence. Damon couldn't make it – he had to take his mother to the doctor.

Detective Dallas Morgan is here; he catches Fairlie's

eye and gives her a nod, reflective sunglasses glinting. At her side, her fingers twitch in a wave. The detective wears middle-age competently, effortless in neatly pressed clothing and comfortably occupying his space.

Fairlie's mother and father flank her. Growing up with white parents, in a white community, Fairlie never felt black. As a young child she thought she had been painted – that she was a white girl dipped in brown ink. Her parents' friends called her *cute* and *fuzzy* and patted her head and talked about the problems with Aborigines: drinking and stealing and welfare-bludging. That wasn't her: she wasn't one of them. But she didn't feel white either.

'Okay there, love?' her mother murmurs. The celebrant's voice drones in the background.

'They're going to bury her,' Fairlie whispers. 'No. I'm not okay.'

After ten miscarriages, Fairlie's mother had stopped counting. Some months the blood arrived on time, other months it would come late – three, four, even five weeks belated. Long enough to have known, long enough to have hoped and for plans to begin to unfurl like flower buds. Pattie Winter was tall, trim and squarish with long bones and broad hips: a robust, strong woman. Medicine could not explain the frailty of her womb.

John Winter, her father, stood over six foot yet his pants were always belted and scrunched at the waistband and his arms were wiry. So while her parents flank her, tall and white like football goal posts, Fairlie hunches between them, short, black and rotund. Oddly out of place yet with the ordinary familiarity of child and parent.

Pattie murmurs something about the weather. Her father's reply is inaudible.

Chubby for as long as she can remember, Fairlie recalls the first time she was referred to as fat. In her late teens, at a sink-hole that doubled as a popular local swimming spot. The water was blue-black and bottomless. Rutted, ancient limestone cliffs eroded away in one section to the water's edge, where brownish reeds sprouted from submerged earth and rock. Atop one of the lower sections of cliff, Fairlie had stared down at the shimmering water with a dry mouth. Where the sun bolted straight down the water looked green, shifting and sentient, impossibly far away. It hadn't looked this high from down there. A shout had come up from below: 'Take cover! Fat boong incoming!' A smattering of adolescent male laughter; Jenna had taken her hand and whooped and they'd leapt together, hitting the water with a smack and roar of white-water in her ears.

Fairlie brings a knuckle to her teeth and bites down hard.

The occasional mutter has filtered through to her: 'Poor Ark', 'He looks utterly awful' and 'Is he going to be sick?'

He's afraid, Fairlie wants to shout. *Mortality is terrifying – don't we all feel it? Don't we feel the terror creeping into our pores? The horror of being alone?*

She realises that she is hoping to see Evelyn. Anger

surges within her at the poignant absence of Jenna's mother. Surely, whatever had happened couldn't be so bad that she would not come to say her final goodbye? Looking up, Fairlie thinks of Jenna's father. Throughout her childhood she had only seen Stephen Walker a handful of times in person – on Jenna's weekend or school holiday visits – but she knows him well, from a lifetime of Jenna's stories. Genuine smile, a voice assured and intelligent but Jenna always recalled it was never raised, no matter how angry he was. Where is he?

Henry is not here. Fairlie thinks of Jenna's child, back at that big house. Who is looking after him? Who is feeding him crackers and wiping his chin and whispering to him that, despite all this, his mother loves him so dearly?

And then, it's over. Clods of dirt are heaped into the black hole in the earth that gapes like a grotesque mouth. Fairlie is overcome with an impulse to leap forwards, screaming, to clamber into that hole and cleave open the coffin and lift Jenna out, shake her, breathe her back into life and call her stupid and inconsiderate and tell her that she loves her like nothing else and that she's sorry, so very sorry, and she can't breathe right now, she can't even breathe. Doesn't Jenna realise that?

But she doesn't. She walks forwards, grasps a handful of damp dirt and drops it into the hole. She hears it scatter and tick across the top of the wooden box, a hollow sound, like the scurry of beetles.

Someone hugs her. Abbey squeezes her shoulders, says she'll meet her at the café. Damon is on his way. Her parents murmur, 'See you there.'

Detective Dallas Morgan approaches, waiting politely until she is free.

'I'm so sorry for your loss, Fairlie,' he says. 'How are you?'

At the sound of him speaking, her mother stiffens. Fairlie senses her turn away from the couple to whom she'd been talking in a low voice. Unsure how to answer when her best friend has just been buried, Fairlie lifts her shoulders. 'I don't know. How should I be?'

Her mother clears her throat and her hand closes over the inside of Fairlie's elbow. 'Let's go, dear,' she mutters, close by her ear.

'Lovely to see you again, Mrs Winter,' the detective says, offering her mother a smile.

'You know my mum?' Fairlie asks, surprised.

Pattie returns the detective's smile, briefly. 'Likewise, Detective Morgan. Come on, Fro. Your father's waiting.'

Fairlie frowns and shakes her mother off. 'It was nice to see you, Detective. Thank you for coming.' Detective Dallas Morgan clasps her hands and tells her to take care of herself.

'I'll try,' she answers, before turning to follow her family.

'I'm calling from Telstra regarding the fifty-two dollars and eighty-nine cents outstanding on your account.'

Fairlie stops mid-stride. 'Again?'

'We need payment of the outstanding amount within the next twenty-four hours, otherwise this call is to notify you that your account will be disconnected.'

'You know what?' Fairlie squints up into the bright ball of the sun. She balances on the kerb and cars trundle past her elbow. 'My best friend just died. I'm standing on the street after her funeral; I'm about to meet some friends for coffee. So we can grieve and remember our dead mate. And her life. Before she died.'

'I'm very sorry to hear that, ma'am —'

'I'm sorry too, I know you're just doing your job. Do you like it, by the way? Thinking about a change of career myself.' She digs her knuckles into her eyes, blotting out the sun. 'That's not true. I do actually love my job. I think it's the only reason I'm still here, to be honest. Even though Jenna moved out and disappeared ... the hospital kept me going. Routine. I just put my head down and worked. You know?'

'Ma'am, would you like to pay by credit card?'

Fairlie nudges an unidentifiable object in the gutter. It looks like a cockroach stuck in old chewing gum.

'Her name was Jenna. She was my best friend. What am I supposed to do?' The sun beats hot onto her scalp. 'It's my fault. I should have been there for her. She tried to tell me but I was mad and sad at her for leaving me for *him*. And his *acres*. I felt abandoned. Like I wasn't enough for her anymore. Isn't that just pathetic?'

Silence from the Telstra employee; phones buzz and voices babble in the background. She can imagine him searching frantically through his instruction manual, looking for the heading: *What to say if dead friend.*

'I can take your credit card details today. Or you can choose BPAY.'

Up ahead Abbey and Damon emerge on the footpath. Abbey waves and Fairlie lifts a hand in return.

Fairlie says, 'I've gotta go. But look, it's been enlightening.' Disconnecting the call, she hurries to catch up with her friends.

Dear Jenna,

The first time I met Pattie Winter, I was actually trying to hide.

I was kneeling in the neighbour's garden, digging in the moist soil, damp agapanthus leaves draped across my head. Suddenly, the pile of rhizomes I'd unearthed had scattered across the lawn as a frenzied blur of white fur whizzed past. I heard a woman screech, 'Cooper! You little shit!'

Shooting to my feet, I watched a woman dive into a daisy bush across the yard — in my garden — then wriggle out, butt-first, clutching a wriggling Maltese Terrier.

Anxious not to be caught, I scuttled across the drive.

'I'm sorry,' the woman breathed, 'I'm so embarrassed.'

Dropping the dog, she kept a firm grip on the lead with one hand and extended the other. 'I'm Patricia Winter. I live around the corner. Number 12.'

When I introduced myself she blurted, 'I know —' and then clapped a hand over her mouth, her cheeks flaming.

Her embarrassment struck me as amusing. Before her I stood with mud-soaked knees, dirt smeared across my face, caught trowel in hand as I scooped rare rhizomes from the next-door neighbour's garden while they were away on holiday. I was supposed to be watering their garden, not looting it.

'Lily of the Valley,' I said, sheepishly offering the bag of rhizomes. 'The scent is divine.'

'And highly poisonous,' Pattie added, holding the dog up

to her face and scowling at him. 'Doesn't sound like such a
bad idea.'

I knew we'd be friends then, Jenna, because she'd
plucked the trowel from my hand and begun a fresh trench.

Only a couple of days later, I found myself at Pattie's
door, in need of her telephone as I had locked myself out of
the house. Pattie prepared tea and fed me lamingtons and
told me about the time she had once locked herself out of her
car in the Target car park and walked all the way home
only to find the keys in her handbag.

We saw each other almost every day after that. The rest,
you know. We're inseparable. I would do anything for her.

Well, you know that, too.

One evening I found Pattie inside my front door, her
body bowed in a frightening deflated curve, her hands over
her face. I could hear her sobbing and she was apologising
over and over. She said, 'I hoped I'd pull myself together
before I saw you.'

After a moment she said, 'My monthly came again
today. This time I wasn't even pregnant. Is that better than
a miscarriage?'

I must have told her I was sorry, or some other thin
and useless condolence. But my thoughts had stolen to the
humble swell of my abdomen – I still hadn't told anyone
besides Stephen. A secret hidden by the ruffles of my blouse.
And here was my dear friend telling me that what I hid she
was being cruelly denied, over and over and over.

Pattie smiled tearfully. 'I wish I could say that after so

113

many years it would be easier, that each month would be less of a bitter disappointment.'

I said something empty and limp, if only to fill the air between us with words so she could know how much I cared, how sorry I was for her hurt. But the space between my hipbones seemed hot and weighted, and it was all I could think about. I felt like a fraud.

She told me, 'I feel like a failure as a woman. Why can't I fall pregnant?'

'Sometimes, there's things we just don't know,' I said, feeling the clench of the truth of it.

Things we don't know. I asked myself, What do you know, Evelyn?

I cannot understand why I chose that moment to tell Pattie that I was pregnant. But when I did, my dear friend responded with a fervent, unconditional delight that only intensified the low ebb of my guilt.

It was on that weekday evening that our friendship was cemented; we clicked with a marrow-deep understanding of each other over the raw grief of loss and the exquisite joy of hope – and of how things out of one's control can turn with the slip of time.

Until next time,
Love, Mum

6

Then

Leaning silently on the bathroom door frame, Jenna watched Fairlie settle the elderly woman over the toilet before she knocked.

Steadying the old woman by cupping her bony elbows, Fairlie glanced up at Jenna and smiled. 'Uh oh, Mrs Pearce,' she said, 'Jenna's here.' Then she added seriously, 'Hide your jewellery.'

'Crack whore,' Mrs Pearce muttered in a voice like sandpaper. 'You killed my father.' It was a common allegation from the 81-year-old. She'd accused two other nurses of the same crime, as well as a teenage boy at the front desk, and the vending machine in the hallway.

'I'm so sorry,' Jenna said good-naturedly. 'It won't

happen again.' She felt her cheeks glow, and her breath came quickly.

'What's with you?' Fairlie asked, ignoring a loud fart trumpeting into the toilet bowl beside her. Squatting, Fairlie shifted her weight to her other knee, groaning as the joint cracked, and carefully clutched Mrs Pearce's robe out of the way. 'Never seen you so keen to start night shift.'

Jenna grinned. 'I have some news.'

'Oh?' Fairlie tore off a few sheets of toilet paper to clean her patient.

Jenna took a deep breath. 'Ark asked me to marry him.'

'What the –'

'I'm not done, you stupid girl,' Mrs Pearce barked.

Fairlie dropped the paper, unused, into the bowl behind her patient's bottom. Straightening, she turned to Jenna. 'I'm sorry – *what*?'

'We're engaged.' Stretching out her left arm, Jenna held her palm downwards and watched Fairlie's gaze fall on the modest diamond on a white gold band. It glinted upon her ring finger in the sterile bright lights.

Fairlie blurted, 'But – you've known him for a month.'

'Four months,' Jenna corrected, softly.

There was a moment of silence. Jenna asked herself what she had expected: happy tears? Hugging? Maybe some shrieking and dancing and hand-flapping?

'Fro?'

'Huh?'

116

Jenna kept her hand outstretched and lightly touched Fairlie's forearm.

'I know it's sudden – but I couldn't be happier. I feel great.'

Fairlie was studying the toilet paper dispenser.

'You excited?' Jenna tilted her face to catch Fairlie's eye.

'Of course,' Fairlie said. 'Of *course*.' After a brief shake of her head, she grabbed Jenna in a hug. 'Wow. I knew you two were happy, but I had no idea *this* might happen yet.' Stepping back, she took Jenna's hand and studied the ring, rolling her hand to watch the diamond catch and toss the light.

Jenna shrugged. 'We love each other. We want to be together.'

'Okay, wow,' Fairlie repeated. 'If you're sure, then I'm sure.' She smiled.

Jenna felt a ripple of irritation, so subtle it might have been imagined. 'I'm glad I have your approval,' she said, dryly.

Jenna watched Fairlie draw her hand back and the space between them seemed to expand.

'She's done, by the way,' Jenna said, gesturing at Mrs Pearce, whose torso tilted towards the chrome railing on the wall, silver curls dipping dangerously forwards.

Fairlie either missed it, or refused to acknowledge Jenna's ironic dig. Instead she balled a large wad of toilet paper. 'This is great news, Jen.' She nudged the commode forwards to clean her patient. 'I'm happy for you. And hey, you never know.' Fairlie straightened. 'Maybe I'll shack up with some dude soon, too.'

'You'd have to keep them longer than one night,' Jenna pointed out.

'It's not for lack of trying.'

Stepping behind the commode, Fairlie rolled Mrs Pearce towards the door. But as the wheels rolled silently across the bathroom tiles, there was a sudden and explosive wet ripping sound. Fairlie cursed and danced backwards, crashing into Jenna as Mrs Pearce let forth a diarrhoeal stream – straight through the open hole in the seat of the commode, and all over the floor.

r—O

It looked to Jenna as though the scent of the freesias was making Fairlie sick. Their heady fragrance filled Jenna's nose like syrup and she watched Fairlie with a sense of sad amusement. The determined set of her smile, invisible fishhooks drawing the corners of her mouth outwards. Fairlie was mincing her knees, trying surreptitiously to wriggle the clinging silk a little further down her thighs – it was riding up, bunching under the billow of her arse.

Jenna turned to Fairlie and saw the tender decades flash between them. How it could come to be that she, Jenna Walker, the ten-year-old who used to hide in the wardrobe with Fairlie trying on her mother's lacy bras and stuffing them with socks, who had once declared that when she was a grown-up she would move to the African plains and run wild with the elephant matriarchs, was now standing in front of a crowd of people she barely knew, in a glimmering white gown, a spray of freesias clutched in her fist, smiling benevolently as though this was something for which she had eternally longed?

Ark was shaking hands, kissing cheeks, clapping arms, moving through the crowd broad-shouldered. As Jenna watched him he laughed and bent down to pick up a small child with a blue bow in her hair. He tossed the girl gently into the air and she squealed with delight. Ark hugged the child and set her down.

Fairlie threaded an arm through Jenna's, brought her in close as the crowd surged in, all air-kisses and a rain of coloured rice.

'Can you believe it?' Jenna said.

'I'm calling the Pope,' Fairlie announced. 'But not before I fling this dress to the op shop. I hope you don't mind, but I'm sweating up a storm here.' She *pfffd* unsuccessfully at a limp curl hanging down her face, before using her bouquet to swat it up onto her crown. 'Do you know *anyone* here?'

Jenna kept a hold of Fairlie with one arm while she was swamped with perfumed embraces and smacked with sticky-lipsticked kisses.

'Well,' she began, 'Ark's mother, Marguile, and his sister, of course.'

'Of course.'

Jenna smiled. 'I'll introduce you. They're lovely. His mother is so sweet and genteel, she's like a lady from eighteenth-century England or something. And his sister, Ness, is just adorable. She already calls me sis ...' Jenna busied herself with her bouquet for a beat. 'Abbey and Damon are over there somewhere.' She stopped talking as a wide, bearded man abruptly appeared and swooped in to hug her, then finished with an assertive squeeze of her bum. Jenna gritted her teeth.

'Oh, there's Tom, Eliza and Mrs Yates from work,' Fairlie pointed out, having missed the butt grope, 'and Mum and Dad.' Fairlie waved to her parents at the back of the crowd, but then dropped her arm, turning to Jenna with an expression of guilt.

'It's okay,' Jenna mumbled. 'I didn't think she'd come.'

'You didn't invite her.'

'Lack of permission never stopped her.'

Fairlie drew back, surprised. 'Did you *want* her here?' Her expression turned soft. 'Jen, you could have invited her.'

'Mrs Ark Rudolph!'

The title panged in Jenna's belly, the erasure of even her first name. Ark's mother breezed over wafting scarves of Chanel, puckering up to kiss the air in front of Jenna's cheeks. Another handful of coloured rice was tossed in her direction and some of it filtered down her cleavage.

'Mrs Rudolph –' Jenna began.

'Oh stop,' the older woman *tsked*, 'Marguile, please.'

120

'Right. This is my dear friend Fairlie Winter.'

Ark's mother clasped Fairlie's wrists and smiled, pearls glimmering on her milky skin. 'Pleasure.'

'Right back atcha,' Fairlie said.

'The photographer wants us over by the roses,' Ark's mother said, turning back to Jenna. 'And the caterer said the first round of hors d'oeuvres are ready.' Clasping Jenna by the elbow, she issued a gentle tug away from Fairlie, towards the crowd.

An anxious flicker stiffened Jenna against Marguile's grasp, like an animal baulking at a gate. 'I'll see you later,' she said hurriedly to Fairlie, 'this doesn't change anything.'

Fairlie squeezed her hand. 'Hey. Don't worry about me. Just focus on losing your virginity tonight.'

Ark appeared, wrapped his arm around Jenna's waist and placed a kiss on her temple. 'I see Mum has got every-thing running smoothly,' he said with a laugh. He made a joke that after the honeymoon, when his mother would stay with them for a few days, she might never want to return home.

'You know me, darling,' his mother chuckled, her cheeks suddenly flushed. 'You might be a big strong boy but your sister still needs me.' She winked at Fairlie, who nodded, as though she had any idea what they were talking about.

'I'm just sorry Ark's father didn't live to see this moment.' Finally releasing Jenna's elbow, Marguile's eyes misted over.

Ark squeezed his mother's shoulder. 'I know, Mum,' he said. 'Me, too.'

Jenna turned away. From Fairlie, from Ark's mother, and she took the hand of her new husband and began to walk down the centre of the gratuitous aisle that some faceless person had spent all morning arranging ivory plastic chairs to create. Two enormous manna gums flung piebald shade onto the lawn. From somewhere above a kookaburra hollered, determined to outdo the lone violinist who whined away from over beside a row of prickly grevilleas.

And Jenna walked away, into her instant family, into her new life.

—O—

Jenna sighed, flinging herself down on the bed.

'Long shift,' Ark said, leaning down to kiss her nose. He straightened and started to unbutton his shirt. 'You work too hard.'

'It was.' Jenna sat up with a yawn. 'But,' she stretched out her arms; the muscles pulled deliciously, 'it's Saturday night and for the first time in three weeks, Fro and I are both free. So, what shall we all do?'

Ark walked into the ensuite and turned on the shower. He reached into the spray to test the temperature, then peeled off his shirt and dropped it into the laundry hamper.

'Sure,' he said, 'it's the first Saturday night you've had off in a month. We should do something special.' He began to undo his jeans.

'Hmm, special in Penola.' Jenna tapped her chin. 'So, the pub? Or, we could go out on a limb, and go to the *other* pub.'

Ark slowly lowered his zipper. 'And that's special how?'

'We'll wear bow ties.' Jenna sauntered over to him and placed her palms over his bare chest. 'And top hats.' She stood on tiptoes and kissed his lips, tasting the sugary tang of fresh grape juice.

Ark ran his hands down her spine, over the swell of her bum. He pulled her against him. 'Let's just you and I do something,' he murmured, his lips moving across her jaw to beneath her ear. He took a deep breath, as though breathing her in, and her body bowed into his.

'But I promised her.'

'So?'

'So?' Jenna said, pulling away. 'It's Fro. I haven't seen her for ages. I'm having withdrawals.'

'You saw her at work today.' He pulled her back in.

'She helped me clean bedpans. Then we shared half a box of Pizza Shapes.'

'That's more than you've shared with me today.' His voice was low, his fingers brushing her collarbone. 'You should put *us* first – you and me.'

Jenna bit her lip. His hand slipped lower, his palm settling over the rise of her breast. Steam from the shower warmed her skin, moisture pricked on her face and throat.

'Please?' His lips moved on her neck.

Hooking her fingers into the waistband of his jeans, she tugged them down his thighs. 'Okay, you've twisted my arm,' she said. 'I'll send her a message.'

'Later,' he said.

━○

Sunday morning, an unseasonably warm day for late March. Jenna waited on the couch. The ceiling fan stirred the pages of the paperback she was reading half-heartedly when Fairlie trumped through the front door without knocking and lifted up her T-shirt.

'Check it out,' Fairlie said from behind the fabric. 'New togs. Slimming, no?' She twisted from side to side.

Jenna chuckled, taking in the wide vertical black and white strips of lycra stretched across her friend's mid-section, tucked snugly into the waistband of fluorescent orange surf shorts.

'Ahh, I see what they're doing,' Jenna said, tossing the novel aside. 'That black section in the middle with the hourglass shape, and the white on the sides – it's like a pseudo waist.'

'Exactly.' Fairlie lowered her shirt enough to peer at Jenna over the fabric. 'I even waxed my bikini line for that extra wow factor. But I have to warn you,' she said, 'we might be fighting blokes off with a bat once I reveal myself in this at the beach.'

'Sorry, I forgot to tell you.' Jenna shook her head. 'We won't be going to the beach.'

Fairlie's shirt fluttered back into place. 'Why?'

'Ark's coming. He doesn't swim, remember?' Jenna shot her a look of apology.

'Oh.' Fairlie looked at her tummy and smoothed down her T-shirt. 'I thought he had some conference call thing on this morning?'

'It's been rescheduled.'

'Right.' Fairlie nodded. 'Dude owes me lunch, anyway.' She plopped alongside Jenna on the couch and dropped a loud smack on her cheek. 'What on earth is this?' She picked up Jenna's paperback. 'Since when do you read . . . ' she flipped the novel over and quoted, '"erotic romance"?'

'Ark got it for me,' Jenna said. 'He thinks I'll like it.'

Fairlie opened to a random page in the centre of the book. Her eyebrows began inching towards her hairline, then she burst out laughing. 'Remind me never again to eat ice-cream,' she said. 'Do you actually *like* this?'

Jenna snatched the book back. 'It's fine.'

'Bow chicka bow wow,' Fairlie sang, shimmying her shoulders. 'Is it supposed to be some kind of subtle hint? I mean, does Ark want you to get a whip and –'

'Hey, Fairlie.'

'Good morning, stranger.' Fairlie didn't miss a beat, launching straight from one sentence to another as Ark came into the room. 'I wore my bathers for nothing, I hear.'

'I'm sure you'll find an excuse to strip and show them off anyway,' he said, holding out his fist. Fairlie leaned forwards and bumped it.

Ark bent to kiss Jenna. Squeezing her shoulder, he said, 'Ready? Let's go.'

'Right now?' Fairlie broke in. 'Can we have a cuppa first? I'm parched.'

Ark offered her a fleeting smile, then directed his gaze back to Jenna. 'I'm not sure what time the call will come through, but it could be as soon as two. So I want to get back in time.'

Taking Ark's hand, Jenna stood and slipped into her thongs. 'Let's go,' she said over her shoulder, as Ark tugged her playfully from the room.

'Hey, wait,' Fairlie said from behind her. 'Where's the fire?'

Sticky air engulfed them as they stepped outside. Galahs tittered in the eucalypts and sparrows flitted about in the grass. Sweat sprung out on Jenna's forehead and she rubbed it with fingertips.

'Perfect weather,' Ark announced. 'Lunch; a beer in the shade. Check out the bikini bodies on display on the sand.'

Jenna scoffed softly, and Ark laughed and curled an arm around her waist. 'None as beautiful as you, though,' he chuckled into her ear. Jenna shoved at him, but couldn't help the self-satisfied ripple beneath her skin.

'Are we taking my car?' Fairlie asked.

'Nah, we'll take the Merc,' Ark tossed over his shoulder. 'More comfortable.'

Jenna smiled at her. 'Come on, you haven't had a ride in it yet.'

Fairlie hastened to catch up. 'My arse can hardly wait.'

The Mercedes purred the hour's stretch of bitumen between Penola and Robe, the sleepy and unassuming beachside town that boasted a population of about 1500 in winter and 15,000 in summer. Most of the tourists had packed up their tents and caravans and dragged themselves home for the year, but a few locals and daytrippers wandered the main street.

Warmed by the friendly stream of banter that Ark and Fairlie had maintained for the whole trip, Jenna lounged back in her seat, the air-conditioner whispering cool air around her ankles. Ark's hand rested on her bare thigh and she stroked his fingers. Shopfronts flashed past the window: a surf shop, bodyboards lined up like shark's teeth in a window; a bakery; a trendy espresso bar that had sprung up in response to burgeoning tourism; a ladies' wear store; another surf shop; a service station. At the end of the main street, the shops gave way to a lawn bowls green, a broad expanse of half-dried kikuyu grass and then the azure of the Great Australian Bight glittered into view.

Ark swung the car in a circle and pulled into the shade beneath a strand of towering Norfolk Island pines.

'. . . entire roast lamb leg,' Fairlie was saying, incredulous. She slapped her knee and snorted.

'You're lucky, though.' Ark looked at Fairlie in the rear-vision mirror. 'I can't get Jenna to make a toasted sandwich – yet you've got a neighbour who leaves a Christmas feast on your doorstep every second day.'

'Oh God, tell me about it!' Fairlie said. 'I lived with her for over a year. I completely understand.'

'You're both full of shit,' Jenna interjected.

Out of the car, Jenna's skirt lifted in a briny gust of wind. Ark drew her in close and kissed her forehead. Children shrieked on a nearby playground. The air smelled of pine sap and salt; slender spiked needles from the pines crushed beneath their feet as they crossed the grass.

Granite boulders crouched at the edge of the park. Beyond, the beach was a finger of sand uncurling into the distance, foam and sea-grass lazily stitched onto the shore.

Fairlie took a deep breath and sighed wistfully.

'Gonna get your gear off then, Fro?' Jenna looked at her.

Fairlie turned her face up to the sky, her expression hidden behind sunglasses and sweat-sticky brown curls. 'Nah,' she said. She dropped her gaze to Jenna and smiled. 'Not the same without you.'

'Time for lunch,' Ark broke in with enthusiasm.

'Excellent. Fish and chips.' Fairlie rubbed her hands together. 'I've been waiting all week. Did you know the management's changed, Jen? Hope they still have that spicy noodle salad.'

Ark, his arm firm across Jenna's shoulders, turned from the beach and made for the street. 'We're going to the pub,' he said.

Jenna wheeled with him. 'Come on, Fro. Ark knows the manager.'

'Half-price drinks,' Ark added. 'On me, anyway.' He aimed his words forwards, projecting loud enough for Fairlie to hear. 'I know you're not one to turn down a free drink.'

Before she turned out of view, Jenna saw an irritated flash cross Fairlie's features. Annoyance? Disappointment? Jenna told herself she had imagined it, but it was several long moments before Fairlie caught up.

———⚷———

The interior of the pub was dim, the air carrying the damp, fermented scent of beer and timber. They made their way through the front bar to the bistro. Ark waved and shouted a cheerful greeting to a thin man with a shining bald crown in a black polo shirt writing specials on a blackboard.

'Rudo!' the bald man cried, grinning broadly and

setting down his chalk. 'Good to see you, mate.' He hurried over, slapping his palms together, and the two men shook hands with bicep-swelling gusto.

'Hey man, thanks for that box of shiraz, eh?' the bald man enthused. 'Bloody generous of you. Bloody generous.'

'Hey, hey.' Ark held up his hands, refusing the gratitude. 'Not at all. I appreciate your support.'

'And this must be the lovely Mrs Rudolph.' He turned to Jenna.

'Yes, this is her. My beautiful wife.' Ark wrapped his arm around Jenna's shoulder and made introductions: the man was Tate Adams, newest manager of the Commercial Hotel and, according to Ark, a great bloke and a man with whom he'd shared many a local wine appreciation event. After shaking Fairlie's hand and giving her a cursory smile, Tate returned his attention to Ark.

Jenna felt, more than observed, Fairlie looking back and forth between Ark and the animated pub manager as they spoke. After some minutes, Fairlie tittered something about her tragically distinct lack of beer and wandered to the bar, leaving Jenna with the men. Jenna made to follow her, but Ark's arm held her in place, and for a beat in time she felt a twist of anxiety. Where was she supposed to be? A moment later, Fairlie, beer in hand, ambled through the back doors into the sunlit beer garden. Jenna exhaled and mentally shook herself.

'You got my order?' Tate was asking.

'You know it,' Ark replied.

'Excellent. Buyer's all set.'

Ark lowered his voice. 'You finalise the deal?'

Something in Ark's clandestine tone piqued Jenna's attention. Nodding, then offering Ark a fist bump, Tate gave a shrill whistle that made Jenna jump. A boy appeared, his white T-shirt damp and stained, a tea-towel tucked into his apron.

Ark fished his keys from his pocket and handed them to the kitchen boy. 'Silver Mercedes,' he said. 'Top of the street.' The kid nodded and left.

'What's he doing?' Jenna asked.

'Nothing. Just delivering something. Hey, babe, why don't you go pick us out a table?'

Jenna considered him, but he just smiled at her nonchalantly.

Outside, the beer garden was walled with low red brick and fringed with potted palms. In the shade of a broad canvas umbrella, Fairlie was seated at a table in the middle of the garden, sipping her beer. Over a crackly speaker, Kenny Rogers' 'The Gambler' was playing. Only a handful of people were scattered about. Seagulls hopped on spare tables and squabbled on the pavers.

Fairlie had gathered the cardboard coasters from her table and stacked them into a pyramid. She hadn't noticed Jenna threading her way through the tables. As Fairlie was balancing the last coaster atop her creation, her tongue sticking from the corner of her mouth, Jenna stopped at her elbow.

The coasters tumbled onto the table.

'Bloody hell,' Fairlie said. 'That took me half a day.'

'Sorry.' Jenna slid into a seat. 'That Tate guy can talk the head off . . . ' She gestured to Fairlie's beer. 'You know.'

'What's taking so long?'

Jenna shrugged. 'Business. I guess. Think Ark brought something for him.'

At that moment, Ark, laughing riotously, barrelled through the back doors and strode over to their table. He grinned and announced, 'Lunch is on the house.'

'See?' Jenna said to Fairlie. 'I told you he's a handy man to have around.'

'Real handy,' Fairlie agreed, taking a swallow of her beer. 'Like a Chux wipe.'

Lunch arrived quickly, piles of golden fried chips stacked with crispy-battered fish.

'Fish and chips, as promised,' Jenna pointed out.

'No noodle salad, though,' Fairlie returned, indicating her inadequate pile of lettuce leaves.

Ark's phone rang. Dropping his fork, he mumbled his apologies and hastily walked to a quiet corner. Jenna couldn't hear him but he spoke rapidly, waving one hand around. When he returned to the table, his face was lit up.

'That was him,' he said to Jenna, bouncing on the balls of his feet. 'New buyer. This is really gonna happen.' He shook his phone triumphantly, like a trophy.

'That's great, honey!' Jenna cried.

'But,' he said, 'I've gotta go.' He slapped his watch. '*Now*. They want a Skype conference in an hour.'

Fairlie looked down at her barely touched meal. 'We can't finish lunch?'

'Fairlie,' Ark said, beaming, 'when this deal goes through I'll buy you lunch for a *month*.' He batted a hand at their plates. 'It was free anyway. Come on. Let's go!'

Taking Jenna's hand, Ark led them from the beer garden, Fairlie trotting to keep up.

As Fairlie's car disappeared into a cloud of white dust down the drive, Jenna smiled and tucked her arms around Ark's waist.

'I'm glad you could come anyway,' she told him, 'even if it was cut short.'

Ark peeled her arms away, glancing at his watch. 'Shit, I've only got five minutes.'

Jenna followed him inside, jerking up a hand to stop the door from slapping her in the face. In the bathroom, she watched him yank off his T-shirt and set the hot water gushing into the sink.

'What's the rush?' she asked, putting her hands on his back.

Ark shrugged her off and glared at her in the mirror.

Steam rose in wisps from the tap. 'I've got four minutes to look half-decent – we're talking potential stocking at Dan Murphy's here, Jenna. Haven't you been listening?'

Jenna blinked, taken aback. 'I'm always listening.'

Ark slapped shaving foam onto his cheeks. 'I shouldn't have come today, I really didn't have time.'

'You wanted to come.'

'What choice did I have?' Water squirted across the tiles as he rinsed his razor under the tap. He cursed. 'I've barely seen you for weeks. You said you were going to the beach with Fairlie on my one free day. How else am I supposed to spend time with my wife?'

Wife. He'd said it like she'd forgotten his birthday.

'I've just missed you so much this week,' he was saying, swiping a hand towel across the bench. The muscles in his upper arms bulged. 'We've barely spent ten minutes together. You're working all hours – taking care of everyone except me – or playing with your girlfriend.' He looked at her sadly. 'We need more time as a couple.' He took a shirt from a hanger and was gone. A moment later she heard the click of the office door.

Jenna closed her mouth, and sat down on the bed to stare at the floor.

━○

Jenna remained silent as the waiter cleared plates from between them. She stole a quick look at Ark and saw that he was watching her, a small smile on his lips, but he thanked the young guy profusely.

'And to think,' Ark said, after the waiter had left, 'six weeks ago we were just Ark and Jenna. Now,' he was rubbing his napkin into a drying squirt of garlic butter on the tablecloth, 'it's Mr and Mrs Rudolph. Sharing a meal like any normal married couple.'

Her fingers traced the rim of her coffee cup, papery-rough with hardened milk foam. She rubbed her thumb and forefinger together, brushing it away. She didn't answer him.

He crossed his arms and sighed. 'You're still pissed at me.'

'No,' she replied at length. 'I'm . . . disappointed.'

He stared at her, tapping his teaspoon on the table. 'You're flirting right in front of me for the entire meal, and *you're* disappointed?'

'This is ridiculous,' she said curtly. 'Come on.' Unhooking her bag from the chair, she made to stand up but Ark remained seated, and so, after a brief, half-squatting hesitation where she was neither sitting nor standing, she gingerly sat back down.

Ark stood up.

Outside the restaurant, a chill had crept into the evening air. Jenna hugged her arms, her shoes clicked across the car park.

'So now you're not going to speak to me, is that it?'

Jenna glared at him. The car door handle was cold

beneath her hand; she jerked the passenger door open.
Snapping into her seatbelt, she replayed the dinner over
in her mind: how contented they'd both been when they'd
arrived, the waiter politely taking their order. Ark's behaviour had turned bizarre when their entrees had been
delivered, after the waiter had set the bruschetta in front
of them – what had she said? She recalled thanking the
waiter, surely she'd smiled courteously. The waiter had
remarked that the bruschetta was one of the chef's special-
ties, told them to enjoy it, and she'd simply said, *Thanks,
I'm sure we will.* Or something like that. Hadn't she? She
swiped her cheeks with the back of her hand.

'You're crying?' Ark said. 'Please don't make this into
a big deal.'

'Of course I'm upset,' she said angrily. 'You harangued
me for the entire meal about doing something I have *no
idea* that I did.'

'Babe, look, maybe it's because of all the wine you had,
but ... you were a bit brazen. I mean, by the time he
brought desserts the poor kid was blushing. You asked him
what time he would be "getting off".'

'I was making conversation! You're taking it the wrong
way. It's stupid.'

'I'm *stupid?* That's nice.'

'I didn't say *you* were stupid, I said –'

'Sometimes you really hurt me, you know that?'

'This is insane! I'm not trying to hurt –'

'Insane? Wow, Jenna. Tell me how you really feel.'

Jenna gaped at him, her mouth opening and closing. Nothing came out.

'And how do you think this kind of behaviour reflects on me?'

'Can you even hear yourself?'

'People know who I am. In that restaurant they sell two of my vintages, babe. It's ... ' He shook his head. 'It's embarrassing.'

Seething, Jenna went quiet. The night rushed past the car, headlights illuminating a blur of ghostly gum trunks, the flash of the dotted line on the bitumen. The engine hummed and Jenna closed her eyes, her jaw aching with the clamp of her molars.

After a while, Ark said, 'I'm sorry.'

Opening her eyes, she glared at him.

'Hey, look, I am sorry that you're upset.' He gave her a brief, conceding glance. 'It's just ... They always say that relationships are supposed to be based on trust and honesty. So I guess I was ... hurt, that you'd flirt so openly with that guy.'

'I wasn't flirting,' she ground out, 'and you're being a prick about it.'

He paused, letting her angry words crash between them.

'Don't insult me,' he said evenly. 'You'll kick yourself for it.'

Jenna turned her face to the window.

'Look,' he repeated. 'It's because of her, you know? My

ex. She . . . ' He rubbed the back of his neck. 'Sometimes I overreact, because she stuck me, you know? She was a bitch – bled me like a fucking pig. So yeah, I guess it's not my fault. I'm a bit damaged.'

Jenna stared unblinking into the night, flicking her wedding band with her thumbnail. 'I know she hurt you,' she muttered. 'You've told me. And I'm always sympathetic. But I wasn't flirting. And it pisses me off that I have to defend myself.'

'Okay,' he said slowly. 'Wow.' Then he shook his head, chuckling. 'Guess you *are* drunk.'

When he didn't offer anything further, she said, 'Are you suggesting all men think basic manners are an invitation for sex?'

'You were sucking your finger at him.'

A single syllable of laughter burst out of Jenna. 'I had garlic butter on it.'

'Hey.' He held up a hand. 'I'm not saying we're perfect. But we're men. We're always looking for an excuse. Especially when the woman in question is so hot.'

Silence fell over the car. Jenna's pulse still fretted in her throat, but she felt it slowing. Something in his point niggled at her. Maybe she *had* flirted with the waiter; he'd been sweet and funny and the meal had been lovely. Had she been single too long and forgotten how to act in a relationship? Or was it genetic – an audacious need for acknowledgement?

'I mean,' his voice changed, settled, 'it's awful, but it's

like what we hear on the news all the time: a woman in a short dress, alone at night – in an undeniable way, she's asking for trouble. I'm not saying it's an excuse – I'm not "victim blaming" –' he air-quoted, '– but if you leave your house unlocked, don't be complaining when your stuff gets stolen, you know?' He gave her a long, almost sympathetic look. 'I'm only saying you have to be careful. You're not single anymore. And,' he added, 'you can't keep taking examples from Fairlie. She . . . well, she gets around. Hey, hey.' He held up his hand again as her head snapped up. 'I'm not being derogatory. She even admits it. *You* call her a whore – I've heard you. I know, I know, you're friends, term of endearment and all that,' he finished.

Jenna's body stiffened. That day, her mother had said to her: *I thought I knew it all. But I didn't – I was blind.*

Ark put his hand on her thigh.

Jenna took in a deep breath and let it out slowly. When she was thirteen, she and Fairlie had been allowed to go to the Spring Show alone for the first time. Jenna recalled the scent of sawdust, frying fat and animal shit; heard the hiss of hydraulics, the emboldening thump of rock music and the screams of revellers on rides. Despite Jenna's pleas, Fairlie had flatly refused to accompany her on the Zipper, a contraption where riders curled inside tiny cages strung around an enormous, rotating oblong arm. Waiting in line, Jenna's heart had pounded. Two boys, tall and lean, their voices cracking with testosterone and their hair a tribute to Kurt Cobain over their faces, had convinced

Jenna she'd be safer snug in a cage with them, rather than loose in a cage on her own. She'd clambered into the cage, giggling, daring, with the boys. And when the cage began to move, and the music beat through her body, and she'd somersaulted, shrieking, Jenna had told herself the hand that had suddenly dug between her legs and remained there, fumbling and gripping, for the whole ride had been inevitable.

As the car slid cocoon-like through the night, Jenna touched the silky back of Ark's hand with the tip of her middle finger, felt the supple rise of the vein there and the pulse, faintly; the beat of his heart thrumming through her finger, up her arm and into her chest. There was a part of her that seethed with hurt; but there was a part of her that stretched out to him, wanting him to come to her, so they might soothe each other's wounds.

The roller door rumbled shut behind them, and the inside of the car fell into a taut silence.

The leather seat whispered as Ark turned to her. 'Don't be upset,' he said. Without the noise of the road his voice seemed deeper; in his tone was a calm, quiet plea.

Jenna rubbed her forehead. 'How do you expect me to feel?'

'Relationships aren't always easy,' he said. 'They need work to get through the bumps. That's all this is – a speed hump. We can work on it.'

'Work on it,' Jenna repeated, more to herself than to Ark. Above him, the mild beam of the interior light rendered his face into light and shadow: the sweep of his brow, the strong line of his nose, the darkened pools of his eyes.

His fingers squeezed her knee. The seat rustled again as he leaned over, his hand moving from her knee and sliding up her thigh. 'Let it go,' he whispered, his breath warm against her ear. Then he kissed her jaw, the touch of his lips sending a bolt of electricity down her middle.

'Easy for you to say,' she said softly. 'You weren't just accused of adultery.' The word smouldered in her mouth.

He chuckled, and she felt it shudder against her. 'I have so much love to give. I need you to love me as much as that.' His hand moved higher, his fingers spreading across the inside of her thigh; his thumb dug into her hip. 'And I love you so much it consumes me.'

Through the windscreen the inside of the shed was dark. The interior light faded, plunging them into blackness.

Jenna closed her eyes as his lips moved to her neck and his hand slid beneath the hem of her shirt, stroking tingling streaks across her skin. Again she heard the soft talk of leather, felt the warm damp of his breath against her collarbone. She made her mind blank as he pressed her against the seat, as he found her mouth with a sudden hunger that mirrored her own.

Because if she thought about anything, she feared she could trust nothing. If she let herself remember any of it she may come apart completely. So, as his tongue pressed against hers, she let it all fall away. Tangling her fingers into his hair, she breathed deep the sharp, spicy scent of him as though she could swallow him with it.

One by one, he deftly tugged at the buttons on her jeans and slid his hand beneath her waistband. She arched towards him, pressing herself against his palm as he found the slippery centre of her.

Her jaw fell open, her breath rushing back and forth hotly between her lips. He urged her thighs further apart. And then she threw herself at him, heard the rapture in her satisfied moan as she took everything she could from him, in order to obliterate herself.

The white netting was heavy and snagged on the vines. Although it was a cool day with a blanket of low grey clouds, Jenna felt a drop of sweat slide down her ribs.

Only a small portion of the grapes had been netted, and Jenna thanked a deity for that small mercy as she heaved the net over the top of the last row and dragged it to the ground. It lay on the ground between the vines, a snarled, long white trail dotted with twigs and leaves.

'Almost done.' Ark gave her a smile as she bent over, her breath coming hard. 'You need to work out, honey. Don't want you getting all unfit for me.' Together they hauled the long rope of net towards them, bundling it into a big pile.

Jenna saw the snake before Ark did.

The thick brown coil of its body was tangled in the net, shuddering as the net lugged along the ground.

'Ark,' Jenna said, dropping the net. 'Look.'

But the snake was dead; its thick muscular body was lifeless. Jenna felt only a fleeting spark of relief before she saw Ark's hands begin to shake.

'It's okay,' she said quietly, motioning for him to step away. 'I'll just get rid of it, okay?'

A pained expression crossed Ark's face: a look of frustration and terror and self-criticism. He lifted his hands to his head and pulled at his hair, tears welling at the corners of his eyes.

'Ark, just turn away. I've got this.'

Swiftly she approached the snake. Wrinkling her nose, she pulled her sleeves over her hands and tried to pick it up, but the slick long muscle was wrapped and twisted into the netting. With some difficulty, and revulsion, she managed to extract the snake – a smallish king brown, only young, but still deadly if alive – and toss it beneath the grapes. She would come back with a shovel later and bury it somewhere Ark wouldn't come across. He had walked briskly to the end of the row and had his back to her.

'It's gone,' she called to him. 'But you know what, why don't you just go inside? We can finish this up later. Besides,' she glanced at the sky. 'I think it's about to rain.'

Back inside the house Ark asked in a quavering voice if she could please shower: he couldn't handle knowing she'd touched it with her bare hands.

Out of the shower, Jenna sank onto the couch next to him, running her hand down the length of his arm. He was still shaken, shudders occasionally rippling through his body, and she could tell he was struggling to keep his breathing slow and even.

'Tell me,' she said.

Ark took a deep breath. 'You know my dad died when I was fourteen.' He swallowed. 'I found him. I found ... his body.'

Jenna picked up his hand.

'I'd just gotten home from school. He was sitting at the kitchen table.'

'And he ... had already passed away?'

'Yeah.' The word came out in a breath.

'Honey, I ... I don't know what to say. How awful.' Jenna fought the urge to collect him up and rock him in her arms.

'I couldn't get hold of Mum. I had to call my neighbours, and they came over and called an ambulance but it was too late. He was dead. They said he'd probably been dead a few hours.'

Jenna bit her lip. It wouldn't help him to start weeping.

Ark's voice had become far away as the memory spilled out. 'His eyes were open. And his lips were blue. Like – a really freaky blue, something from a horror film. I'll never forget that. Whenever I try and picture him now all I can see is that. His blue lips and his eyes open, staring at nothing.'

'I'm so sorry.'

He turned to her, his pupils huge. 'I hated the cunt, did I ever tell you that?'

Jenna started. 'No. I thought you said –'

'No matter how hard I tried, I could never do anything right. He was always telling me off for something. Half the time I didn't even know what I'd done. At home, at school, on the vineyard – I'd try my damnedest to please him but it would never be enough. I was never enough. And my mum?' He gave a kind of mirthless laugh. 'She never stood up for me. She was scared of him, too. She was just his whipping post. Too frightened to say boo. She *never* stood up for me,' he repeated. 'Not even when he belted me. I learned to stop crying pretty fast, because there was no fucking point in it.'

As she listened to him pour out his soul, Jenna tried not to think. Because with each damnation of his mother, Jenna could feel the words her own mother had spoken twisting bands of steel around her heart tighter and tighter until she might never breathe again.

'I've been thinking about something,' he said.

Jenna lifted her head from the pillow to glance at the clock.

'It's 2 am,' she mumbled. 'Why aren't you sleeping?'

'I've been thinking about us,' he went on. 'About the rift that's between us sometimes. We can mend it.'

He found her hand beneath the blankets and curled his fingers into hers. 'We can make something that's only ours,' he whispered. 'You and me. Something no one else can touch or make dirty.'

She waited.

Tenderly, he said, 'I think we should have a baby.'

Dear Jenna,

All of these things I am telling you, it's as if they are greater individually – swollen, somehow – than the sum of them pressed together. When I examine each of these moments alone, I recognise I could have made better decisions; I could have steered into a course less tragic, less destined for a certain doom. But at the time I believed I was nothing more than a hapless passenger, bound inexorably to my fate.

Around midnight on the eve of your birth I awoke to a dull, low pain that made my belly rock-firm. As I placed my hands over my bulging middle, I could feel the tightening of the muscles deep under there.

Oh, how this moment had been one for which I had so fiercely longed, and yet at the same time, dreaded with a quiet, existential fear! You were coming, our beloved baby, and as I curled over the contractions I whispered sweet words down to this child who would change everything. Silent tears rolled down my cheeks and my belly curved out into the night; I knew that it would represent a beginning, and inevitably, an end.

I just couldn't know whose end it would be.

At one point, I believed I would die. The doctor's voice was firm and encouraging, muffled by a green surgical mask as he told me to keep pushing. I had been bemused by that mask. Was the doctor covering his face to shield himself from the fluid and sweat and shit and the obscenities I muttered through teeth gritted so tightly they might splinter and fill my mouth with tiny, fatal shards? When I picture that green mask now, I can almost feel your father's grip on my hand: tentative and clammy; I can almost feel my heart thundering in my ears through the pethidine's foggy haze.

And when I pushed, and Stephen's face went white, the face of my mother flashed before my eyes. I saw her waving madly from the open window of that banana-coloured Kombi of my childhood as my parents rattled off up Jubilee Highway and left me, nineteen and entirely unaware that I wasn't omnipotent. Suddenly, in labour, I wanted my mum. More than anything. My mother would fix this; my mother would make it all stop because that's what mothers do, damn it, they hold you up when you feel like there is nothing left of you but the pitiful, soggy waft of your exhaled breath and the transparency of your unrealised expectations. Don't they?

Isn't that what I, then – and now – was supposed to do?

Do we ever stop needing our mother?

Fixed flat on my back and staring up at the bright lights, the obscene bulge of my gut rising forth between us all and the blue sheet bunched around my hips, I gave a banshee cry that I thought would surely rip open the arteries throbbing thick and hot in my throat, and perhaps then there would be nothing again to fear.

And then something happened. There was another cry. A strange, watery bleat that elicited a cheer from the nurses and a satisfied beam from the doctor.

'Well done,' the doctor said from behind his mask, 'you have a little girl.'

I stopped breathing. Trembling with the strain of it, I raised my head and stared at you – our baby – slick and gooey and defiantly shrieking in the doctor's hands. Your head lolled back, neck gripped between the doctor's blue-gloved thumb and forefinger. A ropey purple-cream cord pulsed from your belly.

Your skin was wrinkled, blotchy pink and blue-white.

I closed my eyes as a thousand kinds of relief sank over me. When I opened them again the room was brighter, softer. A rasp in Stephen's voice as he whispered something strained and prideful in my ear; he ducked his head to wipe his eyes, furtively.

I only knew I was weeping when you, bundled in a soft fleecy blanket, were nestled by a nurse into my arms. Your face, once scrunched and furious, smoothed and quietened as I looked down at you, and then I realised that my expectations had been wrong, all wrong, because everything that felt splintered apart was now glued back together.

My baby. Stephen's baby. Our girl.

The rest of our lives would begin, now. We would start again and everything would be wonderful. This baby – you, Jenna – represented the two of us, Stephen and I. You represented everything that was perfect and laudable and right.

Stephen and I looked at each other. We named you Jenna.

149

And that's when it all changed again. Perfection had surrounded us for a few minutes – a soothing, victorious taste of normalcy – before it all broke apart.

But this will do for today. I need to stop now.

Love, Mum.

7

Now

The main street is quiet, only a few people stroll listlessly under shop awnings. An empty flatbed truck rumbles past, stirring the odour of hot exhaust and rubber from the asphalt.

The traffic light *bip-bips* and Fairlie is rooted to the kerb. Her gaze is trained on the concrete strip of kerbing where Jenna had tripped when they were walking home to the flat one night, cutting her chin like a kid falling off her bike. Squatting, Fairlie touches her fingertips to the gritty surface and imagines she can feel Jenna's warm blood there.

Everywhere. Jenna is everywhere and she is nowhere.

Fairlie goes left. Passing the coffee shop with the welded

tin chooks out the front, where Jenna had always ordered a one-sugar latte, Fairlie holds the door open for Mrs Hurst from the quilting supplies shop, struggling out with a box of takeaway coffees.

Mrs Hurst thanks her. 'I'm sorry to hear about Jenna,' she says, clucking her tongue. 'How are her husband and little boy doing?'

'I don't know, to be honest,' Fairlie admits.

'I ran into Marg,' Mrs Hurst says. 'She mentioned she'd given you some time off.'

Marg Dunbower, Fairlie's nursing unit manager, has left several messages on Fairlie's voicemail. *We're here for you. Come back whenever you're ready.* Fairlie has pondered the word 'ready'. It means something proactive, something that puts you in control. How can she ever be *ready*?

'They miss you at the hospital,' the older woman is saying.

Fairlie's vision wavers. Although Jenna quit before Henry was born, she's scared work will now remind her of Jenna. On the ward, or in the tea room, or in the halls, Fairlie will feel the ghost of her friend behind her, vaporous fingers counting the knuckles of her spine. Because it was Jenna who wanted to leave the larger Mount Gambier Hospital for somewhere quieter. It was Jenna who had found them jobs at the Penola War Memorial Hospital, and rented their little flat two blocks away. The flat where Fairlie now lives, alone.

Mrs Hurst says, 'You'll look after yourself, won't you?'

Fairlie stares at her. How can Fairlie look after herself if she couldn't look after her best friend? Who is Fairlie without Jenna? Jenna was the heritage, the history, that Fairlie has never known for herself. And now she's gone and Fairlie is back to a rootless, unknown nobody, snipped at the cord, untethered.

The woman squeezes Fairlie's elbow in farewell and hastens into the air-conditioning of her store two doors down, disappearing behind the colourful bolts of fabric clustered in the windows.

Without looking at the road, Fairlie steps off the kerb. Tyres chirp to her right but Fairlie doesn't notice.

Lace curtains pattern the glass of the lolly shop's windows, 'Sweet Treats' painted in simple curling script on the door. The rich, syrupy scent of cocoa butter and powdered sugar greets Fairlie as she steps inside. Racks of glossy foiled packets line the walls, free-standing shelves piled with chocolate bars stand on dark timber floors in the middle of the room.

From behind the counter, the owner's daughter looks up to greet her. A silver ring glints in her nose; there is a new stud in one side of her bottom lip.

'Another warm one,' the late-teen says.

Fairlie nods, back-handing sweat from her brow in answer. As she stands in front of a row of chocolate-coated liquorice, she can see the girl watching her from the corner of her eye. Deliberating. Desperate for information. After a moment, the girl thumbs something in to her phone. A hasty SOS to a friend, perhaps: *OMG dead chick's friend here. What do I say?*

Fairlie loads her arms and dawdles to the register, reluctant to leave the sweet, cool hush inside the store.

'It's Dottie, isn't it?' Fairlie asks, pushing white-chocolate-coated raspberry bullets and macadamia toffee across the bench.

The sales girl nods and grins, showing a row of small white teeth like buttons. 'You're Fairlie, that nurse from the hospital.'

'The one and only.'

'You probably don't remember,' the girl went on, 'but you bandaged up my foot a couple of months ago. I cut it on some tin in the backyard. Had to have a tetanus shot and everything.'

It is Fairlie's turn to smile. 'I do remember,' she tells the girl. 'Obviously you came to an agreement with your mother.' Fairlie thrusts out her lower lip and gestures to it with her hand.

'Oh, yeah.' Dottie touches a fingertip to the piercing. 'Took her long enough but she let me in the end. But this –' she sweeps her arm around the store and indicates her own presence in it '– is part of it.' She punches numbers into the register with one hand as she flicks through Fairlie's bounty with the other. 'I promised her forty hours in exchange.'

'Good deal.'

The girl hesitates. 'You knew that lady, didn't you?' Pink rises in her cheeks. 'Jenna Rudolph?'

'I did,' Fairlie answers. 'We were friends. Very good friends.'

'Sorry,' she says, diffidently. 'It's real sad. Kinda hits home, doesn't it, like we don't always know people, do we?'

Fairlie stares at her. 'No,' she says finally. 'We don't.' Fairlie hands her a twenty. 'Keep the change,' she says. 'Save up for your next piercing.'

━━○

The knock at the door startles Fairlie and she bolts upright, pausing *The Walking Dead*. Yodel leaps from her chest and skitters across the floor, shooting her a glare of indignation before sidling away.

The light coming through the windows is muted violet, and birdsong has been usurped by the evening cricket chorus. As she pulls open the door, the energetic chirp of a cricket bellows up at her from the flowerbox by the front wall. Fairlie shoves the screen door and it bangs back against the wall, startling the cricket into silence.

There's no one there, but a rich tomato-wine scent wafts up from a red enamel casserole pot on the doorstep.

'Oh, Mrs S,' she says. 'You've outdone yourself.'

Cradling the warm coq au vin she shuffles to the kitchen. Yodel leaps to mewl plaintively at the pot as she sets the food atop the counter.

Fairlie brushes away strands of cat hair and sets out a single bowl, a solitary spoon. The items sit there on the benchtop, sad and pathetic. Stark evidence of a single woman living alone with a cat. Looking through the room she sees the dimness of twilight covering only her own things – a tumble of meaningless knick-knacks, the lone cutlery in the sink, the nothingness of being alone. A prickling tingle rushes up her limbs and her heart starts to bang beneath her ribs. For a moment she is overcome with a ferocious, pure terror. From somewhere far away, below the rushing in her ears, she hears a rational voice: *This is a panic attack. Breathe. It will pass.*

So she breathes for her life. *In, out. Hold. In, out.* It's all she can do. And when, after a while, the rushing of her blood slows and her fingers ache from gripping the countertop, she lets a few tears slide down her cheeks before she dashes them angrily away.

Fairlie snatches up the casserole dish and presses the weight of it into her chest. She steps outside into the still evening and takes in fat gulps of warm air, almost tasting the tomatoes in the casserole prepared with thought and care. *You're not alone*, she tells herself firmly. Her footsteps seem loud as she crosses the courtyard under a darkening sky, from the paddock across the street comes the mournful bleat of a sheep. Familiar sounds, the ordinariness of every day. She tries to draw some comfort from it as her finger trembles on the doorbell above the tarnished bronze numeral 2.

'Ah, Fairlie,' says a woman's voice as the door is opened, the sprightly tone belying her age. 'I've been wondering when you'd surface.'

'Someone left me this lovely, huge meal.' Fairlie's words come in a rush and she forces a smile. 'I can't eat it all myself. It's a shame to eat alone. Fancy a bowlful?'

The octogenarian moves aside. 'I had a gnat for dinner, that's all I can manage these days. But for God's sake, come in. You look like a dog's breakfast.'

Crossing the dimpled plastic mat in the doorway, Fairlie steps into Mrs Soblieski's living room and her feet sink into thick brown shagpile carpet. Across the room, where shagpile meets faux-timber linoleum, the scent of more cooking floats from the avocado-coloured kitchen and Fairlie wonders if she will ever need to cook for herself again. The kitchen counter is swallowed beneath bunches of wilting-topped carrots, piles of potatoes like mounds of builder's rubble and what looks like an entire side of lamb alongside a leaning tower of clean plastic containers. Mrs Soblieski runs an unofficial one-woman charity, nourishing all the locals incapable of cooking for themselves. Fairlie's limbs still tingle, and she clutches the pot tighter to her chest.

This week, Mrs Soblieski's hair is an energetic shock of fuchsia-pink curls. 'What a goddamn shame,' her neighbour says, digging in the front pocket of a sagging hibiscus-print apron. The old woman withdraws a crumpled packet of cigarettes and offers it out – as always – giving her usual shrug as Fairlie courteously declines.

Mrs Soblieski scuffs across the floor and pushes open the back screen door. Fairlie knows better than to try to help as Mrs S bends awkwardly to prop the door open with an upturned terracotta pot. In the kitchen, Fairlie searches for a place to set down the casserole dish. Beef stock bubbles on the stove, shining thick knuckles of white bone the size of her fist.

In the doorway, Mrs Soblieski draws deeply on her cigarette, blowing the smoke out into the night. After a while she asks, 'You surprised?'

Fairlie glances at her, pulling a bowl from the shelf. 'I – of course I am.' She slops mashed potatoes into the bowl. 'I can't believe it. Why,' she pauses, 'aren't you?'

Mrs Soblieski exhales softly. 'I couldn't say. I've rarely seen her past couple of years. The odd hello in the car park and that. But even that got rarer and rarer.'

Dark red sauce drips from the ladle as Fairlie lifts it in a wordless question; Mrs Soblieski shakes her head, her pink curls bouncing.

'Course I understand why she disappeared,' Mrs S goes on mildly. 'She stopped coming over not long after she moved out.' The old woman crushes her cigarette into a sand-filled pail and the screen door closes with a bang. 'People change. She changed when she met that wine-making man.'

Fairlie feels instantly defensive. 'She was pretty busy. Work, renovations, the baby and all that.'

'Maybe.' Mrs Soblieski shuffles past her and disappears into the pantry, before reappearing with a dark glass bottle. 'Guess the husband took up a lot of her time, too.'

With the back of a spoon Fairlie smacks a well into the centre of her mashed potato. 'Yeah,' she says. 'She was so happy.'

'Obviously not.'

It thumps into her chest like percussion. 'Obviously.'

Mrs Soblieski pours three generous fingers of brandy into two crystal tumblers. 'You're angry at her,' she says, handing one glass over.

'Of course I'm angry,' Fairlie replies, dumping chicken over the mash. Sauce splatters onto the counter. 'How could she do this? Leave everyone? Abandon Henry?' Fairlie blinks back hot tears; she wouldn't want them to fall into the coq au vin and taint the lush sauce with her lousy grief. 'It's so selfish. Why didn't she *say* something?'

'Don't let yourself feel guilty.' Mrs S sips her brandy. 'He was poison to her from the word go.'

Fairlie picks up her drink and gazes into the amber liquid. 'At the start, she was happy,' she says. 'Ark this, Ark that. His love and his generosity. His big house in the vines.' She waves one arm as though painting a huge canvas in broad sweeps. 'But then ... '

'Things changed,' Mrs S says, matter-of-factly.

'I know they argued sometimes, and she would beat herself up for it. Said she had "unrealistic expectations". That she'd been damaged by her mum. And then one day ... '

'How many times did she leave him?' Mrs S asks, gently.

'Twice,' Fairlie whispers. 'That I know of.'

Mrs Soblieski moves to a well-worn armchair and sinks down with a laboured sigh. 'You're blaming yourself. With grief, that's as normal as cow dung in a cow paddock. But you shouldn't. Nothing you could have done.'

Fairlie props her palms on the counter. 'Maybe I couldn't see things were so bad after she'd talked up all the hearts and flowers for so long.'

'You didn't like him.'

Fairlie doesn't answer.

'You didn't think much of him.'

'At the start, she was deliriously happy.'

'And then?'

'And then . . . ' Air whooshes from Fairlie's nose. 'I don't know, exactly. They fought. She faded away.'

'So why are you blaming yourself, and not him? Or her, for that matter?'

Fairlie pauses, chewing the inside of her cheek. 'She loved him. I took her on her word. He was that great guy you always hear great things about – his name in the papers, his successful business, people always drawn to him. But I couldn't help but think . . . '

'What?'

'That the distance that came between Jenna and I was caused by him. Somehow.' She digs her fork into the casserole. 'I was jealous. That's really it. I have abandonment issues, don't I?'

160

The older woman looks at her with furrowed brows.

Fairlie grabs the brandy bottle. 'Or maybe I was bitter? Clearly I was blind.' She lifts the glass again, downs it in one hit and coughs.

'You drifted apart. That makes being vigilant a little difficult.'

'I should have told her to make up with her mum. God knows, she must have wanted to. It was years they hadn't spoken, in the end,' Fairlie says, reproachfully. 'Idiots, both of them. I should have told Jenna to pick up the phone and put an end to the stupid stand-off.' Her voice goes quiet and she adds, 'I saw Evelyn a few times. Maybe I should have said something to *her*, told her to call Jenna.'

Fairlie tries to recall how long it has been since she spoke to Evelyn Francis – weeks? Months? Fairlie had run into Jenna's mother briefly over the years: at the supermarket in Mount Gambier, a glimpse of her face in the car on the street, and once or twice passing her in the driveway or through the front door of her parents' house.

'Stop torturing yourself,' Mrs Soblieski says.

Fairlie stares at her bowl of casserole. Her mouth is watering and she's not sure if it's from hunger or the brandy. 'But then Jenna had Henry, and she seemed ... well, life went on.'

Fairlie tucks the bottle of brandy under her arm, collects her bowl and sits into the second armchair. Its cushions are firm, less used. She sets the brandy on a small glass-topped table between them, and the older woman refills her glass as Fairlie shovels in a few mouthfuls of chicken and mash. It's delicious; she wants to cry.

A moment of silence passes before Mrs Soblieski says, 'It can be a hard thing to admit – that you were wrong about someone.'

Fairlie wonders who she's talking about. Jenna and Ark? Jenna and her mum? Or her and Jenna?

'Try not to blame yourself.' Mrs S swills the brandy in her glass. 'And don't worry, the fury hurts now – believe me, I know – but it eases with time. Try to accept that you might never know.'

Fairlie picks up her glass and tosses down the rest of her drink, welcoming the flame of it in her throat.

Hours later, out in the courtyard, the black sky drapes above her, strewn with diamante stars. Spreading her feet, Fairlie tips back her head, her jaw loose, a plastic tub filled with chocolate cake clasped under her elbow.

'Jenna, you dickhead,' she whispers at the stars swirling above. 'I'm sorry.' She doesn't know why she's sorry but she is – she's so very goddamn sorry.

Her face falls and the world tips. To re-balance herself she stretches out her hand before she staggers across the courtyard. Setting the chocolate cake on her doorstep, she fumbles for her keys before remembering she'd fled her flat carrying only the casserole dish – the door is unlocked.

As she swings the door wide, the far-off sound of raucous male laughter mingles with the twang of country music from the pub on the main street. Stumbling backwards, Fairlie lets the door swing closed. She wheels around on unsteady feet, her vision blurred at the edges, and blinks furiously to clear it up as she sets off. It's only a short walk to the pub. The pub will have more brandy.

The Heyward's Royal Oak Hotel is brightly lit, yellow light pools onto the street through arched windows. Four men stand on the kerb outside, red dots of cigarettes glow and bounce in their shadowed faces. As she approaches, their voices grow quiet.

'Evening,' she calls, holding up a hand as she passes and heads for the bottle shop. 'Nice night for it?' She's never understood that saying. *Nice night for what, exactly? Because it isn't, Fairlie, it isn't a nice night. It's a very shitty, shitty night and tomorrow you're going to feel even worse.*

'Fairlie?' someone says. 'Fairlie Winter?'

Mid-stride, she stops and spins around. 'The one and only. Who's asking?'

One of the men comes forwards, stepping into the light. He walks with a bit of a swagger and is smiling widely, fine blond hair pulled into a low ponytail.

Fairlie thinks he might be the hottest bloke she has seen in a decade.

'It's me, Brian,' he says with a grin. 'Brian Masters. Remember? We were in Mr Overoy's homegroup together in year ten, I think it was?'

'Little Bri-Bri!' she crows, rocking on the balls of her feet. 'From Mr Ovaries! How the hell are you?' Then she slaps a hand across her mouth. 'Sorry,' she mumbles from beneath her palm, 'not so little anymore.'

Brian laughs. 'What are you up to?'

'Brandy,' she fills him in. 'I need more brandy, Bri-Bri Masters.'

His face goes serious. 'I heard about Jenna. I'm sorry. You guys were still friends, right?' His mates have fallen into an amused silence and watch him, nudging one another, from behind his shoulder. When Fairlie bites her lip, he apologises again, and offers to buy her a drink at the bar. Deciding that she can always buy more brandy afterwards, Fairlie praises Brian for his clever idea.

Four more drinks and three games of eight ball later, Fairlie sways on her feet and suggests Bri-Bri considers undertaking the gentlemanly act of walking her to her door. It's just around the corner, after all.

'I'm a gentleman,' says Brian without deliberation. 'So what choice do I have?'

Grinning, Fairlie tips back her head to laugh and grabs onto Brian's shoulder for balance. 'Easy, tiger,' she says to him, as though it's he who stumbled. 'Think there's a step there or something. O, H and S hazard,' she cries, pointing to the plain, smooth patch of carpet.

Outside the night is still warm, the waxing moon bright and high. As they stroll the side streets Brian Masters tells Fairlie about the four years he spent in the navy straight out of high school, wishing he could be on his father's crayfish boat instead of the HMAS *Sydney*.

'So you were called home,' Fairlie says. 'I wish I knew where my country really is.'

Brian doesn't say anything, just watches her in the darkness.

'Want me to carry you over the threshold?' Bri-Bri asks as they reach the doorstep.

'Look, it's tempting,' says Fairlie. 'But one, we're not married. And two, you'd snap your spine like a pigeon bone, Little Bri.'

Brian takes a step back and looks her up and down, eyes narrowed in concentration. 'Piece of cake,' he says.

Fairlie spreads her arms. 'I'm not exactly Tinkerbell.'

'You're not a tank, either.'

'Be still my beating heart! A man who thinks I'm more slender than a tank!'

Brian claps his hands together, rubs his palms briskly. 'Hold onto your britches,' he says, and in one swoop bends and lifts Fairlie into his arms. With a shriek, Fairlie kicks her feet into the air. She clutches her arms around his neck and giggles; he's fragrant with one of those cheap, testosterone-y deodorants, beer and hot skin. She reaches down to unlatch the door and Brian balances on one foot to kick it open, stumbles and they fall together onto the living room floor.

And so it is a matter of moments later, on the scratchy carpet in her living room with Yodel offering judgement from the couch, that Fairlie discovers little Bri-Bri Masters *definitely* isn't little after all, and makes a mental note to tell Jenna. But then she remembers, somewhere amongst her gasping breath and the smoke-scented drape of Brian's ponytail across her cheek, that she can't tell Jenna. Never again will she tell Jenna, and she digs her fingers into the clenching arse of Brian Masters and cries out because he isn't little, and Jenna, who would be scandalised and blush with the verbosity of Fairlie's recollection, will never find out exactly how little he isn't. In fact, he is so very *un*-little that her groin and hips will ache for three days.

In the morning, she remembers him kissing her tenderly, and she's grateful that he's gone.

Later the following afternoon, the hangover pounds in her head in time with the ringing down the line. It rings for so long Fairlie thinks she'll be diverted to voicemail. But as she prepares to leave a message, he answers.

A brief silence and then, 'Oh. Hi, Fairlie.'

'So.' She drums her fingers on her knees. The cat chirrups and butts against her elbow and she pushes him away. 'Just calling to see how you are,' she says, hoping her voice sounds unremarkable. 'How's Henry?'

'He's okay,' Ark replies with a small cough. 'We're both as to be expected.'

'Right, sure, I'm sorry.' Fairlie is nodding. She doesn't know why. She stops.

'So,' she says again, drawing the word out. 'I thought I might come up for a visit. I'm sorry it's taken me so long.' *Damnit*, she thinks, *why do I keep apologising to him?*

'That's fine,' he breaks in. 'No need. I have my family supporting me at this time.'

'Are you sure? I'd love to see him. You. Both of you.'

'Thank you. But we'd like to grieve together.'

A flash of irritation thickens her throat. 'Of course. But can you please –' She breaks off, wipes her nose with the back of her hand. 'Can you please keep me posted? I'm worried. About Henry.'

He goes quiet.

'Ark?'

A heavy sigh blows like a burst of static against the earpiece. 'I don't mean to sound like a jerk,' he says, morosely.

Thinking there will be more to that statement, Fairlie waits, but when Ark remains silent she is forced to concede, 'Gosh, no, not a jerk at all.'

'I appreciate it.' He sounds far away. 'I appreciate your consideration. I was thinking of packing up ... her stuff. Maybe ...'

Again Fairlie waits.

'Maybe you could come over and help with that.'

'Sure,' she forces out. 'I'd be ...' What? Happy? She rephrases. 'I will come and help you with that. But surely there's no rush. Can I come over in the meantime, for a visit?'

His answer is a long time coming. 'Are you free tomorrow?'

Fairlie blinks. 'Yes, yes I am.'

'I should have enough boxes, but bring some if you have any. Come by as soon as you can in the morning. I want to get it over and done with.'

Ark hangs up, and Fairlie stares at the phone, holding it at arm's length. The space between her temples throbs and she resolves never to drink again.

r—O

Fairlie sleeps late the next morning. For breakfast she fries rashers of bacon and eats them from the pan, weeping silently. She drops rinds on the floor for Yodel who hums his appreciation and romances her leg with his arched back.

Midmorning, as she pulls on clean shorts and wrestles into a bra before heading over to Ark's, she receives a text message from her mother: *I'll be up with some dinner.*

Sounds good, Fairlie types in response.

The message fails to send. She tries again, but the same fail error appears.

'Bloody hell,' she mutters, holding her thumb on the power button to restart the device. But when that doesn't work either, she swipes the screen to try calling.

'Your account has been suspended,' a recorded voice tells her. 'Please contact Telstra for reactivation.'

'Oh, *fuck's* sake.'

With a groan she hurries to the fridge, but she hasn't tacked the telephone bill there. She searches the benchtop, rummages through the drawers. 'Where'd I put that damn bill, Yodel?' She slumps back into the lounge room and stares around.

A corner of an envelope pokes out from beneath the couch. Now she remembers. The morning after Jenna's death. Henry was here; she'd kicked the pile of mail away. Recalling the comforting weight of him on her hip, the sweet, still-babyish smell of his hair, her heart gives a twist.

Peering beneath the couch, she fishes out three dusty envelopes, a stale cracker and a sock with a hole in the toe. Another envelope is pushed further back, but she can't reach it. Taking a wooden spoon from the kitchen, she retrieves it after a few attempts, trailing a dusty braid of cobweb.

She freezes.

The envelope is pink. In green ink, her address is penned in familiar handwriting. Jenna's handwriting.

Jenna has addressed this envelope.

With a blunt fingernail she tears the envelope open. She unfolds the slip of paper to reveal more of Jenna's handwriting.

My dear Fairlie,

I'm sorry I can't give you more answers. I know you're reading this and you're probably confused as hell. And you're probably denying it, too. All I can tell you is that I'm sorry. And I am – I am so, so sorry about all of this. About everything.

You probably hate me, but please know that I've thought of you every single day. And I've missed you, too. More than I could tell you. But there was nothing I could do. Please don't worry about me. I'm where I've always wanted to be: in heaven, with the elephants. I love you – please believe me. And please tell Henry that I do love him, too.

Inside the envelope you'll find a key. Store-For-You, unit 8.

All of this? This is between you and me only, sister.

More love again, and always.

Jenna

Fairlie reads the note three times; the brevity of the words inexplicable on the page. Turning the envelope upside down, something small and heavy slides onto the carpet.

A key.

Fairlie stares at it, dumbstruck. The key is small, brass coloured and unimportant looking.

What is this? What the fuck is going on?

'What the fuck is going on?' she echoes aloud.

She can hardly breathe. With one hand she clutches Jenna's letter to her chest, with the other she covers her mouth to stifle her scream.

170

8

Then

Crammed together in the hospital tea room, Jenna watched the biscuit crumbs stuck to Fairlie's bottom lip bounce as she chewed. As yet, Fairlie hadn't responded to Jenna's revelation. Instead she'd simply gazed back at her warily.

At length, Fairlie swallowed her mouthful. 'And ... what did you say to that?'

Jenna poured boiling water over her two-minute noodles. Shaking in the flavour sachet she watched the broth turn a sickly caramel-brown as the powder dissolved.

'Not much.' Jenna's voice was stretched as she answered. 'I told him I wanted to think about it.'

'Having a baby?' Fairlie gave a low whistle. 'Yeah. That one warrants some *serious* rumination.'

The scent of artificial beef and wheaty starch filled the air. Fairlie dug into the jar for another biscuit and stuffed it whole into her mouth, then folded her arms and chewed with considerable force, leaning back against the counter.

'Okay, yes, a baby is a huge deal,' Jenna said. 'But in a way it makes sense that he wants to start a family. He's got such big plans, it's –' she paused, waved her fork in a circle, '– impressive, the way he's thought the future through. Did I tell you he's talking with a potential international supplier?'

Fairlie shook her head. 'I can't keep up with the dude's enthusiasm, to be honest. But a baby –'

'Not only that,' Jenna went on over her, 'he's looking into buying more grapes – some here in Coonawarra, plus a heap of established acres in the Hunter Valley. Eventually, with the income he's predicting, he'll be able to employ managers and the business will run itself, so he'll have more spare time.' She glanced at Fairlie, gauging her reaction. 'More money would be helpful,' Jenna continued, working at the noodles with her fork. 'It will be nice to not have to explain every dollar I spend.'

Fairlie frowned. 'What do you mean?'

'Saving up for the grapes, Ark's a bit tense about what we spend,' Jenna said with a short sigh.

'But a baby? Are you ready for that?'

Jenna's fork stabbed down. 'He's always thinking of us, of our future. He's like a father already, only without a family.'

172

'It's great that *he* knows what he wants. But what about you – hey, Marg.' Fairlie cut herself short as their nursing unit manager strode into the room.

'Good morning,' Marg Dunbower said brightly, squeezing her stout frame between them. 'Isn't this rain depressing?' She filled a cup with hot water and dropped in a herbal tea bag. 'Although goodness knows, the farmers need it.'

'Depressing,' Fairlie agreed around another yoyo biscuit, 'but it's a party for the farmers.'

Beneath Jenna's fork the cake of noodles finally fell apart.

'Jenna, how's that new husband?'

Jenna smiled quickly. 'He's great.'

'And the vineyard? It's going well?'

'Super, thanks Marg.'

'Any plans for children yet?'

Dunk, dunk, dunk, went Marg Dunbower's tea bag.

'Oh, you know,' Jenna said.

'Good, good.' The nursing unit manager nodded.

Fairlie scratched her nose. Jenna coughed and looked at the floor.

'Right. See you.' And Marg was gone.

'Poor Marg's gonna think we were talking about her,' Fairlie muttered. 'Did you fart or something? What's with the tension?'

In Jenna's bowl the noodles had gone flaccid, twisty pale strands waving like bleached seaweed. Even an innocent

173

answer to Fairlie's question evaded her. What could she say? More and more, she found even the simplest eye contact with her friend had become almost unbearable. The weight of what she knew heaved over Jenna like a glacial slide, heavier and darker as time lurked onward. But Ark's recent suggestion that they start a family had grown more insistent with each day, and Jenna's answer as yet had not been forthcoming. The lifelong crutch of turning to Fairlie, her beloved friend, was a habit hard to break. She had always shared everything with Fairlie: from the simplest joys to – almost – the bitterest of hurts.

And yet.

Yet.

There was that one thing. That one enormous, unfathomable thing. Ignoring it seemed only to inflame it, yet facing it seemed impossible. If only that thing wasn't there, and she could turn to her friend for advice and solace. It was at moments like these that Jenna's resentment of her mother stung so viciously she could cry out with it.

As a woman's voice droned nasally over the PA – someone from grocery was wanted at the checkout counter – Jenna shuffled down the brightly lit aisle, her forearms resting on the trolley handle. On a whim she'd come all the way to Mount Gambier, to the larger supermarket. Perhaps the longer aisles and the bigger selection than the local deli in Penola could overwhelm her, dazzle her with inspiration.

Wake her up. Slap her around with choice and colour and life.

Although she knew Ark would frown – the longer trip, the petrol costs, the splurge on foods they might not eat – she hoped a quiet dinner together, something novel, might sweeten them both.

Her bounty of cheddar cheese, stuffed olives, chicken breasts, brown rice crackers, a dozen eggs and a packet of environmentally friendly toilet tissue made from recycled office paper – the literal wiping of one's arse on someone else's hard work – represented a one-item-per-aisle shuffle through Coles. Subconsciously, she also knew she was trying to keep it below one hundred dollars: the smaller transactions were less glaring on the credit card statement.

In the stationery aisle a colourful display of markers and art papers caught her eye. Flag-like flyers proclaiming 'Back to school!' highlighted decimated-looking shelves. She guessed the back-to-school part must have already happened.

Jenna paused in front of a clearance bin at the end of the aisle. Generic, saddle-stitched A5-ruled notepads, fifty per cent off. She dipped in her hand and withdrew the first thing she touched: a purple-and-black striped cover, '240 pages' printed in bold white letters in the top corner.

She tossed it in the trolley, trying not to think about why.

Garlic. And white wine, of course. And something else Jenna couldn't quite place – sage, or perhaps thyme. The fragrance wafted down the hallway, drawing her to the kitchen like a fish on a line.

The kitchen window was covered with condensation, pans steamed on the stovetop and Ark, his back to her, whistled and danced on his feet. Apron straps were tied in a knot at the small of his back.

Jenna smiled and leaned her shoulder against the door frame. For a while she watched him: the quick and sure movements of his arms, the self-congratulatory smack of his lips as he dipped his hand into the pan and licked his fingers.

Jenna cleared her throat. Looking back over his shoulder, Ark's face split into a smile.

'Aha,' he said, spreading his arms wide. 'Mama is home.'

Her stomach dropped. 'Mama?'

He waved his hand. 'Just a figure of speech.' He swept over, kissing her with a mouth tasting of cream and garlic.

'Chicken,' he said, and waggled his eyebrows. 'And I have something else.' He took two pans from the heat and set them on the sink before wiping his hands on his apron.

'Sit,' he said dramatically, gesturing to the set table. Candles flickered on a placemat in the centre. 'And close your eyes.'

'Ark,' she laughed. 'What's going on?' But she did as he asked, a curious flutter in her belly.

'Hold out your hands.' His voice, deep and warm in her ear; his lips on her earlobe. A tingle of pleasure ran up her spine. Eyes closed, she held out her hands. Something firm, velvety, pressed into her palms.

Ark's gentle command: 'Open them.'

Jenna opened her eyes. A navy jewellery box, sitting open in her hands to reveal a pair of glimmering pearl earrings.

'Oh,' she said softly. She looked up at him and he was smiling so tenderly she thought her heart might splinter. 'Thank you. But what is this for? I thought you said we couldn't afford –'

'No.' He stopped her with a finger on her lips. 'We can always earn more money, but I can never adequately express how much I love you.'

Jenna stroked the pearls, cool and silky, shaped like teardrops. He took the box from her hands and removed the earrings. Pressing the pearls into her palm, he curled her fingers around them, and wrapped her hand in his.

'All you have to say is thank you,' he said, his face inches from hers. 'Soon you're going to make me a father. That's the greatest gift of all.'

Jenna's mouth went dry. Impulsively, she sought his lips with her own, his fingers tightening their grip. Breaking away, she said, 'You're going to burn the chicken.'

'Not with that pan,' he said. 'Are you ready for the best meal of your life?'

Jenna stretched her neck to look up at the stove. 'You got a new pan?' She stood and moved towards the bench. 'You got *all* new pans?' Wide-eyed, she turned to him.

'Yep.' He was nodding, puff-chested. 'Nothing will ever stick to those bad boys.'

'Ark.' Jenna's voice was breathy. 'This must have cost ...' *Hundreds*, she wanted to say. *Where did the money come from?*

'Hey, forget it.' He bustled her from the kitchen, urging her again to sit down. 'Tonight is about you. About *us*. Forget money.'

'Yeah, but ...'

He looked at her. 'But what?' His face dropped. 'You don't like the earrings?'

Jenna let out a long breath. 'Of course I do,' she said, shaking her head as though to clear it. 'I don't know what to say.'

'You don't have to say anything.' He returned to the bench, and began to serve the promised best meal of her life.

⚷

The movie finished and Jenna glanced at the clock. Close to midnight. Peeling back the knitted throw rug over her legs, she rolled from the couch and stretched, yawning, before shuffling out of the lounge room and into the hall, pulling her towelling robe tighter around her body.

Light spilled from the office doorway, cutting a bright circle in the dark hall. She poked her head in and squinted at the light.

'Honey,' she said, 'why are you still up?'

It took her a moment to notice he wasn't sitting at his usual place, in the centre of the desk at his computer screen. His chair was swivelled to one side and, balanced on a stack of papers, her laptop sat open. Ark read from the screen, his fingers scrolling on the mousepad.

'Babe? What are you doing?'

Ark's chair rotated slowly as he turned to her. 'Who's Euan Li?' he asked.

'Who?'

'Euan Li,' he repeated. 'You have six emails from him. Quite the chatterbox.'

'Hey,' she snapped. 'Why are you reading my emails?'

'Answer my question.'

'Who?'

'Euan –'

Jenna gave a stiff, exasperated sigh. 'Does it matter? Without knowing what the email says, I can't remember.' She stepped into the room and repeated crossly, 'Why are you reading my emails?'

Bemusement crossed Ark's face. 'I'm your husband. I'm entitled to know everyone you're dealing with. And this guy –' he waved his hand at her computer, '– has sent you six emails.'

She stalked to the computer and leaned over his shoulder. 'Look, it's right there –' she pointed at the screen, '– Euan Li, from Prestige Carpet Cleaning. It's about the steam cleaning we had done two months ago. Are you happy?'

'That's two, maybe three emails at the most. But you sent him more than that. Look here,' he began to read aloud, '"Beautiful job, Euan, I'll definitely contact you again". What kind of *contact* are you going to give him next time?'

Jenna glowered at him. The hall clock ticked; the fridge clicked off in the kitchen.

'Oh, God.' She groaned and put her hands over her face. 'I'm not doing this. No.' She turned and walked to the door. 'Goodnight.'

This isn't normal, she thought as she brushed her teeth. *Is it? Is it normal?* What had she written to Euan Li? Was six emails to a tradesperson excessive? Dates, times, confirmations . . . that's all the emails were. Right? Jenna racked her brain trying to remember what she'd typed. Had she been excessively complimentary? Was it possible to flirt unconsciously over email?

Tomorrow, she would delete the emails – delete *all* her emails, she decided, staring at her reflection in the mirror. Maybe Ark was right, and she was flirting because she needed validation. Her fingers laced into her thick black

180

hair and tugged it from the scalp until it burned, and she asked herself, *What would you even know?*

Jenna watched Fairlie's door open, and the first thing that shot out was Fairlie's foot, poised to stop the cat from escaping.

Jenna couldn't stop herself crying.

'What –' Fairlie stepped outside.

Jenna shook her head, silencing her. A small, flattened-looking suitcase was by her feet.

Fairlie stood aside and pushed back the door, taking the suitcase from Jenna as it began to rain again: prickly, miserable gusts of water.

Jenna lowered herself to the couch, a sad smile crossing her face as Yodel leapt up beside her and headbutted her shoulder. Jenna scratched the soft spot below his pointed ears and the cat squinted with pleasure.

'Coffee?' Fairlie asked after a moment, then, 'Vodka?' when Jenna looked up at her, nose streaming.

'Vodka.'

After clearing a space on the kitchen bench, Fairlie splashed liberal hits of Smirnoff into a couple of glasses. Jenna unwound her scarf and shrugged from her coat, staring at a spot on the centre of the carpet.

Jenna took the drink, held it in her lap as Fairlie plopped onto the other end of the couch with a sigh.

'Are you okay?'

She twirled the glass in her hand, slowly, like she didn't quite know what to do with it.

'You're not, obviously.' Fairlie took a sip, grimaced. They both looked at Jenna's rain-splattered suitcase on the floor.

'I think it's over,' Jenna said.

Fairlie took in a sharp breath and watched her carefully, but said nothing. Glossy rivulets of rain ran down the windowpanes.

'I don't know if he loves me. Like, *really* loves me.' Jenna stared hard into her drink. 'He says he does. But . . . ' She took a swallow, then gazed out the window, eyes filmed over. 'We keep going round and round. Everything's tense, then everything explodes – and it's always my fault – then he's buying flowers and saying he loves me and he's sorry, and I always end up apologising, too.' She set her drink on the floor and scrubbed her hands over her face.

Again, Fairlie said nothing.

Jenna's hands floated down; puppet hands on invisible strings. 'He still wants to have a baby,' she said, her voice thick and thin all at once, 'and I . . . sometimes I think it's the greatest idea in the world – the one thing that could bring us together.'

Ark had always wanted a family. He'd told Jenna that, on that first night in the crowded pub – that he wanted children, he wanted to settle down and give his family *all the things he'd worked hard to provide*. How could she burst that bubble for him? How could she tell him that family was nothing but a load of shit?

'He won't let it go,' Jenna said. 'I keep telling him I'm not ready, and then he tells me I'm selfish. Or immature, Or . . . ' She looked away. 'Or that I need to let go of my mother and "move on".'

She raised her eyes to Fairlie, her knuckles colourless around her glass. 'When he tells me that we belong together, I believe him. When he says we'll get counselling, I believe him. When he says he's sorry, I *believe* him.' She squeezed her eyes shut. 'When everything is wonderful, I feel so *happy*, I feel . . . grateful. Thankful. Maybe he's right. So why am I holding back?'

From the expression on Fairlie's face, it was clear that she didn't know what to say.

Outside, the rain roared. In the bedroom, the heater blasted so fiercely that they were both clammy and flushed, hot-cheeked with vodka as they rolled on the bed, one moment yelling and the next laughing and the next stony-faced and silent.

It had been – how long? A year? Eighteen months? – since she'd moved out but it felt to Jenna as though she'd never left. How ridiculously tiny their flat was! It was never big enough for two, not really – but it had been cosy. Easy.

But then her mother.

And then she'd met Ark. And he was somewhere safe she could put her eyes. All that pain and awkwardness, all that staring at the ground because looking up at anything *hurt* – it went away when she looked at him. Her mother had dropped a grenade on her, and Ark had been a warm, pleasurable respite. The more she got to know Ark Rudolph, the more she doubted how much she knew herself. Or had *ever* known herself. Everything she had believed in changed.

'I'm sorry,' Fairlie said eventually.

Jenna was lying on her back, hair spilling out like coal over Fairlie's pillow, balancing her near-empty glass on her tummy. Sitting cross-legged at the end of the bed, Fairlie put her hand over Jenna's ankle.

'You're doing the right thing,' Fairlie said.

Jenna's glass rose and fell, rose and fell. 'Am I?'

'I think so. I mean . . . ' Fairlie crawled alongside Jenna, resting her chin in the cup of her palm. 'Lately, everything you've said has sounded so . . . miserable.'

Jenna swallowed, didn't say anything.

'You are. You're doing the right thing.'

Over the sound of the rain and the blast from the heater they could hear the dance-beat clatter of Jenna's ringtone from the living room. Every break in conversation for the past hour had been punctuated by that insistent electronic ring, a mortuary stiffness stealing over Jenna's body with each unanswered call.

Jenna heaved a huge sigh. 'I should talk to him.'

'You've tried. How'd that work out for you?'

'I should at least let him know I'm okay – I practically ran out.'

'He didn't know you'd leave?'

Jenna snorted. 'Of course he did. I've been saying it for weeks – *months*. God,' she choked out with a sob, 'even before the wedding we'd been arguing. For a long time, I've been saying things about fixing it.' She put her knuckles over her eyes. 'Honestly, Fro? Why today? Why *now*? I don't know. I just felt . . . desperate. And now,' she sat up so suddenly that her drink went flying, 'I feel like a fucking *bitch*. He's probably sitting at home crying – he always says he doesn't understand why I'm upset, he always says he's trying so hard. Why can't I *see* it? What's *wrong* with me? Are my expectations too high? I'm asking too much. I am, aren't I?' Groaning, she lay back down, arms flung out like a crucifix.

'It's always *me*. I'm crazy. I fly off the handle over nothing – he's always so . . . *calm*.' Her chest heaved. 'Am I stupid for falling in love with him? For getting married?'

Fairlie scooted closer and silently lay her face on Jenna's bare forearm.

'I *feel* stupid. But I want to believe that I'm not.'

The breath Fairlie blew gently on her cheeks smelled of vodka. A disarray that hadn't existed even in their messiest days together had taken over the flat: clothes heaped like molehills, dishes strewn across the sink and bench, weeks of unopened mail papered the dining table.

'You've gotta get your shit together, Fro,' Jenna said.

Fairlie lifted her head. 'What's wrong with my shit?'

Jenna stroked her hair. 'You're drinking too much,' she

said, smiling. 'And this place is ridiculous. I can't even see the floor.'

'You left,' Fairlie mumbled. 'I stopped caring.'

They lay together like that, drunk silences spinning amongst the fretful, jumbled web of spoken condolences, reassurances, confused or righteous self-flagellations. Unpacking Ark's every word, every action, every god-damn time he unzipped his pants, and putting it back together, and Jenna's weeping, weeping until the sun went down and came up and Jenna went home.

The counsellor introduced herself as Karen, but she implored them to call her Kay.

'Okay, Karen,' Ark laughed. The counsellor also laughed, and Jenna wondered if she was too nervous or perhaps too dumb and she'd missed the joke.

With a Masters degree in psychology from Flinders University, Karen Macpherson came recommended to Jenna by another nurse at the hospital. She wore spectacles with bright blue frames so enormous they skimmed halfway down her cheeks. A silver plait trailed over her left shoulder and down the front of her blouse. After they'd navigated the narrow footpath through carefully pruned roses and rung the doorbell, Jenna and Ark were ushered by the counsellor through the front door of a small red brick cottage, and into the first room off a narrow hallway.

The sound of flames crackled from an open log fire and two plush red couches squatted either side of a low coffee table.

This was all Jenna's idea.

Jenna sat on the edge of the couch, her knees pressed together, her hands clamped in her lap. Ark lounged beside her, his knees apart, one elbow on the armrest. He was laughing again.

'So,' Karen said, settling into the cushions. She held a clipboard and pen, and she jabbed her glasses up the bridge of her nose with her ring finger. 'What brings you here today?'

Jenna glanced at Ark; he smiled at her openly.

'Well,' Ark said.

'It was my idea,' Jenna began at the same time.

Ark laughed again. 'You can start, honey,' he encouraged.

Jenna hesitated. She looked at the counsellor, who stared back at her expectantly.

'Okay,' Jenna said slowly. 'I suppose I feel like we've been having some . . . ' She paused again, fidgeting with the buttons of her cardigan. What was she supposed to say? Wasn't it obvious? How many couples came to see a marriage counsellor because their relationships were perfect?

'I guess I want some advice.' Jenna glanced at Ark again. He was still fixing her with an encouraging smile. 'I've been a bit unhappy. I wanted to find out how to fix that.' Jenna felt the words slide back down her throat.

'Okay, sure,' Karen said at length. 'How long did you say you've been together?'

'Two years,' Ark answered.

'About year and a half,' Jenna corrected.

'And you were married recently?'

'Four months ago.' Jenna's thumbnail found her wedding ring.

'Congratulations.' Karen smiled and turned to Ark. 'Would you like to tell me why you've come along to chat today?'

Ark sat up, propping his elbows on his knees. 'Like Jenna said, it was her suggestion.' He sounded thoughtful. 'I'll be honest – I didn't think we needed to be here *already*, like some disenchanted long-married couple.' He winked at Jenna. 'She did have to twist my arm a bit. But,' he rubbed his chin with his thumb, 'what is it they say? "Happy wife, happy life?" I respect her suggestions.'

Karen swivelled her face back to Jenna, her pen poised.

'Yeah, I asked him to come, but not because . . . ' One of Jenna's buttons had come loose. Her fingers found another. 'I guess I just wanted some help . . . like, helping him understand me. And me him. It's like we don't actually hear each other correctly . . . or something.' Being here with the counsellor began to feel like a gross overreaction. Like seeing a neurosurgeon because of a headache. Jenna felt a burn rise in her cheeks.

'That can happen sometimes, when couples have been

together a while,' Karen said lightly. 'People can become complacent in communication.'

One year is a while? Jenna thought. *What happens after another twenty?*

Karen smiled again. 'Would either of you like to share an example?'

Jenna felt Ark shift his upper body towards her, he moved his knees, reached out and took one of her hands. 'Honey?' he prompted.

Jenna swallowed. 'Sometimes I feel like Ark doesn't trust me.'

The counsellor looked at her intently, chin propped on curled fingers, before rolling her hand in a gesture: *Go on.*

Jenna cleared her throat. 'We've been arguing a lot.'

The counsellor turned expectantly to Ark.

'She's right,' Ark replied with feeling. 'We haven't been communicating well at all. I'm working very hard, and with the irregularity of Jenna's shifts at the hospital, it means we don't have much time together.'

'Do you make time for each other?'

'I try, for sure,' Ark went on. 'But Jenna can be so tired, with her night shifts,' he offered her a smile and squeezed her hand, 'so I understand why she gets moody. But she often misinterprets things I say.'

Frowning, Jenna opened her mouth but Karen spoke up again.

'What sorts of things do you do to *make* time for each other?'

'I try and make the weekends about us,' Ark said. 'Sometimes a Sunday is the only day we get together, but Jenna often wants to visit her friends instead. Particularly this one friend, who – I admit – has been a source of conflict between us.' Ark held up his hands as Jenna made to interrupt. 'Look, I like Fairlie and I know she's important to you – but our marriage matters, too.' He took up her hand, twined his fingers between hers. 'Especially if we want to have a baby.'

The counsellor looked at Jenna.

'Of course I want to spend time with Ark,' Jenna said quickly. 'I – I don't think that's the issue.' She frowned. 'And we haven't decided on the baby, yet.'

'So what is the issue for you?'

Jenna glanced between them. Ark nodded at her.

'As I said before: Ark makes me feel like he doesn't trust me. He accuses me of things that aren't true.'

Ark gave a big smile, a knowing sigh. Nodding his head, he said, 'This is a good example of her misinterpreting me. You've been so tired, babe, with working and trying to fit in all your friends – always travelling to the Mount – I think you put too much *pressure* on yourself. You're trying to please everyone, you have no confidence in yourself. You need to stop, to spend some time at home and take care of *you*. With me. Take some care of *us*.'

The counsellor was still nodding, saying 'Mmm-hmm' and scribbling away.

Ark was looking at Jenna, his face etched with

190

sympathy. 'You're too hard on yourself sometimes. I would never say anything to hurt you – I'm only trying to help.'

Karen adopted a contemplative expression, head tipped to the side. 'Can you give me an example of a time you've felt accused or mistrusted, Jenna?'

Jenna opened her mouth, closed it again. 'All right. This is one of many, but a month or so ago, Ark accused me of flirting with a waiter at a restaurant. He often does that – thinks I'm flirting with other men, or leading them on or whatever. And two days ago we had a big argument, about . . . ' She fidgeted on her seat, scratched the back of her neck. Her face felt hot.

'About?'

Jenna looked up. 'Well . . . '

'Sex,' Ark said with a heavy sigh. 'I think, with every-thing she has going on, Jenna has trouble remembering that marriages need intimacy. I often feel pushed away. I wonder if that's why she shows so much interest in other men, because we're not being physically affectionate enough with each other.' He looked pained. 'Do you think that's possible, Kay?'

'What? No!' Jenna sat forwards. 'That's not true. I –' She broke off, frustrated. 'That's not what I was going to say. I wanted to talk about the argument we had a few days ago, about the credit card statement.'

'Ah,' said Ark. 'Yes, I think that's important, too.' He laughed and added, 'Sorry, Kay, you're going to earn your money with us today!'

The counsellor laughed good-naturedly. Steepling her fingertips, she glanced down at her clipboard. 'I want to return to sex in a moment, as Ark's right – physical intimacy is paramount in a marriage, however, I want to address your anxiety that Ark doesn't trust you.'

'Anxiety? I'm not anxious about it. He said I'd sucked my –'

'We can't argue with someone's perception,' Karen said, her face tilted to peer over the top of her glasses. 'If Ark feels that something is happening, then his perception is his reality. Even if he's mistaken, his irritation or hurt is still valid, it's still *real* to him. Can you understand his frustration and sense of betrayal if he interprets you as flirting with other men?'

'I'm not flirting!' Jenna snapped. 'And this isn't the point. Can we *please* talk about the credit card statement?' She glared at them both. Karen and Ark exchanged a look.

'Very well.' Karen made another hand gesture: *Go right ahead.*

'There were some things, transactions, on our Visa statement that Ark ... let's say he took exception to them.'

'Things?'

'A pair of shoes I needed for work. Petrol for my car. Lunch with *Fairlie* – no, don't interrupt – some new undies and a pair of socks. A box of chocolates because I was feeling down. Those kinds of things.'

192

'Hey, hey.' Ark held up his hands, chuckling. 'Of course you can buy what you *need*. But you know we're saving for renovations, more land, and holidays.' Turning back to Karen, he said, 'Jenna wants to go overseas, so we're saving up, she's got expensive taste! Anyway,' his voice softened, 'all I'm saying, sweetie, is that you should include me in any financial decisions.'

'That's true,' the counsellor broke in. 'Finances are a big source of tension between couples. You have to be honest,' her eyes rested on Jenna, 'and you have to make decisions that are mutually agreed upon.'

'I know that. But does lunch with Fro really warrant two days of lecturing about me "leaning outside" the marriage?'

Ark sighed. 'You know what, honey? You're right, I probably was a bit cranky that day. Look, I do apologise. But like Karen said, we have to make mutual decisions.' A look of discomfort crossed his features. 'I know you didn't grow up with married parents, so I understand you might not know what's realistic, or how to maintain a marriage.'

Jenna looked at her watch; still forty more minutes.

Ark smiled and squeezed her hand. 'Look, of course I work a lot. Running the business on my own is a big job – I hire as little staff as possible to keep overheads down. But the profit means I've been able to do some of the renovations that Jenna wanted.' He grinned. 'Like the bathroom? You wanted it re-done and it looks so much better now, doesn't it, sweetheart?'

The counsellor looked at Jenna.

'I guess,' Jenna faltered. 'I mean, yes. The bathroom is great.'

'And we've been researching a trip to New Zealand, pricing flights and hotels, haven't we?'

'Sure, but –' What was happening? The conversation felt like a car on an icy road, fishtailing precariously. 'Can't I make the decision to buy a pair of *socks* on my own?'

'Of course you can!' Ark said with a big laugh. 'I'm not Big Brother.'

Karen joined in his chortle.

'I –'

Ark held up his hands and dropped his head deferentially. 'Ahh, look. I need to say it here.' The room went quiet as he lowered his hands and took time to lift his gaze. 'I had a great childhood. I never went wanting for anything. But . . . my dad was quite strict.' A flicker crossed the counsellor's face. An internal *Aha* moment. 'And my mum often got mad at him, but not in an obvious way. She'd go quiet, and not say anything for days. A kind of punishment.'

'So, when your parents argued, your mother would withdraw affection, is that right?' Karen asked.

He gave a slow nod. 'Yeah.'

'And that made you feel . . . ?'

'Like I never want that to happen to us.' Ark turned to Jenna again. 'I want us to be open with each other. That's all I'm asking. That we communicate. Because I hated the silent treatment. It made my dad angry. And he'd lash out at me for it. Mum never listened when he'd try and talk or reason with her – she just clammed up. So what was he supposed to do? She made him angry.

'And yeah,' he finished, 'I'll admit, it's compounded by past relationships. Particularly my most recent ex,' his voice cracked. 'That left me bleeding a bit.'

They both looked at Jenna expectantly. Was she supposed to respond to this? What was the right thing to say? She *was* communicating with Ark . . . or trying to . . . wasn't she?

'And considering the separate lives we lead – you working odd hours, me busy with the grapes – it's no wonder we're struggling to communicate. Here's an idea.' Ark bent forwards, gazed solemnly into her eyes. 'Let's go away for the weekend. Really focus on us. We'll talk, we'll remember what we love about each other. We've gotten complacent, as Karen said –' his eyes sought the psychologist and he gave her a nod, '– so let's agree to make an effort to spend our spare time together.'

'Does that sound feasible, Jenna?' Karen asked, pen lightly tapping her page.

'Of course – well, yes, I mean . . . ' *Shit.* A button popped from its thread, escaped her fingers and dropped down the side of the cushion. There wasn't any saliva in her mouth. The counsellor was looking at her intently. 'But I'd also like him to stop treating me as though I'm untrustworthy.'

Jenna's voice was wire-thin. 'I want him to stop accusing me of things that aren't true.'

'Ark? How do you respond to that?'

Ark sighed. 'I guess it comes down to communication. Bring it up with me when I do it, because otherwise I don't see it, you know? If I have a sickness, I need to know the symptoms. And I need you to stick by me, help me work on it, instead of threatening to leave all the time.' He smiled sadly.

Jenna's mouth fell open. She turned to the counsellor, unconsciously seeking something. Protection? Solidarity? Answers? The room was swimming, the walls had taken on a shimmer and the open fire was too hot.

'I know it's hard for you sometimes, Jen,' Ark soothed. He stroked her knee. 'With your estrangement from your mother ... you tend to be oversensitive about things. Gosh, I've never accused you of *anything*. But I understand that you've been hurt, and that makes it hard for you to believe me, sometimes. And your dad was never around – no, look, I know you hate to hear it but people are *always* wounded by absent fathers, it's a psychological fact – but Jenna,' he gripped her hand, his eyes welling, 'I'm not your mother, or your father, baby. I love you and I'll never hurt you and I'll *never, ever* leave you.'

Blinking rapidly, Jenna swallowed hard.

'Okay. It sounds like we've hit onto something poignant here.' Karen's voice was like liquid Valium. 'I'm sorry to hear you're suffering some pain, Jenna.' She slid a box of tissues across the table. Ark took one and carefully, lovingly, wiped Jenna's cheeks. She wanted to slap his hand away. This wasn't going right. Irrational projected pain from her estrangement from her mother or some kind of Freudian father issues had nothing to do with Ark's escalating, near-constant fury with her every time she so much as looked at another man; his checking her emails and text messages; his index finger painstakingly tracing each line of the latest Visa statement, his calm, measured demands that each transaction unknown to him be explained and justified in full – and usually to his dissatisfaction – were *his* trust issues, not hers.

And hadn't they had sex four days ago? In truth, Jenna *hadn't* been in the mood for it lately. Not because she wasn't interested in Ark, or because they didn't *make time* for it, but because she'd felt increasingly alienated from him for reasons, amongst other things, she had hoped this counsellor might have been able to illuminate.

Was she being over-sensitive? She began to feel whiney, childish. It was true that she hadn't exactly been raised by a shining pillar of integrity, nor had her upbringing demonstrated healthy, open relationships. Jenna's heart dropped into her stomach, a dead weight of self-loathing.

When the hour was over, Ark handed over his Visa card and thanked Karen Macpherson profusely. He promised to drop off a bottle of his award-winning 2010 vintage shiraz.

They never went back.

A gauzy slat of late-afternoon sunlight streamed through the bathroom window. Suspended in the beam, dust motes hovered a slow waltz, so untroubled that not even gravity could touch them.

Jenna watched where the light splashed down onto the tiles. Ark's strong hands had placed each of those big squares – the colour of an elephant's tusks – with loving care, just for her. Although she could not recall disliking the original floor tiles as much as he claimed she did – smaller, pale blue tiles stippled with white and grey – she couldn't deny that he had knelt there and ripped up the floor, chipped tiles from the wall and pulled doors from the cabinets, within a month of her moving in. For a week, he'd had paint in his hair and grout beneath his fingernails; he'd worked so hard, and now the bathroom was beautiful. Just for her.

The edge of the bath cut into the backs of her thighs. Her feet tingled.

Watching that beam of light coming through the window, Jenna imagined the journey those dancing photons had taken: spewed from a burning ball of gas, hurtling through black empty space towards this lush blue-green planet. Through the upper layers of the atmosphere, through the fluffy clouds, through the rustling gum tree outside and in through the opaque bathroom window to where Jenna sat.

She was so small – an insignificant part of something so infinite and enormous that she shouldn't dare question it.

This was life. People loved each other and hated each other; people were messed-up and happy and everything in between; lives broke apart and came back together; people had secrets, people were flawed and human and sometimes you couldn't control it. Any of it. Or could you? Perhaps, like her mother, she was simply selfish, entitled, expecting everything to happen to her liking.

Between her fingers, Jenna twirled the white plastic stick. She was happy – of course she was happy – but other, more demanding emotions were surfacing as though to eclipse the happiness. Apprehension, quiet and creeping; uncertainty, a cloud of it; and fear, cold and sucking the moisture from her mouth. In Ark's voice, she reminded herself that these latter feelings were ephemeral; she told herself those more hesitant, tentative or subtle feelings never last and therefore can't be trusted. All she needed to do was wait for their trajectory to push inevitably past.

But would they? Could she forget the past and move forwards, truly free of it?

Down the hall, the front door slammed. Ark's boots thumped on the floorboards.

'Jenna?'

Jenna breathed in; she breathed out. Her feet had gone numb.

Closer. 'Jen?' His footsteps in the kitchen. 'Where are you, babe?'

Forearms on her knees, head low. She filled her lungs and straightened.

'In here. The bathroom.'

After a moment from the doorway: 'Hi,' then, quickly, 'hey, are you okay?'

She looked up at him and she smiled, closing her hand into a fist around the stick. 'I'm great.' She stood up and he came towards her.

'What are you doing?' he queried, giving her a quick kiss on the cheek. He was filthy; sweat bloomed in the armpits of his shirt, dust was caked into gritty lines on his sun-reddened forehead. There was dried grass in his boot laces, grass seeds embedded into the folded-down tops of his thick black socks.

'Get all the picking finished?' she asked.

'Yeah, finally. It's going to be a big year. Great harvest.' He smiled briefly, then tilted his head. 'Sure you're okay? You look a bit . . . ?'

Jenna uncurled her fingers, like a flower opening. As Ark picked the pregnancy test from her palm, she felt a real, proper smile tug at the corners of her lips and as he whooped and grabbed her in a hug, she closed her eyes to that beam of light from the sun and remembered that sometimes, there are things you can't control, forces greater than you, and all you can do is go with it. Because only a fool – a selfish fool – would try to control what cannot be.

And maybe, just maybe, this could be the new beginning she needed.

Fog streaked in low clumps across the road, curling through the winter-bare vines and disappearing into the night. Jenna shivered and yawned as she glanced at the illuminated display on the dashboard: 12.08 am. 1.5 degrees.

The heater had barely begun to blow warm air as she slowed off the highway, headlights flashing across the stone gateway. ArkAcres. White gravel stark beneath the front of the car, a midnight tunnel through hunched vines squatting dormant in strips of cold fog.

Parking alongside the shed, she yawned again and squinted as the interior light came on. The thump of the car door closing seemed absurdly loud. On tiptoes she made her way through the house and poked her head into the bedroom.

'You're still up,' she whispered with a smile.

Ark closed his laptop and stretched his arms above his head. 'Had some stuff to do. You look tired.'

Jenna nodded. 'I am.'

Pulling on an old T-shirt in the ensuite, the mirror showed the small paunch of her belly swelling into the fabric between her hips. Jenna dropped her gaze and clicked off the light.

A lamp was glowing on the bedside table. Ark had put aside his laptop, the covers were drawn up to his chest. He watched her as she stifled another yawn and climbed under the blankets.

'Long shift?'

'So long. I'm trashed.'

Ark held his arms open and she leant over and kissed his cheek. She smiled, then drew away, closing her eyes with a low groan of pleasure as her head hit the pillow.

'Goodnight,' she said, contentedly. 'Love you.'

Weight shifted on the bed as Ark moved closer; he slid his hand under the sheets, ran his fingers down her arm.

She smiled sleepily, patted his hand. 'Night,' she repeated.

Nestling closer still, he fitted his body behind her, tucking himself around the curve of her hips. He kissed the back of her neck. Wrapping her hand around his fingers, Jenna squeezed his hand gently and then let go, snuggling deeper under the covers, shifting out from under his touch.

'Have a good sleep,' she murmured.

Ark moved again, catching up; she was right on the edge of the mattress. As he drew a heavy, bare arm over her shoulder she could smell the hot musk of his skin, his warm breath on her ear, the prod of his erection at the base of her spine.

'Sorry, babe, I'm tired,' she said.

'Come on,' he said softly, his lips on her earlobe.

She shook her head, like flicking off an insect. Ark's body stilled, then he snorted and shot away so fast a puff of cool air stole under the sheets.

After a moment, she opened one eye. 'You okay?'

'You're always tired.'

Tension flitted beneath her ribs. 'I'm back on day shift again soon,' she told him. 'Don't worry.' She reached back with her foot and poked his leg with her toes. 'Go to sleep.' Her eyelids felt weighted with concrete.

A laboured sigh. When he spoke again his voice was up higher, closer to her head. 'You're always so tired now – you can't tell me not to worry.'

'Really, Ark,' she said from under the sheets. 'It's okay.'

'You've got no time for *us* anymore. You barely get three words out to me before you're asleep. Don't you remember what the counsellor told you? You need to make time for us. Intimacy is paramount in a marriage.'

Jenna exhaled heavily. Her entire body ached for the relief of sleep, she could feel the teasing tug of it like a cloak, but Ark held the other end. Maybe, if he was quoting the counsellor, she could find the person he'd been in that session all those months ago: loving, compassionate, open-minded.

'You're right, I am too tired these days,' she relented. 'I'm sorry. I know it's important to you. But can we please talk about this tomorrow?'

'Oh sure,' his voice took on a condescension that made her pulse quicken, 'when it suits *you*. It's *your* job that's important, I'm only running an entire business, after all. I've got nothing better to do than sit around waiting to talk about *your* problems.'

'Ark, please.'

'Honestly, Jenna, do I mean *nothing* to you?'

Irritated, she rolled to face him. 'That's ridiculous.'

He blinked. 'So now I'm ridiculous? Yet when you want to talk about how *you* feel, I'm supposed to drop everything and listen? I've told you, I'll look after you. You need to think of our family' He paused. 'You need to resign.'

'We've been through this –'

'Why aren't you listening to me? You don't give one shit about me or the baby.'

She sat up. 'I enjoy my job.' She could hear the dangerous edge in her voice. 'I'll stop when –'

'When what? You fall down from exhaustion?'

'Ark –'

'When you've forgotten about me entirely?'

'Look –'

He pursed his lips. 'Who is he?'

Jenna's jaw dropped. 'Oh my God,' she snapped. 'You can't be serious.'

'It's true, isn't it? You stand around in the hospital tearoom with that fat black whore and swap doctor sex stories?' His face had gone a telltale shade of crimson. 'Yeah,' he said, nodding. 'Now I'm onto something.'

'Ark, that's crazy!' she cried. 'Do you even hear what you're saying?'

He smirked. 'Now you're getting angry to try and hide the truth.'

Jenna didn't know whether to laugh or cry. 'I've told you,' she said hotly, 'I'll take mat leave when the baby is due –'

'No, you'll resign.'

'– and I'll go back after a few months.'

'So your family means nothing to you? You are such a selfish bitch.'

'For fuck's sake!' she shouted, slapping her hands onto the sheets. 'Will you *listen* to me?'

Jenna wanted to throw her head back and scream. She pictured the tendons straining in her neck, heard the satisfying howl of blood in her ears. She imagined the horrified white of his face as her infuriated wail pierced the night.

Ark rolled his eyes. 'I don't have to put up with an outburst,' he said, reaching to snap off the lamp. The room plunged into darkness. 'We'll discuss this when you can talk rationally, without swearing at me.'

Chest heaving, baby fluttering in her belly to the drum of her heartbeat, Jenna sat in the dark. Eventually she laid down and pulled the sheets to her chin.

Moonlight slid sullen beams across the ceiling and she watched them for hours, her longed-for sleep now forgotten. Finally, before dawn, she felt relief in the slackened grip of her muscles, a grey shadow of sleep slinking over her, just as Ark's alarm began to sound.

When he woke, he dissolved any chance of her sleeping as he turned to her and snapped, 'The least you can do is apologise. If you can't love me like I can love, maybe I'll find someone who can.'

⌗

Jenna stepped from the shower cubicle, reaching through the steam for her towel. She watched her belly in the mirror as she dried off; the enormous, round weight of it dragging the small of her back forwards. The ball of her belly had dropped low now like the baby might simply fall out at any moment. Stretch marks bloomed purple zigzags across her hips and under her navel.

Naked, Jenna waddled from the ensuite into the bedroom. A glance at the clock told her Ark would be home at any minute; his flight from Melbourne had touched down in Mount Gambier at seven, and then he'd have a forty-five minute drive home. Barely even 8 pm and she was exhausted. Her shift had been long – an elderly patient had died after a brief battle with the flu had turned into pneumonia – and her feet and back and knees ached, and she was desperate to curl up in bed and sleep. Opening the top drawer of the dresser, she reached in to pull out her favourite oversized T-shirt.

She went still.

The T-shirt was gone. All her pyjamas were gone, but the drawer was stuffed full.

Lace and gauze spilled out like soft foam as she pushed in her hand. Pink, white and black strips of glossy satin. Cool, exquisite fabrics glided between her fingers like air. Finding a thin strap, she lifted her hand, slowly, and the flimsy negligee unfolded as though breathing to life: transparent, barely there black lace cups that would contain little more than her areola; spaghetti straps with tiny crystals that glimmered in the lamplight and a body with a split right up the front, entirely transparent, with a puff of faux-fur around the hem.

NaughtyMama, read the tag. A tremor went through her as she recalled the conversation. *Just because you're getting a big belly, doesn't mean you can't still look gorgeous.* And, *I want someone I can be proud of. My sexy mama.* And, *You used to care about making yourself look good for me. Who are you looking good for now?*

Letting the slip float back into the drawer, Jenna searched the rest of the dresser, but only dug out more lingerie. In the walk-in robe, she rifled through the baskets, searched through hanging suits and coats and dresses, sunk awkwardly to her knees and tossed aside boots, thongs, sandals. Nothing. Her pyjamas were gone. All of them.

Why? Why had he done this? *Was* she letting herself go? Morphing into the sexless, apathetic women who symbolised the burden of motherhood?

On the floor in the robe, Jenna panted, her belly a heavy weight on her thighs. There was a catch in her throat. Taking a firm hold of the shelves, she hauled herself carefully to her feet; the bones in her hips and sacrum crunched and popped.

In front of the dresser, she pulled open the top drawer and withdrew the first thing on the pile: a sheer black baby-doll with red satin trim, a minuscule matching G-string clipped to one of the straps. Raising her arms above her head, she let the fabric whisper down over her breasts, draping over the balloon of her belly, the cutaway front dropping open to let the baby-heavy bulge fall out.

She moved to the full-length mirror and stared at the heavy pendulum of her breasts; the black-inked elephant tattoo on pale skin; wide, hormone-darkened nipples caught in the sheer fabric. Ruffles breezed across her hips as she bent to step into the G-string, thin elastic cutting into her fingers as she stretched it over her hips and shimmied the strap into position between her buttocks.

Ripe, voluptuous, obscene. She gazed at her reflection: wisps of strategically fitted gauze and lace like gilt edging. In the mirror, she saw the outline of the fleshy folds of her vulva, waxed and stripped as requested, to show she loved him. To demonstrate her care and commitment to his needs. Milk-white, pre-pubescent, but shadowed with adult gauze.

Ridiculous. Eight months pregnant, she should be relaxed and comfortable – not trussed-up like an object to wank over in *Penthouse*.

A singular tear slid glistening down her cheek, trembled on her jaw, then fell to her breast and dissolved into the lace.

9

Now

With trembling hands Fairlie picks the key up off the carpet.

Store-For-You, unit 8.

Fairlie re-reads Jenna's letter, over and over. The envelope is postmarked for the day before Jenna's death. Jenna mailed this knowing Fairlie wouldn't receive it until Jenna was dead.

Her phone won't let her open a browser and Fairlie gives an impatient squeak of anguish waiting for her laptop to boot up. When Google finally pops up she types *Store-For-You* into the search bar and navigates to the website. A budget, no-nonsense page boasts cheap rates and friendly service. Fairlie's ribs feel too tight as she searches for the address: 1127 Bay Road, Mount Gambier.

Scrambling to her feet, she shoves Jenna's key into her pocket and races through the flat, snatching up her handbag and knocking Yodel from the bench in a skitter of paws.

Then she remembers. Ark. Packing Jenna's things. Henry. She'd promised she'd be there today.

Without thinking, she keys in a text message to Ark, apologising that she won't be able to make it. Her phone beeps with a fail message.

Fairlie yells a string of curses about Telstra and their unsavoury personal hygiene habits. Then she shoves her phone into her pocket, grabs a package from the freezer, pounds the door open and, in the car, guns the engine and peels from the car park.

Fairlie's hand hovers over the front door. Struck suddenly by indecision over whether to knock or simply walk straight in like she once did, she knocks softly, pauses, looks from one end of the verandah to the other, then raps her knuckles with more certitude. From inside, footsteps thud down the hallway; the low rumble of a man's voice sounds through the wood.

'Hey,' Fairlie says as brightly as she can when Ark opens the door. 'Here –' she holds up a bag of frozen meals '– it's from my neighbour. Beef curry.' Fairlie explains, 'I think she's on a quest for world peace. Through obesity.' Her cheeks grow momentarily hot.

Ark looks uncertain, but takes the bag of food. Henry is hoisted high up on his chest, Ark's forearm gripped around the back of his little thighs. Henry twists to look at her, a box of sultanas gripped protectively to his chest. It takes Henry a beat to recognise her but his features relax when he does, his big eyes soften and he smiles shyly.

'Thanks for coming.' Ark stands aside to motion her in.

'Any time,' she tells him, smiling at Henry and patting his back as she steps over the threshold. Her heart is still racing.

All of this? This is between you and me only, sister.

In the kitchen, Ark offers her coffee. Purple shadows like horrid bruises ring his eyes and his face is creased as though he's slept on the pillow seams, but he still moves around the room with a casual, alpha-male ease. Not even the abrupt and tragic death of his wife could snatch that from him; Fairlie wonders if he is fighting the grief.

Inside her purse is Jenna's mysterious and inexplicable key. Fairlie takes a burning mouthful of coffee and wonders if Ark can see it on her face. Should she ask him? Maybe she could slip it casually into conversation and gauge his reaction.

Hey, Ark, have you ever rented a storage unit?

The coffee is scalding and strong, and while Fairlie tries not to grimace as she sips at it, Ark sits opposite her and they both try not to acknowledge how tragically awkward it is. Between them, Jenna looms large.

So, Ark, I'm thinking of hiring a self-storage unit. Can you recommend a good one?

Fairlie takes a sip of her coffee. 'How have you been?'

'Okay.'

'How's Henry been?'

Ark shrugs. 'He keeps asking where she is.' A muscle in his jaw clenches.

'I can help you.'

'I'm coping.'

'Honestly,' she says, reaching over to touch his hand. 'Please call on me more often. I'd like to help. Both of you.'

At that moment, Henry toddles to Fairlie and lightly pats her thighs. 'Up,' he says. When she lifts him into her lap he immediately begins to poke his fingers up her nose and she laughs, not bothering to remove them. He giggles with her, then moves to knead the flesh on her neck.

'You got a skishy neck,' he says.

'Keeps me warm in winter,' she replies.

She can see Jenna in the curve of his cheekbones, in his thick eyelashes.

They finish their coffee and Ark suggests they get straight to it.

Fairlie agrees hastily. Henry slides from her lap as she stands and scrapes her chair back in. What about: *Ark. Storage locker. What the fuck?*

Henry is subdued and sticks closely by his father as they make their way to the bedroom, but seems happy enough

212

to occupy himself with a basket of Lego that Ark drags into the hallway outside the bedroom door.

Uncertain where to begin, Fairlie and Ark circle the bedroom warily. The bed is smartly made, the sheets smoothed out, two pillows lined up alongside each other. Does Jenna's pillow still smell of her?

'I'll start with her clothes if you like?' Fairlie says eventually.

Ark nods. 'Okay.' He sounds relieved.

She wants to ask him what he's going to do, but the question sounds too ambiguous. So instead she offers him a smile, the kind that says, *Don't worry, it's going to be okay*, even though it feels disingenuous, and then she opens the door to the walk-in robe.

Jenna's things *do* smell of her. Dresses and shirts and skirts fill one side of the robe; Fairlie brushes her hand over soft fabrics and releases a cloud of Jenna's scent: milk and violets, rosemary shampoo and the basic musty undertone of skin. Living flesh that once warmed and stained the fabric.

Her heart thuds as a sense of panic whispers at her. She concentrates on taking several slow, deep breaths. As she slips Jenna's clothes from hangers, memories flash before her. Wearing this purple knitted dress, Jenna had bartered with a salesman at an electronics store and got almost two hundred dollars off their TV. (The TV Fairlie now watches alone.) This chocolate corduroy blazer had been one dollar at an op shop. (That same day, Fairlie had bought herself six

213

pairs of jeans, three jumpers and a T-shirt that said, 'Beam me up, Jesus' for twelve dollars fifty.) The rip in the knee of these jeans, the bacon-splash grease stain on these tracksuit pants: Fairlie knows it all. A longing for Jenna strikes her so hard she grabs a shelf to steady herself.

'You can put her shoes in here.' Ark appears with a large box.

'Thanks,' she says, but he's gone before she can say anything further. A moment later, she hears the scrape of wooden drawers being yanked out, one by one. She peeps out of the robe and watches Ark dumping contents onto the bed and slinging drawers aside.

'Hey,' she says with a frown. 'You okay?'

He looks up at her, his face almost as red as his hair. 'I just want this over and done with.' There seems to be no method to his actions; he pulls and discards, rifles and flings stuff aside.

'Mate, is there something in particular you're looking for?'

He doesn't look at her. 'No.'

'Should I help with that?'

'Please.' He stops finally. 'Please just –' He waves at the walk-in robe.

Fairlie backs away. 'Sure ... '

He looks up again, suddenly. 'But if you see anything in there that isn't clothes ... bring it out here, okay? I'm not looking for anything, but I ... there's something I haven't seen for a while.'

'What is it?'

'Nothing important,' he says, brusquely. 'Just some books.'

'Anything in particular?'

A beat of silence. 'Notebooks,' he answers finally. 'Handwritten accounts. It's just business stuff – boring.'

'I'll keep an eye out,' Fairlie says. His frenzied movements have unsettled her. Is that what's in the storage unit – the accounting books Ark is searching for? Why would Jenna send her a key to a unit containing boring business accounts? Fairlie wants to linger over Jenna's shoes as she stacks them into the box, but she figures the quicker she gets this done the sooner she can go to the storage unit.

When Ark had asked if she would come over and help pack up Jenna's stuff, Fairlie had expected to go through the dresser and put away the odd thing here and there – moisturising creams, paperbacks, old clothes – but it was quickly becoming apparent that Ark wanted to pack it *all* away. Absolutely everything that had once belonged to Jenna was to be boxed up and removed. As though he was erasing her entirely. He pulls underwear from the dresser and tosses it into a box on the bed. Lacy, frilly things – not at all Jenna's taste.

'Wow,' Fairlie says, gesturing to the pile of expensive underwear. 'Racy.'

Ark smirks. 'She was pregnant and feeling frumpy. She bought these to cheer herself up. I told her she was gorgeous in her old T-shirt, didn't need these things, but she insisted. You know how Jenna could be.' He lifts a strap of lace and runs his thumb over it.

Heat flushes up Fairlie's throat. Jenna, always a fan of comfortable cotton, needed a lacy G-string to feel better?

'Well, this is awkward,' Fairlie says.

She returns to the walk-in and picks up her pace. Leaning deep into the back of the robe, Fairlie fishes out the last pair of shoes: a pair of well-worn flat sandals. The sole of one is wedged into the corner, between the back wall and the sideboard.

Huffing, Fairlie crawls further forwards on her hands and knees beneath a curtain of Jenna-scented clothes and tugs at the shoe. It comes away from the wall with the feel of something unsticking. Tilting the shoe into the light, Fairlie sees pressed onto the heel and toe are two pieces of Blu-Tack. With a frown, she peers closer at the back wall. Something glossy is sticking to the wall, tucked between the skirting and the sideboard.

Fairlie shoots a furtive glance in Ark's direction. She can't see him, but she can hear the sound of items being tossed into boxes.

The hairs on the back of her neck prickle as Fairlie silently pulls the small ziplock bag from where it had been tucked behind the board, tacked over with Jenna's shoe. Fitting in the palm of her hand, the clear plastic bag contains a handful of pills.

This is between you and me only, sister.

216

Quickly, Fairlie stuffs the bag into her pocket. Her knees crack in complaint as she rises to her feet.

'Bathroom break,' she offers to Ark as she hastens from the bedroom.

Down the hall; into the bathroom. Her mouth is dry as she locks the door. The tub where Jenna died is clean and white. For a moment, Fairlie thinks she might be sick.

Suicide through exsanguination, Fairlie knows, is monstrously messy. The average adult human body contains about five litres of blood. Severance of the major blood vessels in the forearm by slicing vertically along the limb, as Jenna had done, would result in unconsciousness in a matter of minutes, and death within the hour. Blood vessels, dilated in hot water, draining crimson over pale skin. Steam rising languidly as the colour darkens. Fairlie bites her lip hard to fight the image.

Using her thumbnail she opens the bag and fumbles one pill into her hand. Round and pale yellow, she recognises the generic Nitrazepam – it's the same kind prescribed at the hospital. But on these pills there's no pharmacist label: no prescription.

Blood drains from her face and rushes through her ears. There are enough sedatives here to kill a football team.

'What are you hiding, Jenna?' Fairlie whispers, blinking dry eyes.

The pills safely back in her pocket, Fairlie flushes the toilet, blasts the cold tap on then off, and hurries back to the bedroom.

For the next two hours, Fairlie and Ark work in silence, swiftly removing all traces of Jenna. First the bedroom, then they move to the lounge room: photographs, novels, a few more items of clothing. Fairlie struggles to keep her hands steady and swallows dryly so many times her throat begins to burn.

Eventually, they are done. Fairlie allows herself to linger only when she hugs Henry tightly, feeling the curl of his little arms around her neck, and her eyes fill with tears.

'I'll be back real soon, okay?' she whispers to him. 'I promise.' She gives Ark a stiff smile, and then she hurries to her car.

r—O

Nitrazepam.

Fairlie racks her brain as she pulls onto the highway. A heavy sedative, the drug is only prescribed at the hospital in small doses – and only rarely. It's possible it had been prescribed to Ark to help him cope in the aftermath of Jenna's death. But in that case, it would be in a blister pack in a box with a pharmacist label and Ark's name clearly printed.

And it wouldn't be hidden, stuck purposefully to a wall behind Jenna's shoe.

Yanking the steering wheel, she pulls to the side of the road. Conveniently Telstra's suspension doesn't extend to their account payment number, so after conceding her credit card details, she's finally able to open a browser on her phone.

Nitrazepam: A hypnotic drug of the benzodiazepine class, indicated for the short-term relief of severe, disabling anxiety and insomnia ... Sedative and motor-impairing properties ... Side effects include dizziness, depressed mood, rage, violence ... fatigue, impaired memory, slurred speech, numbed emotions ...

Severe, disabling anxiety and insomnia. Was that Jenna? Depressed mood, violence, numbed emotions. Is that what she'd been going through?

In Fairlie's hand, her phone begins to vibrate, interrupting her thoughts. The caller ID reads *Brian Masters*. Her immediate thought is to silence the call and her thumb hovers over the screen.

This is the third time he's tried to call. Both previous calls she had let go to voicemail, and the messages he'd left were cheery and brief, asking how she was, and if she'd like to catch up again.

Did she want to catch up again? She'd been so drunk she could barely remember: flashes of the heat of his skin, the blurry swim of her vision, the carpet prickly against her back. Why did he want to see her again?

She thumbed the screen. 'Hey,' she said, then listened. 'I'd love to.' Lowering her right foot, Fairlie pushed her car over the speed limit.

10

Then

Jenna's heart was buzzing, a hummingbird caged in her chest as staff moved around her, their actions routine and unhurried. They all seemed so blasé and unconcerned, almost jovial. Nattering and gabbing about this and that, as though the woman spread-eagled on the table before them, skin translucent beneath the blinding spotlight, wasn't about to have her body opened like an envelope.

A kind face appeared in her vision. A woman with green eyes, the rest of her face obscured by a mask and hidden beneath a wildly patterned headscarf.

Elephants.

Pink and purple elephants lumbered in rows across her head. Jenna relaxed ever so slightly. The theatre nurse with the elephants on her head was smiling – Jenna could see it in her eyes.

'All set, darl?' The mask muffled her voice.

Jenna couldn't answer for fear, so she simply nodded once, wide-eyed.

'Don't worry, we'll let Dad know straightaway.'

Somehow, rather than bringing Jenna comfort, it made her heart race even faster. Ark, trembling into the operating theatre earlier, had turned white behind his mask and fled, croaking out a panicked, tear-filled apology, his eyes darting wildly.

How very alone she was; how very inescapable this was for her.

There was pushing and shoving and pressure. She could feel her body being jostled, and the obstetrician's head dipped behind the blue screen that blocked her view of her lower body. With one final pull, the doctor held a baby above the screen, briefly. Its limbs were thrust outwards as though startled, its tiny fingers and toes spread wide like a grabbed cat. Gleaming blueish skin, slick and bloodied.

'A boy. Congratulations,' the doctor said. The baby was whisked away for a few moments; a moist, strangled cry filled the room. Then gowned arms were pressing a heavy, wrapped parcel to her chest, high up near her throat.

A boy.

Too exhausted to move. Her arms felt so weighted she was suddenly frightened she might not be able to hold the baby steady on her chest.

'Do we have a name?' a nurse asked brightly.

Jenna looked up at her. A name. The baby was here – her baby, Ark's baby. It was all real, now. Another squawk from beneath her chin, a snuffling, the blankets moving in and out with jerky, tiny-limbed movements. Could she say it, the name they'd agreed upon? Ark wasn't here. It was his name. Her heart thudded against the cage of her ribs, numb nothingness below as the surgeon – laughing with his assistant about something that happened on television last night – worked inside her open abdominal cavity.

'Henry,' Jenna whispered. She named him so that he could become a real person.

Outside the window of Jenna's hospital room the sky lightened gradually, a smeary purple-grey turning mushroom pink as the magpies began to warble.

The waterproof covering beneath the thin sheet crackled as Jenna shifted on the mattress, trying to get comfortable. A stab of pain flashed across her belly and she winced as her hand found the raw incision, staples like railroad pins studded across her spongy flesh.

Over in the trolley, the baby was squirming again. Little coughing bleats, wet and effortful, small fists and feet and knees prodding at the soft white swaddle from within. The baby seemed so *real* out here – had it really been inside her? Had its limbs poked like that at the walls of her womb?

Jenna struggled into a half-sitting position, feeling the blood drain from her head. Her vision swam; she put a cannulated hand out for the baby's trolley but it was out of her reach. Gritting her teeth, she shifted higher and leaned against the bed rail but a thick rod of pain shot down her middle and she cried out.

The infant's coughs turned mucousy and urgent. Finding the call button at her shoulder, she rang for a midwife. The infant was trying to cry in a voice strangled with liquid. Jenna watched with alarm as bubbly fluid trickled from the wide open mouth. Panicked, she stretched out, thumbing the call bell again and again.

Finally, the midwife strode into the room.

'I can't reach – the baby's choking,' Jenna said despairingly.

Deftly, the midwife plucked the swaddled infant from the trolley and turned him onto his side along her forearm. 'He's fine,' she said, one hand vigorously stroking the baby's back. The middle-aged woman had a broad, kind face and a confident, no-nonsense air. 'How are you feeling?' she asked. 'How's your pain?'

'Is it . . . is he okay?' Jenna nodded towards the baby.

'Perfectly fine. He just has a little bit of mucous to drain, that's all. When they come through the birth canal the normal way, all the amniotic fluid gets squeezed from their lungs. So caesarean-born babies sometimes need to cough it up instead. He'll be fine. Nothing to worry about.'

The midwife plopped Henry into her arms and Jenna,

trying to look capable, fumbled the bundle into the same position in which the midwife had held him.

'Have you put him to the breast yet?' the woman asked, picking up Jenna's chart.

'I tried, but he doesn't seem to want it.'

'Try to do it soon,' the midwife replied, scribbling something down. 'They can be a bit sleepy from the epidural. It's important that you get him fed soon. Would you like to try now?'

What Jenna wanted to do was sleep. Wheeled into theatre yesterday afternoon after twelve hours of induced contractions that had gone nowhere, she'd then spent the night waiting for the sensation to return to her lower body while listening to Henry's squawks and bleats. On and off in the dark, she had held the cross infant to the pale, blue-veined orbs of her breasts and watched him mouth ineptly at her nipple like a clumsy lover.

The baby cried out again – he seemed angry now, as though he'd heard her thoughts.

'Okay,' Jenna said wearily. 'I'll try again.'

Laying the baby between her blanketed thighs, Jenna picked up the cooling toast and bit into the corner. It was under-cooked and bland but it was food, and her stomach was growling. Just as she took her second bite, the door opened and an enormous bunch of flowers was pushed into the room, followed by Ark grinning so widely she couldn't help a small laugh. Lilies and roses, swaying spikes of green leaves, 'It's a boy!' on a floating pastel-blue balloon.

'How's my little man?' Ark leaned into the trolley and picked up the sleeping baby like he'd done it a thousand times, cradling him and chuckling softly, placing kisses on his forehead like gifts. He bent down, Henry in his arms, and kissed her softly. 'And how's my lovely wife?'

'Sore. And tired,' she answered honestly.

Ark frowned. 'That's not good,' he said. 'You didn't sleep last night?'

For some reason, Jenna felt a stab of self-consciousness. She smoothed the blankets over her lap, ran her fingers through her hair, licked at her tacky lips. 'He's been unsettled, plus . . . ' She suddenly couldn't finish the sentence, a hard lump swelled into her throat.

'Hey,' Ark said, sitting down on the bed. 'What's wrong?'

A tear slid down her cheek. With a knuckle, she flicked it away.

'You're tired,' he said, putting a hand on her leg. 'And hurting. Should I ask for something for your pain?' He looked up at the door, as though he could summon a nurse with the thought.

Jenna bit her lip. 'I've asked. They won't give me anything stronger than Panadol.'

'Why not? You just had surgery!'

'Because of the . . . ' she waved at her chest, 'drugs go into the milk.'

'Oh.' He looked sympathetic. 'Maybe it's for the best, then.'

Was it for the best? She felt like she'd been sawn in half, the pain drilled down to her spine. Blood and pee leaked from between her legs. But there were more important things than her now – the baby, the milk in her breasts. The baby might be out but her body was still not her own.

But as she looked at Henry, his rosy red face and womb-curled body cradled so deftly in Ark's strong arms, there it was again: that clenching, fearful ache in her throat, the tearful swim of her vision. How could she even think such self-centred things? Of course it wasn't about her. Pain licked flames along her hips and she gritted her teeth, told herself to feel it.

Ark took her hand and squeezed it reassuringly. The action felt at once grounding and so affectionate Jenna was hit with a wave of what felt like homesickness. A sob escaped her mouth, and she covered her face with her free hand. All she could see behind her closed eyelids was her own mother, and an unavoidable wave of responsibility brought forth by the delicate newborn.

'Babe,' Ark said softly, 'get some sleep.'

'How?' she asked, letting herself sound as miserable as she felt.

'I'll take Henry,' he said brightly. Then, looking at

Jenna's face, he added, 'Don't worry. We'll have fun, won't we, buddy?' Ark rocked the baby, his face shining with happiness. 'Just sleep,' he said to her. 'You need to rest and recover, your body's been through a lot. But look,' he said, lifting Henry's face to his own. 'Look what you've made. You're incredible.' He kissed her again, on the mouth and then on the cheek. 'I could never thank you enough for this gift.' His voice cracked. 'You've made me a father.' Tucking the blankets around her shoulders, he repeated, 'Sleep. I've got this.'

So he took the baby and, after a while, Jenna slept.

'Still sore?' Fairlie asked.

'A little,' Jenna answered. Settling back as comfortably as she could she watched Henry's cheeks, shiny with the lanolin she'd smeared over her stinging nipples for three weeks. But he latched well now, and sucked hungrily. 'At least he's finally started to gain a bit of weight.'

'That'll make your child health nurse happy.'

For a while they settled into a companionable silence. They sat side by side out on the front verandah, looking across the lawn towards the grapes, feet tucked beneath themselves on the day bed. Finches twittered in the grevilleas and far away, down beyond the grapes, the cars on the highway sounded like the rush of the ocean. Between the mildness of the afternoon, Fairlie's easy company and the sound of Henry's swallows, Jenna was aware that it should be possible to feel relaxed. Contented. But as immediately as this awareness came to her – the softened fall of her shoulders, Fairlie's somnolent yawn as she scrolled on her phone – something within Jenna hardened, like a muscular reflex, and she was instantly on guard again. Uneasy and frightened, although of what she was not sure. In her peripheral vision she saw Fairlie drop her phone, stretch and look over at her. Jenna continued to stare out over the vines.

'Everything okay?' Fairlie asked.

'Sure,' Jenna answered quickly. 'I'm just tired.' She offered her friend a smile. 'Everybody says it gets easier eventually. How many times have we said that to women with newborns?'

Fairlie seemed to wait for more. 'I'm sure it will,' she said, reaching out to squeeze Jenna's leg; her hand felt warm on her shin. 'He's only three weeks old, hang in there.' She paused and added, 'Have things been better at all?'

Jenna sniffed. 'It's okay. Ark's busy right now, a few more weeks and they'll be picking the grapes again, so I suppose that makes things more difficult.'

'What's going on?' Fairlie phrased the question casually. 'Are you guys fighting again?'

'He's trying to spend more time at home,' Jenna said, her fingers worrying a loose thread on Henry's jumpsuit. 'But it's difficult when he's got so much to do. I probably

228

am being selfish, needing him here when I should be coping.'

'God, Jen. You just had a baby. You're allowed to find it hard.'

Abruptly incensed, Jenna flung a hand in the air. 'Abbey said I should try initiating sex more; I should be more affectionate. On the BubHub web forum they said I should put Henry into day care and get some time to myself so I don't demand so much of Ark. Bloody hell, Linda Sommerson said I should consider myself lucky, because *her* ex-husband used to flog her with the kettle cord.' Jenna's shoulder slumped and she closed her eyes. 'I'm so tired of complaining, Fro.' She rubbed her hand across her face. 'He says he loves me. That's all that matters.'

'If he loves you, he should treat you better.'

'My expectations are too high.'

'An unwillingness to be whipped with electrical appliances isn't exactly aiming high,' Fairlie pointed out. 'Are you happy?'

Jenna gave her a tired look. What could she say? That she felt trapped? How would she explain that? How could she say that she felt like everything was out of control and that her life wasn't her own anymore? Anywhere she looked, the view seemed unfamiliar – like everything before it had been a ruse.

'Yes,' she said eventually. It was an easy lie, she told herself. Not even a lie, a stretch of the truth. 'I just need more sleep.'

With a soft popping sound, the baby released her breast. She positioned him onto her lap, grimacing as she moved his sleepy weight away from her still throbbing incision. 'Your mum called me yesterday,' Jenna said. 'She wanted to know how Henry is going.'

Fairlie picked up her cup and drained the last of her tea. 'She's always asking about you two,' she said, setting her cup down.

A familiar broodiness descended.

'Jen, why don't you call her?'

Jenna stared down at Henry, swooped with a sudden wave of fatigue. 'No.'

'But she's your mum. You used to be so close. She'd want to know about Henry.'

'It's been too long.'

'It hasn't. Besides, I don't think it matters how long it's been since you spoke to her – she would still want to hear from you.' Fairlie hesitated. 'There's no time limit between mothers and their children.'

'It's not about time.' Jenna raised her eyes to meet Fairlie's. 'I don't know who she is anymore.'

r—O

Evening fell hazy over the grapes. Even from where Jenna sat on the couch, insatiable baby tugging at her breast, she could see the fruit hanging in clumps along the rows. Heavy and ripe. She glanced down at the milky bloat of

230

her breast, at the fattened veins spreading from her tattoo. It was going to be a great vintage. A busy season. Ark would have his hands full: his skin and clothing would be stained purple-black and the phone would ring incessantly with eager buyers. She imagined her milk turning purple in Henry's throat, saw her breast as a bloated, dark grape for greedy suckling.

Inside, the house was a mess. Three piles of clean washing heaped in accusing mountains on the couch; the kitchen floor was scattered with cereal left over from her breakfast, knocked flying as she ate one-handed. Filmy dishes from last night's dinner were piled in the sink and she hadn't even thought about tonight's dinner.

Although he was quiet now, memories of the baby's cries from throughout the day rang in the back of her skull like an echo. The muscles up the back of her neck pinched tight. Her bladder ached. Henry slipped from her nipple. Awkwardly she slithered out from under his body and cradled him in the dent between two couch cushions, then she tiptoed across the room.

And walked straight into Ark.

'Oh!' Jenna exclaimed, laying one palm on his chest. 'You snuck in, I didn't see you there.'

'How could you not?' he replied. 'It's not like you were doing anything.' He glanced at Henry. 'You shouldn't leave him unattended on the couch like that. It's not safe.' His gaze slid down the hall towards the kitchen. 'What's for dinner?'

'I don't know. I haven't had a chance.'

He lifted an eyebrow.

'I've been a little busy.' She gestured to the sleeping baby.

'You're spoiling him,' he told her lightly, as though talking about the weather. 'And while you're spoiling him you're ignoring the rest of the stuff you should be doing.'

She tried not to drag her feet as she followed him to the kitchen. He opened the fridge, selected a beer and flicked its lid into the bin. 'Look, babe. This has got to stop.'

'What has to stop?'

'This . . .' he waved his hand, 'this nothingness.' Dishes clattered as his hands raked over the pile in the sink. 'You need to get up and start doing things. You need to motivate yourself. You're not sick. People can't sit around doing nothing all day.'

'Nothing?' she snapped.

'The house is a mess, there's no food to eat.' He took a step towards her. 'Nothing has been done.' He paused. 'Except the baby has been spoilt rotten. He's got you wrapped around his finger.'

Jenna felt her pulse fluttering in her wrists. 'You try running on two hours of broken sleep.'

'Well then, you need to get him out of *our* bed, and stop letting him suck on your tit all day. Get yourselves into a routine. It's healthy.' He sat on a stool at the bench and began marking off points on his fingers. 'Get yourself together. Tidy up. Have a shower, maybe?'

Jenna wondered if tomorrow she'd see these points

232

written on the whiteboard on the side of the fridge, along-side the shopping list. *Milk. Coffee beans. Tinned tomatoes. Tidy up. Shower.*

'You're being lazy,' he was still going, 'and you're starting to make me look bad. I bend over backwards to provide for you and you throw it in my face.'

Jenna's anger flared. 'Henry is a baby. I had major abdominal surgery five weeks ago. I'm still bleeding.'

But *was* she being lazy? She'd read about all the babies who, within two months of birth, were sleeping through the night, weaned from their mother's breast and shipped neatly off to day care while their mothers went back to paid work and contributed to the household – contributed to society. Why couldn't she get it together? Only three days ago, Ark had driven all the way to Mount Gambier to collect her favourite Thai takeaway and brought it home, wrapped in a towel on the front seat of his car so it would stay warm. Maybe he was right – maybe she *was* being ungrateful. She let Ark's accusations sink home like snooker balls. Lazy. *Clunk.* Unappreciative. *Clunk.* Selfish. *Clunk.*

'I get it,' she said through gritted teeth, 'but you don't have to be a dick about it.'

Launching from the stool, Ark tossed his empty beer bottle into the sink. It smashed into the pile of dishes. Glinting brown shards spat into the air and littered the bench and floor. 'There's two of us in this marriage, and I don't want to carry you anymore. It's pathetic.'

And then something happened. Ark's mouth continued

to move, but no words came out. Instead, Jenna heard a rushing sound, a solid body of white noise; she saw her bare feet moving across the tiles, then the toaster was in her hands. Cord snapping tight, the plug popped from the outlet as she lifted the toaster above her, crumbs falling like brown rain.

She threw the appliance as hard as she could at Ark's head.

Ark yelped and ducked as the toaster smashed into the overhead cabinet behind him.

'Jenna! What the *fuck*?'

Upon hitting the tiles the toaster split into a tangle of plastic and metal. More scorched crumbs burst across the floor. A smudged dent marked the cabinet door. Ark's face was white. He stared at her as though she was a ghost.

The muscles in Jenna's arms sang and her hearing returned; her arms were still rigid above her head.

'You called me lazy,' she said. 'You said I was pathetic.'

He swore again and stared down at the shattered kitchen appliance. 'You could have seriously hurt me.'

Jenna lowered her arms and burst into tears. Great hot sobs bubbled up as if from her bones. Her eyes dropped to the floor, taking in the slack flop of her belly, the long droop of her breasts, heavy with milk beneath her stretched shirt. Disgust curled her insides as she smelled the oil in her hair.

Hesitantly Ark came to her, stepping around pieces of broken plastic. 'Babe, I'm saying this for *you*.' His hand cupped her chin and she let out an anguished moan. 'I'm telling you these things because I love you.'

She glared at him through her tears, her breath coming hard through her nose.

'You know how if you're eating at a restaurant, you'd want someone to tell you that you had spinach in your teeth? It's like that, babe,' he said. 'You've gotta be cruel to be kind.'

Wrenching free from his grasp, she stepped back. His eyes went wide.

'You can clean this mess up,' she spat. 'And make your own fucking dinner.'

She went to the bedroom; the slam of the door woke Henry but she didn't come out.

Ark didn't speak to her for six days. A week of cold, deliberate silence: he made her no meals, offered her no hands to hold the baby so she could shower or shit unaccompanied by a whining infant. On the seventh day she cried, and apologised. That afternoon, he bought her flowers and he cried, too.

Six months passed.

Half a year of the same.

Bars of soap, half-empty bottles of nail polish remover and a litter of hair ties were flung aside as Jenna rifled through the bathroom drawer, searching for a tube of lanolin. Henry was teething; her nipples stung and the cotton of her shirt felt like razors.

She huffed and went to the bedroom. Rummaging through her drawers, through the silky maternity lingerie pushed to the back of the drawer behind the old pyjamas Ark had eventually returned. (*Come on, honey, can't you take a joke?*)

Jenna eyed Ark's bedside table.

The drawer made a soft slipping sound as she slid it open. Her ears pricked up automatically and she glanced at the doorway; Henry was quiet in the lounge room, the soft melody of a children's television programme filtered up the hall. Eight months old and already she relied on the TV as a babysitter. She could almost see the aghast comments from the mummy pages on Facebook.

Her fingers walked over a blister pack of ibuprofen, a coil of iPod headphones, letters from his mother. There was a time when Ark used to read those letters aloud to her, curled up together in bed. Statements like *I miss you* and *Thinking of you* and *I'm so proud of you* that Jenna would savour like treats as they rolled from his tongue. Those times, his arms snug around her, she had imagined what it would feel like to hear those words from her own mother: words of endearment, reassurances, the tenderness of unconditional approval.

Now, she realised, Ark simply read the letters quietly to himself and folded them away.

With care, Jenna lifted the pile of Marguile Rudolph's letters from the drawer. As she flicked through the stack, she came upon a particularly bulky envelope. This envelope was blank, unaddressed, but its creases strained. Peering inside, she let out a gasp.

A thick wad of cash filled the envelope. More cash than Jenna had seen in her life. Wrapped in an elastic band, the bundle was mostly green and yellow – hundreds and fifties. Jenna had only seen hundred dollar notes once or twice – ATMs didn't dispense them, so they only came from the bank. Where had all this cash come from? What was it for?

She pulled off the elastic band and began to count.

The rattle of Ark's LandCruiser pulling up the drive startled Jenna, and she glanced at her watch as Henry crawled to the edge of the sandpit. It was a little past noon, and Ark's arrival gave her a wash of unexpected pleasure and relief.

The lawn was cool and dry beneath her bare feet, prickling her ankles as she crossed her legs. Henry had finished with his crackers and she crumbled a couple in her hand to toss to the few brave finches that flitted towards her across the grass while their kin twittered angry warnings from the grevilleas.

She didn't bother calling out to Ark; he would find them. Soon enough he emerged from the back door, his boots thumping across the deck. Seeing her sitting cross-legged on the lawn, brushing sand from her knees that Henry gleefully flicked into the air, he smiled and waved, and bounded down the steps.

'You finished early,' she observed as he came within earshot.

'I cut out of the meeting,' he said. 'I couldn't wait to see you.' The finches scattered away as Ark crouched alongside her and kissed her cheek. Magnanimously he withdrew his hand from behind his back and held forwards a metallic silver envelope.

'What's this?' Jenna asked. Sliding her finger beneath the flap, she slit the paper open. Inside was a gift voucher from Larissa's, a day spa in Mount Gambier. In flourished pink script the wording on the card read: *This voucher entitles Jenna Rudolph to one three-hour Blissful Body Indulgence session, including eyebrow shaping and bikini wax.*

Jenna's head snapped up. 'What's this for?'

Ark wrapped her in a tight hug. 'For being you,' he said. 'I can see how tired you are, and I thought you could do with a bit of pampering.'

'Three hours,' she murmured into his chest. For eight

months she'd felt obligated to be with the baby, his body attached to hers like an external gestation. The idea of spending time alone, without another human clinging to her, felt like a kind of illicit freedom. But almost immediately, guilt tramped upon her, and she felt the greyness of obligation slink back over.

Ark lounged back onto the grass. 'He'll be fine with me for a few hours, won't you, kiddo?'

Now, she thought to herself. *Ask him about it now.*

She plucked a long spear of grass from the edge of the sandpit. 'Ark?'

'Hmm?'

'I found some cash the other day.'

Ark gave her a look of surprise.

Just ask him.

'A twenty you didn't know you had?' he said, leaning forwards to push a toy bulldozer within Henry's reach. 'That's always a nice surprise.'

'It was more than a twenty.' With her thumbnail she slit the grass spear up the centre.

'Is that right?'

'Ark, there is seven thousand dollars in the bedroom. What is it for?'

He stared at her for a long moment; she felt the skin on the back of her neck tighten.

'Where did you find it?' His voice was measured.

'In one of your drawers –'

'Why were you looking in my drawers?'

'Why do you have seven thousand dollars?'

They stared at each other for a long beat until Ark exclaimed suddenly, 'Oh, that!' He brushed sand from his hands. 'I was just holding it for a friend. His bank was closed, and he didn't have anywhere safe to keep it.'

'A friend?'

'Yes. He sold his car.' Ark smiled.

Jenna's grip on the gift voucher grew clammy. Bitterness crept across her tongue as she realised he expected her to swallow his explanation. But what was the truth? He'd robbed a bank? Stolen it from someone's wallet? Found it washed up in a bottle on the beach? Her fingers curled tighter, the voucher made a crunching noise. A whine started up in her ears, like her brain was swelling inside her skull.

He said, 'Babe, I've just given you a generous gift.'

'Ark, I –'

'The money doesn't concern you, Jenna.'

'But the cash –'

'Is *my* job. Running the business, managing the finances – that's *my* job. Your job is taking care of our home and our son. That's the commitment you made, to me and to yourself and to our son. Stop stressing unnecessarily. Remember what the counsellor said about pressuring yourself?'

'I never –'

'Stop being paranoid!' He rose to his feet. 'You don't know the first damn thing about money. I've just booked

240

you a whole day on your own and you're throwing it back in my face. Maybe I'll take the voucher back, since you're being so ungrateful.' He snatched the card from her hand and stormed across the lawn, up the deck and inside the house.

Henry began to cry. Jenna stared down into her hands; four lines of blood sprang from four stinging cuts across the soft pads of her fingers.

Stupid. *Stupid* for picking at him, for nagging. She should have saved her energy for something that mattered.

Humming white noise rushed through her like static. Jenna was on her feet, sprinting across the grass, hurling her body down the slope and into the thicket of grevillea. Birds shrieked and darted skywards. Bees swirled angrily. Barbed leaves tore at her skin and brittle sticks lashed her face. A thousand tiny rips unwrapped her skin.

And when she was done, the roaring white noise stilled, she heard a sound behind her on the lawn.

Henry was laughing at her.

Under the stream of hot water from the shower, Jenna's body ached with mastitis.

All day her skin had flushed hot and cold, burning where Henry grabbed at her; her head felt fragile and strained. Alone, she had forced down a one-handed dinner of toast and butter while Henry threw his own onto the ground and cried.

Henry wanted to breastfeed, but Jenna refused. A desperate need for her body to be hers alone clawed at her. He had butted her with his head and screeched with fury at her refusals to lift her shirt. Her muscles clenched each time a hand mauled her, wanting, needing. Leaving her hollow. And now her inflamed breasts ached, crass globes of milk, and the fever simmered along her skin.

Ark was at a friend's house fulfilling a month-long promise to help set up a home theatre system. Hours of poker and rum would undoubtedly follow, and Jenna expected Ark to stay out well into the night. Is that where he was getting his cash? Poker? Gambling? Jenna blinked water from her eyes and gazed down at the cuts on her fingers, the raw scratches across the backs of her hands and wrists, washed red from the hot water.

Towelling dry hastily, she anticipated the soft sheets of the bed with longing. Henry was splayed across one side of the mattress as he simply wouldn't sleep well alone. The only chance she had of getting a few hours of sleep was with him in bed. With her. With *them*. Ark would be irritated at the sight of Henry between them on the mattress; he'd accuse her of spoiling the child. But on the occasions she left Henry in his room, crying out into the night, Ark would toss and turn and growl at her to *do something*.

Shivering with fever, Jenna clutched the towel tightly across her shoulders and snapped off the ensuite light.

'Hey, babe.'

The voice gave her a fright. Dressed only in his boxers, Ark swayed with one hand on the door frame. He tottered across the room and wrapped his arms around her, pressing his body into hers as he ran his hands up her back.

'I wasn't expecting you,' Jenna admitted, keeping her voice low. She glanced uneasily at Henry. 'The mastitis is still bad, I'm going straight to bed.'

'Bed sounds great.' He grinned and made a grab at her towel.

Henry snuffled and tossed an arm.

'I've finally gotten Henry to sleep.' She smiled weakly, gesturing towards the bed. 'I just want to go to sleep myself.'

Threading his arm around her waist again, Ark pulled her back to him and pushed his hand up the side of her throat. His palm rested heavily on her cheek. Gripping her chin between his thumb and forefinger, he pulled her face close.

'Aw, come on, babe.' His breath was syrupy with rum. 'Don't you love me?'

'Of course I love you,' she answered, carefully pushing his chest. 'But I'm unwell. I think I'm going to need antibiotics.'

'Always excuses,' he muttered, sliding his free hand

243

under the towel. 'Come on.' His fingers crawled across her inner thigh. 'It's been ages. You mustn't love me anymore.'

'My skin hurts if anything touches it,' she told him. 'My head is pounding. I can't get warm. I just want to go to bed.' Muscles quavering, she pushed his chest again but he held her firmly.

'Please, Ark.'

He stiffened, then dropped his arms to his sides; his palms slapped against his thighs. He took an exaggerated step back.

'Is this far enough?' he demanded. Backing unsteadily further, he stepped into the ensuite. 'How about now?' He held up his hands. 'Better yet, why don't I move out? Move to Spain? Would that be far enough?'

Jenna gritted her teeth. 'What are you talking about? And please,' she warned, shooting another panicked look at Henry, 'please keep your voice down.'

Giving a short groan of disgust, he returned to her and laid his hand on her upper arm. Her skin burned beneath his fingers.

'It's been ages,' he said again, furrowing his brows. 'Months.'

'Come on, Ark.' She hated the plea creeping into her voice. Her legs felt heavy; the bed was so close, but she wondered how long before she'd be able to lie down. 'It hasn't been *months*. Maybe a couple of weeks. Everything is okay. I'm not feeling well. You know that.' Looking him directly in the eye, she added, '*Please.*'

He let her go.

Cautiously, she crawled onto the bed, moving the blankets slowly, desperate for Henry to stay asleep. He whimpered and she froze, holding her aching body on her hands and knees, watching his small body anxiously. He stilled, and she gingerly lowered herself to the mattress. Pain sliced behind her forehead so sharply she felt a wave of nausea.

Ark thumped onto the bed.

Henry jumped and yelped, then began to shriek.

It took Jenna an hour to settle him. An hour of pacing the dark hallway, fever flushing her flesh hot then cold, the heavy child cradled in her leaden arms. When Henry finally went to sleep, Jenna laid him in his cot in the next room. She knew it would be a matter of when – not if – he would again awaken.

She returned to the master bedroom, slipped into bed, and after half an hour succumbed to Ark's whining. Opening her legs to him, she gazed into the dark slab of the open doorway as Ark's hot breath filled her ear. Her reluctance fuelled her self-loathing. She tried feigning something, some feeling, for herself, but resentment churned deep and her energy suffocated. If she could get through this, maybe the Ark she loved would return. If she could stifle her fickle temper, he would comfort and spoil her again. So she chose to ignore the money, the criticisms, the entitlement to her attention and her body. She chose to let it go. Because that choice – the choice to submit – allowed her some element of control. Didn't it?

When Ark was finished, he kissed her and rolled from her body. Down the hall Henry cried out and she was ridiculed by yet another sleepless night.

11

Now

Fairlie grips the wheel tightly for the entire forty-minute drive.

The air-conditioner blasts chilled air from the vents but still she sweats, still her thighs quake with anxiety. Roiling violet clouds gather in the sky and the air bloats with humidity. The highway rolls beneath her car and the dense Pinus radiata plantations sweep the thunderclouds. Twice on the short journey she stops with nervous urgency to wee, squatting in an alcove made with her open passenger-side door, long dried grass poking into her crotch and piss splashing up onto her ankles. During one such stop a truckie blasts his horn and Fairlie holds up her middle finger.

As the crater lakes of Mount Gambier rise into view, Fairlie forgets about Nitrazepam. She forgets Brian Masters and fuzzy recollections of ponytails and carpet burn. Taking one hand at a time from the steering wheel, she flexes her fingers and holds clammy palms to the air-conditioner vents, surveying the skyline of Mount Gambier: a collection of limestone buildings surrounded by the waft of dairy farms and pine chips.

There, alongside a service station: 1127 Bay Road. Her right foot lifts; she gulps. It's all she can do not to haul a U-turn over the median strip.

Fairlie pulls up in front of a squat office made of brown brick. Leaving the engine running, she surveys the lot, cool air pooling at her feet. The office building reminds her of the generic front offices of brake repairers or landscaping supply yards – stuffy boxes to hold an air-conditioner, permanently smelling of microwaved leftovers for lunch.

After a time she cuts the engine and steps from the car. She stands on the kerb, forcing her breath to slow, while thunder growls in the gunmetal sky and the air stills like a stopped clock.

A vibration from her pocket: *Looking forward to tomorrow.* Brian Masters has signed the text message with four Xs. Fingers trembling severely, it takes three tries to key in her response: *Me, too.*

Fairlie inhales, runs her fingers through her hair and steps away from the kerb.

A buzzer sounds as she enters the sparsely furnished

front office. A chest-high counter runs the width of the room, laminated in dark brown vinyl and covered with a couple of faded, curled-edged posters. Behind the counter is a mirrored window and a small access door, which opens at the sound of the buzzer. A balding, middle-aged man steps out. He wears a tartan shirt and navy blue slacks and brings the stale smell of cigarette smoke.

'Help you?' the man asks in a gravelly voice.

'Storage unit eight,' she manages to say. What if he won't let her open it? 'I need to access it.'

What the hell is inside?

His face is impassive. 'D'ya have the key?'

Fairlie withdraws the key from her pocket and holds it up with white fingertips.

The man shrugs. 'Second to last, down the back.'

Is that all? Fairlie realises she was hoping for more resistance, more questions, more answers. More something. So much for security. Perhaps whatever Jenna has stored isn't worth all that much?

The buzzer yells again as she pulls open the door.

Behind the office, a narrow yard runs perpendicular to the road. Surrounded by a chain link fence topped with a sagging strand of barbed wire, a corrugated iron shed extends the length of the yard, roller doors evenly spaced along the front. Fairlie steps warily along a crushed gravel driveway that fronts the shed. Roller door number eight looks the same as all the others, but her mouth feels as though it is full of feathers.

Fairlie looks down at her fist clutched around the key. A lone dandelion grips a crack in the edge of the foundation.

A lock in the door, about waist height, small and innocuous.

As though observing someone else, Fairlie watches the slow, trembling reach of her hand. The key aimed towards the lock, the pause before it slides home, tumblers clicking. Before she can lose her nerve she twists the key.

Fairlie holds her breath, grips the door handle, and gives it a swift tug. With a clunk, the clasp releases and the door lumbers upwards with a loud metallic rattle.

12

Then

'It's an illness,' Doctor Jones was saying as he smiled at Jenna. 'It's quite common. It's not your fault.'

'Depression,' Ark repeated. 'That explains everything. Thank you, doctor.'

'If it's been going on for a while, I'd say it's postnatal depression,' the doctor went on. 'But since Henry is eighteen months old now, we'll call it plain depression. We tend to diagnose the "postnatal" part before twelve months post partum.'

Jenna was trying to name the colour of the carpet. Too light for grey, it was also too bland for silver.

'But you definitely think this is postnatal?' Ark asked.

'If it's been going on for some time, yes.'

'It has. A long time. We should have come to see you sooner.'

Off white? she wondered. No, it wasn't cream enough.

' . . . medication, you should notice a difference.'

'We know a great psychologist,' Ark was saying. His voice had taken on a bashful, almost humbled quality. 'We've been to see her as a couple. Worked wonders.' He gave Jenna's knee a squeeze.

Eggshell, she decided.

The room was too warm. Jenna tugged the neck of her T-shirt. Ark was bouncing Henry on his knee and the child was giggling with delight. Jenna looked away. *What colour is puce? No wait, that's pink.*

'Jenna?'

She looked up. 'Huh?'

Ark gave the doctor an apologetic smile. 'Doctor Jones asked if you are okay with all that.'

'Sure,' she said. 'Antidepressants. Counselling. Got it.'

'I suggest you join a mother's group, too,' the doctor said, scribbling his signature on the prescription. 'Get out of the house more. The support will help.'

'Doctor Jones? What colour would you call this?' She pointed to the carpet.

The doctor exchanged a look with Ark. 'Take care, Jenna,' he said.

After they left the doctor's clinic, Jenna told Ark she wanted to stop by the hospital.

'Why?' Ark asked with a frown.

'There's a form I forgot to sign. For my resignation.'

'You resigned ages ago,' he pointed out.

'Hospital paperwork never processes fast.'

When he pulled into the hospital car park Ark left the engine running. Before she could open her door he grabbed her wrist. 'Five minutes,' he said, eyeing the building with nervous distaste. 'We need to get Henry home.'

Jenna hesitated, her hand on the door handle. 'I might be a bit longer. I thought I'd stop in at maternity and ask about mother's groups.'

His eyes flickered over her face. 'Why?'

'Like the doctor said, I should get out more.'

Ark sighed, his jaw working. 'We'll talk about it later. You need to get more settled into a routine around the house before you try going out. That will just mess everything up.' Reluctantly, he released her arm.

He waited in the car with Henry, and when she returned, clutching her handbag tightly and trying not to look back over her shoulder, she hoped he couldn't hear the hammer of her heart.

Adrenaline sent tremors through Jenna's limbs as she popped pills from blister sheets onto the bathroom counter. Through the locked door she could hear Ark in the kitchen, singing loudly to Henry.

Crumpling the empty boxes and blister sheets into balls, she shoved them deep into a drawer beneath a box of tampons and packets of sanitary pads. Tomorrow, when Ark left for work, she'd burn them.

Jenna sealed the ziplock bag, stuffed it up her sleeve and left the bathroom.

Wails filled the dark. Miserable, angry wails that drilled into her ears and plucked like hands at her heart.

'For fuck's sake,' Ark muttered from beneath the covers. 'How long is this supposed to last?'

Jenna gritted her teeth. 'The book said three nights.'

'It's been a week.'

'I know,' she snapped. 'I'm not deaf.'

'Don't get angry at me. I'm not at fault here.'

She rolled over, her back to Ark as she faced the wall, squeezing her eyes shut.

The wails had morphed into long, drawn-out sobs. *Muum-mma. Muum-mma.* Tears slipped across the bridge of her nose, spreading wet into the pillow at her ears.

It was some time before Henry went quiet – an hour, maybe two, but when silence finally fell she felt Ark's hands slide over her waist, the familiar splay of his fingers across her belly – thumb on one hipbone, little finger stroking into her pubic hair. She resisted as he tugged at her, bringing her hips back to his body, the thick of him pressing against her spine.

'No,' she said. But her dissent mattered not, and when he entered her it was swift and urgent, her T-shirt rucked up around the small of her back. Pressing her face into the damp of her pillow, she held her breath, stifled her useless sobs.

Afterwards, she crept from the bed and tiptoed down the hall, her fingertips trailing across the walls in the dark, trying to ignore the sting and drip of fluid from between her legs. In Henry's room, there was enough moonlight for her to make out his sleeping form. He had grown almost too big for the cot now. She stared down at him, wondering why she felt so blank. Nothing; her mind was blank, her body a discarded carapace.

Snores filled the master bedroom when she returned. The sound jangled up her spine. On tiptoes she crept into the robe and knelt silently. She held a pill between her teeth before swallowing it dry.

Now she could lie down, and wait for the relief of a slack darkness.

━━O

Jenna leaned against the kitchen counter, rubbing her temples as she watched Henry turn buttered toast into a grain-and-saliva mush on the tabletop. Curds of it littered the floor. As she stared at him, he dropped a mangled crust and, after observing it hit the tiles, he looked straight to her, his features twisting in outrage.

Heaving herself from the counter, Jenna hastened to reassure him before his cries escalated.

'Everything's okay,' she told him, 'I'll get it.' Wincing against the throb in her head, she knelt to retrieve the crust. Her stomach rolled as she wiped her hand against her trackpants.

Her left hand stayed curled in a fist. Returning to the sink, she opened her fingers to stare down at the minuscule tablet in her palm. Rain battered against the window, and she thought of Ark driving the muddy lengths of the vines, checking on the labourers he'd hired for pruning. His words from the early hours of the morning swam through her mind. *Don't worry, soon you'll be all right. Back to normal.*

Jenna watched glimmering rainwater chase itself down the glass. At the table behind her, Henry began to whine.

Normal. It seemed such an absurd concept. She knew that she should be longing for it, striving for contentment and happiness, but it was as though all her muscles had wilted away, as though even her mind had turned to slop, like Henry's toast. She was an unrecognisable smear of her former self. Forever altered, forever stripped of form and purpose.

The Fluoxetine weighed nothing in her palm. It rested there, full of promise. The answer! Take this once a day. Tell this person all your woes and, like a fart in the wind, all your problems will miraculously disappear. Your life will *mean* something. As if tablets and a $200-an-hour stranger could erase it all.

For a bit longer than a week she'd swallowed the pill each morning. And for the past few days, there'd been nothing but nausea and headache. No signs of content-ment, no glimmer of happiness. Every morning she awoke, her body stubbornly refusing to accept that there was no point to her existence. Breath kept coming in and out of her lungs; her heart kept up its useless, repetitive beating.

How hard would it be to simply hold her breath, to slip away?

Ark had only approved of her seeing Karen, with the Masters in psychology and the long silver plait. Jenna had insisted that if she was going to do this again she wanted someone completely new, but Ark was adamant: she wasn't going to see a stranger. How could he trust someone with his precious wife if he hadn't already vetted them? *I love you*, he'd implored, her hands wrapped in his. Tears gleam-ing in his eyes. *I love you.*

Acid lurched in her stomach. Jenna tilted her hand and the antidepressant rolled from her palm. It made a small ticking sound as it hit the bottom of the sink. She turned on the tap and watched it spiral down the drain. As had yesterday's. And the day before's.

She knew.

Even before the line materialised to tell her, Jenna knew the inevitable truth of it.

It wasn't just the antidepressants. A week of nausea, the constant headache, the sharp bite of her sense of smell.

So as she stared into her knickers, clean of blood for seven days too long now, even before the second line appeared on the pregnancy test Jenna knew.

She knew she couldn't do this.

Dear Jenna,

So you were born. You were out, pink-skinned and thriving. And for a moment we were perfect, you and me and your father.

But.

But then.

Looking down I cooed at you, but then I frowned, and winced, as the doctor tugged between my legs. I asked him to stop; I told him it hurt.

He apologised, still pulling, eyebrows drawn together over his mask. He told me to push again, said something about reluctant afterbirth. Still the tugging, yanking on my insides. But then – pain drilled up through my body.

The doctor cried, 'Shit.'

Barking orders, nurses flying into action. Stephen's worried voice: 'What's going on?'

'There's another baby.'

Another baby.

Another baby.

I heard it, Jenna, but it must have been wrong. I had just had a baby. Somebody declared something about surprise twins, but the tone in the room wasn't celebratory.

Over the years I have tried to recall events from this point, but I simply don't remember much. I can hear frenzied cries – they must be mine? – the copper tang of blood, the hot gush of fluid and the rough press and jerk of the doctor's hands. I remember feeling flayed in half. Confused, frightened. Panicky. Drugged. Something about a head out. And they said there was blood – so much blood. The doctor roaring at me to push.

So I pushed again.

And the room descended into silence.

I thought it must have been death. Only death could bring the silence so swiftly, like the fall of an axe. But I wasn't dead.

I was very much alive – the aches and raw stings of my body were too furious and hot. Ragged breathing, Stephen's hand clutching mine with numbing fierceness. From the far side of the room you screamed. Amongst it all, the steady bleep, bleep, bleep of a machine that measured the life beat of hearts. The doctor clearing his throat, his eyes looking at a place I couldn't see behind that god-damned bloody sheet.

'It's a girl.' Yet the doctor sounded uncertain; a nurse peered over his shoulder and put a hand over her mouth.

Stephen's voice was thin as he asked, 'Is she okay?'

I wondered who he was asking about – me? You? Who?

Eventually, the doctor looked up. He stared at me with such intensity that I wanted to look away. Then he turned to Stephen and he said: 'There is another girl.'

In the background, you wailed. But – where was our new baby? This second girl?

Then the doctor lifted his hands. And nothing would be the same ever again.

Now, can you see how hard it would be for us?

Until next time,

Love, Mum.

13

Now

When the roller door rattles upwards, Fairlie squeezes her eyes shut. Her heart thumps in her chest, battering at her collarbone as she draws in a shuddery breath.

Is this even real?

Fairlie is waiting to wake up and discover that the past couple of weeks have all been some sort of catastrophic, horrifying nightmare. Thunder cracks and rumbles across the sky again, closer this time. The birds have gone silent.

Slowly, she opens her eyes.

A flat grey concrete floor, swept free of dirt and dust. Plasterboard walls, twin fluorescent tubes in the plasterboard ceiling. In the far left corner, pushed against the back wall, a plain brown cardboard box with *She's Apples* stamped on one side. Otherwise, the unit is empty.

Fairlie stares at the box, hands hanging limp like chicken carcases at her sides. Jenna didn't like apples – the skin got stuck in tiny annoying pieces between her teeth. She flicks a light switch and the fluoros tick and buzz overhead.

The box has no lid. Approaching slowly, Fairlie squats, her fingertips touch the concrete.

Inside the box is a large stack of spiral-bound note-books with hard covers, held together with two giant elastic bands. Fairlie counts eight in total. Pulling one book out, she flicks through the pages. Columns of dates and figures, it looks like old-style accounting books. Headings like *Month, Sales, Cash, Supplier.* Were these the books Ark was looking for? She slots the notebook back in the box and continues to flick through the contents. An A4-sized envelope filled with papers. On top of the stack of books is a creamy yellow manila folder, a large paperclip affixed to the top, from which the edges of a few sheets of paper protrude. Scribbled in red pen on the front of the folder, in Jenna's handwriting, are the words, *I love you.*

Fairlie's hand descends into the box, towards the final item. Small and square, and not much bigger than a teacup, the hinged box is covered in dark, padded red velvet. It's the larger variety of jewellery box, the kind that encloses bracelets or watches. Taking it into her hand, she runs a thumb over the tiny hinges, over the snug closure between the two halves.

Her mobile phone shrills into the silence. Fairlie startles, her fingers snapping tight around the box. Fumbling in her pocket, she withdraws her phone.

It's Ark.

Henry.

When she answers, her voice echoes around the bare walls.

'Fairlie? How does . . . how did Jenna get Henry to eat anything?'

'Oh hey, it's nice to talk to you, too,' Fairlie says.

A frustrated huff comes down the line. 'I can't get him to eat anything.'

Fairlie frowns, unable to tear her eyes from the velvet box clenched in her fist. 'I'm sure he hasn't been starving for a fortnight.'

'Of course he's eaten *something*,' Ark snaps. 'But he mostly just cries. I'm getting . . . ' She hears the resignation in his voice. 'I'm getting tired of it, Fairlie. I need my life back. I need . . . ' He breaks off.

Fairlie's heart squeezes. 'Hey, it's been rough on him.'

'Rough on him?' Ark repeats. 'You have no idea.'

Clamping her teeth, she pushes down a swell of anger.

'You think this is easy for me?' he asks, exhaling forcibly.

Fairlie uncurls her fingers from the jewellery box. A large clap of thunder judders the shed walls and the first drops of rain tick against the tin roof.

'You there?' he says after a while. 'Look, I'm sorry. I got rid of all those boxes of Jenna's stuff today, and I want to get on with my life. With Henry's life.'

He got rid of everything of Jenna's. Everything.

'Give yourselves some time,' she says, running her thumb over the velvet box. 'You can't rush grief, Ark. And try some pear slices,' she adds, clearing her throat. 'Poached in a bit of brown sugar and cinnamon. Oh, and raisins.' She swipes a tear from her cheek. 'Make sure you lay them out in a line or a shape and he'll go nuts. I'm . . .' Her own voice leaves her then; what can she say? Does Ark know about this storage unit, the jewellery box she holds in her hand?

This is between you and me only, sister.

'I'm in the middle of something,' she finishes. 'I'm in the Mount, but . . .' She hesitates, looking out into the sunlight. 'I would like to come and see Henry again. I feel terrible about it,' she admits. 'I've been slack not coming to check on him.'

'He's with his father, Fairlie.'

'Oh. I didn't mean to imply –' She shakes her head. 'Of course he is. But please – I won't stay long. I have some things of Jenna's to drop off, anyway,' she lies.

A short silence issues down the line. 'Actually, there are some things I need to do. If you're really insistent on seeing him maybe I can drop him at your house for a few hours?'

'Yes!' Fairlie says. 'I'd be delighted to babysit. Any time.'

'This weekend?'

'Perfect,' Fairlie tells him. A smile tugs at her mouth.

Hanging up and snugging the phone back into her pocket, she feels a small weight lift from her shoulders.

Her hand flat, she regards the jewellery box in her palm.

She picks it up and carefully opens the lid.

14

Then

'Keep your eyes closed,' Ark murmured, his breath tickling her ear. 'Watch out for the step.' Jenna squeezed her eyes shut and gripped Ark's hand. The warmth of him brushed against her back, their feet shuffled together, toe to heel. He leaned away momentarily to hold open the front door as she clumsily navigated the step.

'What's going on?' She giggled nervously.

'You'll see.'

Their feet clunked across the deck; a delicate breeze trembled across her bare ankles. 'Is this going to take long? I don't know how much longer Henry will nap for.'

'Relax, would you?'

Just as she prepared to navigate the steps from the deck to the driveway, Ark halted. 'Okay. Open them.'

Sunlight flared bright and she shielded her eyes with her hand, squinting against the abrupt change. She searched the front yard: the rustling of new grape leaves, streaky cotton-wool clouds dashing across the sky.

'What am I looking at?' She glanced back over her shoulder at Ark. He was jiggling on the balls of his feet.

'Your car,' he said, smiling.

Jenna looked along length of the verandah to where her car was parked beside the shed. Going on ten years old now, she'd bought the Ford Laser with her first loan when she'd finished TAFE. It had been faithful and reliable and that was all that mattered. Over the past few years the cherry red paint had begun to fade, but now it gleamed. Light bounced from its contours and the alloy wheels shone polished silver.

'You washed my car!' Jenna exclaimed with a laugh. 'Thanks. It needed it.'

He gave a gallant bow. 'There's a surprise for you on the front seat.'

Giving him another quizzical smile, she approached the car and peered through the window. 'Oh, you didn't,' she said softly as she opened the door. A sweet and damp floral scent wafted out. On the passenger seat sat an enormous bouquet of white lilies. Blooms brushed the roof and leaned to the dashboard. A knot formed beneath her ribs. 'Thank you,' she said.

Ark wrapped his arms around her, pressed his lips to her forehead. 'I'm so proud of you, facing the depression,' he said. 'You're trying so hard. I know things have been a bit ... rough, between us, and I'm sorry for that. But I want to make a fresh start.'

'Ark ...' she began.

'You don't need to say anything.' He drew away and gave her a fond look. 'We both say things we don't mean when we're angry. We're both to blame.' He hugged her again, rested his chin atop her head. Taut ropes of muscle running up his spine shifted beneath her palms; he smelled of fresh laundry and cologne.

'It's okay,' he whispered. 'I know you love me, even when you don't show it.'

Irritation flickered through her. She wanted to tell him she was frightened; she wanted to remind him that she had heard this before, that he didn't have to make these dramatic gestures – she just didn't want to fight in the first place. She wanted to feel trustworthy, useful, respectable. Guiltily, she heard an echo of her own harsh words. In her mind's eye flashed the calm mask of his face as her frustration erupted into throwing things, clenched fists pounding her own breast, scathing accusations spitting from her lips like darts.

And as she swallowed a curl of nausea, her thoughts slunk down to what was growing in her belly and she wanted to tell him what could not happen – the truth that could not eventuate.

Despite growing accustomed to it, hitting *send* on yet another rejection to Fairlie still gnawed at her. It had been weeks since she'd seen her. Shoving the phone in her pocket, Jenna drew her legs up to her chest and rested her cheek on her knees, leaning sideways into the couch. From across the lounge room floor, Henry made growling noises as he slammed a wooden block into the colourful toy xylophone.

Her excuses were growing more pathetic: *Sorry, I'm not feeling well; or Ark's out and Henry needs to sleep; or even, I need to go to the supermarket.*

The hard edge of her phone dug into her hip, as though burning a hole in there, and she knew that she wouldn't receive a reply from Fairlie now. Although that was easier in one respect, in another it hurt far more. Because, if she didn't see Fairlie, that was one less thing for Ark to complain about.

But the less she saw Fairlie, the more pieces inside her turned to stone.

Henry stood and ran clumsily to her. The way her face felt slack and expressionless when she looked at him failed to shock her now.

He blinked up at her, then opened his fist. 'Mumma?' Inside his hand was a marble. Clear glass with a toothpaste-like swirl of green trapped inside. Ark had taught Henry to give any small items – choking hazards – he found to

269

adults. As a result, throughout the day Jenna was handed all manner of small items: pebbles, dead insects, hairclips. He was giving her the marble. Not even two years old and he was already more responsible than her.

'It's okay,' she told him. 'You can have it.'

There was a knock at the front door. Jenna paused, ear cocked towards the rear of the house, but there was silence from Ark's office. The knock came again so she sighed and slipped from the couch, stepping over Henry on her way past.

A white van idled in the driveway. A slow rain was falling, swirly and mist-like. The deliveryman smiled at her from under a red cap, holding a thick parcel. 'Jenna Rudolph?'

The package was a book she had ordered online. Struggling to find any motivation to prepare healthy dinners, she had ordered a collection of recipes for the slow cooker. *Set and Forget,* the book was titled.

'How's this weather?' the deliveryman said, rubbing his arms briskly.

'Typical southeast,' she said. 'Wait twenty minutes and it'll probably be too hot.'

'You're Jenna Walker, right?' he said. 'We went to Mount High together.'

Jenna looked him up and down. 'Sorry, do I know you?'

'Jeremy Lukas. I think we had drama together. Or something.'

'Oh! Of course. Sorry, I've still got baby brain.' She hugged the parcel to her chest. In the lounge room, Henry gave a drawn-out whine. 'Anyway, thanks.' She patted the parcel, making to step back. 'I'd better ...'

'No worries.' The man nodded, then shoved his hands into his pockets. 'Great place you got here. Yours?'

'My husband's.' She couldn't help the small swell of pride that rolled through her – the acknowledgement of fortune, of being someone with something to talk about. But almost immediately, as that realisation dawned, her pride turned to shame. The apple doesn't fall far from the tree, she thought bitterly.

The deliveryman whistled, turning to take in the long gravel drive, the picturesque lines of grapes just bursting into bud.

'It'll look better in summer, in a few weeks,' she told him, 'when they're in full leaf.'

Henry wailed.

The boy from high school turned back to her. 'It was good to see you. You're looking well.' He said it genuinely, respectfully.

She rolled her eyes as Henry gave an indignant shriek to rouse the dead. 'Yeah, mashed carrot is great for the hair.'

Jeremy Lukas laughed and started to respond, but a hand appeared from behind Jenna and pulled the parcel quietly from her arms. An arm wrapped around her shoulder and she took a step back, into the doorway.

'Thanks, mate,' Ark said quickly, 'cheers.'

Jenna saw a look of surprise flicker across the delivery-man's face, before the door was pushed closed.

In the lounge room, as Henry cried and grabbed at her pants, Ark raked her from head to toe with his gaze.

'Who is he?'

'No one,' she answered. 'We went to school together.'

He took a step closer. 'You fuck him?'

Jenna's voice was icy. 'No.'

His stare took in her every detail: undone hair, track-suit, tense posture.

'You should pay attention to the men in your life that matter. Your husband and your son. Not some dickhead who comes to the door.'

'Are you asleep, babe?'

Ark's voice sounded muffled, barely breaking through the swampy haze in her head. Swimming: she was swimming. Floating. It was peaceful, and warm, and she ignored the sound of his voice. Blankets slipped away as Ark moved closer, a breath of cold air stealing over her skin. Hair lifted away. Strokes and kisses on her neck.

'I love you,' he was saying in her darkness. 'Let's talk about today.'

She forced out a response so he would leave her alone. 'Don't worry,' she slurred, the words like sticky lumps of dough. 'Tomorrow. Sleep.'

'No.' His voice grew insistent, shards slicing into her peace. 'I shouldn't have scolded you for talking to that delivery guy. I recognise that as a time where you've felt not trusted. It's only because . . .' His lips traced along the line of her shoulder. 'You're so beautiful,' he murmured into her skin, 'and you don't see it. You don't see what I see – every other man looking at you, like he wants you. And you're *mine*,' he finished, pressing his body against hers as his fingers tracked a line down her belly.

Her own hand was heavy and slow to respond as she groped for his, wanting to stop its path. 'I need to sleep.'

'Whatever.' He laughed softly, his fingers delving between her thighs.

Groggily, she tried to move away from him but he followed her, hands roaming her body. She went limp against the press and caress of him, forcing her breath to slow and deepen, to remain unresponsive. But it didn't matter. He still tugged her to him, he still worked himself into her and finished with a self-satisfied cry of triumph.

And she slid away into the narcotic blackness, again.

⚊⚊○

'Where's Henry?' Ark asked as he entered the kitchen.

Jenna plunged her hands back into the hot water in the sink. 'In bed.'

'Already? It's only six.'

'He's been grating on my nerves all day,' she said, with more than a hint of exasperation. 'It took me two hours to scrub all that crayon off the walls. Then he took a shit on the living room carpet –'

Ark sighed. 'Look, I should be around the house tomorrow afternoon, so I can help.'

'Really?' She turned to face him again.

'You can take a couple of hours for yourself. Have a bath, go for a walk or something.'

She stilled, searching his face for a catch. Finding nothing, she let out a breath.

'Really? Because ... ' The words wouldn't come. 'I could use a couple of hours,' she finished, weakly.

'I know; you're tired.'

'Sure, that, but ... ' She hesitated, searching for a way to tell him without spoiling the mood between them. 'I was actually hoping to go to the hospital, see Marg Dunbower.' She scrubbed at a plate beneath the suds. 'Marg emailed me the other day, saying she hoped I might be able to come back and pick up a few shifts.'

It wasn't a complete lie. Marg *had* emailed, and Jenna *did* intend to go and see her old nursing unit manager about returning to work. However, what she didn't tell Ark was that she'd also made an appointment to visit Doctor Jones.

And the clock was ticking.

Before she could lose her nerve she went on quickly. 'I told Marg that I'd come and chat to her. It sounds like a good idea.' The words tumbled out, rolling into one another like stones. 'We could use the extra money, plus the doctor did say I should do things that are for *me*, you know, not just mothering. Work is healthy.'

As she heard her sentence close, she tasted what she'd left unsaid: her appointment with the doctor, the impossible pregnancy she needed resolved. Immediately.

Behind her, she could feel the tension radiating from Ark's body like electricity. The hall clock ticked; a cricket jittered outside the window. The last of the setting sunlight drifted behind the eucalypts, leaving Jenna and Ark standing in the stark artificial white of the kitchen. Hot water swirled up over her wrists as she scrubbed a bowl. She rinsed it under the tap, set it to drain. Washed a coffee mug, rinsed it, set it to drain.

Ark still hadn't replied.

The mood was over. She wondered if her heart would stop altogether.

After a while she thought he might have left the room, so she hazarded a glance over her shoulder.

He was standing behind her, his face thunderous.

'We've talked about this,' he said softly. 'Why are you even bringing it up?'

'Because she emailed me,' Jenna said, as calmly as she could. 'And like I said, my doctor suggested it was a good idea.'

'So you've worked this all out? Behind my back?'

'I haven't worked anything out —'

'You and the hospital and your doctor, all making deci-sions without me?'

'Nothing's decided. I'm just going to talk to her –'

Ark chortled, shaking his head. 'No, you're not. You resigned. You belong here, now. *This* is your job.'

'This?' She flung her hand in a circle around the kitchen. Suds flew from her hands and splattered on the bench. 'My job? Ark, I'm going out of my mind. It's been two years. I can't keep doing *nothing.*'

'Taking care of our son, of our house, is "nothing"?'

'You know what I mean,' she said, snatching up a tea-towel. 'Look, I'll only take on a couple of night shifts, so Henry doesn't have to go into care or anything.'

Ark was still shaking his head but Jenna kept talking. 'I need this. I was good at my job and I miss it. I barely see any other human beings anymore, I'm cooped up in here for days at a time. I'm going crazy.'

'Are you still taking your pills?'

Jenna blinked.

'Are you?'

'I don't see what that has to do with my job.'

'On the contrary – your mental state has everything to do with whether or not you can be employed. How can you work in health care when you're unwell yourself?'

'There's nothing wrong with me!' she cried.

'You just told me you're going "crazy", that you're "out of your mind" – are you going to disclose that information to the hospital?'

276

Jenna threw the towel on the bench. 'I'm going to see Marg tomorrow. At three. I'm getting my life back.'

'This isn't open for discussion,' he said coolly, studying his fingernails. 'We decided this years ago. What's gotten into you?'

Jenna's blood went cold. Did he know?

With a laboured breath, Ark sat down at the table. 'I think we need to go back to the doctor and have your dosage reassessed. You're not making any sense.'

She recoiled as though he'd slapped her. 'You are such an arsehole.'

Ark laughed. 'Insults. Real mature. And you think you should have a *job* with that kind of mentality.'

'Three o'clock tomorrow afternoon,' she hissed. 'You just told me you'll be home.' She stalked from the room.

⌐─O

The next day, Ark left the house at eight in the morning. By 2.50 pm, he was nowhere to be found. Calls to his mobile went unanswered, and he didn't return her calls, despite the four increasingly frustrated messages she'd left on his voicemail.

Jenna wanted to scream.

With Henry whining at the screen, she'd showered hastily. She had dressed in jeans and a silk shirt – she couldn't remember the last time she'd dressed nicely – with Henry clinging to her calves. She had poked herself in the eye with the mascara wand while Henry pulled toilet paper from the roll and heaped it in dampening mounds onto the floor.

Steel rods squeezed against her temples as she stood in the hall. Henry was pulling at her pants and demanding something about a ham sandwich, and it was 2.58 pm and the house was closing in on her, the hugeness of it, all four bedrooms and two bathrooms and the kitchen and living rooms all with their empty promises, the eighty-two acres of grapes that gave her everything but took it all away, the sky and the billion-strong nebula of stars above her – all of it was crushing her.

And all of it had abandoned her.

Hauling Henry to her hip, Jenna picked up her keys. On her way out, she slammed the front door so hard a vase toppled from the sideboard in the hall and smashed across the floor.

On a play mat in the corner of the doctor's office, Henry threaded coloured beads along curled wire strands.

'Are you sure?' Jenna asked, fingers mauling a sodden tissue in her lap. 'I have to have an ultrasound first?'

'I'm sorry,' Doctor Jones told her. 'But ectopic pregnancy must be ruled out before you can have the procedure.'

'And I can't have it done now? Today?'

'No, I'm sorry,' he repeated. 'You need to be at least six weeks pregnant for the ultrasound results to be clear enough, so you have another week until then. And besides, as you know,' he smiled sympathetically, 'we don't have the imaging clinic here. You'll need to go to Mount Gambier for the ultrasound. Once you have the results, you can then book in for the procedure with the women's health clinic there. You shouldn't have to wait too long for an appointment, maybe another week after that.'

'So it could be another two weeks? Maybe longer?' She glanced at Henry and swallowed a rising dread. 'I'm already symptomatic. I don't want to get worse. Can't I just say no? Sign a waiver? Then you can write me a prescription now. Mifepristone is on the PBS.'

'I'm sorry, I can't.'

'What about my right to informed refusal?'

'You don't have one in this instance, I'm afraid,' he said with a sigh. 'In South Australia abortion is still on the criminal code. It can only be done by a licensed practitioner and only after an ultrasound.' Doctor Jones's expression was understanding. 'What does Ark think?'

Jenna baulked.

'I'm assuming he's supportive of your decision to terminate this pregnancy?'

Another two weeks. An ultrasound, all the way to Mount Gambier. And then what? How would she hide the appointments?

'Yes,' Jenna lied. 'But I wish there was something you

could just give me.' Her fists were clenched so tightly her knuckles turned white.

Doctor Jones sighed. 'I'm sorry there's not more I can do.' He regarded her for a long moment, leaning forwards to rest his forearms on his knees. 'Jenna,' he said slowly. 'Are you *sure* you're okay?'

Drawing herself up, she gave him a brisk smile. 'Yes. I will be fine.' Taking her referrals, she thanked the doctor and stooped to collect Henry's hand.

'Please, come back and see me in a few weeks,' Doctor Jones said.

Jenna promised him she would.

Ark was waiting for her when she returned home.

Twelve missed calls on her mobile in forty minutes; the phone vibrated with messages on the passenger seat the entire seven-minute drive home from the clinic.

Henry had fallen asleep in his car seat, his head lolled to one side, a half-masticated rice cracker cradled in a grubby, slackened fist. Pulling into her space alongside the shed, Jenna killed the engine and twisted in her seat to observe him, her seatbelt digging into her collarbone. There *was* something there, she couldn't deny it, but what was it? It wasn't what other mothers had, what mothers talked about online or what it was like on TV. For Jenna it felt like ... remorse. Guilt. Shame. She watched the child she'd brought into this world and knew she should see a whole future of possibilities and timeless joy, but she didn't. Instead, she saw greyness. Bleakness; shackles. An endless drudgery that no one deserved. Especially not this innocent, beautiful young boy. The guilt she felt as she gazed on his sleeping face stabbed her deep inside and she covered her mouth with her hand to stifle the sob. Facing the front again, she took a deep breath and unclipped her seatbelt.

Movement caught her attention and she looked up to see Ark striding across the driveway. Glaring at him, she stepped from the car. 'You promised you'd be home.'

'Where have you been?' he asked. 'You haven't answered my calls. I was worried.'

'Where do you think?' she snapped. 'I went to see Marg. Like we talked about.'

Ark sighed heavily and rubbed his head. 'Oh, Jenna,' he said, so softly she had to move closer to hear him. 'I'm so sad that it's come to this.' He looked at her with something like painful pity. 'There was no such discussion. We *did* talk yesterday about your mental illness – about how you're unfit to work. Do you remember that?'

Anger bubbled up into her throat. 'There's nothing wrong with me.'

'That's not what your doctor said.'

She flinched. Had Doctor Jones called him? Could he do that? She pictured the look on Ark's face as he answered the phone, heard the jovial camaraderie in his tone as they discussed her secrets and decided between them that they knew better than her. No. Surely not?

She said, 'It's just depression –'

'Precisely, depression is an illness.'

'I'm perfectly capable –'

'And it affects your ability to think and make rational decisions.'

'I'd be perfectly fine if you'd just leave me alone!' she cried, flinging her handbag to the ground. Tears spilled down her cheeks and she ground her fists into her eyes. 'Just shut up!' she shouted. 'Fuck off and let me be!'

Inside the car, Henry awoke at the sound of her shouts.

'Marg wasn't there anyway,' Jenna went on, ignoring Henry's muffled cries. 'So I didn't talk to anyone about going back to work.' Her voice cracked with the lie. 'There, are you happy? You own me, Ark.' She held out her hands, palm up, wrists together as though he could handcuff her. 'You control me like a dog.'

'Jenna,' Ark said calmly, pulling a sobbing Henry from the car. 'You need to calm down. You're upsetting Henry.'

Disgusted, she flung her hands in the air.

'Think carefully about what you're saying,' he said, pushing the car door shut with his hip. 'There, there, buddy. It's okay. Daddy's got you.' His eyes never left Jenna's as he patted the child's back and Henry melted across his father's shoulder, quietening. Ark walked towards her. 'Think *very* carefully about what you're implying,' he said as he drew closer. 'You're sounding quite irrational. You think I treat you like a "dog"?'

'I can't,' she muttered. 'I can't do this anymore.' Gravel crunched under her heels as she backed away.

'Can't?' He sounded genuinely puzzled. 'Can't do what?'

'This! I feel like I'm dying, Ark.'

'Babe, listen to me. You're sick.'

Fury shot through her. 'I'm not sick. I'm ... I'm ... *abused*.' The word rang into the afternoon, clashing across the cladding of the shed, the limestone bricks of the house, falling over the grapes like soot.

'You don't let me do anything, you don't let me see anyone.' Her hands curled into fists at her throat, yanking at the collar of her shirt. 'I've lost my family. I've lost my friends. I'm nothing but an empty shell, bound to this house like I'm in chains. I can't eat. I can't sleep – you don't *let* me sleep! I cannot do another day of this. Not another day.' He swam before her, wavering as though in water.

'I want out,' she said, her breath wheezing. 'I want to leave.'

He took a step towards her. 'Jenna, honey. Listen to yourself. Abused?' He looked scandalised. 'I've never laid a hand on you in anything but love. How insulting for those women who *are* abused that you could lower our loving relationship to that.'

'Ark –'

'We've had our problems, I'll admit. But you're taking medication now.' His breath was on her face. Henry squirmed between them. 'Granted,' Ark said, 'I think after this outburst we'll be getting your medicine altered for something stronger, but still. You've lost your family?' He frowned at her. '*We* are your family, Jenna. We love you. Can't you see that? Look,' he put a hand on her shoulder and she burned beneath it, 'I won't deny that you struggle to feel a bond with Henry, but that's the depression and your stubbornness talking. If you'd lighten up and stop fighting everything I suggest, you'd be much happier.'

'No –'

'You would. You're not thinking rationally right now.' His fingers squeezed into her flesh, his gaze bored into her. 'What are you not telling me?'

'No.' She shook him off, stepping back. 'No. I want to leave.'

'Jenna, please.' Henry began to wail again and Ark's expression turned desperate. 'Babe?'

A late-spring shower began to fall; slapping against the vines, drops sliding down her hot cheeks. Jenna collected her handbag from the gravel.

'Jenna?'

She walked towards the car. Ark grabbed her arm and she lashed at him with her keys. He let her go.

'Jenna, wait.' His voice was shrill. 'Please.'

She yanked open the door and he closed his hand over it but she pulled so hard he recoiled, closing his hands protectively around his son.

'We can work this out!' His voice was muffled through the glass. Henry cried. Ark raised his voice over the sound of the engine turning over. 'I'm not perfect, I know. I need help. You can help me! Tell me what to do!'

The accelerator pedal eased beneath her foot. The car picked up speed. Ark slapped at the window.

'*Please!*' he screamed. Henry cried and the rain fell as Jenna drove away.

Her pounding on the screen brought Fairlie to the front door within moments.

'What – Jenna, are you all right?'

Jenna struggled to regain her breath as she fell into the tiny living room. Rainwater dripped from her fingers; her nose ran and she wiped it on her damp shoulder.

Fairlie's eyes were round. Her hair was dishevelled and sticking up at the back, a novel lay open on the couch in front of a muted television. Trying to look inconspicuous, Yodel slunk across the floor, escaping. The air smelled vaguely of cat, but also lived in, familiar.

'I've left him,' Jenna said.

'Okay,' her friend said slowly. Fairlie scratched the back of her head and her T-shirt rode up at the front, exposing the elastic waist of her trackpants. 'Sit down. I'll make coffee.'

Jenna sat. Fairlie boiled the kettle, spooned coffee granules into mugs, added milk. Jenna took the hot cup from her friend and held it between her palms until it burned. She didn't know what to say. Should she apologise? Or should she expect that her friendship with Fairlie didn't need apologies?

'Where's Henry?' Fairlie asked.

Jenna looked into her cup. Steam rose from the murky surface. Her skin howled with pain and she finally set the cup on the floor and then looked down into the reddened insides of her hands.

'Jen?'

'He's fine.'

'He's with Ark?'

'Of course,' Jenna said, curtly. 'I might be a shit mother, but I wouldn't leave him alone.'

The patience in Fairlie's expression remained. Her old friend simply listened and watched Jenna with an effortless understanding and Jenna felt a yearning well up so fiercely she sucked in a gulp of air. Overcome, she covered her face with her hands and wept, messy sobs that came up like vomit.

Jenna doubled over, rocking, as Fairlie folded her in her arms and held her and rocked, too.

At 1 am, a full moon pushed bold, pearlescent light across the bedspread. Jenna lay curled on her side, blankets snug over her shoulders, watching a lock of Fairlie's hair float and sink with the rise and fall of her sleeping breath. The sheet was tucked high around Fairlie's neck like a cowl; beneath the blankets their knees pressed against each other. The pillow smelled of Fairlie's orange blossom shampoo.

Jenna snuck her hand out from beneath the blankets and gently smoothed the lock of hair back. Jenna left her hand there, resting gently atop the heathery spring of Fairlie's curls until her arm ached.

The next morning Fairlie called in sick. The rain clouds dissolved and summer boasted into the atmosphere. They spent the day in their pyjamas, Yodel eyeing Jenna with distrust from behind the safety of the curtains. They heated a double serve of Mrs Soblieski's beef vindaloo and ate from the same bowl, their spoons clinking together and mouths burning from the chilli, bare toes overlapping. In the shower, Jenna soaped herself with Fairlie's bar of frangipani-and-lime soap; she left the bathroom door open when she peed and brushed her teeth with Fairlie's toothbrush. She laughed until it felt like hands wringing out her ribs.

Fairlie asked her about Henry and about Ark. Tea

snorted from Fairlie's nose as Jenna recounted a week ago when Henry had pointed to a hardened lump of bird shit on the verandah handrail and said, 'Bir dit.' Jenna told Fairlie about Ark's new clients, new stockists, newest cellar door awards. She was honest about how tired she was: that Ark insisted they *never go to bed on a fight*, sometimes keeping her awake into the early hours of the morning until she conceded his point of view. But she heard the stories come out abridged, lined with silver and rose-hued. She omitted that night after night Ark demanded, wheedled or coerced her into sex she didn't want to have. Day after day, motherhood drained her to the point of a greyish, hollowed-out hopelessness but she left that out too, her stories clipped like newspaper articles missing final paragraphs.

And the ticking clock deep in her belly – she left that out, too.

Ark knew where she was. Jenna refused to turn her phone on so he had eventually called Fairlie. Stage-whispering reassurances with her face turned away, placating the man with her nurse's tone, Fairlie said, *She's fine* and *I don't know how long – how is he?* and *I'll pass it on.*

On the third day, Fairlie hesitantly dressed for work.

'Are you sure you'll be okay?' she asked, buttoning her shirt.

Jenna reached to mute the television. 'I'll be fine,' she answered, setting her coffee on the floor at her feet. Yodel bathed himself on the end of the couch.

Fairlie smiled. 'It's been nice, huh?'

Jenna's hands stilled. 'Yeah,' she conceded, returning her smile. 'It has.'

Her friend hesitated then, twisting her handbag strap in her hands. 'Look,' she said. 'I think you should call him today. At least talk to Henry.' Fairlie slung her strap over her shoulder. 'He'd be missing you.'

Something inside Jenna kicked. 'I'm sure he's fine,' she said quietly.

'You're his mother.'

Jenna heard a serrated edge in Fairlie's tone and rubbed at her forehead, searching for spots. Finding a clogged pore she dug her fingernail into the skin.

'Jenna?'

'What?'

'Don't you want to see your son?'

'It's not that. It's . . . '

'What is it?'

Why was she *looking* at Jenna like that? Brows set firmly, pupils darting across her face, mouth a resolute line.

'Stop judging me,' Jenna said. 'I know what you're thinking.'

Now Fairlie's brows went up. 'What am I thinking?'

'That I'm a terrible mother. That I'm stupid for falling for him. That I should never have married him in the first place. That I shouldn't *leave my child*.' Yodel scampered from the couch.

'Jenna, woah.' Fairlie dropped her bag onto the table

and lifted her hands. 'I'm sorry, I shouldn't have suggested it. I thought you'd be missing him.' She kept talking, her tone infuriatingly placating. On and on she went, but her words were too sweet. They couldn't be the truth. Jenna had abandoned her child. Only the lowliest of mothers would do that. And after all, why *wouldn't* Fairlie judge her for that?

'Why don't you wait here, and I'll go get Henry?' Fairlie said. 'And some of your stuff.'

Jenna stared at her, finally understanding. Fairlie had been abandoned by her own mother. Jenna could see that in her friend's expression now – disdain and disbelief. How *could* she? What kind of a person selfishly forsakes their own child? This was a woman's lot in life: paying the price of Eve's sin. Life as a woman was devoted to what she could provide: legs to wrap about the thirsty hips of men. Legs to spread to reproduce, to increase the population who would do it all over again. Again and again.

Horror struck her then. She had become her own mother. Egotistical. Self-centred. Brutally arrogant.

Jenna shot to her feet. Kicking her coffee into a brown stain across the carpet, she snatched up her handbag and left, Fairlie's voice trailing pitifully confused behind her.

15

Now

The jewellery box snaps open. Inside are four ID bands for newborn babies. Made of thin, pliable white plastic, they have handwritten labels behind a tiny, transparent window. They are secured on the smallest holes, and a long tail punched with a row of minute circles protrudes from each. All bands have been neatly sliced open for removal. In her palm the four circular bands are weightless, like air.

Fairlie frowns and picks up one of them.

Francis, Jenna, the name says. *Sex: Female. DOB: 09/05/86. 3.05 am.* Alongside *Mother* is printed: *Francis, Evelyn.*

The second band has exactly the same details. These are Jenna's newborn ID bands. Fairlie imagines them curled around Jenna's fresh new ankles, twenty-six years ago. But – *Francis?* Then she remembers that newborn babies, before officially registered with Births, Deaths and Marriages by the parents, are named and filed with their mother's paperwork in hospital. It's easier for record-keeping. Evelyn never took Jenna's father's name – Evelyn Francis and Stephen Walker were never married – so when Jenna's birth was registered, she had been officially given her father's surname.

Fairlie picks up the third band.

The name says *Francis, Fairlie.*

Fairlie blinks.

Sex: Female. DOB: 09/05/86. 3.17 am.

Francis, Fairlie?

She brings the band closer to her face, squints and studies it carefully. Rubs her thumb across the clear window; maybe she is reading it incorrectly. But she picks up the last band, and when she reads it the words are the same: *Francis, Fairlie.* Born twelve minutes after *Francis, Jenna.*

All four bands have listed – *Mother: Francis, Evelyn.*

Is this a joke? She scrutinises the handwriting again, looking for pen smudges, but it is neat, legible. Placing the velvet box on the floor, Fairlie spreads the bands out on her knees and reads the details again. Made out for two babies, born twelve minutes apart, with the same last name. With the same mother.

But one of them is named *Fairlie.*

A perplexed smile twitches the corners of her lips. Did Jenna make these up?

Gathering up the bands, she tucks them carefully back inside the jewellery box. She reaches inside the *She's Apples* box and takes out the manila folder: *I love you* in the slanted loops of Jenna's hand.

Inside the folder are three sheets of paper.

A photocopy of a birth certificate, a child now named *Walker, Jenna Eve.* Just like the ankle ID bands, the certificate lists the birth details as 9 May 1986. District Hospital of Mount Gambier. Under the section titled *Mother*, there is Evelyn Francis, twenty-six years old with occupation listed as *Not recorded.*

Fairlie smiles. Evelyn would hate that. Her job was her life.

And there's Stephen, listed under *Father*. Thirty-eight years old. *Attorney.*

Marriage of parents: Not recorded.

Fairlie skims over the other details, taking in the official header with its spread-winged South Australian Government logo, the signature of the Principal Registrar.

She sets the sheet aside. Over the second sheet of paper, her brows knit. A cold flash pangs in her belly. Because she holds another official copy of a second birth certificate. With all the same details under *Mother* and *Father* and *Date of Birth* but this child is registered as *Walker, Fairlie May.*

Fairlie Walker.

Child of Evelyn Francis and Stephen Walker, twin of Jenna Eve Walker.

'What the hell?' Fairlie says.

Hastily, she flicks the certificate aside.

The third sheet of paper is a black-and-white printout from a Wikipedia website page. The text is cramped, minimised to fit onto a single page. The heading reads: *Heteropaternal superfecundation: Mixed twins.*

Mixed twins – biological twins of separate races.

Mixed twins. Fairlie races over the text. Her breathing is shallow as she turns the sheet over, finds it blank, swears and flips back to the front. Again, she reads over the text. And again. Dropping the paper, she fumbles open the jewellery box, fingers trembling over the soft, white bands.

Heteropaternal superfecundation: Mixed twins.

The article describes a biological phenomenon where two babies – fraternal twins – are conceived in the same womb merely hours apart. Sometimes it happens where the parents of both twins are mixed race – one twin is like the mother, the other twin is like the father. But sometimes it happens with *different biological fathers*.

Mixed race twins could mean one child of Caucasian descent and one child of Asian descent. Or one of Aboriginal parentage and one of European parentage.

One baby with dark skin, the other with light skin.

On the powder-cool concrete floor, Fairlie clutches at the paper as she re-reads the article describing the approximately twelve-hour window of ovulation, where the usually singular egg, ripe and eager, makes its short but hopeful journey down the fallopian tube in search of that single-celled sperm, the carrier of the other chromosome.

Ordinarily, the woman would share the necessary sexual relations with a man and *voila*, the potential for a new life is sparked. Sometimes a woman might share those necessary relations with separate men, close together – perhaps even too close for her to feel confident about parentage.

But in some rare instances – *heteropaternal superfecundation* – *two* separate eggs are released, and – during that brief window – *two* separate sperm await.

Sperm from two very different men.

Could it be . . . ?

'It can't be,' Fairlie says, her voice brittle as blown glass. 'Can it?' She drops the paper and stares down at the ID bands.

'Is Evelyn my birth mother?' She picks up the birth certificate for Fairlie Walker and asks the empty storage unit: 'Is Jenna my *sister*?'

Dear Jenna,

In those early months with both of you, the days and nights were a blur of exhaustion. Your shrill and insistent cries filled the nights.

I won't lie — I often felt like your screaming was a protest, an accusation: that you took Stephen's side, and reminded me that I was little more than a whore. When I patted your padded bottom and murmured for you to hush, that there was nothing to worry about, I wondered: could you hear the fraudulence in my voice?

And while your wails filled my life from one sunrise to the next, always from the second cot came nothing but silence. It was as though you spoke for the both of you — the selected member of the jury who announces: we find you guilty. When I woke to you during the night, I would think of Stephen: the sheets tucked tightly, stridently, around his shoulders as he closed himself off, locking away that caring part of himself that might prompt him to get up, to offer help to the woman he loved.

One day when you were about four months old, my boss dropped by unexpectedly. (You might not remember Jack — he left Channel 8 when you were only a few years old.) I felt humiliated by the mess in the lounge room; Jack had to move a pile of unfolded towels to sit on the couch. You began to cry. I willed you to be quiet — because often your screams would change the silence from upstairs.

Jack hadn't been the first visitor since you were born, nor would he be the last. Bitterly I wondered, how long can we keep this up? I scalded my tongue on my coffee whilst Jack reclined on the couch and the insouciant drape of his arm on the cushions fed my irritation. You bawled on my knee as Jack waxed inconsequentially about my leave having only four weeks remaining, how the station had missed me, and what had happened to my housekeeper? If she'd quit so hastily, why hadn't I found a new one?

Then, I heard a noise from upstairs. It wouldn't be long before Jack heard it, too. I felt frantic. He needed to leave. So I unbuttoned my shirt, tipped you back in the crook of my arm, and fished my breast from my bra.

Jack leapt to his feet. He couldn't get out of there fast enough.

And so this was my life, Jenna. Hiding away in the house like some hole-dwelling mammal; I had sacked the housekeeper and, of course, could not replace her — how could I have anyone else inside?

A strained, uncomfortable distance began to stretch between Pat and I. I feared she saw your birth as a reason for me to disassociate from her, as though her longing for children might have pushed me away. Week by week I watched her recede, and I don't blame her. All the unreturned phone calls, the hastily terminated visits, the polite conversation and diverted questions.

Sometimes, when I knew Stephen would be working late and I would be alone, I brought her downstairs so she could crawl around the kitchen floor, fat little palms smacking the tiles. You would watch her from your mat, legs and arms

297

stilled; sometimes she went to you and hooked her fingers into your mouth. Seeing you interact, to be able to hold you both together in my lap – those are the moments I felt like a real mother. The fragrance from the tops of both of your heads, the heft of you – one in the crook of each arm: everything made sense. I believed in those moments that we could make it work.

But then Stephen would come home and another day of my maternity leave would tick past on the calendar, and reality would come racing back. I argued with Stephen about going out; I was going stir crazy locked inside. But leaving the house was an impossibility.

Mostly, we argued about my job. Rumours were circulating that a new presenter had been hired to replace me – a 'stunning' young girl from Ballarat. I wanted to return, of course, but Stephen wanted me to quit.

'How can we can go back, after this?' he would say anxiously, sourly. 'It won't work.'

I would implore him: surely we could make this work? We loved each other, wasn't that all that mattered?

'No one can ever know,' Stephen would say and I, despite my desperation, could not find it within myself to disagree.

Haunting me through all this time was him. I couldn't see him, Jenna, and it was tearing me apart. Occasionally I would find these small reminders of him: the theme song to Days of Our Lives *that reminded me of midday, the time we most frequently spent together; Stephen's takeaway* coffee cup in the bin, from the café where we'd first spoken; the crushed pine needles I found in the bottom of my wardrobe, shed from a shoe I'd worn on a stolen lunch break encounter.

He tried calling a few times and the sound of his voice felt like a fist in my stomach. I ached for him.

He didn't know.

When he called me the first time after you were born, I told him about you. Only you.

And then one day Stephen came home early.

I had been obsessing over the rumours circulating about the new presenter who was to steal my job. People were saying that I'd had a dispute with the station, that Jack and I had argued over my maternity leave, that I'd had a nervous breakdown. Even caged in my house, I'd still heard whispers that I was being unreasonable – that I was being a bad mother by wanting to return to work. They said I should quit – that I'd had my time. That I was old news.

You were both downstairs when Stephen, without warning, arrived home in the middle of the afternoon. When I heard his car, I had to hurry you both back into the nursery; she had taken to screaming if I put her away without you. On this day, you both quietened quickly. Perhaps on some level you knew what was about to happen.

Returning to the kitchen, I found Stephen hunched over the counter, a tumbler of whiskey in his palm. When he lifted his head, I felt my body go cold. There was a gash on

299

his left cheekbone, crusted purple, and his collar was torn. Drips of dried blood littered the front of his shirt.

He was crying. I'd never seen your father cry.

'Daryl and Mark,' he said, his voice thick.

I frowned. 'Your brothers did this?'

Stephen took a swig of whiskey and winced. 'No,' he answered, 'your boyfriend did this.'

I took a step back. The room went silent.

'Daryl and Mark came into the office this afternoon. They said they had a surprise for me.'

There was a dull rushing sound in my ears. I didn't want Stephen to go on, but his words continued to scrape out.

He said, 'They wanted to pay him a visit.'

My knees buckled. 'Is . . . is he okay?'

He snorted, swallowing the last of his drink. 'I told them about it – about him.' He was staring down into his empty glass. 'It was a mistake to tell them, but I'm completely cut up. They asked what's been going on, so I told them.'

'Stephen?' I could feel my heart in my neck. 'What did your brothers do?'

'They told me not to worry about it,' he went on, 'but I told them not to worry about it, you know? I should have been more insistent.' When he looked at me his eyes were glassed-over, bloodshot. 'I'm not going to say I'm sorry, though,' he said, 'because I'm not.'

Frantic, I tried to interrupt him, but he wasn't listening.

'You think I can just be okay with this?' he asked. 'Just be okay with the fact that you're having an affair? I can't, Evelyn. I'm not okay with it, no matter how much you say you love me. It doesn't work that way.'

'What did they do?' I cried.

Stephen's tone was flat. 'When they first got in there, they were kinda roughing him up a little. Pushing him around.' He sniffed, wiped his nose with the back of his hand. 'I . . . I just reacted. Tried to stop them. But there were fists going everywhere . . . and I got in the way. He hit me.' He looked up at me again, then. 'He hit me. So Mark . . . ' His voice choked off.

'Mark hit him with a piece of wood. I . . . I don't even know where he got it from. When I looked over after I was punched, Mark just suddenly had it in his hands. This piece of two-by-four. Brought it right down on his head and . . . he collapsed.' He paused, lifted his glass, remembered it was empty and thumped it down.

'Then they propped his legs up on the coffee table and jumped on his shins.' Stephen's body had gone completely still. 'Both of his legs are broken. He's in X-ray now, but they possibly fractured his skull, too.'

I slumped to the floor.

I didn't cry. Not for a few days. But when I finally did, Stephen left the house and didn't return until the next day.

Mount Gambier went nuts. The whole state was in a frenzy. The seemingly unprovoked assault of a police officer in his own home was a major offence. It was all over the

301

news. Some were crying racism, others feared random gang attacks. One particularly opinionated individual quoted the attack to justify his assertion that all police officers should be white, eliminating any potential racially fuelled violence.

My lover claimed he couldn't remember his attackers; he filed a statement that said his assailants had hit him from behind and the rest happened when he was unconscious.

He was lying. He was protecting me.

And it was all my fault.

I can only hope that the passage of time has made this easier to hear.

Because it certainly hasn't made it any easier to remember.

Love, Mum.

16

Then

Summer had arrived in full. Dry mornings, lingering afternoons. Grapes fattened beneath the sun's rays. Jenna paid no attention.

Henry clutched Jenna's hand and precariously navigated the three steps from the deck to the driveway. On the last step, he stumbled. Jenna observed his hands thrust outwards, his fall onto the gravel. His head bounced forwards, fluffy blond hair falling over his face. Almost instantly he began to cry.

Jenna bit back her irritation. Her bladder was full and urgent; she glanced at her watch. One hour. One hour and the doctors would have their ultrasound results and she'd be ready for the final step. She sighed as she knelt and hooked her hands beneath Henry's arms, picking him upright. He stopped crying, looked at her with tear-streaked cheeks, then turned away to continue stumbling on without her. She stood and dug in her handbag for her keys.

'Car, Mumma,' she heard Henry say.

'Hang on,' she called. 'I'll be there in a sec.'

'Car, Mumma. Car.'

'Yeah, yeah.' Searching through the mess of receipts, washcloths, a disposable nappy and the odd stuffed toy – wishing there was a way to do this without Henry.

'Car, car, car!'

'Just wait, Henry,' she snapped. Where the hell were her keys? Kneeling again, she began taking items from her bag: purse, notepad, a toy giraffe.

'Car!' Henry screamed. 'Car! Car! *Car!*'

'What, Henry?' Jenna cried, finally looking up. '*What?*'

Alongside the shed that housed Ark's Mercedes and LandCruiser, the tidy patch of mowed lawn with the well-worn wheel ruts was bare.

Her car was gone.

The police officer said there was little they could do. No witnesses, no other theft, no evidence. The uniformed young man was polite, but resigned and efficient.

After the police officer left and she heard Ark's car

in the driveway, she looked at her watch and saw where she was supposed to be. In Mount Gambier, at the ultrasound. She'd missed it. Now she'd have to make another appointment; more waiting, more planning. Racing to the bathroom, Jenna locked herself inside and wept with fury.

Leaving the door ajar, Jenna crept from Henry's room and padded into the kitchen. Black blocks of night filled the windows.

Ark had returned. He was sitting at the dining table sipping a cup of coffee, finger swiping absentmindedly across the iPad screen. When she sat across from him he looked up.

'I found it,' he said.

Jenna's eyes widened. 'Where?'

He reclined in his chair. 'Mulligans Road, up near Burke Swamp.'

Jenna frowned. 'Where?'

'Behind Wynns Estate. Not that far.' He slurped his coffee.

Jenna made to stand. 'Great. Let's get it. Did you call the police?'

'It's gone, Jenna,' he said. 'Burnt out.'

Jenna felt the breath leave her body. 'What?'

'Your car – there's nothing left of it. It's burnt completely to the ground.'

305

They went in the morning.

Mulligans Road was a rutted dirt track bordered by waist-high bracken between two sagging, rusted barbed-wire fences. On one side a vast irrigated pasture swept towards the horizon, dairy cattle were black and white dots in the distance. On the other side a verdant lucerne plantation rolled in the breeze.

What remained of Jenna's car slumped in the centre of a charred circle on the edge of the track. The surrounding weeds and grass had been burned away. A million fragments of glass glinted in the dirt around the blackened metal shell – the windows blown out by the heat. Rubber hung in melted black tongues across bare wheel rims and the car's belly squatted on the dirt. Inside, a tangled mess of wiring hung from beneath what was left of the dash and the hood-lining dangled in shreds.

Chips of charcoal ticked and sifted from the metal as the breeze undulated across the lucerne and swirled through the burnt-out hollow of her car. And as that same breeze pressed against her ankles, her wrists, her face, it carried a smell that wouldn't ever leave her: an acrid, repulsive smell of blackened rubber, of scorched metal, of white-hot destruction.

Jenna turned and was sick into the bracken.

Jenna stared at Ark through the steam from her coffee. His jaw worked slowly as he chewed, his gaze on the iPad screen, a strip of bacon in his hand.

'I don't understand,' Jenna said. 'If the insurance payout has come through, why can't we use it to buy a new car?'

'Because, babe, we don't need another car.' He smiled at her, reaching across to pat her hand. 'We already have two. Most families manage perfectly fine with only *one* vehicle – three is just ridiculous. The only thing we need to replace is Henry's car seat. Careful, Henry,' he added as the toddler slopped milk and cereal onto the tabletop.

'But . . . it was *my* car. Now I don't have one.'

Ark leaned to save Henry's bowl from tipping to the floor as he chased it across the table with his spoon. 'Like I said, you don't need one all of your own.'

'So I'll just drive the Merc?'

Ark stopped chewing, took a sip of his coffee; the cup made a *plonk* sound as he set it back on the table.

'Actually, I'm going to sell the Mercedes. It's an extravagance we don't need.'

'And replace it with . . . ?'

'Nothing.'

'Leaving us with only the LandCruiser?'

'Sure. It's reliable, cheap to run.'

'But it's a ute.'

'Exactly. It's functional.'

Jenna looked at him. 'It only has two seats. Where will we put Henry? In the back? With the hay?'

'There's no need to be argumentative,' he said. 'It's a bench seat. Child seats can legally be installed on a bench seat if there's no passenger airbag.' He smiled.

Her foot began to tap on the floor. How would she get to the clinic in Mount Gambier without Ark finding out? 'It's your work car,' she pointed out. 'What if I need to go somewhere while you're not here?'

'Where would you need to go?' he asked dubiously, like she'd suggested she needed transport to the moon. 'We'd work it out. Like all those other families do. Don't obsess about it – you know how you get.'

Henry let out a wail as his bowl tumbled from the table and crashed onto the floor. Milk and wheat flakes splattered an asterisk upon the tiles. Furious, he flung his spoon and it bounced across the table and clattered against the far cabinet.

Ark stood, leaving his plate and coffee mug on the table. 'You don't need to go anywhere, honey,' he told her lightly. 'You've got plenty to do right here.' He kissed the top of her head, his thumb brushing her collarbone. 'I'm sure we'll work out how to share just fine. I'll be home around seven. Make something nice for dinner, maybe that chicken saltimbocca? Text me if you need ingredients, I can pick them up while I'm in town.'

He left.

For a long while, Jenna sat at the table. Unmoving, she stared out the window, her gaze roaming the lush lawn that swept away to the gum trees, to the quilted rows of vines stretching towards the thin ribbon of highway in the distance. Even walking down the drive to the highway tired her out, let alone the six-kilometre walk into Penola. And even then – what? Call a taxi to Mount Gambier? There's a two-hundred-dollar round trip that would demand explanation. Wait for the once-daily Stateliner bus to Adelaide?

She could call Fairlie.

The thought ripped through her. No, she could never see Fairlie again. She remembered the horrified look of judgement on Fairlie's face: her insistence that Jenna not leave her son, her contempt that Jenna could even contemplate such atrocity. No. Like Ark's mother had abandoned him when he needed her protection from his father, like Fairlie's birth mother had abandoned Fairlie when she was a helpless infant, Jenna too must fall prey to the unthinkable. Severed ties, the rupture of lifelong bonds.

This was her punishment.

Jenna dug her phone from her pocket, thumbs uneasy as she pressed in the letters of the text message. Before she could change her mind, she hit *send*. Chewing her thumbnail, she stared at the screen, telling herself it had been too long.

But it was only a matter of moments before the phone lit up and buzzed in her hand. Jenna's heart kicked up into her throat.

Jenna. R U OK?

She hesitated, her mouth dry. Then she replied: *NO*

The starburst of cereal remained on the floor for three days. At first she left it there, unmopped in a kind of protest, but in the end it was nothing more than a hardened, gluey mess that she bruised her knees scrubbing away.

It was one of those dreams where a thread of lucidity crept in to remind her that she was dreaming. But rather than bring comfort, all it did was make her dream more difficult – because she knew she was asleep, but she couldn't wake herself up.

Jenna was groping her way through an old house. The mould-dampened ceilings were warped, the floor swayed and the walls juddered dangerously as she dashed from room to room, searching for an exit. She didn't know what floor she was on, only that she was a long way from the ground. At any moment the house would come crashing down upon her, burying her in a pile of plaster and timber beams, asbestos cladding sending lethal shreds into the air to ensure no one would search for her. In her dream she cried out as hands grabbed at her, dragging her into a darkened room off a narrow hallway.

Disoriented, Jenna fought to catch her breath, realising only too late that she was awake. Ark was on top of her, grappling at her skin. Jenna shoved at him, but he grabbed her hands and pinned them above her head.

'Ark, no.' She whipped her head to one side. She said it again, *no*. Didn't she? He muttered something unintelligible, a dark laugh in her ear. Twisting her hips, she tried to move out from beneath him but he pinned her with his weight, forcing her legs apart with his knees. Panic surged through her. She opened her mouth to scream – but what would be the point? There was no one to hear her. A scream would only wake Henry, and it wouldn't stop Ark.

'Keep still, babe,' Ark growled. 'You'll make it hurt.'

'No,' she whispered. 'Please no, Ark.' This couldn't be real. She must be dreaming.

'All right then, if that's the way you want to play it.' He laughed again. It took him two rough, searing thrusts to force himself inside her, and she knew he was right. It would only hurt more.

So she let it happen. Although that might hurt more later, right now, she needed to do everything she could to keep from screaming.

Because there was no one to hear her cry.

⚬━━O

The man at the door didn't have a neck and he was completely bald. Not through age, but through a razor. He was dressed in head-to-toe black: polished black boots, black suit pants. A leather jacket was unzipped and open over a black open-collared shirt, its buttons straining across a substantial torso. A fine dusting of blondish hairs covered the backs of chunky hands. Gold rings adorned several fingers.

'Hello, Mrs Rudolph,' he said, sliding opaque sunglasses to the top of his head. The smile he gave her undressed her. He didn't wait for an invitation, he just stepped inside. With one hand she gathered her shirt closed over her neck.

'Can I help you?'

'Not at all, Mrs Rudolph,' he said, strolling into the living room, gazing at the furniture like a fine art dealer. 'I know Ark's out. I've just come to chat about the shipment he owes me.'

'Are you a buyer?'

'Something like that.' His smile broadened and he swept the length of her languidly with his gaze. 'Where's Henry?'

Her mouth went dry. 'I'm sorry I can't help you. Why don't you come back this afternoon when Ark's home?'

The man stepped closer. He gave off a strong scent of cigarette smoke and something else, furtively sexual, like women's perfume and new cars. Again his gaze dropped to take her in, lingering where her hips pressed into her pants.

'Please tell him he's three weeks late. I have buyers of my own who don't like waiting. If he can't supply the stock, we're open to negotiating a loan of some other ...

goods ... while we wait.' He lifted a lock of her hair from her neck and tugged it gently, before smoothing it down over her breast.

Jenna jerked away from his touch.

'I'll see myself out. Have a nice day, Mrs Rudolph.' Laughing, the bald man replaced his sunglasses and walked from the room. The front door clicked behind him.

Bent low over her phone screen, Jenna's thumbs worked hesitantly. *Send.*

A few moments later, the phone vibrated silently in her hand with a reply. Back and forth messages went; she imagined their words spinning stealthily through the atmosphere until they spelled out their humiliating message at the other end. Could she trust the recipient? No, she could not. That had been made abundantly clear. She couldn't trust *anyone*. Human egos were simply too powerful.

But she didn't have anything else.

In an hour or so, when the conversation was over, she would delete the entire thread. She had to do this right.

Jenna pushed pasta around on her plate, arranging and rearranging it into meaningless shapes.

Ark had been only fleetingly concerned about the frightening visit and strange threats from his bald-headed buyer. *Forget it*, he'd said when he came home that afternoon, dismissing her alarm with a wave of his hand. *Just a friend playing a joke.* Instead, Ark was excited. His voice carried that energised and emphatic timbre he used when plans for the business smacked along at a rate with which she could barely keep up. Enthusiasms of *us* and *our family* and *our future*. Pride swelled from him so perceptibly she could almost taste it. She *could* taste it – he'd cooked this dinner. This was his olive branch, delivered by way of linguine with a rosé sauce.

Honey, I do it for us. *Here, have a bowl of carbohydrates.*

He would want to fuck her tonight. She knew it with the certainty one knows the sun will sink behind the horizon, and inside she fought desperately against the dread of it.

As she watched his fingers work his fork into a slippery twist of linguine, her skin crawled with the thought of those same fingers pawing at her flesh, later. He opened his mouth wide to take in the food and she gritted her teeth at the fervent press of those lips, that tongue.

Quiet acquiescence was the surest way for it to be over in minimal time. Give in, open her legs, let it happen – swallowing a sleeping tablet that she had stolen from work, so that she could at least fall numb. But that didn't stop her from hating herself for that resignation. The gut-ripping pain of it was almost as strong as the sear of his thrusts. Every single time.

Her self-loathing had swooped to depths lower than she'd imagined possible. Trying to recall the last time she'd felt joy was like trying to imagine what it might be like to sprout wings. She poked at the grey mass of her self-loathing with the skeletal fingertips of her mind and it sank and pitted like oedema. Bottomless.

Jenna pushed her bowl away.

And gave up.

Dear Jenna,

Pattie came to visit. She didn't call beforehand because I'm sure she knew by now that I would cite some pathetic excuse to decline. So she just showed up.

When I opened the door, Pattie said, 'Hey, stranger. It's been a while.'

I told her that time was slipping away from me and I realised that for the first time in months – years, perhaps – I was telling the truth. That was why I hadn't seen her: the ineluctable slip of time, passing around me whilst I hid, cowardly and hoping for . . . what? A miracle?

Following Pattie into the kitchen, I could feel the trepidatious drag of my feet, the nervous dart of my gaze up the stairs. But here was human company, here was the warmth and solicitude of another person – a dear friend – and on that day I was so desperate for her that I thought my heart might burst in my chest, and in that case would it even matter if she found out?

I wanted to tell her the truth that I hid within the hulking solidity of these stone walls. I wanted to weep for my lover, fighting for his life in hospital. As Pattie gathered things for tea, as I sank into a chair with exhaustion sapping my bones, I opened my mouth to speak the words: tentative, stretching, desperate for liberation.

I swear this, Jenna, I was sick with the repression of it.

And yet, despite my desire to confess it all, despite how much I missed my friend, and the companionship and exquisite pleasure that comes with the simple touch and sound of another adult, I couldn't help but look briefly at the clock. Still, that familiar clench of anxiety beneath my ribs, the thin edge of panic that rushed in every time someone came to the door.

Whilst I, for months, had tried to conceal the colossal mess of my life, Pattie undoubtedly had worried what she had done wrong to cause this distance between us. Of course the lapse of the months had widened our gap – but everywhere I turned there was nothing but these walls. What could I have done?

Pattie asked when I was to return to work. When I answered that Jack had extended my leave, Pattie raised her eyebrows, but said nothing.

Finally, I said, 'Are you okay?'

With a sigh, Pattie lowered her teacup, her fingers tracing the rim. Her lips drew into a line, and then began to quiver.

'No,' she answered at length. She couldn't look at me as she said, 'I was pregnant.'

Was. Past tense. It felt like a bullet. And even before she said it, I knew.

'I miscarried. At ten weeks.'

As she wept, I held her and I held her. The breaking of my heart was surely so loud that it caused the ripples spreading in the top of my tea. But when I dropped my face, I saw it was the steady drip-drip of my own tears.

Love, Mum.

317

17

Now

The stately limestone home, unchanged for a century but for fresh paint and the constantly morphing garden sprawled around it, is set back slightly from the road, nestled into the side of the hill that swells the southern end of Bay Road as it rises onto the lip of the crater lake.

Fairlie feels nothing as she pulls into the gravel drive, the tyres crunching as she gazes up at the house that has been like a second home to her for almost her entire life. Inside, she will smell the familiar scent of stone and memories, a century of life whispering from the walls adorned with so many photographs of Jenna.

But when she finally steps from her car, and slams the door, and hears the birds twittering in the wattle where she knows she will find a littering of rusted, forgotten Matchbox cars if she digs in the steel-coloured sand at its shallow roots, she feels a surge of nervous anger in her chest. When she swallows, it tastes coppery.

At the top step, the front door is open.

For a moment the two women stare at each other. Fairlie takes in the face of Evelyn Francis, once almost as familiar as her own mother's, now framed with silvering hair tucked behind an elegant neck. Red knitted cardigan drawn tight across narrow shoulders, bird-like arms. The rise of proud cheekbones, the confident jut of a slender chin. Evelyn is a projection of intelligence, of shrewdness, but there's a disguised depth to her gaze and a filtered note in her voice suggestive of a hidden backlight, an inner glow. All of this is carefully controlled, perfectly balanced. Fairlie realises she has never considered Evelyn as flawed or fallible or capable of mistakes in any way.

Sweet Jesus, Fairlie thinks, how things change in a heartbeat. Is this what happened to Jenna four years ago? Is this how she had felt – as though the earth had begun to spin backwards?

'Fro Winter,' Evelyn says. Her voice is unchanged, and as its calm, assertive melody drifts across the verandah, something inside Fairlie jolts.

'Evvie,' she says.

Evelyn watches her. 'It's okay,' she says with a dry smile. 'I know it's been a while, but loyalties lie where they will.

So,' she says, her spine lengthening. 'You're here. Come in.'

The hallway is dimly lit. Slate tiles covered with a Persian hall-runner of maroons and ochres, worn dull with footfalls. There, a few steps in from the door, is the small scorch mark that Jenna had made with a dropped candle when she was ten years old.

'I'd like to say "what brings you here", but it sounds boringly clichéd, don't you think?' the older woman says as they enter the kitchen.

Fairlie doesn't know how to respond.

'There's no need to stand there like a visitor.' Evelyn gestures to the table, bare apart from a pair of knitting needles and a ball of red yarn, what looks like a half-finished scarf.

'Can I offer you tea?'

Nausea washes over Fairlie and she feels at once exhausted and beyond frustrated. *Sure, I'd love some tea. By the way, Jenna killed herself and left me a note and lo and behold we're actually twin sisters. Which means you're my mother. What the actual fuck? But an Earl Grey would be ace.*

'Sure,' Fairlie croaks. 'Tea. Super.'

Evelyn fills the kettle; glasses clink in the sink with the sound of rushing water and it's all maddening to Fairlie. She finds herself looking at the photographs atop an antique buffet running the length of the far wall. A dozen small, framed images aim towards the centre of the room. One is a photograph of Jenna as a toddler, grinning widely, her chubby cheeks flushed pink as she holds her hands together under her chin, cupped around a pink camellia bloom. In another photograph, Jenna is older, in her late teens, her arm slung casually around Fairlie's shoulder. Their faces are close to the camera, both smiling with the blithe indulgence of adolescence.

Everything is different. Everything. Oh, my God.

There is a picture of Henry as a newborn. But it isn't a photograph – it's a clipping from *The Border Watch*. The local paper had run a short story after Henry's birth on the success of a regional vigneron, now starting a family. ARKACRES CELEBRATES NEW DROP, the cheesy headline read.

Evelyn sets a teapot on the table and sits down, lacing thin fingers beneath her chin. 'So,' she says.

Fairlie picks up her cup. It's empty. She sets it back down. A pause bloats between them, heavy and electric. Fairlie says, 'Jenna left me a note.'

Evelyn watches her, says nothing.

'There was a key with the note.'

Evelyn pours tea; Fairlie's first, then her own. Perfectly composed, she asks, 'A note? What does it say?'

Fairlie watches the curlicues of steam from her cup. 'The key is to a self-storage unit, just up on Bay Road. It's a budget, dodgy place,' she adds, as though that somehow matters.

Evelyn blanches. She reaches for her cup but her fingers tremble and tea sloshes into the saucer. She blots it up with a tissue.

'You know what?' Fairlie says, brightly. 'Excuse me a sec. I'll be right back.' She slides from her chair and hurries down the hall, out into the afternoon. A clammy, lukewarm breeze pushes her hair around her face as she strides to the car.

Clutching Jenna's *She's Apples* box to her chest, she returns to Evelyn, who waits serenely in the kitchen.

'Here.' Fairlie drops the box on the bench. It *thunks* onto the laminex with the harsh, undeniable snap of a bomb bay door dropping open. Everything surrounding it would be altered. Evelyn stares into the box, her hands clasped at her chest.

'I suppose there's some things,' Fairlie says, her tone loaded, 'that we need to discuss.' One by one she lifts the items out: jewellery box, folder of birth certificates, the A4 envelope as yet unopened by Fairlie.

Propping her hands on the countertop, Fairlie fixes Evelyn with a hard stare. There isn't anything more she needs to say.

Just like Fairlie did, Evelyn first picks up the jewellery box. She opens it and falls still.

Briefly, Evelyn's shoulders hitch. With the tips of her fingers she strokes the ankle bands; the demonstration is exquisitely tender, as though the bands are made of delicate silk threads.

'Well,' she says softly. 'I suppose now you know.'

'Now I know?' Fairlie fumes. 'Know what, exactly? Evelyn, is this legit?' Fairlie snatches up the manila folder and waves the birth certificates in the older woman's startled face. 'Because if it means what I think it means . . .' She can't finish.

'Fro, I'm so sorry you had to find out this way.' Evelyn gathers the identity bands into one hand and shows them to Fairlie on an extended palm. 'Two of these were Jenna's.'

So it's true. It's true. And Fairlie can't bear it.

'And the other two . . .'

'They're yours.'

The whiskey burns away the lump in Fairlie's throat. They've moved into the lounge room. Abandoned the tea. A bottle of Johnnie Walker Blue sits on the coffee table. Fairlie grips an empty tumbler and stares at the bottle.

Evelyn glances at her hands. 'It should never have gotten to this,' she says. 'If I had known she was struggling so much . . .' Jenna's mother closes her eyes, coming as close to tears as Fairlie has ever seen her. 'Oh, Jenna. Henry. I'm sorry.'

Fairlie swills her drink. 'All these years,' she says, not quite trusting the sound of her voice. 'All these years and no one said a thing.' It doesn't sink in, floating like oily murk on a pool of water. 'Those birth certificates – they're actually *real*? You're my . . . and I'm your . . .'

Evelyn nods. 'And Jenna is your sister. Your twin.'

'But ...' In her mind's eye Fairlie conjures Jenna: milky-skinned, lithe and gangly, impossibly round blue eyes behind that straight dark fringe; and then Fairlie looks down at her own bare arms, her corpulence deflating into the couch, nutty-brown skin and thick fingers. She pats the explosion of curls atop her head. A memory of the two of them as teenagers skims across her mind: Jenna striking poses in shop windows, Fairlie admiring Jenna's reflection while consciously avoiding her own.

'How?' Fairlie says weakly.

'You read that article,' Evelyn says. 'About mixed race twins.'

'I did. But I don't understand.'

'Well.' Evelyn drops her eyes, clears her throat. 'When two eggs are released, and two different men –'

'I understand the mechanics, Evvie,' Fairlie breaks in, holding up a palm. 'I just don't understand anything *else*. How. The situation.' Her jaw aches. 'My mother – what about my mother? I assume she knows?'

Evelyn nods. 'Yes. Of course she does.'

Fairlie opens her mouth, closes it again.

'I tried,' Evelyn says softly. 'I tried so hard. For six months. I was desperate to make it work.'

'But it didn't.'

'No.' Evelyn looks at the bottle on the coffee table. 'It didn't.'

'Bloody hell.' Fairlie takes a drink, winces, sloshes in

324

more whiskey. 'Bloody hell.' She huffs out a long, trembling breath. 'All right then. You'd better tell me what happened. And I mean all of it. You've got twenty-six years worth of explaining to do, Evelyn. I want to know. You owe it to me. And you owe it to Jenna.'

So Evelyn begins to talk.

Dear Jenna,

On the night it would all change, I slurred awake to a velvety black and the sound of the wind howling at the window panes. There was a snap of lightning, the crash of thunder, the shudder of the glass and then — your shrieks carried into the room.

My body felt swampy and leaden as I sat up. What time was it? Almost 3 am. Only ninety minutes ago, I'd been up attending to you. Again. Alongside me, Stephen muttered something incoherent and I stifled a broad wave of resentment as the temporary, sleep-induced blindness slunk off and reality came rushing back: hurt. Exile. Pattie. Him. In hospital, pumped full of painkillers and antibiotics as his body lay bruised and torn, his bones broken, all because of my selfishness, my lust and greed and petulant inability to understand reality.

The years-long depth of Pattie's suffering, alone and in silence, as her longing to create life dripped from between her legs month after month in bloody waste.

And here: me. Crippling shame.

I was tired. I was tired of waiting for Stephen to hate me, and I exhausted myself waiting to hate him. Because I couldn't, Jenna — I didn't hate him. Instead, I loved him and it shackled me. Sleep deprived, yes; tired of running alone after the babies all day, yes; but most unbearably I was tired of upholding all the lies, tired of using the walls of my house to hold off the weight of the world.

In the nursery, I lifted you from the cot but you refused

to be placated; you stiffened in my arms, face screwed into a furious knot. I pulled aside my gown but you turned away, little beast, refusing the comfort of my breast.

A whimper sounded from the other cot. I stilled, my attention refocusing. The other whimper grew, rolling into a cry, and as a shower of rain rushed against the windows, both of you yelped in tandem. The urgent, impatient sound of it threw spikes along my nerves.

'Please,' I moaned.

You babies cried on. I hiked you higher onto my hip and reached into the second cot with my free hand. I hefted her onto my other hip and your concerto cries whistled into my ears and rattled my brain.

The rain drummed on the walls of the house, its roar the accusation of thousands of lips; the charge was clear and it cut to my marrow: they knew. Everyone knew. They would always know who I was – that I was no one, really, just another set of lungs sucking the air and another body to warm a man's bed.

I felt the sobs of my babies rack my body, I let your cries pummel my heart into a fleshy pulp. My knees crumpled under the weight of my own shame, the realisation of my own selfish idiocy.

Stephen was devastated. My lover could die. Pattie was driven to despair.

Jenna, I saw it so clearly right then: this would never work.

I only became aware of my own cries when Stephen was

a sudden silhouette in the doorway. Three strides across the room and he was beside me, on his own knees, his face a mask of misery in the flashing light.

Automatically he put his hands out, as though to comfort us, but I saw him freeze, I saw his expression twist with anguish as he restrained himself, lowering his hands back to his sides. He looked away.

I was alone. I was so brutally alone, my arms weighted with the consequences of my own humanness. 'Please, take her,' I begged.

Stephen's eyes shot from child to child, finally resting his gaze on me.

'I can't,' he said. 'I just can't.'

And as you girls cried on, my own sobs cut like knives in my throat, and I knew then what I had to do. I had to leap. I felt like I'd been stalked to a cliff's edge by wolves. You may think I had a choice, but it was leap and maybe survive, or face the pack and be torn apart.

So, here's what happened.

My rap on the door was loud and harsh, and the baby jumped in my arms. But I bent my head, whispering into the blanketed bundle, and the child stilled, as she always did – so easily placated, so trusting.

Rain sluiced my face, dripped from my hair. I hammered on the door again, harder, gripping the child in my arm.

Pattie came to the door in her nightgown, her voice high with alarm. She dragged me in out of the storm.

'It's the middle of the night,' Pattie cried. 'It's pouring.

What on earth are you doing here?' Then her voice faded. 'Who is . . . that?'

I extended my arms, and was surprised at how easily they floated to my dear friend, as though buoyed on the air. I said: 'You have to help me.'

'You mean,' Pattie's voice snapped tight, 'it's yours?'

I nodded.

'And Jenna is . . . ?'

'Her twin sister.'

Pattie staggered backwards. 'You had twins?'

'Yes.'

'But . . . ' She looked panicked, her eyes darting between me and the child. 'How can she be . . . How?'

'It's possible.' I whispered it.

Pattie's body was rigid, her hands clenched and unclenched at her sides. Then, she closed her eyes and when she opened them again, there was something new there. One door closed, but another opened.

I held firm, against the myriad bewildered accusations Pattie flung at me, against the gut-wrenching rip of my every muscle fibre, yanking me away, out the door, begging me to return home with our baby.

'What do you need from me?' Pattie croaked.

'I need you to take her.' Finally, my voice cracked. 'I can't do this anymore, Pat. Please take her so I can make it all go back to the way it was. To the way it's supposed to be. Not like this anymore.' I was weeping now, tears falling onto the blanket wrapping my sweet, sweet baby.

And as my bones gave way, and I sank to the floor, my child was lifted from my arms and the emptiness flayed me open.

Before I hit the floor, I prayed. And I told Pattie: 'Her name is Fairlie.'

And now you know.

Love, Mum.

18

Then

Jenna stood in the centre of the living room, staring down at her bare feet on the plush carpet. She wriggled her toes and watched them sink into the soft wool, but she didn't feel it; they looked like someone else's toes, in someone else's house.

A cloud of bright sunlight streamed through the bay windows and glossed the polish of the piano, warmed the leather couch. Henry was lying on his belly on the floor, kicking his feet to The Wiggles on TV.

But Jenna was cold. And as she stared down at her pale toes she realised she had forgotten who she was. Who was this person, standing in this room, watching ambivalently over this child? A living-dead creature shuffling from one room to another. What motivated her? What maintained her? She couldn't remember the last time she had laughed. And she realised she didn't care. Images came to her in lazy flashes: Ark, a random midnight years ago while the rain hammered on the roof, standing in the pool of light from the open fridge and laughing with her as they'd taken bites of mint chocolate straight from the block. He had wrapped his strong arms around her and she'd thought she would never fall. The heat of his body, the earthy smell of his skin. There had been a time when Ark's love for her had seemed so certain, so completely flawless, so forsaking that she'd wondered if she was dreaming.

The image of this unconditional midnight embrace engrossed her until she was roused by movement in the doorway. Ark trudged into the living room. Exasperation heaved from him in a sigh and Jenna followed his gaze to Henry's mess: Lego strewn in a wide half-circle, chewed crescents of apple skin scattered from an upturned plastic bowl.

Ark turned on Jenna with a scowl, leaving the beginning of his sentence unsaid as he gestured at the floor. 'And you're just standing there?'

Jenna's fingernails cut into her palms. She said, 'I want to separate.'

Ark flopped onto the couch and kicked off his shoes. Henry jumped up and toddled to his father, launching into an immediate babbling rhetoric about the dead grasshopper on the back step.

'Separate?' Ark picked up the television remote, aimed, and The Wiggles flicked into an image of prawns sizzling on a hotplate. 'Separate what?'

'Us. I would like for us to separate.' The cliché sounded so frail it might dissolve in the bright beams of sunlight.

'This again.' Ark rolled his eyes. 'Whatever, Jenna.'

'I'm serious.'

He turned up the volume. 'You've probably got your period. You say this every month. Go take a couple of Panadol and lie down.' Henry was trying to take the remote control from Ark's hands, demanding the return of his television show. Ark feigned defeat against Henry's strength, animatedly giving up the remote. Henry crowed, clambering over his father's body.

Jenna grimaced. 'I mean it this time.'

He looked at her sideways; the sudden flash of his attention skittered her nerves. Henry tugged at his hands.

'Jenna, give it a rest. You don't want to leave – I know you don't. And to be honest, I'm getting pretty sick of this conversation.' He flung an arm across the back of the couch and regarded her with narrowed eyes. 'We've been through this. You have nowhere to go.'

She had his attention. 'I'll get my job back. Then I'll get my own place.' She left out the hidden truth growing inside of her, resisting the urge to dig a thumb beneath her pubic bone.

'All right, buddy,' Ark said to Henry, 'Daddy's gotta talk to Mummy for a sec, okay? Go watch your show.'

Jenna went on. 'I'll start packing –'

'Jenna, cut it out.'

'You can't stop me.'

Something changed; a shadow stole across his features. 'I hope you're joking,' Ark said quietly, 'because if you're not,' he leant forwards and began to tap his fingers on his knees, 'we have a real problem.'

Jenna lifted her chin. 'I'm not joking.'

'Why?'

'Do you even have to ask?' Jenna said. 'Because I'm not happy. *We're* not happy.'

Henry approached Jenna and began to whine. She ignored him. 'This isn't working, Ark. I'm miserable. You're . . . ' How could she say it? He was abusing her? He was *raping* her?

She was pregnant again, and it was impossible?

'I'm not making you happy – I'm not living up to your standards. This isn't working anymore.' It all sounded pathetic.

Calmly, Ark stood up, picked the remote from the floor and turned off the TV. The room plunged into silence, punctuated by the sounds of Henry's plaintive requests to go outside and look at the dead grasshopper. Jenna forced herself to hold Ark's gaze.

'Who is he?' His voice was like steel.

'Who is who?'

'Don't act dumb,' Ark said. 'You're obviously fucking someone. I'm asking you who he is.'

Jenna wailed and dropped her face into her hands. And then, right there, she knew she could never tell him about the impossible pregnancy because she could already hear his accusations: the nasty, vile, abhorrent charges that would rain upon her like exploded glass.

He advanced on her so quickly she took two steps back.

'You can forget it,' he said. 'We belong together, you and me. You selfish bitch – have you forgotten everything I've done for you? Everything I've given you? My grandmother *died* to leave me this place, I've *given* it to you, and you want to walk away?' His voice cracked and he grabbed her hands. Henry began to cry. 'And you expect me to believe it's because you've changed your mind or some shit?' He wouldn't release her hands, despite her tugging to get to Henry. '*Who is he?*'

'Ark, you rape me,' she finally blurted, hot pressure between her legs as she fought an urge to urinate. 'You've treated me like shit for years. I can't stay here.'

Ark recoiled as though she had slapped him.

'Rape you?' He frowned. 'I'm your husband. You think wives aren't supposed to fuck their husbands?' He gave a short laugh. His face crumpled. 'Babe, listen to what you're saying.' He released her hands and turned his back.

Jenna sank to her knees and allowed Henry into her arms, forming a shield for them both. For a time, the room was filled with Henry's hiccups and Jenna's murmured assurances. When Ark finally faced her again, he was a restored picture of composure.

'Nothing has happened that you didn't want,' he said. 'I know what you like. You were always up for that kind of play.' He smiled. 'Do you think anyone will believe you, babe? It's my word against yours.'

'Look, I just want to leave, Ark. I don't intend to tell anyone –'

'I've seen *all* of you, every little deep and dark place.'

'I just want some space. Some time to think.'

'There are parts of you that I know like the back of my hand – that *no one else* will ever see or touch.'

'I need to go.' Jenna closed her eyes against him. 'Please.'

'You're not going anywhere.'

He had moved so close, towering above her, that she could smell the laundry powder from his jeans. When Henry began to whimper again, Ark joined them on his knees.

'And how do you think you'll get where you need to go?' He laughed again. 'What do you think,' he said after a pause, 'really happened to your car?' He was smiling at Henry and the child grinned in return.

Jenna's bowels twisted. 'You did it?'

'Mmm-hmm,' he said it slowly, like he was humming.

'Oh,' was all she could manage. *My car. He burnt my car.* Of course, it was right after they'd argued about her returning to work at the hospital – the day she'd missed the ultrasound she was legally required to withstand, first.

She had no control. There was nothing left of her but a hollow, repulsive shell; nothing but an obscenely beating heart, a blood supply, hot flesh for someone else. Her life was a farce.

'Hey little buddy,' Ark said warmly to Henry. 'You love your mama?'

'Ark –' It came out like a weak groan.

'Guess what?' he said brightly, fake. 'She wants to leave. She wants some *space*.'

'Don't,' Jenna said. 'He's too young.'

Henry, confused by Ark's disingenuous sing-song voice, frowned and reached for his mother, but Ark took him up under his arms and stood, pulling Henry away. Henry launched into a loud wail.

'You want to leave?' Ark raised his voice over Henry's cries. 'Fine. Go right ahead. But he stays here.'

Jenna thought she might dissolve. Another child torn from their mother.

'Off you go then,' Ark continued. 'But remember this: no one will believe you. I will take you to court and tell everyone you're crazy. I'll show them your health records. He will be mine. And one day, who knows . . . ' He clucked his tongue. 'You might never see him again.'

On her knees, Jenna begged, 'It doesn't need to be like that –'

Henry's cries escalated, his face red and his arms stretched desperately towards his mother. Ark took a step forwards but kept Henry out of her reach.

'Fathers have rights now, Jenna. I'll never give up. My family has money – you don't even *have* a family anymore. I'll throw tens of thousands into this. I know court psychologists, I know cops. You will get nothing. One day, he will disappear.'

Jenna's limbs trembled. 'Please. It doesn't have to be a big deal.'

He stepped closer to her, his boots under her nose. There was dried grass stuck to the laces.

'Face it, babe,' he said, holding Henry screaming above her head. 'As long as you're on this earth, you're mine.' He lowered Henry a fraction further, and then dropped him into her lap. The child landed with a thud, startled from his crying for a moment, and then he bawled even louder.

Ark strode from the room.

Jenna held Henry on her lap and felt her eyes glaze over, her breath scrape back and forth across the roof of her mouth. He was right. She could never leave.

Henry's skin was hot beneath her fingers, his body stiff and indignant. When had his limbs grown so long? He wasn't a baby anymore. Another mother and child, living yet estranged. Could she cope with that? A lifetime of Henry shuttled back and forth, in and out of court – never having a real home, real roots? At one time they had shared a body, would she forsake him now? Rip him loose like a wild animal caught in a trap might gnaw off its own limb rather than face capture?

338

Ark's final words rang through her mind: *As long as you're on this earth, you're mine.*

Gently, Jenna lifted Henry from her lap and set him on the carpet. Then she rammed her fist into the soft space between her hips.

And then, with the blinding flare of pain, the solution came to her.

19

Now

'I was enamoured with Stephen Walker,' Evelyn says, 'from the first moment I met him.'

'I've already heard this story,' Fairlie breaks in. 'The supermarket thing?'

Evelyn gives a far away smile. 'My trolley had become wedged on the kerb, and he helped me haul it back onto the footpath.'

'How quaint.'

'Isn't it?' Evelyn either doesn't notice Fairlie's sarcasm or chooses to ignore it. 'In the beginning, it was an endless stream of dinner parties, weekends in Adelaide or Melbourne and gilt-edged occasions. He was such a successful, older man!'

'Is this going to take long?' Fairlie refills her glass.

'Stephen Walker offered me a place in upper-middle-class normalcy – where people I had never met knew my name. We just were, Fro. In this small town, we were *that couple.*'

'Spare me.'

'I know how pathetic and conceited it sounds. But you need to know that I was swept up in being someone.' She wrings her hands in her lap. 'More than just a hippie kid from a Kombi van. No roots, no connections.'

Fairlie glares at her. 'Poor white girl didn't know her heritage?' she snaps. 'How truly awful for you.'

Evelyn has the grace to look ashamed. 'It wasn't about Stephen's money. Never. I know that's what everyone has said, but it wasn't like that. We loved each other. I *always* loved him.'

This, Fairlie knows. As soon as she was old enough to notice, she could see the pain on Evelyn's face at any mention of Jenna's father. Stephen's absence had been normal for them all – but it had never become comfortable for Evelyn.

'And then ...' Evelyn's voice takes on a strained tenor. 'I hadn't intended for ... things with *him* to last. It was just a ...' Fairlie's gut churns as Evelyn searches for the right word, '... a bit of fun. Two people in the moment.'

'Some fun,' Fairlie repeats, robotically.

'I never meant to maintain anything underhanded. I never meant to hurt anyone.' She looks to Fairlie again with a gaze that prickles Fairlie's spine. 'Haven't you ever loved anyone? You can't control it. And the thing is, Fairlie . . . ' Helplessly she spreads her hands. 'I loved him, too. He is a beautiful man with a dear heart.'

Fairlie thinks: *My father. She's talking about my father.*

Jenna's mother (*her* mother, Fairlie corrects herself) recounts the guilt and shame of loving two men in a world that frowns upon such generosity. (At this, Fairlie clenches her teeth and thinks *narcissist* and takes a heavy hit of Johnnie Walker.) The inevitable pregnancy; her struggles to retain the job she adored, and by which she – and the society around her – defined herself. The anxious nine-month wait, unknowing. Deep down, knowing that the answer would be immediately apparent upon her baby's birth because skin colour cannot lie.

'And back then,' Evelyn says, 'we didn't have routine ultrasounds and so on. I had thought all along that I was only having one baby.'

'And it would either be black or white,' Fairlie says.

Evelyn looks up, her expression pained. 'Exactly.' She clenches her fingers together. 'When I went into labour I was terrified.' She closes her eyes. 'But then the baby came out, and she was creamy and pink and shrieking. I was so relieved.'

Nausea washes up Fairlie's throat. 'But it wasn't over.'

'No. It wasn't.'

Because a second baby emerged. A baby no one had

known was there. And Evelyn's secret became hopelessly clear.

That second baby, with her betrayal of dark skin, was her.

Fairlie.

The silence has stretched so long Fairlie cannot remember who last spoke.

'I'm sorry it's taken me so long to come and see you,' Fairlie says, eventually. Slumped into the couch, she has finished her fourth whiskey. So much for her resolution to drink less.

'It's my fault,' Evelyn says. 'I never got in touch with you after she walked out, for the last time.'

'Neither did I though,' Fairlie admits. 'I mean, I know Jen and I are close –' the present tense grabs at her '– but I shouldn't have written you off because she said so.'

Evelyn inclines her head, a half-nod of acknowledgement. 'I went to the funeral,' she says softly.

Fairlie frowns. 'You were there?'

'I stood within a clump of trees at the edge of the cemetery. You had your back to me during the service.'

'You should have come closer,' Fairlie says crossly. 'You're her mother.'

Evelyn lets out a long breath, and the two sit in silence for a time.

'Is that why she was so angry four years ago?' Fairlie asks. 'Because you'd told her about . . . ?' Fairlie sweeps her hands up and down herself.

'Yes.' Evelyn takes a deep breath. 'But she never let me explain. I don't know why, but she just ran out. Shock, I guess.' Evelyn looks desolate.

'So why did you finally decide to tell her, that day? After twenty-two years of lies?'

Overhead the ceiling fan spins lazily. Evelyn's finger-nails make soft scuffing noises on the fabric of her pants. 'I had a health scare,' she said. 'A lump in my breast. It turned out to be nothing. But it was quite the reality check. I suppose you could say I became aware of my own mortality.'

'You weren't aware of that before?'

Despite herself, Evelyn smiles wryly. 'I panicked, real-ising that I'd been taking life for granted. What mattered before suddenly didn't seem to matter so much. So finally I told her the truth.' She goes on to explain her conversation with Jenna that fateful morning.

'I find it hard to believe she never said a word to you,' Evelyn finishes.

'No,' Fairlie says, picking at the hem of her shorts. 'She knew for four years and never said a word. Sure she acted a little different – but she'd met Ark, you know? I thought maybe meeting him . . . and then Henry. I thought,' she shrugs sadly, 'I thought maybe all that was causing the distance between us.'

Evelyn gives a sad sigh. 'All these years. She kept it to herself.' Her eyes go glassy. 'Just like her mother.'

Fairlie fixes her gaze on a spot on the far wall; the spot moves, a fly scuttling across the stone. 'Maybe I didn't know her quite as well as I've always thought I did.'

'People can surprise you,' Evelyn says, without even a hint of irony.

'The day you told her? That night, she met him.'

'I figured as much.'

'She was upset. Vulnerable. Maybe if it weren't for . . . '

'I know.' Barely a whisper.

Fairlie feels a flush of anger. 'I can't believe it. All those years. Fuck.' Her head shoots up. 'This is nuts,' she cries, leaping to her feet. Whiskey slops onto her shoes. Before she can stop herself she's dialling her mother and when Pattie Winter answers, Fairlie hears herself yelling, sobbing down the phone for Pat to *get her arse over here right this minute.*

Light is fading from the sky as Fairlie waits on the front porch. Pattie had promised she'd be right over. One hundred and fourteen steps. Every time Fairlie had walked those one hundred and fourteen steps each one had reinforced a bond that had been kept from them, but that they'd shared anyway.

Her and Jenna. Sisters.

Fairlie touches her hand to her curly hair, her fingers brushing the tip of her nose, the bulge of her hips. Was that why they'd always been so close? Because they shared a womb? Her head hurts. And then she sees her mother striding up the road, skirt flowing in the evening breeze and Fairlie is running across the lawn.

'Is it true?' she pants.

Pattie nods briskly. 'It's true.'

Fairlie's legs sag.

'Let's go inside,' Pattie says. 'It's getting dark and the mozzies are coming out.'

Pattie meets Evelyn's eyes and the two women exchange a long look, a thousand words passing unsaid.

After seating Fairlie on the couch, the two older women disappear into the kitchen. The susurrus of their voices slinks across the carpet like toxic fumes and it infuriates Fairlie. 'Stop with the whispering!' she shouts. 'You have no right to hide anything anymore!' The murmuring stops. Pattie comes through first, Evelyn following with a tray of coffee. 'I don't want coffee,' Fairlie says, petulantly. 'I want answers.'

Evelyn speaks first. 'What do you want to know?'

Fairlie laughs, flinging her hands in the air. 'Where should I start?' She tops up her drink, slamming the bottle onto the coffee table. The other women jump. 'Let's start with *why*.'

Evelyn takes in a shaky breath, lets it out so slowly that Fairlie fights the urge to snap her fingers.

'Fro,' Evelyn begins. 'The first thing I need you to try to understand is that I never wanted any of this to happen.'

Fairlie opens her mouth to retort but Pattie flings her a pleading look, lifts her hands and lowers them gently, as though stroking an imaginary animal. Fairlie closes her mouth.

'I know that's a dismal excuse,' Evelyn continues. 'And I'm aware that I have no right to expect you to understand, or even to forgive me. But if you'll do one thing for me,' she pauses, gathering herself, 'please keep in mind that none of this was my intention. And if I could take it all back I would.

'My reasons are ... well, they sound so trivial on the surface. But I stood to lose everything. It meant you both would have suffered.' Evelyn spreads her hands. 'I had to do something. It was the eighties, and this is a very small town. Conservatives still have the strongest voice, even today. For heaven's sake, we haven't had a Labor member for parliament since –' she glances at Pattie, who only shrugs, '– the seventies? And Stephen and I were ... well.' She smiles ruefully. '*Everyone* knew who we were. They still do. Would you believe I *still* have people at the shops asking me questions about what happened between Stephen and I? Why he left when Jenna was only a little girl?'

Fairlie digs her fingers into her palms. She doesn't give a tiny skidmark about local political history and people in the shops. 'Bullshit!' she cries. 'This is about the colour of my skin. You couldn't fucking hide it. Black people stick out amongst all your white privilege.'

Evelyn shakes her head furiously. 'It's not that.'

'*Balls* –'

'Fairlie,' Pattie scolds. 'Just listen.'

Fairlie bites her tongue until red spots appear in her vision.

'After you were born, I tried. I tried to make it work for months. But we were prisoners inside the house. Eventually, Stephen couldn't cope, and I couldn't cope, and it all began to fall apart.' Evelyn swallows thickly. 'I loved Stephen, and I was committed to him. But that other man?' Her sigh quavers dangerously. 'God, I loved him. But people don't get that – you simply cannot love two people. They don't see that it's possible – all they see is a slut.'

Jenna's mother goes on. 'I loved two men. But because of that I betrayed them both. I betrayed *you* both. Could I have hidden it forever? No. One day the truth would have come out. And I'd hurt *everyone* I loved.' Evelyn presses a hand beneath her nose. 'I couldn't be a good mother to you. You deserved a life – a great life – and this way you could have it. You deserved a good mother. So I found her.' Evelyn finishes, weeping silently. Pattie reaches over to squeeze her hand and Fairlie feels like she's wandered onto the set of a soap opera.

Evelyn continues, 'Watching you grow up, so close ...

There was part of me that was grateful that I never really lost you. But seeing you every day was like rubbing salt in the wounds.'

'You poor thing.' Fairlie's tone drips sarcasm.

'I get it, Fro,' Evelyn sobs angrily. 'You can be mad at me. But watching you every day was an utter joy. I felt so lucky to be a part of your childhood. You grew into this amazing person and it was a . . . ' she searches for the right word, '*gift* for me to even observe that, let alone play such a big part as Jenna's mother. I was your best friend's mother.' She dashes tears from her cheeks. 'It felt like an undeserved mercy. I got to be with you.'

The room goes quiet.

'I was right around the corner for nineteen years, Ev,' Fairlie says at length. 'Why didn't you ever tell us earlier?'

Jenna's mother deliberates, taking her time to answer. 'We wanted to tell you both. But . . . ' A shudder racks her body. 'It was an awful time. Recalling it became more and more traumatic. With each year that passed, the scars just seemed too strong to pick open.'

With her long fingers, Evelyn rubs at a seam on the upholstery; outside on the street an engine revs momentarily and then quietens.

Evelyn says, 'There's something else I haven't told you.'

'Evvie,' Pat warns. 'Maybe that's enough for today.'

'No, it's time.'

349

'Evelyn's right.' Fairlie sits up straighter. 'All out in the open. What happened?'

Pattie grips Evelyn's hand firmly, gives it a fortifying shake. Then Evelyn says, 'They tried to kill him, Fro.'

Then Evelyn looks into Fairlie's eyes and begins to tell her about her father.

20

Then

The elastic bands snapped around the pile of books. Jenna lowered the bundle into the box, then stuffed balls of newspaper to secure them. Long strips of packing tape peeled from the roll with screeching sounds. Wrapping the strips tightly around the whole box, she picked up a marker and wrote on the cardboard.

The sound of the LandCruiser rumbled up the driveway. Hastily, Jenna ripped the last strips of tape between her teeth, securing the flaps down tightly. She fought the urge to hide the box.

Her heart was knocking back and forth as the front door opened and closed, Henry exclaimed 'Dada!' from the lounge room, and Ark strode into the kitchen.

Henry was clutched high on his chest; Ark had one arm slung effortlessly around his small body, veins standing up in his bare forearm. Four years ago, at the pub, it had been the same smile: promising, convivial, almost peaceful, like upward-held palms. Promises. Reassurances.

It was all bullshit. All shattered.

But Jenna smiled back because it eased the fisted knot at her sternum. She masked the tremor in her hands by smoothing the tape down snugly over the box, then busied herself gathering tape and scissors and markers from the table.

'I had an excellent day,' Ark said. He came to kiss her, leaning down to linger over the kiss, Henry giggling and puckering up at his father's cheek. 'Found a dozen pickers easily.' He set Henry down and the toddler immediately fastened himself around Ark's leg. 'What you got there?' He tilted his head to read her handwriting on the cardboard. '"Birth kits"? What are they?'

'Donations,' Jenna answered smoothly, resting her hands on the parcel. 'Women in third world countries give birth in terrible, infectious conditions. A charity is asking for donations – sterile scissors, suture kits, scalpel blades –'

Ark shuddered and turned his face away. 'Okay, that's all I need to know.'

Internally Jenna apologised to women worldwide for using their trauma for her own lies, then said aloud, 'Sorry. Will you take me to town so I can drop these at the post office?'

A pause. Her heart thumped. Then he nodded.

She exhaled. 'So. You found enough pickers?'

'Yes! And even better,' he said, heading for the fridge and dragging a giggling Henry on his leg, 'I'm paying them the same wage as last year.'

Jenna said, 'It's all working out for you.'

'Jen, have you seen any workbooks around?'

Nausea flushed her skin. 'Workbooks?' she asked. 'Like what?'

He came into the lounge room and his whitened face terrified her. 'Spiral-bound notepads with hard covers,' he was saying. 'They're ... really important. Records of stuff. Business things – finances and important dates.'

'No, sorry.' She frowned and tried to look concerned. 'Important?'

'Very,' he said, raking an agitated hand through his hair. 'Eight years worth of records.'

'Shall I help you look?' Jenna held her breath.

He swore quietly. 'No.'

He left the room.

Jenna breathed out.

Two weeks later.

Jenna waited for Ark to emerge from the fridge with his beer and then asked, 'Can we go for a quick drive?'

'Where to?' He flicked the bottle-cap into the sink.

Clearing her throat, she forced herself to casually hold his gaze. 'I want to stop by the cemetery, actually.'

He stiffened. 'Why?'

The lie came out easier than she'd thought. 'It's the anniversary of Jennifer's death – you know, the nurse I used to work with on night shift? I wanted to pay my respects.'

'Oh, I'm sorry to hear that, babe,' he said with genuine sympathy. Of course, Jenna thought sourly, he always had sympathy for everyone else. Maintaining the 'good guy' façade meant adhering to social responsibility – sympathy, kindness, joviality. Being considered by others as anything other than a *great guy* was simply unthinkable. Ark's shoulder hitched. 'Someone you knew well?'

Jenna shook her head. 'Not really. But I wanted to do the right thing, you know?'

'Sure.' He nodded slowly. 'I can't ...' He tore a strip from the label of his beer, looking at her with apology. 'As you know, but ...'

'It's okay.' She took the scrap of label from him and balled it in her fingers. 'I'll only be a minute. You can wait in the car with Henry, perhaps?'

Relief crossed his features, then he made to set his beer on the counter. 'Now?'

'Oh, no,' she said, 'finish your drink.' She flicked the

ball of paper into the sink. 'Did you find those books you were looking for?'

—O

They pulled up at the top of Old Cemetery Road. Ark rolled two wheels onto the knotty grass shoulder, leaving the engine running. When he turned to her, she could see his terror in the set of his jaw.

Ark took hold of her arm.

Leaning across Henry, strapped snugly between them, she kissed her husband's cheek with all the affection she could muster. 'I'll be fast. Are you sure you don't want to take Henry for a milkshake or something?'

'We'll wait here.' He released her arm, leaving clammy impressions of his fingers on her skin.

'Won't be long.' She stepped from the car.

It took her twenty seconds to come into view of the cemetery. Gum trees surrounded summer-drying lawns, a jumble of tilted old headstones amongst newer, shining granite markers with gold engraving. *Rest In Peace; In the arms of Jesus; Much loved and dearly missed.*

Jenna didn't need to glance over her shoulder to know she was out of sight of Ark in the LandCruiser – he wouldn't be in view of the cemetery. He couldn't stand to face such blatant reminders of death: the headstones, the dried and rotting bunches of flowers on coffin-shaped sunken ground. The inevitability of it.

Puffing, she jogged through the main gate, thongs slapping against her heels, clutching her handbag against her chest. She slowed, glancing around. Gravel crunched beneath her feet as she strode up the centre path.

Reaching the middle of the plots, Jenna came to a halt beside a tall marble headstone: a deity of some sort kneeling atop a thick pillar. A warm breeze whispered first through a tall pine tree at the edge of the yard, then swooped and skittered across her feet. Something nudged against her bare toes. Looking down, Jenna saw a faded red silk flower resting against her foot. Stemless with cupped sun-streaked petals, it paused there, pushing softly against her skin, before the breeze plucked it again and sent it tumbling away.

She took an instinctive glance back at the road. The LandCruiser was nowhere in sight.

A stillness surrounded her: the warmth of the sun, the uninhibited chatter of the birds, and the calm nothing-ness of the end of life. The unassuming oblivion of death. There was a peace there, and it felt undemanding and inexorable. Jenna filled her lungs, her head lightening as though she were already moving up and away, out of her body.

Then she turned right, aimed at the side street, and bolted from the graveyard.

The mailbox was only a hundred metres away. Jenna sighted it, red like a homing beacon, and sprinted, her breath rasping, the contents of her handbag jostling against her ribs.

Dropping to her knees on the pavement, she pulled out the battered, almost-filled purple-and-black covered notebook and slipped it inside the envelope she'd already addressed to her mother. A few days ago Evelyn had sent her the message Jenna had been tearing strips from her fingernails awaiting: *Storage unit all sorted.*

Jenna had wept with relief. The evidence would be safer there. Safer than with her mother. What if Ark went looking and confronted her mother? How could she trust Evelyn not to sell her out?

With shaking hands, Jenna pulled out the second envelope. Smaller, letter-sized.

Pulling open the chute, she dropped in first the parcel with the notebook.

Lifting Fairlie's letter to her lips, the key inside slid into the corner. She kissed it, then dropped it tremblingly into the letterbox

21

Now

'Both of his legs?' Fairlie puts her hand over her mouth. Evelyn nods. Tears stream freely down her face. 'He needed one knee reconstructed. But both legs were broken in several places. After they knocked him unconscious, they propped his legs up on the coffee table and jumped on his shins.'

A gutful of whiskey makes a second appearance up Fairlie's throat. Twenty-five years ago, Evelyn is explaining, her lover was violently assaulted in his own house. 'Stephen's brothers did it?' Fairlie manages to croak out. 'Jenna's uncles?'

Again, Evelyn nods tearfully.

Pattie squeezes Evelyn's hand, rubs her arm. 'It's hard

for her,' Pattie breaks into the taut silence. 'She hasn't talked about the attack since it happened. He almost died. She blames herself for that. But it's not your fault, Ev. It never was.'

Jenna's mother fiercely shakes her head, then tilts her face up and wipes away her tears.

'Did Stephen ask them to . . . do the assault?'

'*No*,' Evelyn answers with a vehemence that almost spills Fairlie's whiskey. 'He would *never*. After the birth, when he found out about the other man, Stephen kept it to himself for months. But when it all became too difficult, and he decided to leave, he confided in his brothers. I think he was just looking for support. But his brothers are thugs. Stephen is *nothing* like them.'

Fairlie says, 'So after the attack . . . '

Evelyn squeezes her eyes shut. 'The assault was the catalyst for my decision to give you up, yes,' she whispers. 'I realised how selfish I had been. I had to think of others. You were all suffering and it was my fault – I had to make it right, somehow.'

Pattie leans forwards, stretches out to take Fairlie's hands in her own. 'Fairlie,' she says earnestly. 'Look at me. You were a gift. I am eternally grateful for you. And for Evvie.'

Fairlie pushes the last dregs of her whiskey away, sickened. She doesn't know what to say.

'When I was little, I thought I was painted,' Fairlie says. 'I thought my skin was white underneath, but I'd been painted brown.'

'I know.' Evelyn gives her a small smile. 'Pat told me. I thought it was cute.'

'Cute? What fucking drugs are you smoking?'

'Fairlie,' Pattie scolds.

'No, Mum. You have no idea what it's like to grow up not knowing your heritage. So Evelyn didn't want to be like her hippie parents? So what! At least you know who they are. Me? Every time a new study came out linking some disease to genetics, I'd have to worry if it would apply to me, if my genetics carried some bomb. Breast cancer, heart disease, mental illness. Who am I? Who are my ancestors?'

Fairlie bolts upright. 'Wait a minute.'

Pattie and Evelyn both jump.

Fairlie's heart hammers like a racehorse. Nostrils flare in and out. 'My biological father is a local black man,' Fairlie says. 'His identity had to be protected. And he has severe, old leg injuries.'

Evelyn's lips quiver as she nods. Pattie erupts into sobs.

Fairlie says, 'It's him, isn't it?'

'I'm so sorry,' Evelyn says. 'I am.'

'Little comfort, Evvie.'

'I might never be able to make it up to you, but I will try.'

'It just hurts.'

Fairlie knows she is drunk. It's likely she's not making any sense to anyone – she certainly isn't making sense to herself. Her head is spinning, spinning, spinning like a carousel. Her sister, her mothers, her father.

Sister. Mother. Father. Heteropaternal superfecundation.

Outside, the sounds of nightfall have taken over from the day. Traffic from the street has quietened, the birds are silent. Off in the distance a car alarm sounds briefly then stills. They hear the low click and hum of the hot water service.

Evelyn says, 'I suppose Jenna got her ultimate revenge.'

'How so?'

'She finally escaped that arsehole.'

Fairlie can't help an irreverent snort. 'You never met him. Bit stiff to be hurling insults. Although,' she adds, 'I've often shared your sentiment.'

In the silence that follows again, Fairlie's phone beeps with a text message. Stretching her legs out she fishes her phone from her pocket. It's from Ark: *Can I drop Henry 2U tomorrow afternoon?*

Henry. Fairlie sends back: *Of course. Any time.*

'You're right,' Evelyn agrees. 'I've never met Ark. But I know him.' Strangely, Evelyn smiles. 'Just recently Jenna began to send me text messages, the occasional email.' She looks wistful. 'I thought we were getting there. After four years of silence, I thought she was coming back. She was opening up to me about things.

'The storage unit?' Evelyn goes on. 'I arranged that for her. She asked me to, a few weeks ago. We worked out all the details together through text messages.'

Fairlie's eyebrows draw together and she sets her glass down. 'Wait – *you* arranged the storage unit?'

'It was Jenna's idea. She sent me everything in the post, I arranged rental of the unit and then mailed her a key.'

'Why?'

'Honestly, Fro, I don't know.' Evelyn sighs. 'Why send it all the way here only to have me put it somewhere else? But she was terrified of Ark finding out. And she didn't trust me. Can you blame her?' The older woman traces circles around and around the rim of her cup. 'I thought she wanted the books in storage so that once she'd left him, she could collect them without having to see me.'

At this, Pattie offers a sad sigh and shakes her head. 'I wanted her to trust me,' Evelyn goes on, 'so I just did as she asked. No questions. It was the least I could do.'

An uneasy roil starts up in Fairlie's belly. 'Hang on. What exactly was she so terrified of Ark finding?'

Evelyn eyes her calmly. 'I think Jenna has more to tell you.'

'The books? I saw them.'

'Yes, those too but –'

'Honestly I was side-tracked by the my-twin-sister-was-separated-from-me-at-birth phenomenon. Forgive me for not giving too many rats' clackers about a whole heap of dates and figures.'

'Those books are more than that,' Evelyn says fervently. 'They're evidence.'

'Of what?'

'Ark's been hiding income.'

'Big deal. Don't all businesses do that?'

Pattie and Evelyn exchange a glance.

'There's more, Fro. There's something else Jenna wanted me to give you.' Evelyn stands up and moves across the lounge room to the sideboard covered with photographs. Sliding open a drawer, she retrieves something and comes back to Fairlie.

'Here,' Evelyn says. Before she hands the item to Fairlie, she sits alongside her on the couch. 'You've had a lot of shocks today,' she says. 'It's a lot to take in. But Jenna was adamant: she said this was for you. Only,' she pauses and her voice drops, 'I thought *she* would collect it from me, one day, and then give it to you.'

She hands Fairlie a notebook, A5-sized with a purple-and-black striped cover – the kind sold for a dollar at the supermarket. The cover is lined with creases, lifting away from internal pages rumpled and swollen with ink. Inside, the pages are filled with Jenna's handwriting.

'What's this?' Fairlie asks softly. She glances at Pattie, who is frowning curiously.

Evelyn looks faintly terrified. The colour has disappeared from her cheeks. 'It's Jenna's diary. I received it in the mail last week. She must have sent it to me before ... There was a note with it – instructions to give this to you. I guess she knew you would arrive on my doorstep once you'd been to the storage unit.'

363

Fairlie looks down at the notebook in her lap, runs her hand over the ridges and valleys of the strokes of ink, made by the pressure of Jenna's hand. The first page is dated at the top in Jenna's looped scrawl: *12 May*. Almost four years earlier. A sad smile wells in Fairlie as she begins to read Jenna's diary.

The first entry outlines a conversation with Ark. With a kind of no-nonsense precision, Jenna describes her initial ambivalence about Ark's suggestion they have a baby. A lump forms in Fairlie's throat; she remembers that day, in the tearoom at the hospital, when Jenna had told her that she and Ark were considering having a baby.

Fairlie reads on. Days and then weeks of tumult as Jenna struggles internally about beginning a family, and as she and Ark grow increasingly discontented. Jenna's narrative has a literal feel, unembellished by fanciful, emotional stretches or conjecture. *This happened, and I felt like this.* But as Jenna's handwritten words paint a picture of day after day, Fairlie skims ahead, the smile slipping from her lips. Her throat dries, and cold fear strokes up her spine.

Pattie and Evelyn speak quietly to each other, fevered tones, hushed words rushing at one another.

But Fairlie can't hear them. Their voices fade, then blur, then drain away completely, like water sifting through sand to leave a cracked and parched earth. The room is silent and stuffy as Fairlie turns the pages in the notebook.

'Fro?' Evelyn is saying. 'Honey, please. Say something.'

Fairlie lowers the notebook. 'He killed her.'

The room plunges into a silence so complete they can hear the crickets outside. Pattie and Evelyn stare at her. Finally, someone prompts her for more.

'This is a diary.' She waves the notebook at them.

'I know –'

'It's Jenna's diary from the past four years,' Fairlie rushes over her. 'I can't believe I never saw any of this, she never told me this much. I knew she was unhappy but this is bad, it's all so bad, oh my God the things that he did to her . . .'

She can't breathe. There isn't enough air in the room. Her lungs are squeezing tight and Jenna's gone and she's never coming back because Ark killed her.

Breathe. In, hold. Out, hold.

Someone gently touches the back of her head; she puts her head between her knees. They're murmuring again, those two. Why does everyone seem to know everything and she knows nothing?

'I knew it was bad, I knew she was unhappy, and I worried that he was being an arsehole but nothing like this, nothing like this.'

Breathe.

After a while, the murmuring stops. The rushing sound in her ears fades. When she looks up, they're both watching her, waiting.

Her *mothers*.

Picking up the notepad from where she'd dropped it to

the floor, Fairlie opens it at random and reads: '"Monday, October ten. Things not good. Ark angry, I left food scraps in the sink drainer but I can't reach it over my belly. Called me lazy and dirty."' She flips the page.

'"Saturday, January twelve. Things quite bad. Ark called me selfish and said I was a bad mother, took Henry out and I was scared he wouldn't bring him back. Laughed when I suggested counselling."' Her voice begins to shake as she flips through more pages.

'"Wednesday, February tenth. I'm scared and tired. I'm sick. I don't know how much longer I can take this. He won't let me leave."'

'"Friday, June third".' Fairlie swallows, puts a hand over her throat. '"Raped again. Always my fault, this time because I've been too tired lately.' Her eyes skim over the words. Words like bad mother and my fault and rape.

Fairlie closes the book. 'I had no idea,' she whispers. 'Fro . . . '

'Mrs Soblieski knew something wasn't right!' she cries. 'Did you both know? Evelyn?' She shakes the notebook at her. 'You just said "she escaped that arsehole". Well? Did you know?'

Evelyn nods quickly, once. 'Yes. But like I said, only very recently. She started sending me messages –'

'And you did *nothing*?'

'I begged her to get away!' Evelyn says, suddenly furious. 'I thought we were planning her escape! Once she was out safely we were going to make an anonymous tip to the ATO so he could be charged with tax fraud! Look,' she yanks the box over and removes items, one by one, 'she stole his books, look here. Eight years worth of hidden income. Prick was so arrogant he kept a record of exactly how much he was earning – how much he was getting away with. He'd been selling truckloads of wine on the side, illegally, to some *very* unsavoury people.' Evelyn slams the pile of books held together by elastic bands onto the coffee table. 'And in here –' she yanks out the A4 envelope filled with paper '– these are printouts of emails, conversations between him and his dodgy buyers. She wrote a statement about a man who came to the house just recently, asking for Ark and making threats. She even collected a list of staff he paid in cash, tradespeople who'd purposely over-invoiced so his expenses would seem higher.' Streaks of pink shoot up Evelyn's neck as she slams more pages onto the coffee table. 'Do you really think I'd do *nothing* if I had known she was so desperate that she might ...' Disgusted, Evelyn makes a snorting sound in her throat.

'I swear to you, Fairlie,' she finishes earnestly. 'I didn't know that she was planning to end her life. I thought she was planning a new start.'

A saddened, cold, quiet falls, a stew of shared complicity. When Pattie finally beaks the silence she voices what they're all too scared to admit: 'Jenna was ill. No one could have seen it.'

Fairlie says quietly, 'She tried to tell me.'

'Don't do that –' Someone reaches a hand for her and she bats it away, lurching to her feet as she pulls out her phone, hits Ark's number. Pattie and Evelyn stare as she backs herself into the corner of the room, the bookshelf digging into her back, her free hand held palm-out towards them and her face wild.

Ark doesn't answer. A recording of his jovial, forced-friendly voice instructing her to leave a message and have a great day enrages her even further.

She'll never quite remember it, what she says then; she won't recall what she shouts, drunken and banshee-like down the line. But her words blanch the colour from the other women's faces and Evelyn sinks to the couch, a trembling thin-boned hand over her eyes.

22

Then

When Jenna suggested they lie down together for his nap, Henry didn't ask why. Although it had been months since she'd slept with him, at only two years old the primitive instinct to nestle alongside his mother hadn't been quashed from him yet.

'Go lie on Mummy's bed,' she said, smiling at him. Henry giggled and clambered onto the sheets as she drew the curtains against the midday sun.

She lay alongside him. Her fingers stroked the length of his small back; she buried her face in his soft hair. He smelled of strawberries and green grass, and she swallowed it.

Time slowed, sluggish in the growing summer. Silence

filled the house and Henry quieted in her arms, his breathing slow and even, moist on her throat. His little arm went slack around her neck. Quietly, she took up his hand and pressed his small palm to her lips. A tear slid down her cheek and she wiped it, tenderly, with his tiny fingers.

'I know you don't understand,' she whispered to him. 'All I can hope is that one day you will. I'm sorry I couldn't be what you deserve, but you have lots of people who can.' She smiled, her vision swimming as she touched the pale, exquisite skin of his neck. 'Your dad,' she told him, 'your grandmas Evvie and Pat.' She swallowed and finished, 'And Aunty Fro. She'll always be here for you.'

Jenna crept out from under his grip, smoothed her hand over his sleeping body. 'I do love you,' she said.

In the kitchen, she made a raspberry jam sandwich, sliced it into even triangles and removed the crusts. She filled a yellow plastic cup with water. Removing the iPad from the charger, she tucked it beneath the wing of her arm and carried the items down the hall, back to the darkened bedroom. Silently, she set the food and iPad along with a basket of blocks on a colourful mat on the floor, where Henry would find it on the unlikely chance he awoke before Ark returned.

She looked down upon Henry, the rise and fall of his chest, his blameless, sleeping face. The crescent of his eyelashes. She closed her eyes and the picture of him stayed, solid, and with it she felt relief and gratitude and the warm glow of love. He was still so young; he wouldn't remember her. And it was better, this way. Without her.

He would be okay.

The hall clock ticked. For a while, she stood in front of it. Outside the magpies cried to one another and a mild summer breeze rattled in the gums. She pictured the grapes growing ripe and fat in the sun, rich with their bounty of juice. In her mind's eye she saw Ark, schmoozing in the swanky restaurant in Warrnambool, across the border in Victoria, an hour's drive away. Swilling wine in bulbous glasses, laughing his booming laugh, clapping shoulders and shaking hands.

Jenna picked up her phone. Her hands were calm as she sent him the text message.

It was the last time she thought of Ark Rudolph.

She went back to the bedroom doorway and peered into the darkened room. Henry was deeply asleep. She did love him, she knew that. That was enough.

Jenna went down the hall, into the bathroom, where the light was filmy and white-gold and the water from the taps ran hot.

She locked the door.

23

Now

Nerves flutter through Fairlie's body so insistently they almost obscure her hangover. The morning is crisp and clear, towelled dry with the scent of pine chips from the timber mill on the edge of town. The fresh air gently cleanses the whiskey from her blood but does little to ease the throbbing pain between her temples, nor the anxiety wringing out her insides.

Only a short walk to the Mount Gambier police station from Evelyn's house; Fairlie counts the steps with a sense of irony.

Last night, for the first time in years, she'd spent the night at Evelyn's. Eventually, semi-passed out, she had curled beneath a blanket on the couch in Evelyn's lounge room and slept; Pattie and Evelyn keeping watch over her until dawn fingered pink smears into the sky.

As Fairlie walks, a clutter of imagery crowds in her mind, each picture jostling for attention. Evelyn Francis gave birth to her. She knows her biological father. Ark had been abusing – raping – Jenna. Henry is without a mother. Jenna is her sister – her skinny, white, *twin* sister. And adhering it all together in a miasma of awfulness is the relentless grief: Jenna is dead.

She misses Jenna more than she can physically bear. More than anything in the world, she wants to talk to Jenna about all this.

Her sister. *Her sister.*

The police station looms before her, a hulking box of grey stone attempting to look modern and edgy yet formidable, a place for criminals to cower. Fairlie's mouth dries up and she clutches the box tighter to her chest as she pushes through the door.

Bright artificial lighting and the warble of telephones and voices. A girl who isn't nearly physically imposing enough, and certainly cannot be old enough to be a police officer comes to the counter. Hands on jangly belted hips, hair gelled back into a tight bun, she gives Fairlie a bright, questioning look.

'Is Detective Dallas Morgan around?' Fairlie says.

The girl playing police dress-ups looks Fairlie cautiously up and down and picks up a phone. Holding it slightly from her ear, she asks, 'You are?'

'Fairlie. I . . . I'm a friend. I have something for him . . .'
She lifts the box like an offering.

The girl looks unconvinced. She speaks briefly into the
phone, listens, and hangs up. 'Sorry,' she says. 'He's out.
Can I take a message? Or . . .' Gesturing to the box, she
holds out her hands.

Jenna's diary, the newborn ankle bands and the birth
certificates are all tucked safely into Fairlie's handbag.
Secrets kept within the folds of family. Fairlie slides the
box of evidence – eight years of tax avoidance, records of
Ark's illegal dealings – across the counter into the police
officer's waiting hands.

Roasted coffee scents the warm fug inside the café. From
behind the counter comes the whirring grind of beans,
spoons clink against china cups and chair legs grate upon
floorboards. Voices and laughter.

Beneath the table, Fairlie's knee jiggles. Swiping her
thumb across her phone screen, she glances yet again at
the time. Still, it's not quite ten.

The bell above the door jangles and a roar of street
noise rushes in.

Fairlie stands. Unsure what to do with her hands she
clasps them in front of herself, then lets them fall to her
sides. Clasps them again.

'Hello, Fairlie, it's good to see you again,' he says. His

smile is as warm as the room. 'I hear Evelyn told you everything.'

Fairlie shakes her head. 'It was Jenna. Jenna told me everything.'

Detective Dallas Morgan offers his hand and she takes it tentatively. *Where do we start? Twenty-six years ago? Or now, today?*

The detective seems to be reading her mind. 'I know we have some catching up to do, but would you like to hear what's happening with Mr Rudolph's case?'

Fairlie exhales, relieved. Ark's tax evasion seems like safe territory. 'Yes, please.'

Dallas waits for a man pushing a toddler in a stroller to pass their table. 'Investigators for the ATO are handling it from here,' he begins. 'Ark will have a visit from the Feds any day now. The investigation could take some time, many months. But —'

A waiter approaches, a teenage boy with an eyebrow ring. 'Here for lunch?' he asks cheerfully. 'The soup of the day is *divine*. Pea and ham —'

'Yes, please,' Fairlie and Dallas answer simultaneously.

The waiter looks back and forth between them as they stare at each other. Fairlie adds coffee, Dallas a cup of tea. The waiter retreats quickly when the two of them stop responding.

'I wanted to get rid of him,' Fairlie says first, when the waiter has left.

'Me, too,' Dallas says. 'But also, I love pea and ham soup.'

Fairlie bites her lip and looks down at her place setting. She fiddles with a napkin, picks up her glass of water for something to do with her hands. Can he curl his tongue, like she can? That's a genetic trait. Are her grandparents still alive? Who are her ancestors? Where does her mob come from? A sense of inadequacy sweeps through her. What if he's disappointed in how she turned out? Fat, slothful, living alone with only a cat for company? Yet at the same time, she feels a conflicting anger bubbling through her limbs. Because hasn't he known about her all this time? And had he never felt the need to give her a call and say, *Hey, just thought you might like to know where you came from?*

'It's likely Ark will go to jail.'

Water sputters up her nose. 'Jail? Seriously? I thought he'd just hidden a bit of income.'

'A lot of income – one and a half million dollars in eight years.'

Fairlie's jaw drops. *One and a half million dollars?*

'How, where . . . ' she stutters. 'Where has he been hiding it – in a mattress?'

Dallas's face creases with something like amusement. 'In plain sight. He's just been spending it – living it up. Probably on expensive household items, gifts, renovations.'

'Jenna always said he was strict with money,' Fairlie says with a frown. 'They always seemed to be watching every penny.'

'It's a cover. If he's telling the tax office he's not earning

376

much, he has to tell that to everyone else, too. And,' his expression softens, 'it was one of his control tactics over Jenna.' Dallas takes a deep breath. 'Unfortunately for Mr Rudolph, it's not just the hidden income. He's also been illegally selling his stock to a few individuals we've been trying to find for a while. Jenna led us to quite a crime ring breakthrough.'

Fairlie grips the tabletop to steady herself. Tax crimes, black market alcohol sales. Bloody hell. 'What about Henry?'

Dallas looks rueful. 'Mr Rudolph has already mentioned that.'

'He'll be without a parent!' Fairlie cries, panicked. 'He can't go into foster care. Oh how *awful* –'

Dallas says, 'Ark wants you to take care of Henry.'

'So Ark was selling wine illegally? Like, on the side?' Fairlie sets her coffee down and pictures Ark with shady-looking characters, clandestine meetings in dimly lit car parks on rainy evenings, handing over duffle bags of alcohol and grabbing briefcases of cash in return. Leather jackets and black SUVs and gruff, grunty conversation. Inexplicably, she bursts out a kind of hysterical, disbelieving laugh.

From inside her handbag her phone beeps, and Fairlie excuses herself to check. A photo message from Brian, a close-up of his face, brown eyes squinted, grinning, holding a tiny grey kitten to his cheek. *My new friend*, Brian has written. *Would Yodel like a play date?* Fairlie's immediate reaction is to stall, but then she pictures Henry. *Henry.* He would love to play with a kitten! Already she can see herself tidying up the spare room, throwing out her junk to make space for Henry's things. In the lounge room she'll put a row of baskets beneath the window for his toys and storybooks, like he has at home. Just around the corner from her flat is a family day-care centre with a leafy backyard and a sandpit shaped like a turtle where she can leave Henry while she goes to work. Mrs Soblieski will help, and her parents, and Evelyn. And Dallas.

Her entire family. Henry's family.

Fairlie writes back to Brian, *Yodel says yes.*

The waiter returns with two steaming bowls of soup and the conversation softens. Dallas asks about work at the hospital; Fairlie regales him with tales of her neighbour's epic doorstep feasts. But, emboldened by peas and ham, Fairlie says, 'How come you never contacted me?'

He sets down his spoon. 'I wanted to.'

'So why didn't you?'

The waiter sweeps in with more water, and Dallas offers him a brief smile. But Fairlie's gaze remains trained on the man across from her: the scattered curve of tiny moles below his right eye, the salty flecks in the stubble across his jaw, the laughter and the old, old sorrow in the lines tracking his eyes, lips and throat.

Dallas clenches a loose fist, runs the heel of his hand over a scratch in the tabletop. 'I didn't want to interfere,' he says finally. 'I didn't want to upset or confuse you in any way.' He smiles sadly. 'Your parents are wonderful people. I know you had a great childhood.'

'I did,' she breaks in, 'but I always waited for one of my real parents to come. Every time the phone rang I wondered if it would be my birth mum, calling to make sure I was being looked after. Like a real mum should.' Fairlie knows Pattie would wince to hear it, but no matter how devoted and loving Pattie was as her adoptive mother, Fairlie never stopped wondering. Waiting.

'Evelyn was scared,' Dallas says. 'She was terrified of this town and how it might hurt you. She made me promise to wait until she was ready. But that day never really came.'

'But we did get hurt,' Fairlie says. 'Jenna died.'

Anguish creases his face. 'Evelyn never stopped talking about either of you. She loved you both. Equally. That this has happened is . . . ' He pushes his bowl away and wearily rubs his face.

Fairlie twirls her spoon in her fingers. Across the room a woman exclaims something about a new car. A basket of bread is delivered to the table alongside them and a young boy politely asks for more butter.

'The day Jenna died,' Fairlie begins cautiously. 'When I came to the house. You knew who I was.'

He looks at her. 'Yes.'

379

'Bittersweet.'

'That doesn't even come close.'

'I vomited on the floor.'

'A very understandable reaction.'

Fairlie looks up at him. Her biological father 'I miss her,' she says. 'I don't know if I can stand it.'

Dallas reaches across the table, turning his hand so his palm faces up. He's offering it to her. Asking for her consent. Though his skin is marginally darker than hers, his eyes are the russet of her own and he has the same barely discernible dust of spots over the bridge of his nose.

'Can you curl your tongue?' she asks.

Dallas pokes out his tongue. Curled.

Fairlie hesitates, then puts her hand in his.

Yodel finds the idea of a play date with Brian's new kitten less than ideal.

While the kitten gambols around on Fairlie's lounge room floor, chasing after a hair-tie, Yodel has flattened himself beneath the television cabinet and emits a high-pitched whine from the back of his throat, hissing any time the fluffy grey kitten comes within reach. The kitten, in its naivety, is unperturbed by such a frosty reception.

Brian Masters is lying on his side on the carpet, propped up on one elbow, head resting in his hand. Tendons line bare feet, knobbly ankles. Dark blue jeans and a loose

T-shirt. Bands of frayed leather around tanned wrists. A blondish three-week beard that scuffs her lips but is silky beneath her fingers. Jenna's coffee stain ends beneath his arm.

'What was it like?' Brian asks, tugging a long strip of paper for the kitten to pounce upon. 'Ouch,' he adds, as the kitten digs tiny claws into his fingers.

'Weird,' Fairlie answers honestly. Although amongst finding out she is Jenna's twin sister, Ark swindling the government out of 1.5 million dollars, and watching Brian Masters go from drunken sex to sober play with a kitten on the same spot on her carpet, 'weird' seems to have become a normal concept. Fairlie shifts her weight and wraps her arms around her knees. 'But also kind of easy. Like I've always known him.' What is she doing? Why is she relaxing on her lounge room floor, playing with a kitten and a guy from high school? Brian's pony-tail drapes forwards over his shoulder and the kitten pounces at it.

'He told me my great-grandmother was born beneath a rocky outcrop at the base of Mount Shank,' Fairlie blurts out.

Brian extracts the kitten from his hair and looks at her, listening.

'I'm Buandig mob. Local,' she tells him, picking up the kitten and holding the squirming, fuzzy bundle up to her face. 'Lots of my ancestors are from around here. It's incredible to know I have roots here. I didn't know how many pieces of the jigsaw were missing until now that I can see them. Where I'm from. Where my family is from.'

Her phone starts to ring and she reaches to grab it from the couch. 'Speak of the devil,' she says at the caller ID. She lifts the phone to her ear and says, 'Yo.'

Dallas says, 'Ark's just been raided by the AFP.'

24

Seven Months Later

Butterflies flit about in Fairlie's belly as she stands on the kerb. A cooling breeze lifts the hair from her neck and she tucks stray curls behind her ears, then smooths her palms over her jeans.

They are five minutes late. Craning her neck she looks down the street, but it is still empty. A car appears at the end of the street and her heart jumps, but it doesn't turn, it slides on past.

Behind her, Yodel meows plaintively through the screen door and she turns and calls to the cat, 'I'll be right there.' Through the flyscreen she can see the tidy living room carpet – with a brush and a foaming carpet cleaner she's even managed to remove the coffee stain – and the clean expanse of the kitchen benchtop. The fragrance of fresh bread reaches her even out here.

Turning back to the street, she watches a white sedan turn the corner and glide up her street. Marguile Rudolph's car. For the past week Ark's mother has been staying out at ArkAcres, helping to take care of Henry while Ark's case has been in front of the judge. Fairlie imagines how arduous the week must have been for them all. Does Marguile know that Ark had chosen Fairlie to take care of Henry instead of her because he believed his own mother too weak, too pitiable?

It has been eight long months since Jenna's death.

The car pulls into the driveway and Fairlie sees his little face peering out the back window. She grins and waves.

Ark's mother steps from the car. Smoothing her silvery hair down, she looks as though she could blow away in the breeze. She busies herself opening the boot and lifting out bags and boxes, placing them onto the driveway.

Ark unfolds his bulky frame from the passenger seat. He looks awful. Worse than when Jenna died. His skin is grey, like the underside of a dead fish and his hands are shaking. A small pang of sympathy flickers through her, until she remembers the contents of Jenna's diary. Ark watches his mother remove Henry's things from the car, like he's watching her on TV.

They stand in an awkward triangle: Ark, his mother, and Fairlie.

Fairlie speaks first. 'Last day tomorrow.'

'Yeah.' Ark runs an agitated hand through his hair, nails bitten and scabbed. He's lost weight so rapidly that the flesh on the underside of his arm hangs from the bone.

'Any idea how long . . . ?'

Marguile's cheeks suck in angrily. Fairlie wonders if she's angry at the judicial system, or at her son for being such a law-breaking arsehole.

'Not sure exactly. Lawyer says it could be years. If I'm lucky, I might be out in seven.'

Holy shit. Seven years in jail.

'Listen, I . . . ' Ark's voice shatters. He looks at her desperately. 'You can think what you want of me, but I know you'll look after him.'

'Of course I will,' Fairlie answers. 'He's my nephew.'

Ark lifts the boy from the car and sets him down. He wears brand-new sneakers and his red tracksuit pants are rolled up at the ankles.

Crouching to her knees, Fairlie opens her arms and Henry toddles towards her. In front of her he comes to a halt, suddenly shy.

'I not two,' he says, in his charmingly inelegant toddler voice.

'You're not?' she asks animatedly. 'How old are you then? Forty-seven?'

'Two-a-*half*,' he says, laughing at his own joke. Then he launches himself abruptly, his weight thumps into her body and she rocks back, kissing his cheeks and his hair.

He smells like Jenna.

Acknowledgements

I am grateful to my wonderful publisher Haylee Nash for her enthusiasm and dedication to this story right from the beginning. Warmest thanks to Alex Lloyd for his exceptionally clever and patient editorial expertise, to Deonie Fiford and Kylie Mason, and to all the staff at Pan Macmillan Australia.

My deepest gratitude to Pippa Masson for being utterly brilliant in every way, to Dana Slaven and everyone at Curtis Brown Australia, and to Kate Cooper at Curtis Brown UK.

To Meg Vann and the Queensland Writers Centre I am grateful for the opportunities. Thank you to Paul Lucas and J.M. Peace for answering difficult questions about police work; to Monica Murfett for offering legal information; to Jill Buck for schooling me on bookkeeping; and to Gypsy Whitford for sharing personal experiences. *Black*

Chicks Talking by Leah Purcell and Lundy Bancroft's *Why Does He Do That? The Secrets of Angry and Controlling Men* were useful to me in the writing of this novel. At times I heeded advice and at times I favoured creative license – errors are mine.

Many thanks to Hayley Prentice and Kevin Massey for hours of creative childcare. Thank you to Anna Solding and Lynette Washington for the writerly companionship, chocolate, and midnight political discourse at Meningie.

As always I am grateful to those who read drafts: Julie Lock, Stacey Lock, Renee Lock and Amber Mount. My adoration to Leisa Masters and Kelly Morgan who always go above and beyond in areas of advice, friendship, and high-pitched encouragement. Thank you to my talented writing group buddies of 'The Eight': Laura Elvery, Kathy George, Mhairead McLeod, J.M. Peace, Sarah Ridout, and extra thanks to the magnificent Les Zigomanis. You are my people and you are superb.

Thanks to my parents Peter and Julie, my family and friends – you know who you are. Your cheering keeps me going. And love to Ben, Addison and Leo – for getting it.

Join us at

For competitions galore,
exclusive interviews with our lovely
Sphere authors, chat about
all the latest books
and much, much more.

Follow us on Twitter at
🐦 @littlebookcafe

Subscribe to our newsletter and
Like us at 🇫 /thelittlebookcafe

Read. Love. Share.